SLEEP STATE INTERRUPT

T.C. Weber

See Sharp Press ❧ Tucson, Arizona

For more information contact

See Sharp Press
P.O. Box 1731
Tucson, AZ 85705

www.seesharppress.com

Weber, T.C.
Sleep state interrupt / T.C. Weber – Tucson, Ariz. : See Sharp Press, 2016.
324 p. ; 23 cm.
ISBN 978-1-937276-97-3

1. Anarchists—Fiction. 2. Musicians—Fiction. 3. Dystopias—Fiction.

813.6

Cover design by Maria Francesca Roca. Back cover graphic by Kevin Patag.

For my wife Karen,
my brother Dan, and my parents

Acknowledgments

Thanks to Alicia Kelley, Eric Bakutis, Sherri Woosley, Lilian Weber, Alexander Harris, Robert Brandon, Rob Savidge, Bob Neufeld, Amy Kaplan, Robert Niccolini, Virginia Smith, and Eric Callman for reading drafts and providing feedback, and the critique circle at the Baltimore Science Fiction Society (http://www.bsfs.org/). Thanks to Robert Brandon, Eric Callman, Eric Bakutis, John DeDakis, and James Madigan for technical advice.

0

Waylee

"Protesters have gathered since early this morning," Waylee told her Comnet audience as she exited the *Baltimore Herald*'s downtown building. "They won't go quietly."

Above the white rectangle delineating the camera view of her data glasses, the cloud metrics read "Live Reach 139." Even her house parties had bigger audiences. But beside the current count, the thumbs up clicker steadily increased. If she got enough upvotes, she might make the print edition and priority digital feed. Maybe impress her bosses enough to keep her on when the re-org jackals arrived.

The bone conduction transducers on the glasses' arms blasted polythrash from her playlist, rattling her skull with battleship guns and tortured jet engines. Her pink-calloused, black-nailed fingertips played imaginary chords on imaginary guitar strings. Her scalp pulsed with harmonics as new song lyrics and pieces of story assembled themselves, moving too fast to consciously organize.

Waylee passed from the building's shadow into midday sun, which washed out the data overlays. *The paper should have sprung for a fancier model.* The data glasses weren't just cheap, they were ugly, with thick obsidian frames and an obvious, intimidating camera lens. The nightlife section lived on scraps, though, and even at twenty-seven she was one of the youngest people on staff. She yanked up her hands and adjusted the brim of her stretch hat until she could see.

The Independent News Center, the region's biggest nonprofit for investigative journalism, was a few blocks south. They launched on the old Internet. After the transformation into the much faster Comnet, the new gatekeeper—Media Corporation—imposed access fees that indie media couldn't afford. INC went into debt, then made the mistake of attacking MediaCorp.

Guitar riffs broiling her inner ears, Waylee marched down a cracked sidewalk along a deserted street. Sticky heat radiated from the asphalt, autumn yet to provide any relief. Just beyond, the expressway rose on columns above the city, an apartheid scar to get suburbanites to and from downtown offices without having to interact with scary locals like her neighbors and friends.

Ahead, Baltimore police cars lined the curbs, blue-striped white sedans bristling with antennae and lights. Three slate-grey armored vehicles sat beyond. Two bore SWAT insignia. Glossy black tubes—*what are those for?*—rose behind the roof flashers. The third was unmarked, with a big vertical plate mounted on top.

"So far," she told her audience, "I see… ten squad cars, two SWAT carriers, and a mystery vehicle. I'll get a full count when I'm closer."

The Live Reach jumped to 180, and upvotes—minus downvotes—reached 66.

"DG," she told her data glasses, "audio transmit off. DG, top trending stories, Baltimore."

Hottest local submission at the moment: Ravens game predictions, with a net score of 3803.

Aliens could bombard the city with carnivorous Pikachu and even that wouldn't tear people away from their sports fixations. None of the other submissions were insurmountable, though. With a little post-event coaxing, maybe some organized downvoting of the competition, the *Herald* would have to publish her story, and let her do more.

She passed a corner, then spotted the three-story red brick building that housed the INC's offices and studios, plus classrooms, a library, and a dozen community groups—the heart of progressive Baltimore. People were gathered outside, several holding signs, and someone had torn down the big *Future Home of Charm City Condominiums* banner that was hanging from the roof last week. Impatient to drive INC out of business, Media-Corp had bought their building and tripled the rent, then evicted them when they couldn't pay.

Police blocked the streets on at least two sides of the building, hemming it in. Waylee saw Baltimore Sheriff's deputies, city cops in flexible body armor, and three people in suits standing off to the side. Another mystery vehicle with a metal sail perched up the road. Both, she now saw, were manned by men in grey combat gear with no insignia.

"DG, stop music." Silence echoed through her skull. Then she heard cars racing oblivious on the overhead expressway and a din of voices up ahead.

"DG, audio transmit on." She stared at the weird vehicle and swiped a finger along one glasses arm to zoom in.

The camera had pretty decent pickup—not high-def, but good enough for vlogging. Beneath the view frame, numbers indicated exposure, focal length, and other stuff she couldn't be bothered with. "DG, identify."

A black and white circle spun in the upper right corner, then "No matches." Either she had a bad angle or the vehicle wasn't in the public databases.

She looked around and spotted two INC journalists, both twenty-somethings like her, speaking to police. Judging from the way they moved from one cop to another, they weren't getting many comments. As far as she could tell, she was the only other journalist here.

Big surprise. This story should be huge, standing up to the biggest bully in America, but MediaCorp owned every news outlet in Maryland—including, as of last month, the *Herald* and its subsidiaries.

The highest ranking officer was a thin, dark skinned woman with lieutenant's bars. Waylee whispered to her glasses. "DG, search Baltimore Police Department, identify."

A short bio of Lt. Janette Rixson appeared. She commanded a Special Weapons and Tactics unit. She was conferring with the second ranking BPD officer on scene, a sergeant from Central District.

Some of the police turned to look at her. The Comnet icons disappeared from her overlay, replaced by a flashing "Connection lost."

I'm press, they can't jam me! She'd have to work offline now.

Waylee approached the lieutenant and sergeant. The sergeant, a beefy man sprouting long tufts of nostril hair, scanned her with motel room eyes. Waylee wasn't a model like her sister, but had high cheekbones, full lips, and other conventions of pretty. Further down, faux-leather pants clung to athletic legs.

Waylee wasn't desperate enough to flirt with Sgt. Nosehair. She flashed her laminated press badge. "Waylee Freid, *Baltimore Herald*. Can you tell me what's going on here?"

The lieutenant frowned. "I'm sorry, you're going to have to talk to Media Relations."

A press badge wasn't the access key she'd fantasized about in journalism school. "And is there someone here from Media Relations?"

"No." Lt. Rixson snapped fingers in the sergeant's face and they proceeded to ignore her.

Waylee considered inserting herself between the two officers. She raised her voice instead. "Why are you jamming the wireless? The public has a right to know what's going on in their city."

The officers turned and narrowed their eyes. "This is a crime scene," the lieutenant said, "and there's potential for confrontation. The safety of my officers comes first."

"What does that have to do with the wireless signal?"

The lieutenant thrust a finger at the people surrounding the building. "It's procedure, in case they're calling reinforcements. Now if you'll excuse me." She turned away again.

If these glasses had a bullshit detector, the meter would be off the scale. Waylee strode over to the ranking Sheriff's deputy, hoping for less intransigence.

The deputy, a balding black man, glanced around as she spoke.

"Sorry," he said, "I'm not authorized to speak to the media."

She tried the armored vehicles next, but couldn't even get close before being shooed away by men with guns. That left the woman and two men in suits, whom she couldn't ID without Comnet access.

"Excuse me," she asked them, "are you with the city?"

One of the men, ginger-haired with big eyebrows, eyed her up and down. He stank of aftershave or one of those body sprays that were supposed to make women tear off their panties.

"And you are?"

"Waylee Freid, *Herald.*"

"We're with Charm City Realty."

A subsidiary of Media Corporation. "In what capacity?"

"This building is our property. It's being unlawfully occupied." He pointed at the big windows. Angry faces stared back. "They've had thirty days to vacate, and as you can see, it looks like they have no intention to do so."

"Why did you decide to buy this building? And isn't a 200% rent increase unusually harsh?"

The man—realtor, lawyer, what?—stepped closer, his love spray making her nose twitch. "We're on the same side, you know."

"I'm sorry?"

"We both work for Media Corporation."

Not by choice. "I'm a journalist. I'm not supposed to take sides." She almost believed it.

The woman pulled out a comlink. Like her data glasses, the palm-sized handheld computers tied their users into the shared techno-haze of humanity, as long as they had an overpriced account with MediaCorp or one of their dwindling competitors. "You say-id"—her voice drawled Virginian —"your name was Waylee Free-id?" She typed something on her comlink. "How do you spell that?"

Trying to intimidate me? "Could you tell me your names and why you're here?"

"I'm sorry, Miss Free-id," she said, "I decline to comment." The other two looked away.

A familiar voice projected from a bullhorn over by the building's main entrance: "Whose streets?"

A semi-unified chorus responded: "Our streets!"

Waylee gave up questioning Authority, and turned her attention to the faces gathered outside the INC building. She recognized most of them, people who worked or volunteered for the media, community groups who'd also been evicted, and a handful of supporters. About a hundred altogether, many holding signs with their group affiliation, like "Food for All" or "Baltimore Workers Association." And at the windows, two dozen more.

One hundred and twenty people out of a city of 650,000.

"Whose streets?"

"Our streets!"

The police lined up, helmet visors down and big plexiglass shields held in front. Restraint cables hung from their belts. Most gripped long rubber batons, but a few held shotguns and assault rifles.

Her friend Dingo, a 21-year-old self-proclaimed revolutionary with uncertain ancestry and unruly dark hair, had the bullhorn. After a couple more repetitions, they switched to another time-worn chant: "The people united, will never be defeated! El pueblo unido, jamás será vencido!"

Waylee flashed her press ID again and elbowed her way through the line of cops. She pulled off her black floppy hat, folded it to pocket size, and shook her mulberry hair loose.

Dingo lowered the bullhorn and grinned. "Oh goody, the nightlife section is here."

"Go fuck yourself, Dingo. Is Pel here?"

"Your boyfriend went home after they shut off the power. What's an IT nerd gonna do without power?"

"He's not a nerd. What about Shakti?" One of her housemates, a tireless organizer for the People's Party.

"Here this morning, coming back after work."

"Anything to say to the press?"

He whipped up a hand, blocking her view. "Get that spy shit away from me."

"Your revolution won't be televised, then." She jerked a thumb toward the police. "They're serious, you know. Do you have a plan?"

Dingo shrugged. "I'm not in charge. No one should be in charge."

Waylee spotted Willard Ramsey, the grey-bearded INC director, just outside the front door. She hadn't seen him since handing off her story describing Media Corporation's secret deals with the government, which *The Herald* had refused to publish. That was months ago, but nothing positive ever came of it.

"Hi."

His lips curled down. Not happy to see her. "Hello, Ms. Freid."

"What's happening here?"

"What's happening?" Narrowed eyes transfixed her camera lens. "What's happening is this city, this country, this whole planet, are in deep shit."

No doubt Baltimore was sliding downhill with a banana peel on its ass. She saw it every time she took the bus home—the boarded-up row houses, the homeless crones pushing shopping carts full of junk, the mounds of trash and discarded needles against the curbs.

"All because of top-down fiscal crises and ideology-driven 'belt tightenings,'" the director continued. "And vicious predators like MediaCorp."

Waylee zoomed in to a head shot.

"What's happening," he said, "is the convergence of government and corporate power to benefit the wealthy elite and crush any dissent. Crush any independent, uncompromising voices like ours."

"DG, pause recording." This is a disaster. "Is this my fault? Retaliation for showing how MediaCorp co-opted Congress and the president?"

He shook his head. "We've always challenged the hierarchy. You just added an extra thorn. Your documents were fantastic and we were happy to run with them."

"It didn't propagate."

"Not many people saw the broadcast. MediaCorp blocked our Comnet access the day before it aired, and back channels are too slow. Then they turned their lawyers on us."

"All these organizations evicted. I'm really sorry."

He softened. "How about you? Pel told me *The Herald* put you on probation."

"Not exactly. I just got an unfavorable performance review. We're quite the bureaucracy."

Her editors were mad she 'aided a competitor,' but relieved it wasn't *The Herald* under attack. She'd worked hard to try to salvage her career. She'd be the number one target, though, once MediaCorp sent hatchet men to impose 'efficiency measures' on their new acquisition.

"Well I'm glad they sent someone to cover this," he said.

"Actually I sent myself. But I'm here and I'll try to get the word out."

More cops arrived, wearing full combat gear, including helmet visors and gas masks. "DG, record."

The director pointed up the street. "The police are supposed to serve the public, not MediaCorp."

"What's your plan?" Waylee asked him.

Sweat beaded on his forehead. "Honestly?...I'm not sure." His eyes shifted back and forth. "I didn't think they'd be so heavy handed."

In the building windows, faces retreated.

Lt. Rixson spoke in a wireless mike, amplified through speakers mounted on the SWAT vehicles. "You are trespassing on private property. You must disperse immediately or you will be placed under arrest."

The building's defenders linked hands, first a few, then almost everyone. The INC director bit his lip, grabbed the bullhorn, and cleared his throat. "We're not leaving, but we're not violent. Let's keep this peaceful, please."

Waylee zoomed in to Lt. Rixson, standing behind the line of riot police. The lieutenant tapped fingers against her temple, then put the mike to her mouth again. "This is your last warning. Disperse immediately."

The building defenders murmured. An INC production assistant—Waylee couldn't remember her name—started a chant. "We won't go!"

More voices joined. "We won't go!"

The police waited through several repetitions, then pulled back, well away from the building.

In the crowd, fingers separated and faces relaxed.

"Yeah, go back to the donut shop!" Dingo shouted. A dreadlocked girl kicked his calf. Dingo grimaced and cursed.

Diesel engines grumbled. The mystery vehicles with the looming plates shuddered, then inched forward.

Waylee's stomach shrank into a pit of ice.

Smiles disappeared. Feet shuffled backward. Waylee swept her head around, trying to record as much as possible.

The vehicles halted well short of the crowd.

"What the hell are they doing?" a protestor behind her said.

Waylee heard a low buzz and a series of clicks. Black stripes streaked across her view, scrolling irregularly from top to bottom.

Now they're jamming my video. She pulled off the data glasses. Her vision cleared, but the buzzing and clicks intensified. They weren't coming from the data glasses. They were coming from the center of her skull. Her eyeballs twitched, rattling her vision like a bumpy train.

All around her, people clutched their heads and fell to their knees. Some screamed, some writhed like epileptics. Police raised thick guns and fired canisters toward the building windows. They crashed through the glass and white smoke billowed out.

The street, the building, the sky, spun in circles. Waylee fell to her knees, smacking her hands against hot asphalt. Her stomach contracted and her breakfast spewed out over the pavement, leaving the taste of bile and the stink of rancid milk. She threw up again.

Her twitching eyes started to sting. *Tear gas.* She forced them shut. The cacophony of shouts and buzzing tore at her brain.

Finally the noise inside her head faded away, leaving only external groans. She blinked and forced herself to look up.

None of the protestors were still standing. Vomit spattered the street and steamed in the sun. White plumes of tear gas wafted down from the broken windows overhead.

A school-aged girl lay nearby on her stomach, arms and legs jerking up and down. An older woman crawled over and cradled the shaking girl's face, which streamed blood from a mashed nose.

With a chorus of shouts, the dark-armored stormtroopers charged from both ends of the street. They hit the disoriented building defenders like a tsunami, slapping instant-lock cable ties around wrists and ankles, and swinging batons at anyone who resisted.

Dingo rose with clenched fists. One of the cops raised a shotgun and blasted a wooden dowel at him. It glanced off his forehead, leaving a bright red gash. Dingo howled and cupped a hand against streaming blood.

Still on her knees, Waylee slipped her data glasses back on. No more striping, and the camera was still recording. Comnet signal still blocked, but no matter— she'd upload the video as soon as she got back to the newsroom.

A bulky cop rushed toward her, shield up, baton raised. Pale blue eyes gleamed behind a pig-snout gas mask. "Hey, you!" The voice from his helmet speaker sounded tinny, more machine than man.

She held up her hands. "I'm press." She tried to remember where she'd put her badge.

Her attacker thrust out a black glove and snatched the data glasses off her face.

"Fuck you!" Waylee forced herself up, then grabbed the edge of the cop's shield. She shoved it aside and reached for her glasses, hoping to pry them out of his fingers.

Behind his mask windows, the cop's eyes widened. His baton swung down.

Her temple exploded in pain, and the world went dark.

* * *

"That bald patch looks awful." Waylee's teenaged half-sister, Kiyoko, averted her almond eyes and twiddled one of the silk bows in her long rainbow-hued hair.

Waylee's boyfriend, Pelopidas, patted her hand. "You're still the hottest scenester in Baltimore."

"Whatever." She felt a little relief, though. *He must not have found someone else yet.*

Kiyoko reached into her big Sailor Moon carry bag and pulled out a shoulder-length wig with black bangs and metallic blue dreads.

Waylee didn't bother rising from her bed to reach for it. "I hate blue." The walls of her hospital room, shared with a dwarfish woman who spoke neither English nor Spanish, were pale blue. Her detergent-reeking bed sheets were also blue. Even her flimsy gown, which offered no protection against the freezing air conditioning, was blue.

Kiyoko spread the wig apart in her pink-nailed hands. Its dreads drooped like jellyfish stingers. "It's cybergoth. It'll look awesome on stage."

"I hate goth too. And anything cyber related stinks of MediaCorp."

"I'm just trying to help, Waylee. This cost me fifty bucks."

Pel, who had transformed himself for the band with a buzzcut, long sideburns, and braided Jack Sparrow beard, snatched the wig from Kiyoko's hand. "Just wear it for now. Or don't. It's the least of our problems."

Waylee wanted to rail against the police department, about how she'd sue them for cracking her skull, but tears poured down her cheeks and she couldn't talk.

Pel grimaced. "We're here to pick you up. Threw that PowerPack in the RV today, maybe we can make some money street racing it." He smirked, but didn't barrage her with details the way he normally did.

We're both unemployed now. What the fuck are we going to do? Unemployment benefits were one of the first casualties of the *laissez-faire* Congress. "The enemy won," she managed.

Pel raised a pierced eyebrow. "The enemy?"

"MediaCorp, who do you think? Their enforcers put me here. Their hatchet men fired me." She was first on their list, and they didn't even give fair notice, just an email to come pick up her shit. No one at the paper defended her.

Her young doctor waddled through the open doorway, data pad in left hand, abdomen bulging with late pregnancy. "Good morning, Ms. Freid." She spoke with a precisely enunciated Nigerian accent.

Waylee sat up and wiped her eyes and nose on a sleeve of her gown. "Hospital coin counters evicted me this morning." Even a shared room was way too expensive without insurance. "Are you sure I'm good to go?"

The doctor stared at her data pad and swiped her fingers along its screen. "Your skull will take three to six months to heal, but it can do so at your home." She didn't look up while speaking. "In the meantime, do you play sports, anything like that?"

"No."

"It is important that you protect your cranium while it heals."

Avoid bullies with badges. Got it.

Kiyoko plopped down in the visitor chair and fished her pink-framed virtual reality headset out of her carry bag.

The doctor glared at Kiyoko and Pel. "Would you mind waiting outside while we consult?"

"They can stay," Waylee said. "They're family."

She shrugged.

"Now, any changes since yesterday? Headaches, ringing in the ears, memory troubles, mood changes?"

Waylee hesitated, then answered, "No."

The doctor swiped the data pad again. "I am sending your post-operative instructions to your Comnet account. I encourage you to visit our hospital site and you can confer with our virtual doctor with any questions you might have."

"I prefer real people."

The doctor looked up. "I assure you that the virtual doctor can access every unclassified medical database on Earth and is therefore much more knowledgeable than anyone on staff. We would, however, like you to come in for a follow-up examination. Say, in three weeks?"

"I lost my insurance."

"You can buy medical insurance on the exchange. I encourage you to do so as soon as possible."

"With what money?"

The doctor fiddled with her data pad, ignoring the question. "Now, your MRI scan showed no brain damage, that's the good news. However, the functional analysis indicated some anomalies that we'd like to examine further."

Pel frowned and rubbed a thumb against two of the beads securing his chin braids. Kiyoko wasn't even listening, her smooth Asian features half engulfed by the VR headset.

Waylee's throat snapped shut and tears blurred her vision. *Some strong female I am, crying like a baby whenever something goes wrong.* She turned away, toward the heavy curtain separating her from the other patient. *I wish that pig had killed me.* She still had life insurance then, enough to send her sister to art school.

"What sort of anomalies?" Pel asked.

Waylee swung her head back toward the doctor. "I have a pre-existing condition. Check my records from College Park."

Cyclothymia, the doctors called it. Milder than bipolar disorder, but still a hard beast to ride. They diagnosed it when she was in journalism school and having trouble focusing. But probably her brain turned against her long before, somewhere in the darkness of Philadelphia.

Pel inched forward. "Are they related, or is this something new?"

The doctor wagged a brown finger at him. "Please sit. I will consult her records."

Pel looked around. Still oblivious in her headset, Kiyoko occupied the only chair.

The doctor tapped a cadence on her pad and stared at it. "I see. This information is quite old, but it might be congruent with the functional data."

"Doctor visits were a waste of time," Waylee said.

The doctor slid fingers along the screen. "It says here that concussions could make your condition worse; amplify the depressive phase. There's a forty percent probability, and it doesn't always manifest right away. I will refer you to a psychiatrist on staff, and our virtual doctor has psychiatric options."

"Is the app free?"

"It is very affordable. As for in-person visits, the hospital has a number of payment plans. If you sign up for a credit card, you get ten percent off your first visit."

Why bother? Cyclothymia had no cure, and medicine didn't help, not that she could afford it anyway.

The doctor left, and a smiling nurse pushed a black wheelchair into the room. Pel shook Kiyoko out of her virtual world and helped Waylee out of the bed.

The wheelchair embarrassed her. There was nothing wrong with her legs.

The nurse guided her into the chair and patted her shoulder. "Hospital rules. It's just to get you to your car."

"My stepfather bullied me," Waylee said as Pel and Kiyoko packed her things into the Sailor Moon bag.

Pel turned and nodded. His eyes searched for context.

"Knocked me down day after day, year after year. And he paid the price."

Kiyoko stared and bit her lip.

* * *

June
(9 months later)

Gunshots woke Waylee from a haze of choking tentacles.

Pop! Pop pop! Pop! Pop!

Printed pistol by the timbre, professional disagreement by the tempo. Distant—other side of U.S. 1.

Waylee glanced at the grimy window of the crowded, musty bedroom she shared with Pel. It wasn't even night yet.

Survival of the fiercest in West Baltimore. Their geriatric two-story house was in a patrolled DMZ, but she and her roomies still had to be careful. Not everyone respected the zone system, and she'd get no favors from the police after her failed lawsuit.

Two more gunshots, then silence. Mission accomplished or weapon malfunction. 3-D printed pistols weren't terribly accurate or reliable, but they were the latest weapon of choice. Cheap, no serial numbers, and acetone soluble.

She threw aside the sweat-drenched sheets and half-rolled out of bed, her trim body clad in zebra-print panties and one of her dozens of unsold band T-shirts. *Dwarf Eats Hippo—we were high as clouds when we came up with that.* She edged past piles of used books by Goldman, Foucault, and a hundred other social theorists, and snatched up a pair of tattered jeans from the floor.

Her comlink sat in the charging station on a shelf by the door, along with Pel's chrome-framed data glasses. She could do just about anything with her comlink once hooked to the Net, and the screen could stretch to six times its current size. At the moment, though, this fancy piece of technology served as a clock, with faux-analog hour and minute hands.

5:30. She'd slept twelve hours. *I can't believe Pel didn't wake me.*

Waylee trudged into the hallway, gritty floorboards creaking beneath her bare feet. Guitars rang in her head and the day's first lyrics spilled forth.

Aching meat bleeding for meaning,
Tattered banners 'neath a dark moon...

Behind Kiyoko's door, marked with a rainbow and unicorns, a piccolo voice spoke, "I will never abandon my realm to the likes of Vostok."

Immersed in BetterWorld again. Even her own sister was ensnared by MediaCorp's virtual world, their number one manufactured distraction. Waylee lost the thread of her song.

Further down, explosions and screeching tires leaked past the reinforced door of the game room. Pel and Dingo, their latest housemate, practically lived in there. She knocked, but no one answered, no doubt dreaming like her sister in cyber cocoons.

All alone. Shakti, her most reliable friend, was out tonight, off at a People's Party meeting.

Waylee's chest tightened. She should be out there organizing, not sleeping life away. Gravity pulled her down the stairs to the living room.

The metal-plated door of the storage closet was unlocked. She grabbed the lap-sized Genki-san Comnet interface and nested in the living room recliner, cat-lacerated sofa and chairs flanking her on either side. Her stomach grumbled, but could hold out until dinner.

She pressed a small button on the Genki-san, transforming its glassy surface into a touchscreen and virtual keyboard, then activated the huge display skin fastened to the opposite wall. She logged onto the Comnet, using her real account, planning to check the responses to her latest freelance proposal.

Working in blinding spurts, Waylee had spent the past nine months researching MediaCorp's relentless march to monopolize information, their suppression of critical analyses, and their empowerment of an international plutocracy. Her latest story, about how they warped news coverage to elect their political supporters, was nearly done. She just needed funding for undercover work, to access hidden documents, interview people, and get some choice quotes. A little money and recognition would boost her morale, too.

She'd pitched her story to every independent outlet in the U.S. and Canada that paid their contributors. There weren't many, and the number dropped each month.

Still no responses. Not one.

Waylee didn't know whether to scream or cry. Not one paying gig all year. Well, there was the band, but that barely covered equipment costs. She wouldn't even have a blog, with its handful of subscribers, if Pel hadn't arranged free space on the Collective's shadownet. She was twenty-eight years old with nothing to show for it.

The *why* homunculus stirred inside her head and activated her fingers. Why hadn't anyone written back? Waylee pulled up the list of outlets.

The first, *Platform*, was her favorite, at least after the demise of *Democracy Now* and the Independent News Center. They published 'edgy' news and analyses, but had high standards and a sizable budget.

Someone had redesigned *Platform*'s Comnet site since her last visit. It had a slicker look, and the articles were all about "viral innovations" and "trend reports." The lead article heralded, "BetterWorld Passes One Billion Subscribers," followed by fawning praise of "the Comnet's crown jewel."

Waylee almost dry heaved, then tapped the search icon. "*Platform* acquisition," she told the Genki-san's hidden microphone.

The most relevant response on the screen read, "Media Corporation Buys *Platform* and Subsidiaries."

Waylee sat motionless for a while, too exhausted to feel sad or angry. Then she continued down her list. *Stirrings* and *The Daily Read* didn't exist at all anymore.

The rest... maybe no one but her cared that a handful of sociopaths controlled the world and used MediaCorp to tighten their grip every day. Or maybe no one would fund her research because she lacked the creds and followers. *I'm nobody, why should anyone take a chance?*

To the right of the wall screen, Pel clomped down the stairs, clad in grease-stained jeans and a *Pirates 4 People* T-shirt. "I presume by the volume you were the knocker?"

"You could have answered. Or would something awful have happened, like having to pause your game?"

"You can't just pause online combat; you'll get fragged. Whatever. I'm gonna work on some tracks." Instead of asking what she wanted, Pel took the lower stairs to the basement.

The loneliness stopped circling and settled on her like a bloated carrion bird. Waylee decided to check the news before going back to sleep. Even though it barraged her with propaganda, she always kept a national news portal open in the lower right corner. 'Know thy enemy,' Sun Tzu advised across three millennia of dog-eat-dog history.

The talking heads were spewing their usual pablum, this time about curtailing the power of local governments to restrict development. "They are just infringing on our rights," a man in a suit said, "the fundamental right to do with our property as we please."

Sometimes she argued with the anchors and commentators, as if they could hear her point of view. Today, the notion seemed absurd.

"And now," a female anchor said, "we turn to President Rand on the campaign trail."

The whitebread jock-handsome president strolled through a crowd of homogenous Anglo-Saxon supporters, smiling and shaking hands. "With polls showing overwhelming support," the anchor narrated, "it looks like his re-election's in the bag."

They cut to his speech du jour. "America has never been more prosperous than today," the president proclaimed from a podium. "People around the world see us as the land of opportunity."

Too bad none of that trickles down.

Waylee's lyrics homunculus dipped into her deep well of anger.
Bend over, chattel;
Pretend you like my ride.
Kneel when I say so,
And swallow my pride.

Something caught her eye, something out of place. Fingers flying across the touchpad, she expanded the news portal to fill the wall screen.

After the lottery numbers, the moving ticker on the bottom read: LEVEL 3 ZOMBIE OUTBREAK DOWNTOWN WASHINGTON D.C. AVOID CORDONED AREA. RESIDENTS IN AFFECTED AREA URGED TO STAY INDOORS.

Lights exploded in her head. She laughed so hard, the Genki-san slid off her lap and thudded onto the dusty rug.

Her nemesis, which Pel considered impregnable to hackers, had chinks in its armor.

She didn't need journals or publishers. She could reach a bigger audience without them, maybe millions of people, and tell them whatever she wanted. Why play a fixed game when she could kick the table over?

On the wall screen, President Rand had disappeared, replaced by green reboot messages as the Genki-san recovered from its fall.

Nerves humming with electric fire, Waylee pumped a fist and shouted. "Get ready, you bastards! I am gonna stick the biggest firecracker on Earth up your ass and light it with a flamethrower!"

1

December

Waylee

"Superheroes don't get stoned before they go into battle," Pel insisted from the parked van's passenger seat. He whipped out a latex-gloved hand and tried to snatch the fattie out of her fingers before she could light it.

Waylee was too fast for him, though, and jerked her prize just beyond his reach. "You're a mere mortal, my dear Pel, and can't possibly defeat the likes of Storm."

Triumphant, she ignited the joint, thrust it between the lips of her mask, and inhaled. Friendship Farm's finest—smooth as a glissando and 100% organic. Jagged edges melted off her nerves as she exhaled a thick cloud of acrid, piney smoke. *And to think, this used to be illegal here.*

Too bad she wasn't really Storm from the X-Men, the African sorceress with white hair. Or anyone with superpowers, able to right the wrongs of the world merely by existing outside the confines of science.

Shut up. I can do anything. Especially after six months of planning. With Dr. Doom, a.k.a. Charles Marvin Lee, the only person to ever hack a MediaCorp broadcast, on her side, she could reach enough people to make a difference. To loosen, maybe destroy, the grip of the plutocracy. All she had to do was break him out of jail.

"M-pat said this would be easy," she said.

Pel sputtered through the lips of his lifelike mask. "Compared to kidnapping the president, maybe." He turned away.

Waylee hit the joint again, hoping to calm her hyperactive neurons. She wouldn't smoke enough to dilate time and fog her memory, only enough to keep her hands from shaking.

Storm wouldn't shake. She would call down lightning or tornadoes to smite her foes, the plutocrats and their yes men who couldn't bear to share with others, for whom the world was a personal grab bag. Her weaselly bosses at the newspaper—*zap!* The utility companies and their collection thugs – *zap!* MediaCorp, the great crushing beast—*ZAP!*

Waylee emptied her lungs toward the windshield. The cone of smoke broke against the invisible barrier and recoiled into a confusion of eddies. When it dissipated, she scanned the dilapidated section of Eager Street ahead of them. No police cars. Baltimore's finest rarely patrolled anymore, relying on the cheaper option of streetlight cameras and remote-controlled quadcopters. And this stretch of boarded-up businesses, vacant lots, and dead trees contained nothing worth watching.

Beneath the mask, her skin oozed clammy sweat. She looked over at Pel. He was lost in his data glasses, monitoring his microcameras and probably the traffic. A wire-thin microphone boom snaked down from the dorkishly wide frame arms and terminated just short of his lips.

"What do you see?" she asked.

"Nothing yet."

Behind the glasses appeared a stranger. Kiyoko had artist friends who owned a large-format, high-precision 3-D printer, and created photo-realistic masks—right down to the hair and skin pores—for a living. Pel could have been anyone, but asked for a thirty-something ginger with day-old stubble.

"You should have been a Greek god," Waylee said. You couldn't get more Greek in Baltimore than the Demopoulos family. "Apollo, maybe. You look like Prince Harry with a five o'clock shadow."

Pel faced her and sighed. His brown eyes glared at her through translucent overlays of buildings and maps. Beneath his right eye, a tiny clock, mirror-imaged, approached the point of no return. "The idea behind disguise, Waylee, is to blend in with your surroundings. Someone's gonna see you and say, 'Hey, isn't that Storm from the X-Men?' 'Yeah,' their companion will say, 'only the X-Men are an invention of Marvel Comics and don't actually exist in present-day Baltimore. Therefore, that must be someone hiding behind a mask.'"

"Well played, Dr. Snark. But you're assuming anyone will notice or care. Besides, I don't look anything like Storm in real life."

"That's not the point," he said.

"Whatever. Just give me the satisfaction of burning your mask when we're done."

"After I've taken it off, I hope."

"Yeah, I wouldn't want it to melt to your skin and have to lock your frightful ass in the attic."

He smirked. Their masks were thin, flexible, and internally contoured to their real faces, and weren't bad at showing expressions. "The attic doesn't have any locks."

She didn't bother responding. The trouble with Pel's type was that they took everything literally.

His smirk evaporated. "You know, it's not too late to back out. If anything goes wrong, if we get caught…"

Anxiety surged through her veins. Pel had never been enthusiastic about her plan. "Even without money, we've got a decent life here," he said when she'd first proposed it six months ago. "Why risk prison just 'cause the president's an ass and MediaCorp ruined journalism?" A strange comment from someone who broke computer laws every day.

"Nothing will go wrong," Waylee told Unshaven Prince Harry/Pel. "We planned every detail. Besides, Charles expects us. No way am I breaking my word." *Or going back to pointless complaining on a blog with no readers.* "We're committed."

Pel stared at her through a still image of a red brick facade with rein-forced glass doors and windows shadowed by an overhang. It took her a second to decipher the mirror-imaged lettering on the front of the over-hang: *Baltimore City Juvenile Correctional Facility*. Two blocks to the east and half a block to the south, less than a quarter mile away. "We're not committed," he said, "until M-pat flips that switch."

"We've already been through this, Pel. What happened to your love of challenges? Fortune favors the bold—"

"So does a pair of cuffs."

She nudged the joint toward him. "Want some?" He never did, but it might help.

He frowned. "You're our getaway driver. Focus, would you?"

She withdrew her offer.

"Besides," he said, "I thought you didn't like that stuff."

"Well, depends. If I'm charged, pot dilutes the energy. And the bad times, I don't need the added introspection. But Shakti thought I'd need it today."

Pel said nothing, his artificial face blank. Beyond, the sun peeked over the tired skyline and breathed fire into the dust on the dashboard.

"And in case you're wondering, I'm not being crazy, and I'm not gonna fuck things up. I'm more alert now than I've ever been in my life." Even faint wisps of engine grime and stale plastic stood out.

His shoulders drooped. "Waylee…"

"We're doing this, that's all there is to it." Drums pounded in her head, only slightly muffled by the pot. "We all agreed, there's only so much we can do in the neighborhood. We're constrained by the system, by global economics and culture, and more and more that's controlled by a self-serv-ing elite."

"Duh."

"The political system's rigged," she continued. "MediaCorp decides what people see and hear. The whole game needs changing if we want to control our destinies. And that's not gonna happen without direct action." Dingo, of course, was all for it. The others had taken longer to convince.

"Okay, let's just focus." He turned away and peered into the side mirror.

She patted his arm, then took a third drag. This would be her last, so she let the smoke chill in her lungs, get comfortable, hang out with the alveoli a while.

A city bus, sides plastered with lottery and fast food ads, passed their parked van and stopped at the institutional-looking public tenements a couple of blocks up the street. Pel tapped the arm of his data glasses. "Anything?" he said into his microphone.

He paused, presumably listening to his bone conduction transducers. Dingo and M-pat—who had the tough job—waited in the other white cargo van they had rescued and refurbished.

"Just say when," Pel said in the mike.

He turned back to her. "It's almost time."

Waylee coughed out her last cloud and gripped the steering wheel. She peered ahead, then in the side view mirrors. Almost no cars now, their drivers shackled for the day in some human warehouse. She pressed the power button.

A ragged man clutching a brown paper bag shuffled toward them along the cracked sidewalk. On the other side of the street, rats foraged through trash in front of a shuttered bail bond office, whiskers twitching as they fought for scraps.

"I see them," Pel said, gazing through his remote eyes. "They're coming out." His voice was tense as a ready-to-snap guitar string.

Waylee pulled the van onto Eager Street and sped toward the jailed hacker who would help her change the world.

2

M'patanishi

"Go now," Dick Clark said from the cargo van's passenger seat, his eyes half-hidden by a mirror image of the Baltimore Juvenile Correctional Facility. It wasn't really Dick Clark, of course, but Dingo's mask pretty much passed for real. That is, if Dick Clark wore thick-framed glasses with a voice tube.

"You sure? They ain't crossed yet." M'patanishi, masked as a fiftyish Little Italy type and wearing a brown suit from Goodwill, couldn't see anyone at the crosswalk almost half a block up Greenmount Avenue. They'd be a lot closer if someone hadn't taken their damn traffic cones. Despite the morning chill, his hands sweated inside the double layer of surgical gloves.

"Yeah, kicks!" Dingo said, moving the lips of his mask. "Step it up!"

Their main microcamera, hidden in a shrub just past the front doors, gave a perfect view. So as much as it pained him, M'patanishi—M-pat to most—decided to trust Dingo. They were crew, after all.

He waited for a dented red Toyota to pass, then pulled out behind it.

This is crazy. This wasn't like slinging product or beating some thief's ass, neither of which worried the po-boys these days. This, he'd do hard time if they got caught. And he had a family now.

It was his fault they were here. He told the others it would be easy. That PrisonCorp, who managed the state's correctional facilities, was a joke. Waylee had it right, PrisonCorp and all the big corporations thought only about their bottom line and neither knew nor cared much about the real world. About people like him, who could be pretty damn lethal if they put their minds to it.

Dingo swiped a gloved finger along one chrome-colored arm of the data glasses Pel bought him for the mission. "They're counting them all up now. I see the target."

The timing had to be perfect. M-pat eased off the gas a little. He passed the red brick pre-release unit on the right, fenced parking lots on the left. Empty cars lined the street on both sides. No one on the sidewalks, only the Toyota ahead, no one behind.

He reached the fortress-like Juvie compound on the left side of the street. Up on the right, he saw the Occupational Skills and Training Center—institutional red brick like everything else. That's where guards escorted Charles and a couple dozen others every morning to make furniture and fix cars for the state. Still no sign of them.

He slowed even more. The Toyota disappeared ahead.

"My grandma drives faster than you," Dingo said. "And she's dead."

M-pat ignored him. In the mirror, a pickup closed from behind. A big metal top covered the bed. *So much for no traffic.*

There they were. Teenagers caught in the system, wearing bright orange coveralls, filed out of the juvie entrance overhang and past the white columns holding it up. No chains, no handcuffs—this was a minimum security facility. One of the guards walked in front, a skinny white boy wearing a PrisonCorp uniform. And a holster with a .38. *Where's the other guard?*

M-pat glanced down at his metallic Faraday bag. Still strapped on, still closed to protect the stun gun and handheld comlink inside. *I'd feel better with a Glock.* The stun gun only had two charges, and only put them down a few minutes.

"Gonna stash my glasses," Dingo said. He opened his Faraday bag, threw his data glasses inside, and refastened it.

The van drew close enough to make out faces. *There!* Charles Marvin Lee, a.k.a. Dr. Doom, the now seventeen-year-old hacker who'd added a zombie invasion to MediaCorp's news ticker and got a two year sentence for his trouble. No mistaking that puffy cocoa face. "Ready?"

"You know it, chief."

Breathing deliberately, M-pat pulled up just past the thick glass doors of the Juvie entrance, and blocked the vehicle tunnel they used to transfer prisoners.

A few paces up the sidewalk, the second guard, a middle-aged black man, hurried stragglers toward the crosswalk. More guards would be inside. One at the reception desk, one at the monitors, the others probably sipping their morning coffee.

Dingo flipped a switch Pel had installed on the dashboard.

The capacitors in the windowless back of the van made no noise whatsoever as they discharged their energy into a modified power transformer and released a massive electromagnetic pulse. M-pat felt nothing. *Pel said it'd be safe.* But the van died. So did the truck behind them. And so, hopefully, did every security camera, comlink, radio, and other unprotected bit of electronics within sixty feet. The guards would have to pry the entrance doors open, and wouldn't be able to call for help.

The prisoners and their guards kept walking, oblivious.

M-pat pulled his blocky-looking stun gun out of its Faraday bag. The standby light glowed green. *Still working.* "I got the black guard. You get the cracker. Don't miss."

Dingo checked his gun and nodded. He slipped out the passenger door.

M-pat opened his door at the same time. Gun in hand but down at his side, he strode toward the black guard. The man turned, fear in his eyes.

Just a little closer. He broke into a sprint and raised his weapon. The guard fumbled at his holster, hand shaking. Some of the prisoners turned to stare.

M-pat pulled the trigger. The stun gun clicked, barely audible, and the guard crumpled to the ground. Temporarily paralyzed. He shot him again for good measure, then ran over and took his pistol.

He looked over at Dingo. The white guard was also down. *Rent-a-cops. One day a year of training.*

Charles ambled toward them. He waved the boy closer. "Hurry up."

Dingo addressed the rest of the prisoners, who all looked confused. "You're free! Go forth and—ah, just get the fuck out of here!"

* * *

Waylee

Waylee turned the getaway van onto Greenmount Avenue, the heart of the city's correctional industry. Teenage boys in orange coveralls ran down the street. None looked like Charles.

"We should be up there already," Pel said from the passenger seat, swiping the left temple arm of his data glasses to magnify the image.

"Seconds away." Waylee gunned the engine. She swerved to avoid a bike messenger, bounced over a pothole, and passed ugly brick buildings with blue plastic covering the windows.

She saw their first van parked ahead to the left, blocking the Corrections Center driveway. Orange-clad teens fought with a pickup driver stopped in the road. Two guards lay motionless on the ground.

There! Two fiftyish men in cheap suits stood on the sidewalk and looked her way, feet tapping the concrete. One was brawny with Italian features, the other, Dick Clark.

A short, pudgy kid with coffee-hued skin paced back and forth behind them. *Charles!* A dozen other prisoners waited nearby, apparently too cowed to run. "What the hell is their problem?"

Pel glanced at her.

"Ignore that." Waylee screeched her van to a halt, but kept it in drive.

M-pat and Dingo ran for the back, Charles following. A pair of oranges sprinted toward the passenger door. Pel locked it just as they got there. They banged on the door and window. "Lemme in, yo!"

Pel squinted at Waylee. "Should have brought more stun guns."

More banging. "Yo, bitch, lemme in!"

"Sorry," she shouted at them. "Get your own ride."

M-pat's muscular frame appeared behind the two juvies. He reached out big hands and smacked their heads together. They dropped.

Dingo stuck his Dick Clark face in a rear door window. He opened the doors and jumped in, followed by Charles, then M-pat. "Let's go," M-pat said. "Don't run over those bitches I put down."

Dingo sniffed the air. "Someone's been tokin' in here."

"I'll pass it soon as I get a chance." Waylee took her foot off the brake and accelerated, trying not to hit any prone or running figures.

"Woo kiddies!" Dingo shouted from the back. "That was too easy! B'more's first mass jailbreak."

"Welcome to freedom, Charles," Waylee said, keeping her eyes on the road. "Or do you prefer Dr. Doom?"

"Charles is a'ight," came the faint response behind her.

She passed the crosswalk. Staring out the passenger window, Pel shouted, "Guards coming out of the Training Center door! Two."

"Step on it, they goin' for their guns!" M-pat said, probably looking out the back.

Damn it. She pushed the gas pedal down, but the van responded reluctantly. *Come on.* They passed a parking garage and approached the ten-story New Inmates Center.

"Down!" M-pat shouted.

They wouldn't shoot, would they? Ahead, the light at Madison, the first intersection, was red. *Run it or turn right?* The plan was to go straight, then head northeast. Madison went one-way west.

A gun blasted behind them and echoed off the buildings, a lot louder than the *pops* she heard at home now and then. Waylee gripped the steering wheel, not in terror, but knowing that she should feel terror.

A guard ran out of the New Inmates Center as they passed, eyes wide.

Another gun blast. Something tore through the rear of the van and smacked through the windshield between her and Pel. He yelped. The bullet left a circular hole amid a web of cracks.

Another shot. The passenger side mirror shattered. Pel hunched down, trapped by the seatbelt from moving any further.

Waylee slowed at the intersection, and spun the wheel to the right. The tires squealed as the van hopped over the curb, smacked a garbage can, and sent it barreling it off toward the building. She scraped a lightpost and skidded onto Madison.

"Yeah!"

Brakes screeched somewhere behind her. Someone honked and kept honking. *Asshole.* Up the street a bus stopped, blocking half the road.

She didn't want to be on Madison. They'd pass more prison complexes and more guards. And like half the streets downtown, it was under perpetual construction. The expressway, where all the cars were probably headed, was only a few blocks ahead.

But would they make it? And wouldn't the cops expect them to take the interstate?

Fuck Madison. Waylee spun the wheel to the left toward Forrest Street. Someone clipped the rear fender and they veered off course, facing oncoming traffic. She yanked the wheel to the right, trying to correct. "Get us out of here," she yelled at Pel. "Where does Forrest go?"

More horns blew. She entered Forrest, which was empty except for parked cars, and accelerated over cratered pavement. "No sirens," she said to Pel. "Your EMP bomb must have worked."

Pel didn't respond. From the back, M-pat shouted, "Yeah, it worked. But them guards that shot at us was past sixty feet. Better believe they squawkin' now."

"DG, directions," Pel said at the same time. Staring forward, his voice trembled. "Follow Forrest one block and turn left on Monument. Then we can take Ensor to Harford and we're out of here."

Waylee reached Monument seconds later. One way east, a better choice than Madison. The light here was red too. *Naturally.* She decided not to run it, and checked the mirror, the one that hadn't been shot out. No pursuit yet.

As soon as the light changed, she floored the van onto Monument. Not a whole lot of traffic. After a couple of blocks, she turned left on Ensor Street, three lanes in each direction, and headed out of the city. To the rendezvous point.

3

Waylee

As Waylee drove the getaway van north on Ensor, row after row of red-brick public housing on either side, Charles's voice sounded behind her. "Which one of you is Aunt Emma?"

That would be me. Waylee focused on the road. But at the first red light, she unhooked her seatbelt. "Pel, you drive."

His eyes widened. "What? We're in traffic..."

Waylee made her way into the back of the van and Pel scooted over to the driver's seat.

The back had no seats, just a black plastic mat. Charles huddled against the metal siding.

Sitting next to a 'Green Baltimore' reusable bag, Dingo grinned and thrust up a fist. M-pat stared out the rear window without the bullet hole.

She pointed at Dingo and jerked a thumb over her shoulder. "You're shotgun now."

"I'm down. You could have brought cushions, you know." He didn't look scared at all.

Waylee shrugged and handed him the rest of her joint.

"A'ight then." He headed to the passenger seat.

"Watch for cops." *And keep Pel from freaking out.*

The van jolted forward. Waylee tried not to fall as it bounced over fractured asphalt. She sat next to Charles, the floor mat hard against her ass. She pulled off her gloves, but kept the mask on, and reached out a fist for him to bump. Citywide gesture for solidarity and respect. "I'm the one who messaged you."

Charles hesitated, then tapped a fist against hers. "And now you want my help," he said. "Bad, to scheme up so much trouble."

He looked so young. And flabby—he must not exercise much. And why the hesitation? "We made an agreement. Freedom for yourself, freedom for everyone." *An awakening, anyway, then others can do the rest.*

He shrank away. "What if they catch me? They could try me as an adult, then I'd never get out."

She closed the distance and touched his arm. "They won't catch you. They catch you, that means they catch me, and I got enough problems as it is. Trust me, we planned this out. No way is BPD or PrisonCorp going to find any leads. These are the best masks made."

Normally only movie studios could afford Baltimore Transformations, who didn't even have to advertise their services, but her sister, a legend in the local cosplay scene, fabricated a batch of anime costumes in return.

His eyes roved across her face. "You do look real."

"Plus, no fingerprints, no DNA, and both vans were hulks we found and fixed up."

Charles still looked scared. "They got me from a snitch, someone from school."

"Well, you shouldn't have bragged about your hacking there."

He nodded.

"I know my friends," she said. "They all hate authority, they all have principles, and we're tight like family. No snitchers."

Music blared from the front. A neo-grindcore cover of Son Volt's "Medicine Hat." *Dingo.*

"Knock it down a bit," Waylee shouted. "We're trying to talk."

"C'mon, this shit is apropos," Dingo said.

The volume dropped. "Thanks, Pel."

M-pat stared at her.

Shit, I gave Pel's name away. Charles would have to commit, no other option. She turned back to him. "You're the only one who's ever gotten through MediaCorp's defenses."

"Still?"

"Yeah. The Collective considers Dr. Doom quite an elite." Like Pel, he was in their inner circle, the closest they had to any kind of structure.

Charles beamed.

"You're local," she said. "And you passed our test."

"What test?"

"Getting back to me."

Once Pel discovered Dr. Doom—Charles Marvin Lee in the real world—was behind the MediaCorp hack, and was sent to Baltimore Juvenile for being dumb enough to brag about it in school, Waylee had mailed an old-fashioned letter from his fictitious Aunt Emma. She wrote that he had always been clever, and she held him in the highest regard. She advised him to learn a trade like car repair, and closed with, 'Hope to hear from you soon. Auntie_Emma.'

It took a while, but Charles acquired an Occupational Training slot, accessed the Comnet through a car wireless and an unencrypted hotspot, and posted a private waypoint at the intersection of Charles and Eager Streets, tagging @Auntie_Emma. They exchanged coded texts from there, the best medium they could manage via the China Autotronics All-in-One Control System.

"Gave me something to do," he said. "Deleted the evidence afterward."

"We were impressed. And the guards never noticed?"

He smirked. "Them minimum wage monkeys? Only thing they know 'bout computers is how to find porn."

The van shook, jolting down and up. Her arms clutched Charles as she fought to stay upright. "Geez, be careful!"

"Not my fault the roads are shit," Pel responded in staccato tones.

Charles's face flushed.

She let go of him. "Sorry." She searched for the overlay of stillness from the pot and embraced it. *Focus.* "Before we go any further, I need to know for sure, are you with us?"

He looked her in the eyes. "I told you in my texts, yeah, I'm down with you, you got my word. And get back at MediaCorp and the cops for jackin' me primetime and takin' all my shit?" His nostrils flared. "Yeah, sign me up."

He looked sincere. She might have jumped up and danced if not for the pot. "You, sir, are the best. We'll go over the plan when we get to the house."

"And you'll show your real self?"

Why not now? Waylee peeled off her mask. The air—even Baltimore air—felt good against her face. "I'm Waylee."

At his sentinel post by the rear window, M-pat shook his head a few degrees to either side. She decided not to introduce anyone else.

Charles's eyes drifted, then fixated on her hair.

Oh yeah. She'd dyed her long cornrows red, white, and blue for that gig at Le Chat Noir in DC. She felt a little naked without her piercings, which had to come out to get the mask on.

He finally responded. "Charles. Can't use Dr. Doom anymore." He fidgeted. "You know it ain't gonna be easy, taking over the MediaCorp feed. Why you wanna hit 'em so bad?"

She fought a surge of impatience, knowing there was no cause for it. "It's been a long fight. I got this job at the *Herald* after graduation. This was like six years ago. They always gave the noobs the lamest assignments. In my case, nightlife." *Never should have bragged about my bands.*

"I'd pitch meaningful stories," she continued, "but the editors wouldn't give me a shot. So I met... uh, my current boyfriend, and he got me interested in the Comnet and how it's destroying free expression and democracy. MediaCorp cut these secret deals with the government during the national upgrade to highspeed fiber optics. Not just to speed up the old Internet, but to make it more efficient and secure."

Charles smirked. "Ain't as secure as they think."

I love this kid. "That's why I need you. Anyway, because of these deals, everything's integrated. MediaCorp took over the backbone and switches, and they're using that to control the content. No regulations except to prohibit public competition.

"I got some specifics, like who they spread money to and how their lobbyists called the shots. Pel recruited some Collective hackers to help me get emails and documents."

Even though he wasn't involved, Charles held up a fist in solidarity or appreciation.

"Did the paper run it?" she continued. "No. MediaCorp was planning to buy the paper and my bosses were scared for their jobs. In fact, the VP yelled at me for billing hours to something outside my beat. We had some words and they put me on probation. Then—did you hear about the police attack on the Independent News Center?"

Charles squinted.

Of course not. "INC was the last independent voice in Maryland. Media-Corp tried to buy them, but they wouldn't sell. So the bastards hiked their Comnet fees, then bought their building, raised the rent, and evicted them when they couldn't pay.

"Well, they decided to stay, and MediaCorp brought in the cops. I went to cover it. They used military crowd-control weapons—pulsed micro-waves and classified stuff. I heard we were a testing ground."

He leaned toward her. "What happened?"

"Dozens of people hospitalized, some of them just kids, everyone else arrested. This BPD thug stole my recordings and fractured my skull, took months to heal." She still had a scar beneath her hair. "The paper fired me while I was in the hospital."

"Why?"

"Corporate cost savings." Her fists clenched. "So that's the end of inde-pendent journalism. MediaCorp sold everything in the building or trucked it to a landfill. It's all condos now. What they did should be a huge scandal, but corporate news spun it as a victory of law over 'militant radicals.'

"I've been writing about this threat ever since, but no one will publish it. In a Comnet without MediaCorp—let's call it the freenet—I could support myself, my boyfriend could work a legit job, and we wouldn't have to steal oil to make it through the winter. And it's not just me we're talking about. MediaCorp is destroying journalism itself, critical inquiry, everything de-mocracy needs to survive."

Charles slapped his right palm with the back of his left. "I feel ya. Free-dom of information. I'm down, I follow the code."

The van turned right. *We must be getting close.* She reached into the 'Green Baltimore' bag and handed Charles a pair of jeans, a Jesus fish T-shirt, a faded Ravens hoodie, and generic white tennies. Goodwill's finest. She hoped they fit. "Alright, Charles. Here're your new clothes."

He grimaced.

"Better than a bright orange jumpsuit. Change. We're gonna switch vehicles soon, then I'll show you your new home." She turned away to give him some privacy.

Once Charles said "done," Waylee tested his resolve.

"This op we're planning could take a couple of months."

He threw on the shoes and started lacing them. "Where am I staying?"

"With us. They'll be looking for you at home."

He tightened the left shoelace. "Ain't nothin' for me there anyhow. Just overdogged gramma, drunk-ass aunt, and more kids than we got beds. And no gear, nothin'."

She felt a strange mixture of relief and pity. "We'll get you whatever you need."

"Yeah? Money too?"

"What you need and what we can get." *Another challenge.*

"We're almost there," Pel shouted.

Waylee scrambled up front, threw her arms around his seat for balance, and peered through the bullet-cracked windshield. Putty Hill looked like every place else on Baltimore's periphery—wide roads, impersonal tract homes, lawns either neglected or mowed down to the roots. She wasn't sure where Putty Hill's boundaries were, or even if it had boundaries.

Pel followed a side street to Paulo's corrugated metal auto garage, tucked among scraggly, vine-choked trees, and almost impossible to find if you wanted a car repaired. Someone had rolled open one of the four bay doors.

Inside, Paulo, his black hair slicked back, pointed to the lift ahead. Pel parked and switched off the ignition. Paulo slapped a red button on the wall, and the garage door descended. Three assistants, no name tags on their polyester shirts, converged on the van with rags and squeegee bottles.

Pel pocketed his data glasses, peeled off his mask, and hopped out. Waylee followed Dingo out the passenger door.

The garage smelled like oil and spray paint. Their ancient Class C Motor Home sat to the left. Kiyoko bounded toward them, wearing a long pink wig bound in bows, her almond eyes shadowed and fake-lashed into Anime Big. She wore one of her frilly silk dresses, as if Paulo's grease-stained chop shop was just another cosplay club. *24/7 fashionista.*

Kiyoko hugged Pel, then Waylee. "You made it!" Her cartoonish eyes drifted to the bullet hole in the windshield. "Oh." She stepped back. "What happened? Everyone okay?"

"No worries. PrisonCorp's finest took some pot shots at us. No one got hurt."

Dingo pulled off his Dick Clark mask, returning to a 23-year-old punk with an inch-wide semi-circular scar on his forehead. He stared at the mask's empty eye sockets. "You, sir, are getting lucky tonight."

M-pat yanked off his Mafia capo mask and rolled it into a ball. He couldn't look more different now—Waylee's age, with dark brown skin and a chin strap beard.

Charles darted his eyes from one person to the next, fingers twitching.

Kiyoko tilted her powdered face toward him. "That's him? The super hacker you're risking our lives for?"

"That's him," Waylee said. "And he is a super hacker."

She frowned. "He's just a kid."

Dingo looked over. "You're one to talk."

"I'm almost twenty, Dingdong." She strolled up to Charles and curtsied. "I am Kiyoko, Princess of West Baltimore."

Charles took a step backward, then scanned her up and down. He smiled and nodded, but didn't say anything.

Speaking to each other in Portuguese, Paulo's crew wiped down the cargo van. They would take it apart next, etch off the serial numbers, and sell the parts or have them melted down at Sparrows Point. They did this every day, who knew how many stolen vehicles each year, and moved like choreographed dancers.

Pel threw his ginger mask and gloves into an old oil drum with a flame decal on the side. He looked at Paulo.

"Yes, we take care of that right after the van cleaned."

Waylee slapped Pel on the butt. "I thought I was burning that."

"Same thing." No smirk on his face.

She clambered back in the van and retrieved Charles's orange jumpsuit and her Storm mask. With empty holes for eyes, her mask looked grotesque, like a demon. "Goodbye, Storm. You're still in my heart." She threw it in the drum along with her gloves and the jumpsuit.

"Keeping my Dick Clark mask, yo," Dingo announced.

M-pat frowned and crossed his arms. "The fuck you are. I told you and Waylee to pick anonymous faces but you had to go ahead and be some kind of celebrity. Pel and I the only ones that got sense in this crew."

Pel threw up a solidarity fist.

M-pat pointed at Dingo's mask. "I expect you to burn that goddamn thing lest you get caught with it."

Waylee glanced around. "Can I change in private?"

Paulo pointed to a wooden door marked *Sacos/Bucetas*. "Over there."

She wasn't sure what the words meant, but guessed they were unsavory. "There better not be any peepholes."

She halted after a couple of steps. Charles couldn't seem to keep his eyes off her sister, who was examining the bullet holes and dented fender. He probably hadn't seen a girl in months, and Kiyoko had somehow hit the genetic jackpot, but she was off limits.

Pel, still unsmiling, interposed himself and shook his hand.

Good job.

"Charles," he said, "it's an honor. I'm Pelopidas. Pel for short. I'm the one who tracked you down."

"How'd you do it?"

"Asking around, mostly. I'm in the Collective's inner circle too."

Charles's eyes widened, and he grinned. "You got through all the puzzles?"

Pel took a second to respond. "With a little help."

Charles smirked. "I didn't need any help. What's your avatar?"

"William Godwin."

Charles squinted and didn't respond.

Pel's lips pressed into tight disappointment. The "inner circle" contained thousands of vetted hackers, ones who solved a series of cryptic puzzles, then proved themselves against selected targets. He was pretty touchy about his lack of status among them. "William Godwin's an eighteenth century philosopher. An early thriller novelist too, believe it or not."

Charles scratched his head. "Well thanks for bustin' me out. I ain't typed for jail."

M-pat trudged over to Charles. "You in fo' sho'?"

He nodded. "Yeah."

M-pat tapped fists with him. "M'patanishi."

Dingo followed. Charles stared at the eyes tattooed on the backs of his hands, but returned his tap.

"What do you call fifty bosses at the bottom of the ocean?" Dingo said.

Having lived with him for over a year, Waylee knew all his jokes, especially the tired ones. Charles, though, shrugged.

Dingo laughed out the answer. "A good start."

Waylee walked into the grimy bathroom and changed as fast as she could, then ushered everyone toward the motor home. "Let's go."

Kiyoko jumped into the driver's seat and fiddled with her wig in the mirror.

The RV was their only transportation. They could fit all their band equipment in, but it guzzled gas, especially after Pel, ever the gearhead, threw in a big V8, a 'PowerPack,' and a turbocharger. They decaled the band name, Dwarf Eats Hippo, on both sides and the back, but that was the limit of their agreement. Waylee got the "starboard" side, and wrote quotes from Rousseau, King, Goldman, and a dozen others. Kiyoko picked the left. She was a talented artist, but her tableau of manga elves and fairies spoiled the gestalt.

Pel had ceded the back to Dingo and Shakti. They worked at a graphics shop, and printed a giant sticker of MediaCorp's CEO morphed into Cthulhu, rising monstrously from the sea. Waylee smiled every time she saw it.

She started to shake Paulo's hand, then hugged him. "Thanks for everything."

"*Boa sorte.* Thanks for the van."

She climbed into the back with the rest, then heard the garage door open.

Headed home. They were 100% committed now.

4

Charles

Charles had never actually been in West Baltimore, at least not past MLK. From the camper window, it looked as shitty as East Baltimore. His broken-down neighborhood anyway, which somehow got worse every year.

He wondered how Gramma kept all them kids in school and off the corners. His mom just had him. Then she passed, close to five years ago now. Septicemia they said. Should have been treated early on, they said. Father—AWOL from day one. Probably in jail somewhere.

He might have hustled dope then, likely capped by now. But he discovered the Internet as a kid, back when the libraries were open. The Internet was like caveman tech—slow, clunky, and two dimensional. You had to hand it to MediaCorp—its replacement, the Comnet, was a million times better. Especially if you ordered immersion gear on a stolen credit card.

Charles turned away from the window. Sitting next to him on a red velvet couch, Pelopidas stared forward while Waylee rubbed his hand. The other two, M'patanishi and Dingo, shared a matching couch directly opposite. The rest of the camper was crowded with coiled cables, tool boxes, rolls of duct tape, and cardboard boxes full of Dwarf Eats Hippo T-shirts and crap.

Ahead and a little below, that girl Kiyoko sat behind the wheel, humming to herself while driving. She was weird, but beautiful like no one he'd ever seen. Like an angel. Forgetting the pink hair, she looked kind of Chinese, with some European mixed in. He wondered what her body looked like without that dress on.

As for the others, Waylee was either white or Hispanic, kinda thin, and had a pretty face. In fact, she'd be fine if she was younger and not so punked out. She seemed to be the leader. She had these eyes you couldn't turn away from.

Her man, Pelopidas, was the first Collectivista he'd ever met in person. You could tell he was a performer by his braided beard and all the tats. Like Waylee and Kiyoko, with their bright-colored hair.

With his old white guy mask gone, the one called M'patanishi was a brother. One look at those muscles and eyes and you knew he was lethal. Not someone you'd want to fuck with.

Waylee turned to him. "We've got a room set up for you. More than one, actually."

They must be rich. Either from rhyming or stealing. "So you're all in the Collective?"

Waylee smiled and shook her head. "No, no. Just Pel."

"But you said in your texts you're a hacktivist."

"Well, yeah, sort of. Pel's the hacker, I'm the activist. So together..."

Charles nodded. *Half and half, huh?* To the butt-tards in juvie, on his street too, women were just hos and bitches. Maybe Pel was her bitch. He laughed inside.

Maybe he should have toughed out another year. But it was too late now. Might as well enjoy the freedom, and make the best of it.

He pointed at M-pat and Dingo. "What about the soldiers?"

"They're friends. They're not soldiers."

They drove past endless townhouses, some boarded up. People sat on stoops or stood on corners, quite a few sucking on electronic drug vaporizers. Then they passed a thick band of trees and turned left, onto a street of standalone houses with yards.

"We still in B'more?" he asked.

Waylee glanced out the window, then back at him. "Yeah, we just passed Gwynns Falls. We're in a warehouse and factory district, but this is a nice little neighborhood sandwiched in."

"For Ballmer, anyway," M-pat said from the opposite couch. "We still get some shootings and break-ins, but mostly West Ballmer turf is all parceled out and we in a DMZ."

"A what?" Charles asked.

"Demilitarized zone. 66 detached homes, 63 townhouses. Workin' folk with families, mostly. And some retirees. I'm the Chief Facilitator."

"What… What does that mean?"

"Mostly it's conflict resolution and fixin' problems. Sometimes I got to bust some heads, though." The big man smiled for the first time. "It's my Ujamaa contribution."

"Say what?"

"Ujamaa's about families and communities comin' together and takin' care of each other and not lettin' outsiders tryin' to run things for you. Julius Nyerere invented it for Tanzania after he threw out the colonial occupiers."

Dingo leaned forward. "I'm the chief deputy." He punched the air. "Krav Maga!"

Charles backed into his seat. In his hood, crazies were usually high on something, and sometimes they attacked people and bit their faces off.

"We're here," Kiyoko said, her voice high and musical. She pulled up next to a two-story corner house with white peeling paint and drawn curtains, surrounded by a tall chain link fence topped with barbed wire.

Pelopidas hopped out and unlocked a heavy gate, then Kiyoko parked on a gravel driveway inside, scraping bare tree branches in the process.

The front door opened. A young Indian woman, like the type you saw behind corner grocery counters, rushed onto the porch and down the brick stairs. She wore one of those bright wraparound dresses and couldn't run very fast. Dingo ran out and they hugged.

Charles stepped out next. A loud bark shook him nearly out of his shoes. Right next to the motor home, a massive pit bull bared sharp teeth and barked twice more. *Shit!* He tried to back into the camper, but couldn't seem to find the door.

The Indian girl clapped at the beast. "Quiet, Laelaps. This is our guest. Now sit." The beast obeyed.

She turned to Charles. "Don't worry, he's never actually bitten anyone. He even leaves the cat alone." Her voice sounded kind of Caribbean. "I'm Shakti by the way." She offered her hand.

Before he could respond, someone slapped a palm against his back and nudged him toward the narrow side yard. "Can't be seen out here." Pelopidas's voice. "Shakti, could you let us in the back?"

Dingo snickered. Pelopidas muttered something and led Charles along the side of the house. They entered a big backyard with lettuce and other shit growing on raised beds, a wooden dog house just past, and more chain link fence, overgrown with vines.

Shakti opened the back door and ushered them into a kitchen crammed with cabinets and half-bare shelves. She thrust her hand in Charles's and shook it. "Shakti. Pardon Pel's interruption before." She smelled like coconut and vanilla.

Waylee entered from a dining room, followed by Pelopidas, Dingo, and M-pat. Pelopidas grabbed a can of beer out of the refrigerator. He yanked the tab back and chugged, not even stopping to breathe. *He should meet my aunt.*

Waylee frowned. "Don't drink them all." She slapped her hands into a prayer position. "Welcome, Charles." She waved toward Shakti. "We're at the edge of the zone, so someone has to stay here in case some scavenger gets desperate."

"Took a couple days off," Shakti said. She was short and soft looking, though, not very intimidating.

Waylee seemed to read his mind. "Shakti's another of M-pat's deputies. Knows how to handle herself. And she's a big player in the People's Party, in case our project needs more help."

Shakti spread her hands. "We don't believe in big players. It's bottom up."

Waylee waved him forward. "Let me show you around real quick." Pelopidas finished his beer and they led him through a dining room, living room, and bathroom on the first floor. They passed three bedrooms, a game room, and a bathroom on the second. M-pat lived down the street, Waylee said. The rest lived here.

Kiyoko's room was obvious. She'd painted her name on the door and topped it with a rainbow and unicorns. Charles looked behind him, but she hadn't followed them up.

They had two more bedrooms in the attic. "You can have one of these," Waylee said, "whichever one you want. They're crash pads—"

"Like for touring indy bands," Pelopidas said.

Waylee nodded. "But no other guests while you're here."

The guest rooms looked more or less the same—walls slanting to a triangle, small window, mattresses on the floor, wires and ductwork everywhere, cardboard boxes and piles of college textbooks against the sides. The rooms smelled a little musty. Better than jail though. And they were air conditioned.

Charles picked the one with the most outlets. He looked around but didn't see any roaches. No way was he gonna wake up with a roach on his face again.

"Basement's a practice room for the band," Waylee said as they walked back down the stairs to the ground floor. "We throw parties there too, mostly fundraisers."

"Thought y'all was in a band."

"Yeah. Me, Pel, and Kiyoko. Used to be a fourth, J-Jay, but he sold out."

They arrived back in the living room, where the others, except for Princess Kiyoko, stood talking. Dingo and M-pat were drinking beers. They passed cans to Pel and Waylee.

"What's your band like?" Charles said. "Camper says Dwarf Eats Hippo, that the name?"

Pelopidas opened his beer. "Yeah. It's more or less random. Our music, I don't know what you'd call it. Waylee does most of the writing, and she's always changing things." He started guzzling.

Waylee turned. "'Post-industrial neuro-punk,' the City Paper reviewer said. Back when there was a City Paper. 'Alternating between slow-tempoed doom and rapid-fire multi-prong attacks, often in the same song.' Really, I just write what's in my head, play what I feel. Best to hear for yourself."

"You big?" Charles said.

"If we were, would we be living here?" She took a swig of beer.

"Seems a'ight to me." Pretty damn big, actually.

Waylee jerked a thumb toward Pelopidas. "Thanks to Mr. Fix-It-Up here and his generous parents."

Still no sign of the Princess of West Baltimore. "So Kiyoko," he asked, "is she joining us?"

Waylee frowned. "She's probably in BetterWorld or playing with her cat. She's not really a part of this."

The mention of MediaCorp's three-dimensional social and gaming network tightened his stomach. BetterWorld was his real home, the only place he ever felt easy since his mom passed. He even had his own island there until the feds ganked it along with his gear. He wondered what Kiyoko's avatar looked like, and how to find her. "Is she really a Princess?"

Dingo started laughing.

Stupid question. I never say the right thing.

Waylee put her beer down on the living room table and slapped her hands together in front of Dingo's face. "Zip it."

He shut up and stared icicles.

She turned back to Charles. "She's a princess in BetterWorld. She takes it way too seriously..."

Waylee kept talking. At the same time, she unlocked a sheet metal-reinforced closet door and pulled out a Genki-san interface unit. It could process Comnet data packets as fast as they came in, and had a big touchpad you could stretch into any shape you wanted. She sat in a recliner, turned on the unit, then powered on the huge screen covering one of the walls. "Let's see what the cops are doing."

The others plopped onto the sofa or chairs. Charles decided to stand for now.

The MediaCorp News logo appeared, 'Your Trusted News Source' beneath, then it dissolved to a couple of suits behind a desk. Shakti tapped the volume icon on the wall skin.

"And so polls indicate overwhelming support for the police intervention," one said.

Wha?

"Really, we are seeing the last vestige of unionism here," the other said. "The union bosses know they're irrelevant now, but just like spoiled children, they're paying thugs to act out and try to disrupt things, when most people just want to go to work and pay their bills."

Not about him. Charles looked at the ticker beneath. "PRESIDENT RAND UNVEILS NEW WEAPONS IN WAR AGAINST TERROR ... BEAUTY QUEEN SCANDAL UPDATE..."

"Switching to local," Waylee said.

A news broadcaster, some white woman, appeared on the wall. Eleven male faces, including his, lined the space beneath. "—contact the police immediately if you see any of these—"

"Hold on, let me go back," Waylee said. She swiped a finger along the Genki-san.

The screen showed a street blocked off, police cars and uniforms crowding the other side of the barricades. Another woman spoke in a microphone. "This is the scene where eleven inmates at the Baltimore Juvenile Correctional Facility escaped around 8:30 this morning. All the others are accounted for. The details are sketchy at this point, but apparently the inmates were aided by outside persons."

A popup showed a close-up of a white van, swarming with glove-wearing authority types. "According to police, the outside persons arrived in this cargo van, jumped out, and disabled the guards. Thankfully—"

In her recliner, Waylee mouthed something and threw up her hands.

"—both guards," the reporter continued, "are now recovering. The perpetrators then escaped in a second van, also white, license plate AMM513." The numbers appeared over the video. "They were last seen driving west on Madison Street. Back to you."

The studio anchor reappeared. "Thanks, Inez. And now, Lieutenant Harris from the Baltimore Police Public Affairs Office has a few words."

A thirtyish black man in uniform appeared. "We've got a massive manhunt under way, and hope to have all the criminals in custody soon…"

How massive?

Computer sims of M-pat's and Dingo's masks appeared in a side window, their heads turning like demons.

Dingo slapped his thigh. "Cracklin'! They don't know it's Dick Clark!"

"Who's that?" Charles asked.

"If you see either of these two people," Lieutenant Harris said on the screen, "please contact the police immediately. They should be considered armed and dangerous."

Dingo laughed so loud, Waylee paused the feed.

Charles sat down in a chair well away from him.

When Dingo stopped laughing and Waylee resumed the video, eleven faces popped up below, with the text "Click the photo for more information." Lt. Harris read names, descriptions, and convictions of escaped inmates. Text and rotating heads appeared in a column to the right. "…Charles Marvin Lee. 17 years of age, African American, black hair and brown eyes, 5' 5" tall and 160 lbs. Convicted for felony computer trespass, computer fraud, wire fraud, and criminal mischief…"

It was just for lulz. No one got hurt.

"…Again," Lt. Harris said, "please contact the police immediately if you see any of these persons."

"Charles," M-pat said when the piece ended, "I suggest you stay inside."

Fine with me.

Waylee put the Genki-san aside, stood, and claimed the center of the room. "So let's talk about the next phase." She met his eyes. "Charles, you said you're in."

"Yeah, but I don't know what we're doing."

"I'm gonna fill you in. Everyone else still in, right?"

Dingo threw up a fist, creepy eye on the back.

Shakti raised a hand. "Dingo told me you got shot at. Why didn't you tell me that?"

Waylee looked at Dingo, who shrugged. "No one was hurt," she said.

M-pat shook his head. "I didn't account for them guards to come out and clap iron. Bullets flyin' an' shit, we lucky no one dead."

Waylee bounced on her feet like she was gonna throw a karate kick. "We're not repeating that. But we need you. Not to break in or anything, but your advice and contacts if nothing else."

M-pat leaned forward. "It's one thing to take on rent-a-cops. But Homeland?"

Charles felt shaky. Homeland Security had a vendetta against hackers, and they were the ones who'd put him away. Lucky he was a minor.

Waylee waved her hands. "We're not going to take on Homeland Security. Give me some credit. They'll never know we're there."

M-pat crossed his thick arms and sat back on the sofa.

"Never know we're where?" Charles asked.

Waylee grinned. "On New Year's Eve, MediaCorp's co-sponsoring a special fundraiser in DC for the president's re-election. The biggest movers and shakers in the country will be there."

"Like a billionaire's ball," Shakti said.

Waylee's eyes sparkled. "We're gonna sneak in."

Charles looked at the weird hair and tattoos in the room. They didn't exactly pass for rich old men.

Waylee sat back down at the Genki-san and brought up a menu of video clips. She clicked one.

On screen, a big green helicopter landed on the White House lawn. A door near the front swung down, and a Marine in old-fashioned dress uniform marched out. He stood at attention, and a couple of white men in suits walked down the stairs. One was President Rand. The other was shorter and older.

"That's the president and Bob Luxmore." She pointed at the man next to the president. "Founder and CEO of Media Corporation."

The two ignored the Marine and walked across the lawn together. Waylee paused the video. "They meet all the time, but no one knows what they say to each other. In fact, there's surprisingly little on Luxmore—what he's like in person, what his agenda is, and why he has such extraordinary access to the president. I seem to be the only one who cares."

"Everyone here cares," Shakti said.

Waylee kept talking. "Luxmore will be at the New Year's gala. And the president, of course—it's his fundraiser. I want to hear what they're up to."

"We already know that," Dingo said. "Privatize the world and enrich their cronies."

"But people need to know specifics, and hear it from their leaders' own lips." She stood tall and waved her hands around. "The elites are like anyone else. When they're just among friends, their own kind, they let their guard down. We'll get to hear them talk straight up, say what they really think. And even more important, copy what we can from their comlinks. It'll be like a remote cam in a rattlesnake nest."

It sounded fun, but was probably more trouble than it was worth. How would they copy comlink data without the Secret Service noticing?

Waylee's eyes locked on to him like laser cannons. "Then, we're gonna broadcast it everywhere. That's where you come in, although we need your help with the first part too."

Maybe I shouldn't have agreed to this...

"We're gonna spread the truth. Expose the plutocrats for what they are." Her voice pounded the air like B'more Club hip hop. "Destroy public support for their agenda. Wake people up, create a trigger event."

It sounded like she was done. "Uh, what's a plutocrat anyway?"

She moved closer. "Plutocrats are the super-rich elite—they decide who gets elected and what gets done. And not just here—their trade agreements shackle the whole world. They set the rules and I'm tired of playing by them."

Shakti started to say something, but Waylee kept going. His heart pounded to the tempo of her voice.

"Did you know the richest fifty people on earth control more wealth than half the world's population? Four billion people?"

"You're shittin' me."

"Look it up. And the trend is accelerating. There's plenty of money and resources to solve the world's problems—lift people out of poverty, provide education and health care, stop global warming and the extinction crisis. Why isn't this happening?"

Charles shrugged.

"Because the people who control wealth and power live in their own stratosphere and want to keep it that way. MediaCorp and their allies channel more money to political campaigns than the rest of the country combined." She looked around. "Sure, some of the super-rich sympathize with the suffering masses, but on their own terms, terms that won't challenge their position. And MediaCorp is their biggest mouthpiece, manufacturing pseudoreality and keeping people distracted and divided."

Soo-doo-what?

"Information," Pelopidas said, "should be open and shared."

The Code. "Know that."

Waylee spoke at the same time. "And accurate."

Shakti stood. "Can I talk?"

Waylee shut up and stepped back. "Of course."

"You know I love you and I'm always there for you."

Waylee threw up her palms. "What is it?"

"You and M-pat said today would be easy, but you got shot at. And it only gets harder from here."

Waylee huffed. "You're not backing out, are you? Where's your sense of adventure?"

Shakti shifted her feet. "Look, the People's Party is accomplishing real things in Baltimore. Co-ops, labor exchanges, food gardens, volunteer doctors and lawyers…"

Waylee fidgeted as Shakti continued. "And we won a seat on the city council last election. We'll take over before long."

Waylee sliced the air with her hand. "Not likely. The two major parties are changing the laws state by state, including Maryland next year, to keep us off the ballot. Electoral politics is a dead end."

Shakti flinched. "But you were such a big supporter. As long as I've known you—"

"Let's focus on the mission, alright?"

Charles stepped in. "So the People's Party organized this breakout?"

Waylee shook her head, waving cornrow ends the colors of the flag. "No, most of us are members, but this isn't their operation. Direct action isn't their thing."

"Not true," Shakti said. "It's just breaking the law that's the issue. And I really don't think you'll accomplish much. I mean, trigger social change with a video? Come on."

"That's because you haven't studied journalism. The Watergate investigation. The Pentagon Papers. Wikileaks. Silent Spring. The Jungle. Das Kapital. The Rights of Man. I could stand here for hours listing stories and books that changed the world. Have some faith."

She fixed her eyes on Charles. "Things have to change and I'm done being irrelevant, preaching to the margins with no hope for the future." Her teeth glittered white. "We need you to take over the MediaCorp broadcast at a peak viewing time. See, less than half a percent of Americans follow independent news, and that's declining fast. But public opinion shifts require audiences between thirty and forty percent. So that's the size we're shooting for. We'll replace their program with ours."

"Take over the whole broadcast?" *Was that even possible?*

"Long enough to get our video out, to give people a dose of the truth. 'Enlighten the people,' Thomas Jefferson wrote, 'and tyranny and oppressions of body and mind will vanish like evil spirits at the dawn of day.'"

5

Charles

Waylee's crew argued detail after detail about their plan and how to keep him hidden. At first, he worried that his rescuers were crazies, like the ones who slept under bridges and shouted gibberish to themselves.

But the more he thought on it, the better Waylee's idea sounded. It was the ultimate hack. If he could pull it off, he'd be famous forever. And they obviously had skills and connections of their own; it wouldn't all be on him. Like his past ops where he tapped the Collective for cracks and tools.

And he owed them. He'd never say it, but the others in juvie bullied him nonstop, shoving him around and calling him Chubby Charlie Thunderbutt, Dr. Chunkenstein, and a dozen other moronic names. 'Cause he was a little out of shape and couldn't fight.

M-pat took off, then Waylee turned to Charles. "Ready to get started?"

"Guess so."

"First thing we need to figure out is how to get in the fundraiser." She wrote down a link that would take him to the event site. Then she led him and Pelopidas back upstairs to the game room. Pelopidas unlocked three deadbolts.

Inside, sheet metal covered the window. He saw another Genki-san and wall skin, and some standard control boxes. A transparent red cube packed with chips and blinking lights sat on the floor next to a small pile of black data cubes and a rolled-up keyboard and screen.

Best of all, a virtual reality system filled half the room. Not just a helmet and gloves like he used to have, but a full suit. It stood upright on a bowl-like treadmill, connected by strands to a cylindrical cage of arcing beams. Except for the shiny faceplate, the entire setup was matte-black. Probably the most stylish thing he'd ever seen. "Damn."

Pelopidas finished off his beer. "This was state of the art when I bought it." He unhooked the sleek, almost featureless helmet and handed it to him. Fiber optic and power cables trailed behind. "It's got stereoscopic and peripheral 3-D vision that follows your view, surround sound audio, and a microphone with real-time voice changing."

Charles started to say his helmet had all that, but Pelopidas kept talking. "Boots have minimal friction so you can run in place on the treadmill. Data gloves have inertial trackers and tactile feedback, and so does the rest of the suit. But the best part is the carbon nanotube muscles." He waved a finger at the fibers holding it up. "They can change length almost instantly, and support your whole weight, so you can run, jump, even fly in place. There's nanotubes inside the suit too. They stiffen when you sit down, and with the support fibers it's just like having a chair. And they can apply pressure, so you can feel where you've been hit."

Hit? Oh, in a game... Charles had never been a big gamer but you definitely needed immersion gear for BetterWorld. "How much?"

"Less than a grand now."

Really? The helmet felt smooth and a little warm in his hands.

"Which is still a fortune for most people 'round here," Pelopidas continued.

"No doubt." No way that frame would fit in his gramma's house anyway.

"I'm an early adopter, so this setup cost a mint. That is, it cost some insurance company a mint."

Charles tapped fists with his fellow Collectivista. "Know that." He'd mostly bought on stolen credit cards but there were lots of ways.

"Just to let you know, I only take what I need, from those who can afford it, and try to keep a low profile."

That's bitch talk, but whatever. Charles pointed to the transparent red cube on the other side of the room. "What's that?"

Pelopidas smiled for the first time. "Supercomputer I built with an old classmate. Sixty-four processors. Cheap but it flies." He grinned. "I call her Big Red."

"Now there's a decryption tool." *Gotta respect someone who builds their own supercomputer.*

He nodded. "I've got a computer science degree. Hardware and operating systems are my specialty. Which is why we need you. I can do the basics online, but you're at a whole other level there."

"I know my way around." He had a knack for code and operating systems. He figured he knew Qualia, the BetterWorld programming language, better than English. Same for Edict, the language of the Comnet, and Unix/Linux, the ancient operating systems its servers still relied on. Sometimes he dreamed in Qualia or Edict, commands weaving together like songs.

As Dr. Doom, he roamed the Comnet at will. Firewalls, locks, detection sensors, not a worry. Well, sometimes a worry, but if he wanted something, he found a way to get it. He traded passwords, account numbers, and back doors with other members of the Collective, or the buyers who'd been vetted into the Emporium.

The secret to his success in BetterWorld was an army of AI bots that scoured the virtual clubs for him. They had different exteriors, but ran the same basic code, making them easy to replicate. You couldn't tell them from humans without a Turing test administered by professionals. Basically his bots were vampires – if they touched your avatar, they'd transmit a packet of viruses that would infect your account and computer. He could transmit someone's BetterWorld credits to a dropbox which he could empty at his leisure.

Pelopidas pointed at the helmet. "Ready to get started?"

Charles couldn't wait to test everything out. "You know it."

Pelopidas held up a finger. "One last thing." He handed Charles two plastic spray bottles numbered '1' and '2' with a Sharpie, and a box labeled 'Kimwipes.' "Spray and wipe everything you touch, including the immersion gear. Bottle 1 has a diluted bleach mix. Spray that first, let it sit, then wipe it up. Don't spray it on colored fabric."

Charles nodded.

Pelopidas grinned. "Bottle 2 has a solution of preserved DNA from our dog Laelaps. If you spray that on afterward, it will disguise what little DNA is left."

"Dog DNA?"

His grin widened. "Yeah, I'd love to see a lab tech telling his superiors, 'Sir, this VR gear was last used by a dog!'"

Charles laughed. "Damn, you too much!"

"I made a ton of it so we shouldn't run out."

Charles set down the bottles for now. He sat in a swivel chair and put on the helmet and gloves, not bothering with the full suit. That could come later.

He could see normally through the visor, although the room looked a little darker, like wearing sunglasses. See-through icons floated to the sides, and a keyboard filled most of the bottom.

"You can give voice commands," Pelopidas said. "Just like data glasses. Say VR first, then tell the helmet computer what you want to do."

"Yeah, mine worked the same way."

First thing was to get rid of the distractions. "VR, opaque."

The game room blinked out, leaving him in complete darkness except for the icons and keyboard. "VR, gloves."

A pair of solid-looking hands appeared in front of him, poking out of long black sleeves, like part of a funeral suit. The hands were a white man's, and finely rendered, showing not only the main knuckle creases, but the webbing of creases between. "VR, hand transparency 50%."

The hands and arms lost some of their solidity, so he could see through them.

"VR, give me black man hands."

They darkened to a chocolate color, still see through. Charles experimented with the gloves, waving them around until he got the hang of how the computer translated his movements. Then he clicked the Comnet icon.

The familiar barebones interface of the Collective Router popped up and generated a fake Comnet address, computer ID, and geographic location. It then opened a portal into the Comnet, displaying a galaxy of new icons and pathways, and shoving the offline ones to the side. Unlike normal browsers, it would encrypt everything multiple times, then route the data through random relays controlled by the Collective. Each relay would decrypt one layer, so only the destination computer could see what he typed, and it would have no idea who or where he really was.

He found another familiar program and created a new Comnet account. Using Dr. Doom would be a bad idea. He wasn't feeling particularly imaginative, and so Joe34567 sprang into existence. Then he brought up a virtual keyboard and typed the link Waylee gave him.

The link brought him to a 2D site administered by the Campaign to Re-elect the President, titled "Celebrate the New Year with the President: An Exclusive Gala." It would be held at the Smithsonian Institution Building (aka The Castle) from 8 pm to 2 am. *Thank God it's not in the White House.*

Charles explored the site. Samples of lame-ass music. Menu of fancy food. No price listed for admission, just a dropbox to return invitation responses.

There didn't seem to be any way to list the invitees, although he saw a link to contact the administrator. It being invite only, Waylee wouldn't be able to get in. Unless she was a barmaid or something. Or musician; she could do that.

Charles set up sniffers outside the target to copy any incoming or outgoing data. He ran a script to duplicate the entire site so he could examine the code at his leisure. Then he went on a virtual tour of the Smithsonian Castle. It did look like a castle. Built in the 1840's... the first Smithsonian building... now housing various executive and law offices. The event would probably be in the Great Hall.

He hoped he wouldn't have to go.

* * *

Waylee

Once Charles had settled in, Waylee grabbed Pel's hand and marched him to their bedroom. She shut the door, and not bothering with words, pulled their clothes off as fast as she could.

He didn't look as enthusiastic as usual. He started to say something but she buried her tongue in his mouth and pulled him down on the bed.

His instincts took over and she crashed against him like a tsunami. They varied positions and kept at it, each climax demanding another, until her lover was too spent to continue.

Pel gazed at her with those sappy eyes he always got after a vigorous session. "I love you, Waylee." Despite his tats and buzzcut and braided Jack Sparrow beard, Pel was about as fierce as a kitten.

She kissed him, tasting her own salty musk on his lips, chased with stale beer. "You're a godsend."

Indeed, Pel was an inestimable gift from a generally hostile universe. Her first years in Baltimore were rough, especially with Kiyoko to take care of. Waylee was sixteen, and her sister only seven, when they fled Philly and the drunken fists of her stepfather and mother. Baltimore, though only a two hour bus ride, was as far as the contents of her mother's purse could take them. They squatted, stayed in shelters, or lived with her boyfriends or musician friends, never the same place for long.

But Pel, just a bandmate at first, fell for her hard, and brought stability that none of her prior boyfriends managed. He didn't have a drug habit, for starters. He convinced his parents to buy this house off foreclosure, a great investment he told them. Best of all, Pel stuck with her despite her past, despite her condition.

"You're the only one who's been able to put up with me," she said. *Five years now.*

Pel lay back on the bed, still gazing at her. "You've been incredible ever since you saw that zombie message."

She looked him up and down. "You haven't been bad yourself."

He smiled. "I meant in general." He propped his head on an elbow. "It's like you're on a plateau. Some dips now and then, but barely noticeable."

She sat up. "Today was certainly spectacular." She had finally graduated from a lifetime of futility. Her enemy, the people's enemy, wasn't invincible after all, and she'd bring them down.

Pel's glow disappeared.

"What's wrong?"

He held his thumb and index finger a few inches apart. "I was this close to getting my brains blown out."

"Come on, it wasn't that close."

He averted his eyes. "I just about crapped myself."

"Well it's a good thing you kept your sphincter shut. Charles would have bailed for sure."

Pel pressed his lips together.

She twined her fingers into his. "I'm sorry. I know it wasn't funny." She kissed him.

It looked like he wasn't ready for more sex yet, so her hand moved to the toy drawer in the night stand.

He ran fingers along the curve of her hip. "Want some help?"

"Nah, I got it." But she put the vibrator down. It bored her anyway.

He's right. Someone could have been killed. "Pel, do you think I use you?"

"You mean like a sex toy, or 'cause I'm a master chef and do most of the cooking?"

She laughed. "Your cooking sucks. It's just mine is worse, and Kiyoko is completely useless at anything practical."

Pel looked hurt.

"Sorry, I was just being snarky." She gripped his pec muscles and tweaked his nipples. "You can cook. But I meant, you're right, we took a big risk today. And there's bigger to come."

He slapped her ass, a part of her body that obsessed him. "We all agreed to it. Don't feel guilty."

Waylee slid her hands down the smooth skin of his torso. "You do so much for me. What do I do for you?"

He pointed in the direction her hands were headed.

She chuckled. "Besides that, I mean. You can get that from anyone. That Greektown sweetie your parents want you with, for example."

"Audrey? That's ancient." He entwined his fingers with hers. "You're the only girl for me now. You're like a blazing sun. You can change the world. And we have each others' backs."

Waylee kissed him, then focused on prepping him for another round.

"Aren't you worried?" he said after a couple of minutes.

She was busy, so she just shrugged. Her brain told her not to worry about anything, but her brain couldn't always be trusted. Another reason to have Pel around.

Waylee sat up when her lover looked ready.

"I hope Charles…" he started to say.

I can't believe he's thinking about Charles. She straddled him, shivering at the sensation. "Shut up and do me again. We've barely started."

On a plateau, he said. She hoped this ride would last, but deep inside, knew better. Even if she couldn't see the precipice, it was out there, waiting.

Charles

Charles finished poking around the Smithsonian site, then downloaded some programs from Collective servers that Pel didn't seem to have. Ninety percent of hacking was having a good toolkit.

His stomach growled. He didn't remember seeing snacks in the game room, though. And he wanted to check out BetterWorld. At least for a while.

Pel's virtual reality helmet already had the Collective's software for viewing BetterWorld. Like their Comnet browser, it masked the user's identity and location. And it wasn't full of spyware like the "required" MediaCorp version.

Once Charles confirmed he couldn't be tracked, he opened a portal to BetterWorld. Joe34567 didn't have a virtual home yet, so he started in an anonymous white room full of ads for destinations, avatar mods, and opportunities to trade outside currency for BetterWorld credits. He ignored the offer to install the latest viewing software, and started building an avatar, Big J.

He scrolled through the options, and made Big J an up-and-coming rap artist and private eye, built like a linebacker, and dressed as stylish as the initial wardrobe allowed. *I need some credits to step this chump up.*

He brought up the software's teleport interface. Unfortunately, you couldn't teleport just anywhere in BetterWorld, only to fixed destinations, like property you owned, public sites, or places you got permission to visit. Some of the advertised destinations looked pretty cool—adventures, combat games, all kinds of clubs... He ignored them for now and brought up a search box. "Princess Kiyoko," he said. Might as well find out more about her.

An avatar portait appeared. It looked just like the real Kiyoko, pink hair and all. 'Course, her looks were hard to improve on.

He selected the "my site" link beneath her picture. A doorway appeared and he stepped through, finding himself in an upscale shopping mall, with several levels arranged in nested rings. Other avatars walked around, most wearing costumes like cartoon characters.

The entry level sold clothes and accessories, all designed by her. The level above focused on her band, Dwarf Eats Hippo. Video clips played on the back wall. Kiyoko, who played bass, looked out of place in such a hard-edged band, but seemed to enjoy being on stage. Pel stood in the back with his mix decks and shit. Waylee, though, pounded her guitar and jumped around like a human tornado. *Girl could be a star, why's she risking that?*

He took an escalator to the third level, devoted to her kingdom, called Yumekuni and located over on the Fantasy Continent. He pulled up a search window. 'Yumekuni' was Japanese for 'dream country.' A sign explained that you could visit with permission, "as long as you weren't affiliated with Prince Vostok."

And above this, he hit the jackpot—fan hangouts and a gallery of modeling photos. He flipped through the photos. Unfortunately, no nudes, not even bikini shots.

He started feeling like a stalker and returned to the teleport. "Swagspeare's," he told the search engine. It was no doubt the tip-toppest virtual club on the continent of Urbania. Dr. Doom's homies hung out there—not many hacktivists, mostly profiteers and torchers. Besides checking out who was still in the game, maybe he could scratch up some help.

A portal opened and he walked onto the sidewalk in front of the club. Like everything in BetterWorld, Urbania looked as real as Baltimore. 'Cept no rats or puddles of piss. You could see why BetterWorld took more server space than the rest of the Comnet combined. Only thing missing was the smells, but they were working on that too. No doubt they'd be good smells, like frying fish and sweet potato pie. They'd just rolled out taste technology, but you had to be hardcore and stick electrodes on your tongue.

Even outside the door, dance music thumped. He recited the password to the bouncer, a simulated gorilla just like the ones they had in zoos, but wearing shades and gold bling. The gorilla made a series of hand gestures. Big J responded in kind, then walked into the small lobby.

What…? Along with flyers of upcoming events, there was a note on the lobby wall for him, "Dr. Doom" in big letters. He edged closer to read the smaller print. "Need to talk…"

He froze as soon as he realized what he had done. *Stupid!* He stopped reading, then stared at the flyer next to it. It listed the week's guest DJs. He spent a good minute or two examining all the flyers, then moved on toward the bar and dance floor.

The music got louder, lots of bass and percussion. Same old crowd inside for the most part. They didn't recognize his new avatar of course. But the barmaid, a half-naked party girl, stared at him, and it wasn't the friendly type of stare that meant "What you having" or "What're you doing later?"

Better get out of here. He turned around.

The gorilla stood right there facing him, canines bared and massive fists clenched.

Big J tried to shove past the gorilla, but it grabbed him by the collar and lifted him off the floor. The club district wasn't a combat zone but obviously it didn't know or care.

He threw a jab at the gorilla's face. It didn't even flinch when his fist connected.

He landed more. No effect.

The ape grasped his neck with both paws and began to squeeze.

Teleport time. He didn't have any locations saved, but he could go back to the starting point. Normally you couldn't teleport out of combat, but this didn't seem like a regular game.

The teleport command didn't work. Neither did anything else.

Warning signs popped up. His avatar was being taken over.

Time for the nuclear option. *Peace, Big J.*

Charles switched off the immersion unit. Complete darkness.

He waited a minute, then turned it back on. He'd create a new account, purge Joe34567, and erase all traces of his last visit. He'd have to be careful from now on, avoid his old haunts.

Peace, old gang.

* * *

Pelopidas

When finally Waylee lay back sated, Pel noticed the sun dying on the other side of the window. You wouldn't know it was almost winter from the temperatures, but the days had definitely grown short.

His stomach growled. Normally he and his housemates ate dinner together, but they'd forgotten all about eating today. He turned to his lover. "Food?"

"Yeah. And beer."

They threw on enough clothes to avoid embarrassing Kiyoko if they ran into her. Waylee re-inserted the silver nose and eyebrow rings she'd taken out that morning. She had the face of a supermodel—high cheekbones, full lips, unblemished skin…

She returned his gaze and raised her pierced eyebrows. "What?"

"Chicken butt."

Waylee leapt on his back, and he carried her out the door. She remembered to duck this time.

Pel peeked in the game room on their way to the stairs. Charles sat in the swivel chair, immersion helmet bobbing back and forth, gloved hands waving like a conductor's.

"Hard at work," Waylee said, and hopped off.

"Let's not bother him." *Hard to believe he's one of the top Collectivistas and barely seventeen. All I could do at his age was play video games.* He squeezed Waylee's hand and led her downstairs. The morning's near-death felt like a childhood memory, or something he saw in a movie.

They couldn't find much to eat in the kitchen, and only four cans of Natty Boh. They downed all four, accompanied by bowls of lentils doused in Skankin' Fred's Volcano Sauce.

"Should have gone shopping yesterday," Pel said when they finished.

Waylee raised an eyebrow. "With what money?"

"Shakti's got cash. She and Dingo can go. Can't have our guest starve." He crushed the empty cans, then tossed them toward the recycle bin. Three out of four made it in. "Six cents richer."

Waylee picked up the errant can and dropped it in the bin. "I'm gonna hit the guitar. I may actually write a love song, as sappy as I feel now."

He kissed her, tasting hot sauce and beer. Not much she could do now. The Comnet work was mostly on Charles. "I'll be down later. Thought I'd start getting gear together." It would be expensive, but maybe Charles and Kiyoko could help trade for it, like Kiyoko did for the masks.

Waylee took the stairs down to the basement and he headed back upstairs to the game room.

They needed good A/V equipment, and hoped to rip data off the guests' comlinks. They'd have to be careful with Secret Service present, though. They couldn't broadcast signals of any kind.

No masks this time. As good as Kiyoko's friends were, that was way too risky. They'd have to go as themselves, only bland looking. They'd need appropriate clothes. And they'd need security clearances and fake ID's.

How about designer drugs? Something to relax inhibitions without being obvious, make their targets confess every sin. It would have to blend in with an alcohol buzz. *I'll put Dingo on that.*

Back in the game room, Charles typed on an invisible keyboard. Pel threw on one of the other game systems—3-D goggles, headset, and gloves —and plopped into the second swivel chair. He immersed himself in the Comnet and donned his Collective avatar—William Godwin, the eighteenth century utilitarianist, anarchist, and novelist.

The Collective moved the Emporium, their virtual trading center, at random intervals to random servers scattered around the world in attics and basements. You could only access it using the Collective Router and its decryption algorithms, and you had to know the current address. As an insider, Pel received the new link whenever it changed. He checked the credentials and reviews of the electronics sellers, then sent a contact message to his first choice.

A portal opened after about five minutes, revealing a dark-paneled study. The Emporium ran on Qualia, the same 3-D platform as BetterWorld. A distinguished silver-haired gentleman sat in an overstuffed burgundy armchair, smoking a cigar. He looked photorealistic, as good as Pel's avatar.

"How may I be of assistance?" the gentleman asked in House of Lords English.

"I need some electronics. First, video recorders with top of the line pickup, but undetectable. I was thinking mini pinhole cameras I can embed into clothes. They need to store the data, not transmit, and have to be emission shielded."

He snuffed out his cigar. "Easy enough, Mr. Godwin. How many?"

"Three. No, make that four."

He nodded.

"I also need some ghost snares."

"What kind?"

"One to record comlink transmissions, and one to intercept and analyze radiation leaking from comlinks. Inconspicuous like the cameras. Let's say three of each. And decryption software. Doesn't have to be real time." It would be nice if they could install spyware, but they'd need the comlinks long enough to crack the passwords.

The gentleman leaned back and folded his hands. "That's not as easy." He paused. "But I can do it."

"Your reputation is deserved."

"Now, shall we discuss price?"

"I have a database of unused Comnet ID's I can trade—"

He waved a finely creased hand. "You're wasting my time."

Started too low. "How about BetterWorld credits?" Kiyoko sold virtual clothing and stuff there, and her kingdom had paying tenants.

"You don't have real money?"

"BetterWorld credits are real money. It won't be long before BetterWorld's bigger than the physical economy."

He shrugged.

"I'll throw in some wireless keys."

Which I don't have, but we can put Charles on it...

"Whose, exactly?"

"Enterprises worth accessing. I'll get back to you with specifics."

The gentleman nodded. "Come back in a week. I'll have your cameras by then, and possibly the rest. I'll need a down payment of two million credits."

About $5000. Damn. Hope Kiyoko has that much. "I'll get it for you. I need everything by three weeks, tops."

* * *

Charles

The cleanup process took about an hour. Last step, Charles deleted the sniffers outside the New Year's Gala site and deployed new ones.

He routed the sniffer output to a traffic program. The data packets were all encoded, so he couldn't read them directly. But he could see where they went. The traffic program would copy all data packets entering and leaving the New Year's site, follow outgoing packets to their destination, and back-track incoming packets to their origin. He'd check back in a couple of days and map all the interconnections in a visual program. Maybe they could find the caterers and guests that way.

As for BetterWorld, who'd been operating the barmaid and the gorilla? BPD didn't have the imagination for it. No reward had been posted, so unlikely a freelancer.

They put a lock on his avatar to stop him from teleporting. That meant a programmer or someone else with special privileges. Maybe the law told MediaCorp about his escape, and they sent cybermercs after him on BetterWorld. Well, that was the last they'd see of Big J or Dr. Doom.

He'd wait a bit before creating a new avatar. Then he'd see if he could get programmer privileges for himself. And flip the situation on his invisible foes.

7

Waylee

Waylee finished speed reading her Naomi Klein e-book and joined Pel in the kitchen. He lit their ancient gas stove and poured globs of banana pancake batter in a 12-inch skillet.

Shakti and Dingo had stocked the shelves last night, spending a big chunk of their meager paychecks. The smell of frying bananas brought everyone but Kiyoko running. *Strange, usually she's the first one in line.*

Laelaps padded into the kitchen and squatted next to the stove, summoning the Force to deliver an errant pancake into his mouth.

"My pops wants to come over next weekend," Pel said.

I thought I could rely on you. "You know that's impossible with Charles here."

He shrugged. "Yeah, I know." He nudged a pancake with his spatula, peering underneath.

"Tell him we've got gigs," she said. "What's he want? Make sure we haven't trashed his property?"

Pel whirled and pointed the spatula like a gun. "Don't be a bitch. Not everyone's parents are like yours."

"Unfair." Not that she felt any loyalty to the fuckwits who birthed her. Her statuesque Celtic-Latina mother had shown little interest in childcare. She'd worked mostly at bars, possibly for the free drinks.

Waylee couldn't remember what her father looked like. He would pace their basement apartment in his underwear, shouting about who knows what and waving his hands like he was besieged by clouds of invisible flies. Then he'd cry in bed for days while her mother trudged off to work or wherever. When Waylee was six, he jumped off the Walt Whitman bridge, 153 feet into the Delaware River.

And then her mother fell in with Feng.

"When's the next news update?" Pel asked, eyes focused on the griddle.

"If you mean real news, when I get my video on the air." She'd woken up before dawn and checked the local feed, but saw nothing new about the breakout. Just a fluff piece about the mayor's latest campaign to promote the city. Mayors and Chambers of Commerce had concocted one inane slogan after another to attract businesses and tourists: 'Charm City,' 'The City That Reads,' even 'The Greatest City in America.' Her musician friends called it 'The Gritty City.' Waylee had once emailed the city council suggesting 'The City That Has a Few Redeeming Features If You Know Where To Look.'

Pel grunted.

"How much did you say we need for a down payment?" she asked.

"For the electronics and decryption 'ware?" He slapped the pancakes onto a big plate.

"Yeah."

"Two million BetterWorld credits. About $5,000 on the exchange."

"I'll go get it." Kiyoko could manage it, considering how many people shopped at her online store.

In the adjacent dining room, Shakti and Dingo set out mismatched silverware and cups on the table. They'd been sharing sheets for five months now, and made an odd couple, a pacifist political organizer from rural Guyana and a fight-loving agitator from the streets of Baltimore. *If Pel and I can do it, though, anyone can.*

Shakti frowned. "It's so gloomy in here."

Waylee shrugged. "Go outside." She'd drawn the house's faded red curtains to keep their guest out of sight.

Charles stood in the corner, fingers fidgeting. She waved at him.

He nodded but didn't smile.

Waylee trudged up the stairs and knocked on her sister's door.

No response. She eased it open.

Of course. Even banana pancakes couldn't compete with hyper-reality. Encased in her black immersion suit, Kiyoko sat in midair, hanging from a network of fibers, legs spread apart. Barely moving, she looked like a spider perched in its web, or maybe a trapped fly, its situation so hopeless it didn't bother struggling.

The support cylinder was a lot narrower than the one in the game room, hemmed in by tall Ikea wardrobes packed with clothes and costumes, and display cabinets crowded with Japanese toys and stuffed animals. It was bolted to the ceiling for added stability.

Still in her strange position, Kiyoko rocked back and forth.

"Kiyoko," Waylee said.

No response. "Kiyoko!"

A muffled voice leaked from her helmet, "Be right back." She pulled off the black spheroid and shook her rainbow-streaked hair. Still suspended in the air, she faced Waylee. "I can't believe you interrupted me while I was flying on my dragon friend. This had better be important."

"What are you, eight?"

Kiyoko's face flared with anger. "Why don't you get out of my room."

Waylee regretted her words. This wasn't the time to argue. "Sorry. Listen, I have a big favor to ask."

Her sister's cat, Nyasuke, jumped off the antique bed at the end of the room and navigated the narrow pathway between the sewing machine, cabinets, and wardrobes. He announced his arrival with a loud *meow*. Kiyoko looked down at her cat and smiled.

Just the defusing she needed. "You said you wanted to help out, right?"

Kiyoko nodded. "I drove yesterday, didn't I? And worked my ass off to trade for those masks."

"Yeah, thanks. So, Pel and I need a lot of BetterWorld credits, and you've done well with your virtual fashion line."

"Costumes and accessories. Everyone needs them."

"And marketing our music."

Kiyoko planted her feet and stood. "I'm the only one who cares whether we're successful or not, so you should be grateful. All that money's invested in advertising and equipment."

Took a wrong turn. "And you rent out BetterWorld space?"

"Tenants in my realm, yes."

"Like a feudal lord?" Waylee regretted her words again. It was too easy to fight with the ones you loved.

Her sister frowned. "I suppose. The Fantasy Continent has a medieval motif, and that's how medieval Japan and Europe were structured. Look, I need to get back."

"This is important. We need two million credits to help buy what we need for the president's fundraiser. Can Pel borrow it? He promised the broker he'd have it today."

Kiyoko's frown deepened. "And how's he gonna pay me back? Anyway, the timing's bad, I upgraded my suit last month." She smiled. "It's got an electric field that stimulates the skin receptors, pretty much the coolest thing ever."

The porn industry will love that. "So you spent all your money on that?"

She squinted her left eye. "No, mostly I've been equipping my army. Prince Vostok, I tell you, is the bane of my existence. He is evil personified, and he wants the Vale of Waterfalls, the best part of my kingdom. I told him no way, I spent two years creating it, but now he's trying to steal my tenants away and goads me into these battles…"

What the hell is she talking about? Waylee tried not to scream. "Please, can you get the credits together?"

Kiyoko sighed. She twirled a gloved finger in her hair. "I think I have an idea, but I'll need help."

* * *

Dingo

"Zoom!" M-pat's three-year-old son, Baraka, pushed a friendly faced locomotive along a brightly colored plastic track. M-pat had snapped the course together that morning before Dingo arrived. It filled the entire living room floor of his family's narrow townhouse.

From the sofa, Dingo gave Baraka the thumbs up. "You go, little man." He snatched another Cheeto from the bowl that M-pat's wife, Latisha, had set on the sparkly clean coffee table. *Fuck knows what's in these things, but damn they're addictive.*

For some reason Latisha had decided to run the heat even though it wasn't that cold outside. The faint smell of burning oil wafted up from their basement. Dingo felt like unlacing his boots and freeing his toes from sweaty confinement, but settled for unzipping his hoodie.

M-pat knelt next to the meandering track. "You got to hook up the freight cars, son. Whole purpose of a locomotive is to pull cars along."

"Gaaa!" Baraka let go and fumbled with the coal cars and flatbeds he'd left behind.

M-pat returned the locomotive to its starting point and showed his son how to hook them together.

"You should get one of those electric train sets," Dingo said.

M-pat turned and nodded. "Yeah, maybe next year. They expensive though, and we only had this a couple months."

A birthday present, Dingo remembered. He and Shakti—actually, everyone in the band house—had bought Baraka toys.

Latisha walked in from the adjacent kitchen, where she'd been chopping something. She stood at least a foot shorter than M-pat, and had much lighter skin. "Why not a Christmas present?" She looked at Baraka and smiled. "Maybe Santa could bring it."

M-pat sighed. "I already bought zawadi gifts for Kwanzaa. Santa's a white thing." He glanced at Dingo. "No offense."

Dingo shrugged. "A, I ain't white but maybe a little, and B, Christmas is corporate-religious bullshit."

Latisha put her hands on her hips. "You two just say some foolish non-sense sometimes." She pointed at M-pat. "We celebrate Kwanzaa 'cause you insist on it. But we do Christmas too, like everyone else. That means church, that means a tree, and there ain't no reason we can't have Santa."

"I'm pretty sure Santa's not in the Bible," Dingo said.

M-pat glared at him, then looked at his comlink. "We gotta go. Appointment's soon."

Latisha frowned. "Where y'all goin'?"

"Business, baby."

"In other words, you ain't gonna tell me?"

Dingo decided to intervene. "We just goin' to a meeting. Only worry is we might fall asleep."

Latisha glanced at him, then returned her attention to M-pat. "When you comin' back, then?"

M-pat kissed her. "Back by dinner. Gotta make the rounds after the meeting."

Dingo turned to Baraka and waved. "Alright, smell ya later, little man."

He waved back. "Bye!"

M-pat picked up his son and kissed him on the forehead. "Back before you know it."

They hopped into M-pat's black electric Honda and headed out of the neighborhood. Dingo threw on his data glasses and checked his messages. Nothing. "So what's this Rosemont crew like?" he asked as M-pat turned onto U.S. 1.

M-pat kept his eyes on the four-lane road. "They like all the rest, they just got the best chemist I hear."

"How big's their zone?"

"Rosemont neighborhood. That's why they called Rosemont."

"So they got this great chemist but they only got—what—twenty blocks?"

"More like thirty."

"Either way, that's not a lot of territory. Not a lot of income to support a hot shot chemist."

M-pat turned right on Caton Avenue and headed north. "They producers, Dingo. They export. Which means they a lot bigger than their home turf." He looked even grumpier than usual. Had been since the breakout yesterday.

"What's up, kicks? Why the frown?"

"Just don't like taking my car on shit like this."

He washed that damn car every other day. "Well we can't exactly take the RV. You sure worry a lot."

M-pat glanced over with that homicidal expression he got sometimes. "Easy for you to say. You ain't got a kid."

"And thank God—or the lack thereof—for that. But a'ight, I get you. Baraka, he's a cool little dude."

M-pat scratched his sorry excuse for a beard. "Gettin' popped at gave me cause to think on this whole thing. You do know Waylee's crazy, right?"

"No crazier than anyone else."

"Well, I got a family to think on. I'll help out—I keep my word—but no way am I breakin' into a presidential fundraiser or matchin' moves with Homeland." Red brick townhouses gave way to vine-choked trees and the makeshift tents of squatters as the road entered Gwynns Falls Park.

"Your loss." Dingo went over Pel's specs in his head. The drug had to relax inhibitions quite a bit but not be obvious. Make whoever drank it at the gala open up and feel talkative. Dissolve quickly. No taste or odor.

They exited the parkway and stopped at the end of a street lined with more two-story townhouses. Discarded plastic vials lined the curbs. "Here we are," he said. "Leave your gun, if you got one. Including stun guns."

"So we'll be defenseless?"

"So we get in. And put your glasses away."

"What for?"

"Makes folks nervous, they think you recordin' 'em."

Pel showed me how to disable the camera indicator light. But maybe lots of people did that. Dingo unzipped his hoodie and stuffed his data glasses in the inside pocket, where they'd be hard to steal. He stashed his stun gun under the seat and followed M-pat toward a townhouse on the corner.

It looked like the ground floor was once a store of some sort. Two serious-looking men in stiff jackets with big pockets sat in folding chairs outside the front door. Soldiers, no doubt. Both wore data glasses with dark mirrored lenses but no voice tube. *Double standard here, but it's their turf.*

"I was expecting something grander," he said to M-pat as they approached. "Like a mansion or somethin'."

"What you want, white boy?" the soldier on the left said, not moving from his seat. He looked to be Dingo's age, early twenties.

"I ain't white," Dingo said. "I'm Latino an' shit. Different check box on the forms. We're here to—"

M-pat slashed the air with his hand. "Tell your captain," he said to the soldier, "M'patanishi's here to see him. We got an appointment."

Neither soldier moved. "DG, Captain," the one on the left said. He paused, eyes on Dingo and M-pat. "These two want in. Say they've got an appointment."

After a couple of minutes, Dingo heard the front door unlatch. An unsmiling woman opened it. A large common room lay beyond, a pool table visible with the balls racked and a man standing to the side. The front window was barred and blinded.

The woman waved them in. The man frisked them while she stood there with a hand in one pocket. Apparently satisfied, he pointed at a leather sofa. "Sit."

They hadn't been sitting long when another man entered from the interior hallway. He was about thirty, trim, dark. Head shaved and buffed shiny. He smiled and exchanged West Baltimore peace shakes with M-pat, fists morphing to skin slides turning to interlocked fingers. M-pat designed the shake five years ago during the truce talks, and people still used it.

"M'patanishi, the living legend. Welcome to Rosemont."

"Thanks."

He grinned. "Back when you called yourself Midnight, you beat mo' ass and nailed mo' ho's than anyone in West B'more. You the master of B&E, like a ninja. Got all special forces an' shit holdin' yo' crew's turf. Now you retired and playin' peacekeeper."

"Latisha, she straightened me out. And Nyerere. You gotta read him. And now we got a kid, my seed's what I sow. Know what I'm sayin'?"

Mr. Shiny Head clenched a fist to his heart. "I feel ya."

M-pat pointed at Dingo. "This here's Dingo. He's the one lookin'. I can vouch for him, he's one of my deputies." He gestured toward Shiny Head. "This is Noah. Operations Captain. Just below the boss."

"'Sup," Dingo said, and gave Noah the peace shake.

Noah's eyes narrowed. "Ain't never heard of you."

"Been living 'round West B'more near five years. Wanderin' here and there before that."

"Street thug, huh?"

"Ain't no thug. I'm out doing the people's business, givin' Authority the smackdown."

Noah smiled. "You do look a gutterpunk."

"Ain't no gutterpunk neither. Not for years. I'm with a People's Party crew, we're settled like family, but—"

M-pat held up a hand. "He respectable."

Noah nodded. "A'ight then. So M-pat says you got a special order in mind?"

"Yeah. I got a special concoction that needs brewing, and heard your chemist's the best."

"And discreet," M-pat added.

"Both true," Noah said. "Follow me."

He led them down a flight of stairs into a finished basement that smelled faintly of vinegar and smoke. A big iron furnace squatted on stout feet in one corner. Several people, mostly old, sat at tables squirting liquids from big bottles into plastic vials. They screwed little caps on the vials and labeled the sides with sharpies. An attractive dark-skinned woman in a pressed jacket and skirt sat in front of a wallscreen, swiping a touchpad and moving clusters of colored balls around the screen.

"This your lab then?" Dingo asked Noah. "I expected tubes and Petri dishes and shit."

M-pat rolled his eyes.

"No, we got a proper lab," Noah said. "Different location, obviously."

"So we going there to see your chemist, or is he coming here?"

The woman, made up like a model, turned and smiled, showing gleaming teeth and perfect legs. She stood. "I'm the chemist."

Whoa. Hello, sexy scientist.

"Got a Ph.D. and everything," Noah said. "We pay better than academia, and Big Pharm's mostly outsourced these days."

"Well, you certainly got chemistry," Dingo told her. "I'm Dingo, that's M'patanishi."

She narrowed her eyes at him and turned to M-pat. "Pleased to meet you." She didn't offer her name.

Bitch is rude.

"We talkin' here?" M-pat said.

"We all family here," Noah said. "But…" He motioned for the sexy scientist to follow them, and they walked up two flights of stairs to an office. No one sat.

Dingo described the drug they wanted, and said they needed it in three weeks.

The chemist pursed her lips and tapped a high-heeled foot. She turned to M-pat again. "Well, we have something like that, clubsters like it, but it's probably too euphoric and sensory for your needs. Why does it need to be so subtle?"

"It just does," M-pat said. "Can you do it?"

She crossed her arms. "In three weeks? I'd have to drop everything else and bring others in. It'd be expensive."

Uh oh. "How expensive?"

She glanced at him and shrugged.

Noah stepped forward. "Gotta confirm with the boss, but I'd guess 50 G's down, 50 on delivery."

Dingo's anus contracted. "You're fuckin' joking."

"Lab time's crucial for everything we do," the chemist said. "So of course it's going to be expensive. On the other hand, once the R&D's done, the product might be relatively cheap."

Kiyoko

Princess Kiyoko surveyed the army before her, arrayed along the highlands in concentric semicircles. Red banners fluttered in the wind as five thousand armed men and women awaited her command, by far the biggest army she'd ever assembled. Their leaders included nobles, samurai, magicweavers, healers, unicorns… even a dragon. Matching the banners, Kiyoko had donned red hair and robes to bring luck.

She risked everything. Prince Vostok sought to dominate the entire Fantasy Continent of BetterWorld, and her realm of Yumekuni bordered his. Six months ago he offered a pittance to buy its richest part, the Vale of

Waterfalls. Of course she could never let it fall into the hands of a tyrant like Vostok.

Even though Kiyoko owned her land legally, and he couldn't actually seize it by force, Vostok tried to wear her down by drawing away her supporters and goading her into battles that she always lost. When she complained to the BetterWorld administrators that he was harassing her, they said he wasn't breaking any rules. Vostok and his equally obnoxious followers then called her a 'baby' and 'carebear' on the message boards.

Good never bows to evil, she decided, and she raised an army to crush him, recruiting allies and purchasing non-player soldiers and equipment. After her sister's plea for credits, she increased the stakes.

"If you want the Vale so bad," she challenged Vostok in public, "see if you can take it from me." She proposed a battle on a duplicate of their terrain, which only the combatants could access. Battlefield success and relative casualties would determine the winner. Not an unusual challenge except for the bet. If Vostok won, she'd give him legal title to the Vale of Waterfalls. If she won, she'd get an equivalent combination of land and development points from Vostokia, Prince Vostok's narcissistic and unimaginative name for his kingdom.

Vostok had responded immediately. "Name the time."

Selling his land would take time that Waylee and Pel didn't have, so Kiyoko bet her remaining credits on the BetterWorld gambling market. Given that Vostok long ago reached maximum level as a fighter, and had beaten her three times already, the odds started at 2:1 against her. She encouraged friends to post messages saying she was clueless when it came to combat. As Vostok liked to point out, she was just a girl after all.

The official odds were now 4:1 against her.

Kiyoko lifted a brass telescope to her eye. Vostok prepared his army just past the Neutral Zone, on both sides of the Sylvan River, which began in the Vale of Waterfalls and widened beyond. He'd gathered player guilds and mercenaries, and around eight thousand non-player combatants. Ten-foot tall ogres stood strapped to two dozen wheeled trebuchets and carts of boulders. Others carried long ladders or giant wooden shields.

Long ago, Kiyoko erected a stone wall across the mouth of the Vale and up the adjacent slopes, but it wouldn't withstand an assault like this. The wall was especially weak where the river flowed through an iron grate.

Well, they—and by "they" she meant Pel and Dingo—said the best defense was a surprise attack, so her force of vassals, allies, and mercenaries, along with their computer-controlled troops, would crush Prince Vostok's army before it could launch its assault. Pel, Dingo, and Charles would hold the walls. But cloaked by magic, her main force would hit the enemy's flank and rear.

Atop her giant unicorn cat, Nyasuke, Princess Kiyoko addressed her army. Their loyalty could be her biggest advantage. "My people, my friends. I thank you with all my soul for coming here to my defense."

She pointed to the winding river valley below them and its green farms, magical woods, and thatch-roofed hamlets. Waterfalls cascaded down the cliffs on either side and imbued the air with glittering mist. "You can see how beautiful the Vale is, how peaceful its people..."

Pel's avatar, a high-level knight, appeared in a translucent popup to the right, the glyphs "Accept incoming private call?" underneath.

Bad timing, jerko. "Be right back," she told her army. "I must commune with those who hold the wall."

She tapped Pel's see-through forehead with her finger, accepting the call. Her avatar on the highlands would appear as if in a trance. She used her royal command voice. "Make it quick."

Pel's knight bowed and twirled a finger. "Yes, your majesticness. Everything is ready here." His voice, run through a real-time modulator, sounded deeper and older.

Pel and Dingo had played Fantasy Continent wargames enough to develop high-level characters, but they lost interest long ago, and she'd never seen them in action. "You're sure you can split the enemy?" she asked. Charles offered to reprogram her army's stats and make them invincible, but if the admins saw any sign of cheating, she'd forfeit the wager. So instead, he had come up with something more subtle.

"Yes, yes, we made more than enough," Pel said.

"Tell Dingo not to pull a Leeroy Jenkins on me and rush in early." His avatar's name, Berserker Bob, worried her.

"Don't worry, we've got things under control."

She ended the chat and returned to her attack force. "In his avarice," Princess Kiyoko spoke, "cruel Prince Vostok gathers his foul army to swoop down on this land, destroy all that is good, and put its people to the sword." She met the eyes of her followers and allies. "Only we can stop this terrible fate. And stop it we will!"

A cheer arose from the gathered troops. Swords and polearms pointed skyward. No guns on the Fantasy Continent—against the rules.

Princess Kiyoko patted her unicorn cat. "Forward!"

Her army followed her west on the plateau, away from the Vale and Vostok's army. They entered a forest of tall pines. "We have to win this battle," she spoke privately to Nyasuke.

The unicorn cat responded with a ☺, as he always did.

They halted well to the west of the Vale, still near the escarpment down to the Neutral Zone, but hidden in the pines. She checked the time. The battle would officially commence in ten minutes.

Princess Kiyoko addressed her army again. "And now I bestow upon you the gifts of luck and stealth." She tapped into the *qi* – natural energy – produced and stored by the forests, streams, and minerals of her realm. She weaved all the available energy into invisibility, silence, and bless spells, cloaking and protecting her entire army.

The colors faded from her followers until they looked molded from glass. They could still see each other's outlines, but the enemy wouldn't see them at all. Nor would they hear them. And the bless spell would increase her army's probability to hit and avoid being hit. Of course, Vostok had magic-weavers too, and detect magic was a pretty standard spell, but with luck, they would be amidst the enemy before they could react.

A chime sounded in Kiyoko's ears. "The battle begins," she announced. They were now permitted to enter the Neutral Zone.

Kiyoko's ally Aburatsubo, a powerful mage who lived to the west, had gathered *qi* from his realm and stored it in a crystal-topped staff. He walked to the edge of the cliff marking the border of Yumekuni. He tapped his staff on the ground, traced a sigil in the air, and spoke a few words Kiyoko didn't recognize. A wide column of air thickened, taking on the consistency of water. "You may proceed," he said.

Kiyoko led the way, coaxing Nyasuke past the cliff. It was a long drop, but they fell slowly, slower than a feather. Her map display showed her troops following. Nyasuke landed no harder than a footstep.

The transparent cavalry, including two dozen *qi*-bearing unicorns and their mage riders, gathered at the bottom. Their commander's shouts rang in Kiyoko's ears, but no one outside her army would hear.

The computer-controlled foot soldiers formed into phalanxes with spears and tall shields, each group commanded by a player. Samurai with bows, *naginatas* and other polearms, and *katana* swords took the front positions.

It would take about an hour for the enemy to get their trebuchets in range of the Vale. Kiyoko's forces had to cross miles of open country and hills in less than that. Kiyoko activated the voice override and shouted. "For Yumekuni!"

The horses charged north across the grassy fields of the Neutral Zone. They would hit the enemy from behind. Her friend Jayna from Baltimore, cross-gendered as a male half-elf, rode point.

Nyasuke carried Kiyoko east with the foot soldiers. They would hit the enemy's side.

She'd keep out of arrow range, at least for now. One of the nicest things about BetterWorld was that death wasn't permanent. You could respawn indefinitely. But if you died in challenges like this, you returned to your login point, and couldn't rejoin the battle in progress.

Kiyoko barely noted the immediate scenery, focusing most of her attention on her map display, making sure all her units went where they should, and searching for any sign they'd been spotted. The cavalry forded Amity Creek, which separated the Neutral Zone from Vostokia. Water sloshed silently around the knees of their horses. Kiyoko felt a pang of regret as the first horses exited onto the opposite bank. She had just invaded another realm.

Her cavalry commander, one of the top warriors on the Fantasy Continent, popped up in her vision. "Enemy scouts one mile to the east," the fur-clad woman said.

Kiyoko looked through her telescope. They looked a lot like her horsemen, but wore black boiled leather. They carried long bows and curved swords on their backs. None seemed to notice her invisible army.

Bypassing the scouts, Kiyoko's cavalry continued into the low grassy hills on the far side of the creek. Then they swung east through Vostokia. Her infantry jogged east through the Neutral Zone. *I've split my forces. I hope this works.*

Kiyoko opened a view from the gold dragon, Abrasax. They were good friends in BetterWorld, but had kept her participation top, top secret. Abrasax flew high over Vostok's army as it departed from its camps and construction sites and entered the Neutral Zone. She zoomed in.

So many. Vostok's forces marched along the Sylvan River plain behind a rainbow of banners featuring elaborate coats of arms. Mostly human, but also dwarves, elves, half-orcs, trolls… the usual suspects. Most continents had rules against non-human avatars. They were meant to replicate Earth.

That is, her sister liked to say, if Earth were a world where no one starved or grew sick or died, a world with a stable atmosphere and endless resources.

Kiyoko opened the rest of her views and looked from one to another, also charting her army's progress on the map.

Vostok's army halted, still three to four hundred yards from the Vale wall. *Do they know we're coming?*

Ogres placed boulders in the trebuchet slings. Leather-clad trolls yanked ropes that dropped the counterweights and flung the boulders impossibly far. They smashed against her wall and sprayed shards of stone, leaving ugly scars. More ogres winched the lever arms back in position, and the bombardment continued.

The wall defenders scrambled for cover. "We're under attack," Pel said.

"I see that." Vostok's catapults had a greater range than she expected. "Fire back."

Her counterfire fell well short. *Vostok, you jackdog.* He could just sit there and smash down her walls with impunity, and then send his troops through the gaps.

Should she send in Abrasax? It was still too soon, and the dragon would have no support.

"Got an idea," Pel messaged. The defenders placed flasks of lamp oil in their trebuchet slings and lit them. Orange fire arced through the air and exploded randomly among Vostok's troops.

"Yeah!" she screamed. Lighter projectiles meant longer distances.

Her invisible army neared striking range of the enemy. "Pel," she said, "tell Charles to hop to it."

"You got it." Charles had fudged something or other to increase her stores of lamp oil by over a thousand fold. He'd insisted the "exploit" was undetectable.

Charles's magic-weaver avatar pulled a rope and clear oil poured down a chute and into the Sylvan River, where it floated downstream. He faced Pel and bowed. "Long live Princess Kiyoko."

"Don't tell Shakti about this," she told Pel.

Pel rolled his avatar's eyes. "It's not a real river."

"Problem," Jayna announced in her faux-male voice.

Kiyoko switched her entire view to match her friend's. A picket of enemy scouts, mostly human fighters, stood watch on the final ridge above the river plain. An elven magic-weaver amidst them peered at Kiyoko's cavalry. He shouted something, too faint to hear.

"They can sense us," Kiyoko said.

"I think you're right," her cavalry commander replied over the voice link. "Take 'em out?"

"Yeah, especially that magic-weaver."

Four score horsemen drew their bows and fired a volley at the enemy scouts. Arrows pierced their throats and chests. The elf staggered and dropped.

"That's what I'm talkin' 'bout," Jayna shouted.

The enemy captain, limping from an arrow in the thigh, lit a torch and tossed it into a large open barrel. It exploded, throwing up a huge fireball and plume of black smoke.

There goes our surprise. "Attack!" Kiyoko shouted.

The cavalry, still invisible, charged over the ridge and down the slope beyond, closing the distance to the enemy supply wagons and healers at the rear of their columns. Her infantry sprinted east through the flat Neutral Zone. Kiyoko focused most of her attention on the dragon's view and the map.

Vostok's followers reacted inconsistently. Some commanders looked toward the plume of smoke. More continued to face the Vale wall, apparently unconcerned about an attack from the direction they'd come from. But a handful of silver-robed magic-weavers rode wolf-beasts to the rear of the enemy formation, accompanied by burly looking fighters.

"Target those magic-weavers," Kiyoko told Abrasax.

The enemy had no dragons, which wasn't surprising. As avatars, they were almost impossible to come by, and the computer-controlled dragons kept to themselves. Her friend Abrasax, one of the rare exceptions, swooped into action.

Too late. Multispectral rays burst from the mages' fingers and illuminated her charging cavalry. Transparent armor turned silver and banners waxed crimson.

Untouched and still invisible, Abrasax reached the enemy mages. Orange fire jetted from her mouth and engulfed the nearest figures. The dragon turned visible, her own magic dispelling Kiyoko's. Abrasax strafed the mages and their guards, searing them with a line of flame. Soldiers scattered like ants.

The enemy reacted in earnest, firing bows at the dragon and scrambling to meet the cavalry charge. Abrasax climbed high into the sky, several arrows protruding from her scales. Magic-weavers looked in the direction of her still-invisible infantry and prepared spells.

"Arrows," Kiyoko ordered. "Aim for the player characters. Especially the captains and magic-weavers."

Her infantry turned visible. Arrows arced across the sky in every direction. "Fall, foul fiends!" Jayna shouted over the voice link.

Where's Prince Vostok? Kiyoko looked for a tall figure in black spiked armor on a three-headed hell-horse. If killed, his forces would be uncoordinated, even with vassals and allies there.

Through Abrasax's eyes, she saw him on the far river bank, ordering troops across. Ogres entered the water, unrolling bridges of rope and wood planks as they waded across. Vostok plunged into the river on his hell-horse, followed by the rest of his cavalry on the far side.

Kiyoko told Abrasax, "Ignite the oil."

The dragon folded her wings and dove. Just short of the river, she threw them out to brake, and spat a jet of flame. The river exploded, setting the ogres, the bridges, Vostok, and his cavalry on fire.

Kiyoko screamed for joy and pumped a fist. "Call me a carebear, will you!"

"I'm hurt," Abrasax said. A ballista bolt protruded from her stomach, a lot more worrisome than the arrow pinpricks she'd received.

"Fly to the healers behind my infantry." They were poor fighters but could get injured characters, even a dragon, back in action.

Kiyoko's cavalry smashed through the thin line of sentries and other defenders at the rear of Vostok's army and attacked his healers. Her foot samurai, supported by archers, hit the low-level infantry in the center of the enemy column. They slashed through pikes and cut off limbs and heads.

Vostok's players fought without coordination. They and their followers charged the nearest opponent, and the battle turned to confusion, individual soldiers locked in fights to the death. The clashes, the shouts, and blinking lights on her map grew too numerous to follow. Kiyoko's bless spell gave her side an extra edge, and they pressed forward over the corpses of the fallen. She followed on her unicorn cat, surrounded by guards.

Damnation. Vostok emerged on the near bank of the river, accompanied by two dozen riders, scorched but alive. The bridges had burned at least, trapping most of his army on the other side. And scores of burnt non-player corpses floated downstream.

Astride his three-headed horse, Vostok shouted inaudible orders. Ogres turned some of the trebuchets toward her infantry and their troll commanders fiddled with the release fingers, presumably adjusting the range.

Her own catapults ran out of oil flasks, and switched to small rocks, which served only to irritate.

A human figure arced through the air. Kiyoko snapped up her telescope. Berserker Bob, screaming and waving a sword. *Dingo.*

She messaged Pel. "What's that fool doing?"

Pel chuckled. "Loaded up on armor spells and climbed in one of the slings. Said he wanted to slay some nerds."

She looked back at the battle. Dingo crashed into the middle of the enemy troops, got up, and started swinging his sword left and right.

Abrasax returned to the air. "Health back to normal," she messaged.

"Abrasax," Kiyoko replied, "catapults are top priority."

"On my way." She attacked the enemy trebuchets, igniting huge fires that blackened the sky.

Blue energy streaked toward Kiyoko. Her surroundings flashed red and her skin tingled, although she felt no pain per se. Her health indicator dropped by half, and faint wisps of smoke curled from her robes.

Shit. Someone must have targeted her. She unhooked her shield from Nyasuke's back and held it in front. "This is Princess Kiyoko. I'm under attack by a magic-weaver."

Abrasax took another ballista bolt and two surges of magic lightning, and had to withdraw.

A streak of fire hit Kiyoko's shield. It blocked the damage.

"I'm deploying archers," one of her captains said.

Kiyoko sent Abrasax a private audio message. "How's health?"

"Almost gone."

Another fire blast. Some of the flames curled around her shield and scorched her arm. Her health indicator dropped more.

"Can you stay overhead, so I can watch the battle?" she asked Abrasax.

"Can do."

Through the dragon's eyes, Kiyoko watched her tormentor, a raven-haired woman in indigo robes, collapse from enough arrows to make her look like a porcupine.

Not far away, Dingo's avatar staggered from a dozen wounds, surrounded by enemy dead, plus a few still living. She messaged him. "Well done, Berserker Bob."

He grinned. "M'lady. I believe my work is about done here." He transmitted his external view. "And here comes the coup de grace." A three-headed hell-horse galloped toward him, bearing a figure in black spiked armor.

Vostok.

Berserker Bob raised his great-sword. The charging horse filled his field of vision, crazy-eyed heads spitting froth. On top, Vostok swung a glowing, rune-covered sword toward his head.

Dingo's video feed flashed red, then disappeared.

Kiyoko returned to her personal view. Vostok rallied his remaining cavalry and with him in the center, they charged. They headed straight for her, ignoring everything in between.

Her guards and the other nearby fighters formed a protective ring, but Vostok's horsemen cut them down one by one.

Vostok sliced off her guard commander's head and shouted, "Will you fight me, Kawaii Princess? Or are you afraid?"

She was afraid. He was the top ranked fighter on the continent, and he'd killed her before. But honor demanded that she accept the challenge. Besides, her vassals and allies would carry on without her. Most had bet money on the outcome.

Kiyoko pulled her long naginata from its saddle sheath and pointed it at her nemesis. She summoned *qi* from Nyasuke's horn and wove a protective spell. "Have your minions step aside."

"Leave the otaku to me," he shouted. His horsemen drew back.

"Tell me, Prince Vostok," she said, "do you have to practice day and night to be such an enormous asshole, or does it just come naturally?" She hugged Nyasuke, and they charged. Vostok sat motionless on his horse, holding his glowing sword in the air.

As she closed, Kiyoko wove a light spell directly into her enemy's eyes. *Cheating, maybe, but I need every edge.* She thrust with the naginata as she reached him.

"Sorry, no effect," he said, swinging his huge sword down and severing her naginata's blade from its wooden shaft.

No! I'm so stupid.

His hell-horse clamped onto Nyasuke, two sets of teeth biting into the unicorn cat's flank. Kiyoko screamed for him. Vostok swung his sword again, and Nyasuke's head tumbled from his body. Kiyoko fell from her saddle and hit the ground hard. Her vision flashed red and her immersion suit stiffened against her back.

Vostok laughed. "+5 vorpal sword, bitch!"

Kiyoko stared Nyasuke's severed head in the eyes. She couldn't help it. She cried. It was like he killed the real Nyasuke, her soulmate.

The tears wouldn't stop. Her father, Feng, wore that black suit of armor.

Kiyoko was five when her sister brought Squeaky-Squeaks home. "A friend for you," Waylee said. The cutest calico kitten in Philadelphia.

But Feng snatched up Squeaky-Squeaks during one of his tirades, saying the kitten wouldn't shut up and was driving him crazy. "Just like you, you little brat," he told her. She cried and Waylee kicked him in the shin and then Feng beat the crap out of both of them and she never saw her kitty again.

Feng loomed over her on his three-headed horse. "Cry all you want, it won't do you any good." He raised his huge sword. "And now I'll have your head, little Princess. And your realm with it."

She had always been small and weak compared to Feng, a burly Manchurian transplant who claimed to have never lost a bar fight. She couldn't even stand up to her mother. All she could do was pray.

Vostok and his hell-horse slid backward, away from her. *Abrasax*. Her fangs gripped the hell-horse by the right rear leg. The horse thrashed and gnashed at the air as the dragon pulled it away from Kiyoko. Vostok twisted in his saddle, but the dragon kept just out of sword reach.

Oh, thank you.

Abrasax shook the horse violently. The leg ripped from its socket and the horse collapsed, spilling Vostok to the ground.

He leapt to his feet, charged Abrasax, and brought his glowing sword down on her neck. It sliced off her head.

"No!" She'd lost Nyasuke and Abrasax now. She'd never heard of a weapon that could behead every opponent, every time, but somehow Vostok had one.

Vostok grinned. "I'll trade a horse for a dragon any day. I can salvage this battle yet." He sprinted toward her, sword raised.

Kiyoko pulled her katana out of its scabbard. At least she'd die on her feet. Waylee fought Feng year after year, and in the end, she beat him.

And Waylee said, *if the game is fixed, change the rules.*

She threw her katana aside, knelt, and gripped Nyasuke's spiraled horn. She emptied its huge store of *qi*, undissipated by death, and added the rest of hers, weaving a spell she hadn't used since reshaping her realm years ago. *Transmute earth to water*, used to create stream valleys and other topography.

The ground beneath Vostok turned liquid. "May the very earth you tread on refuse to support you anymore," she said, "and swallow you whole."

Vostok's legs sank into the soupy mire. He cursed and waved his vorpal sword, but his heavy armor dragged him downward. Still clutching his sword, he tried swimming. But his dark torso sank beneath the surface, then his arms, and finally his spiked helmet, leaving only ripples.

She felt no sense of triumph. Only relief. "Goodbye, Vostok."

A glowing sword thrust up from the mire. It traced circles in the surface and flung bits of muck into the air. Kiyoko stepped back and shouted for help.

The tip sank lower with each slice, though. Then it disappeared entirely.

Reinforcements arrived. Kiyoko ordered her troops to drive off and kill Vostok's remaining cavalry. She summoned one of the unicorns over, tapped its *qi*, and reversed her spell, turning the liquid mud back to solid earth. Even Prince Vostok couldn't escape burial deep underground.

With Vostok and his top lieutenants dead, Kiyoko's cavalry and infantry tightened the noose and drove his remaining troops back against the river. *We need some stirring music for this.* By now, a real army would surely surrender. But no one ever surrendered in BetterWorld—they always fought to the death.

Which is what Vostok's forces on the west side of the Sylvan River did. Kiyoko's army splintered them into uncoordinated groups, which they overwhelmed one by one. They killed his remaining player characters first, then finished off their passive automatons with volleys of arrows. While the players disappeared after death, non-player corpses littered the ground. Kiyoko and her allies collected their possessions.

Vostok still had forces on the other side of the river, but without bridges or horses, they couldn't cross. They'd have to strip off their armor and swim, and thereby present easy archery targets. Their commanders didn't seem eager to attempt that.

Kiyoko moved her forces closer to her walls, healed her wounded, and waited. Her casualties had not been light. But three of Vostok's died for every one of hers, giving her a victory even if neither side possessed the Neutral Zone.

After a while, the BetterWorld admins declared the battle over and Princess Kiyoko the victor. The Vale was safe, and she now owned some of Vostok's territory, which she'd split among her allies.

Her reputation would eclipse all others on the Fantasy Continent, and Pel and Waylee would get the money they needed. She hoped this was a good thing, hoped they knew what they were doing.

Kiyoko

The taxi driver dropped Kiyoko off right at the house gate. Red regalia on, she had gone out celebrating her victory over Prince Vostok. From her winnings, she'd given Pel the money he needed, saying not to worry about paying her back. Next thing was to buy augmented reality glasses, if she could find any that didn't make her look dorky. Maybe she'd buy a bunch and invite people over to play live action role-playing games.

Her friends inside and outside BetterWorld had toasted her as a military genius, even though she had done nothing special except use surprise. At Club Kuro Neko, her favorite downtown club, she bought her friends glasses of boba tea and matcha, and boxes of Pocky biscuit sticks. Her friend Jayna used her fake ID to buy a round of plum wine. Kiyoko had almost accepted.

"This good?" the driver asked in some Old World accent.

"Yeah." She paid him, then unlocked the gate. The floods were on, but none of the interior lights. *Everyone's asleep. It is almost four, though.*

Club Kuro Neko catered to the cosplay and Otaku scenes, and stayed open all night, but even it got boring after a while. It was still Baltimore, after all, not Tokyo or Shanghai, the centers of world culture.

And besides, Nyasuke needed her. He'd be waiting. Her cat wasn't treacherous like boys. Or girls for that matter. Kiyoko couldn't help it—once she opened up, she opened up completely. If her body was naked against someone else's, her soul followed, seeking to merge with the other, to bond at a fundamental level. But no one she'd met wanted that—she was just another conquest.

This was all just temporary, though. Their band would land a contract, enter the market, and move someplace real. They had a lot of fans, locally anyway. If they moved to New York or Tokyo, and had a professional manager, they might actually make some money. She'd hire her own limo driver, and maybe a posse of ninja bodyguards.

Kiyoko watched the red tail lights of the taxi recede, and then she was alone. Such silence. No one talking, no one shouting, no gunshots, no sirens, nothing.

She latched and locked the gate behind her. And then saw something moving up in the sky. Not a bat, obviously. Hadn't seen a bat since forever, and it was way too big. It looked like a floating truck tire, silhouetted against the city's eternal glare as it silently banked back and forth over the neighborhood.

She set her comlink video to low-light and maximized the magnification and image stability. It took a couple of minutes to find again, but there it was—a large, black, wheel-shaped object, bristling with antennae and lenses. *Some kind of police drone?*

The flying object changed course again. But this time it glided straight toward the house. Toward her.

Her first impulse was to run. But Princesses didn't do things like that, and certainly she wouldn't. She put her comlink away and waved at the machine. "What do you want?"

No answer. It descended to about twice rooftop level and came up the street.

"I am Kiyoko, Princess of West Baltimore. Who are you?"

It stopped directly overhead and pointed lenses at her.

The thing gave her the creeps. But no way was she going to let it intimidate her. She waved again. "I'm in a band. Dwarf Eats Hippo. I play bass. Check us out, we're playing two sets at Bar Zar on Friday."

On the second floor, her sister's bedroom light switched on. *Oops.*

"We're waking everyone up. Go home, flying machine. You're drunk."

Instead of leaving, the machine descended to rooftop level. It made a faint whirring noise like a blender wrapped in a towel.

"Look, I don't even know you. I'm not gonna invite you in. I'm not that kind of girl. Go home. Come by Bar Zar on Friday and you can watch us play and buy me a drink." *I'm underage, and don't drink anyway, but whatever.* She waved goodbye.

Once inside the house, she couldn't help but peek past the living room curtain.

The machine was gone.

"What the fuck are you doing?" Pel's voice behind her. "Everyone but you is trying to sleep."

She whirled. She hadn't noticed him come down the stairs, clad only in briefs and his Philosoraptor T-shirt.

She averted her eyes from the bulge in his underwear. "You missed it. Some kind of flying machine was stalking me. I'm guessing police drone."

"What?"

She described the black wheel-shaped object and how it flew back and forth across the neighborhood and fixated on her when she pointed her comlink at it.

"BPD can't afford something that fancy. All they got are the toy helicopters." His forehead furrowed with worry. "Did you take video?"

"Yeah, so I could see it better." She played it back for him.

"Lemme borrow your link." Pel yanked it out of her hand, not waiting for a reply.

Jerk. "You're as rude as Dingo sometimes."

He ignored her, sat down on the sofa, and started fiddling with her comlink.

She sat next to him, not touching though, and peered over his shoulder. "What are you doing?"

"I grabbed the best still and I'm searching the net for a match."

A manufacturer's photo appeared next to the video grab of the machine outside their house. The objects looked identical.

Pel tapped the reference photo, and scrolled through text and diagrams. "It's called the Watcher," he said. "Built here in the U.S." He followed a link. "It can see and hear pretty much anything. Even has giga- and terahertz scanners."

"What's that?"

"They can see through walls."

"And clothes?"

He scoffed. "Probably, but I doubt gawking at your nether regions is their top priority. Now the question is, who uses these things?" He navigated a series of pages. "Oh."

"Who is it?"

"Homeland Security."

10

Waylee

Waylee was still a little pissed at Pel for not telling her about the Watcher until the next morning.

"Why didn't you tell me right away?" she had screamed, wanting to punch him in the mouth. "Didn't you think it was important?"

"Not an emergency. And you know you need regular sleep to control your condition," he insisted.

"Fuck you."

She apologized later. Pel knew her better than she knew herself, and didn't deserve her abuse.

Cyclothymia had two cycles, the virtual doctors said—hypomania and depression. The hypomania was good, she thought. It made her more energetic, creative, and optimistic. Perfect for writing and composing. Pel and her prior partners loved what it did for her sex drive.

Then there was the depression. The better her good times, it seemed, the steeper her descent into hell. It was like a cosmic see-saw.

All she could do was try to stay calm. If she didn't, especially after that blow to the head, it could turn into full-blown bipolar disorder, with racing thoughts, delusions, and suicidal urges. Then she'd really be fucked.

She felt her energy draining away, down into the floor. They couldn't possibly afford the drugs they needed. And Homeland Security had jumped in. Homeland had unlimited resources to track people down and crush them...

"Waylee?" Pel waved his hands, trying to get her attention.

"Sorry." They were all gathered in the living room—her, Pel, Shakti, Dingo, M-pat, Charles, even Kiyoko. Except for Shakti, no one sat. Rain pattered down beyond the drawn curtains.

Waylee tried to keep the fear out of her voice. *Hope for the best.* "So first off, we're sure Homeland Security is nosing around our neighborhood, and we're sure they're looking for Charles?"

Pel drummed his fingers together. "Only the feds have Watchers."

"Maybe we shouldn't have used the EMP bomb," M-pat said. "Not exactly your typical prison break."

Pel turned to face him. "Wouldn't have worked otherwise. They would have gotten video. And called up reinforcements, with drones and helicopters. Too dangerous in the middle of the city without getting a big head start."

"Think they got DNA or anything from the van we left?" Waylee asked.

"No chance. No skin or hair exposed."

"So why are they looking here?"

Alone on the sofa, Shakti leaned forward. "Maybe they're looking everywhere."

Let's hope. Feeling a little better, Waylee powered up the living room wall screen, sat down with the interface unit, and navigated to the local news site. The others plopped onto sofas or chairs.

The top story was titled "Councilman Cutler's Ties to Drugs and Organized Crime." Bryan Cutler, an African-American community organizer, was elected to the Baltimore City Council three years ago on the People's Party ticket. He was a rabble rouser on the council and the major parties wanted him out. He was feuding with MediaCorp too, pressing for public media and free Comnet access.

Shakti screeched and pointed at the wall screen. "What's that?" She was Cutler's last campaign manager, and they were still pretty tight.

"Just another hit piece," Waylee said. "The Party raises most of its funds growing pot at Friendship Farm, but it's perfectly legal. As for organized crime, they're probably talking about the gang truces he and M-pat coordinated."

"Well, let's see what they're spinning."

"Later." The news site's "Corrections Center Breakout" banner flashed red, indicating an update. Waylee tapped the on-demand link, taking her to the top of the story.

An immaculate woman sat behind a news desk. *I wonder if she's real, or an avatar?* To the right, windows revealed seven faces overlaid by green check marks, and below these, four faces inside red boxes. One of these was Charles.

"This update on the corrections center breakout," the broadcaster said. "Police have captured most of the escapees. Four are still at large." She went into details about the manhunt and how police caught the seven, none of whom showed much imagination after their unexpected release. Then she described the four remaining.

"Yesterday," she continued, "the Department of Homeland Security began assisting the investigation. Their main focus is Charles Marvin Lee."

Charles's face rotated slowly in the center of the screen. Text appeared alongside, listing details of his crimes and identifying features, with links to more information. No link to his actual hack of MediaCorp, which must have been deemed too embarrassing. "Lee is a convicted cyberterrorist—"

Charles jumped out of his seat. "What? It was just a prank! No harm done."

"—who fled alone in a van driven by the instigators of the breakout..." The woman recapped earlier coverage of their operation. Links to prior broadcasts appeared on the right, along with simulations of M-pat's and Dingo's masks.

"Thanks to descriptions from captured inmates, we now have these images of the getaway drivers." Recreations of Storm and Pel's quasi-Prince Harry rotated on the screen.

Dingo pumped a fist. "Woo-ee, kiddees! They're chasing a superhero and don't even know it."

The news broadcaster reappeared. "Corrections officers exchanged gunfire with the culprits—"

M-pat pointed at the wall skin. "That's a lie! We didn't shoot back."

Waylee tapped the pause icon. "You expect accurate reporting? This is a MediaCorpse outlet."

"Aren't they all?" Kiyoko said.

"Pretty much." Waylee looked at M-pat and the others. "And since when are we the culprits?"

Pel shrugged. "Well you know, breaking someone out of jail is against the law."

Waylee resumed the feed. "It isn't known if any of the culprits were hit," the broadcaster said. A simulation followed of their second van's escape down Greenmount and onto Madison.

"Baltimore police say the breakout was meticulously planned. And federal authorities say Lee's accomplices may be terrorists."

The main window switched to a middle-aged man wearing a generic suit. Text beneath stated Dennis Fecthammer, U.S. Department of Homeland Security. "Lee's accomplices set up miniature surveillance cameras outside the detention center. And they set off an electromagnetic pulse bomb to disable cameras, communications, and other electronics in the area."

Footage of the van interior appeared, followed by a short animation of how EMP bombs work. "In this case, massive capacitors released current into insulated copper wires coiled around an iron core. This created a powerful electromagnetic pulse that fried nearby electronics, much like a bolt of lightning. On a larger scale, such a weapon could paralyze an entire city."

"That's an idea," Dingo said.

Waylee cut him off with a slash of the hand.

Fecthammer returned. "This is obviously not the work of amateurs, and even falls outside the capabilities and M.O. of organized crime, Baltimore's drug gangs for instance. The culprits are as yet unidentified, but we believe they may belong to a terrorist cell, and freed Mr. Lee to assist an upcoming operation. Most likely, Mr. Lee was already a member of this group. As such, Homeland Security is assisting the investigation. We take this threat extremely seriously, and have posted a $100,000 reward for information leading to their capture."

A link appeared where viewers could provide information and collect their $100,000.

"A hundred G's," Dingo said. "More than all of us put together make."

"We've gotta find out more," Pel said. "See what they're doing. Charles and I can see what kind of chatter we can intercept from BPD."

Charles nodded.

Excitement returned to Waylee, stomping the creeping fears into submission. Their mission was too important to fail. Nothing would ever change without tearing down MediaCorp's propaganda machine. "Maybe check out other parts of the city. See if they're being searched too."

"I can upload my video of that Watcher over our 'hood," Kiyoko said, "and ask if anyone else's seen one."

"That would draw attention to yourself."

Dingo jumped in. "Who's less likely to be taken seriously by the Injustice League than Princess Kiyoko?"

Kiyoko scowled. "I'm trying to help, Dingus. You should go get an enema to clear all that shit out of your brain."

"Only if you eat it afterward."

M-pat threw up his hands. "What professionals!"

Waylee leapt out of her chair. She glared at Dingo and Kiyoko. "He's right. Quit acting like two-year-olds." She changed topics. "Kiyoko, would you mind running your message by me before you post it?"

Her sister tensed. "You don't trust me?"

"Of course I trust you, but writing's what I do, and we can't take any chances."

Shakti raised a hand.

Waylee locked eyes with her friend. *Ever the believer in Robert's Rules of Order.*

"Yes?"

"So do you think we're under surveillance now?"

Pel butted in. "Nothing since last night. But we should be careful."

"Could they hear us talking?"

He shrugged. "Possibly."

"I'd know if there was po-boys in the neighborhood," M-pat said. "And there's nothing flying around now."

Waylee paced the wooden floor. "Well, we should figure out what to do if the drone returns. And where to go if we have to run."

Charles poked his hand up to ear level. "Uh…"

"Yes?" Waylee said.

"Someone set a trap for me on BetterWorld and I had to jet."

Waylee managed not to scream. "Why didn't you tell us?"

"I thought I covered my ass well enough. Took the emergency exit. You know, switched the power off. Then I went back and deleted my accounts. But maybe someone got a sniff of my location."

"Okay," Pel said, still calm. "How would we know?"

"Not sure. I can look around." Charles leaned forward. "And I could spoof myself over in Jersey or somewhere and throw them off."

Pel nodded. "Nice."

They seemed to have things under control. "Alright then," Waylee said, "You boys hop in the net and do what you gotta do. M-pat and Dingo, make sure Authority isn't skulking around the area."

Dingo crossed his arms. "Since when are you my boss?"

"You're right. I'm not anyone's boss. Take it as a suggestion. You got a better one?"

He stood. "No, we on it."

Shakti raised her hand again. "Maybe Charles should relocate? Just to be safe?"

She's not being very helpful. "This is the safest place for him," Waylee said. "Trust me."

Pel leaned back in his chair. "I'll put out more cameras. And prep our gear for emergency exit, if it comes to that." He tilted his head, then smiled.

"I'll search the Comnet and see how to make caltrops. No shortage of scrap metal with all the junkyards nearby."

"I'll see where we could go," Waylee said. She'd have to ask around without letting anyone know what was going on.

No way would Homeland Security stop her.

* * *

Charles

Charles returned to the game room. He hopped in the immersion suit, which he'd been using for a couple of days now. It smelled faintly of bleach from all the cleaning, but at least the dog spray was odorless.

The suit took some getting used to, and some coaching from Pel. But it added a lot, walking through virtual landscapes instead of just watching it happen. It was like he'd been confined to a wheelchair all his life, but some preacher cured him with the power of the Almighty. If he didn't have so much scripting and poking around to do, and had more time for gaming or BetterWorld, maybe he could lose some weight with this suit, and look finer for Princess Kiyoko.

Once he got everything on and hooked up, he entered the Comnet. Maybe it was a little obvious, but he posted a message on /snarknet, one of the public boards popular with Collectivistas, seeming to originate from a wireless router along the New Jersey Turnpike. "On the run and free, they can't stop me. Dr. Doom got the jump, Authority just a chump." A spy would no doubt report it.

Next stop, the Baltimore Police Department. Homeland was too risky; they took hackers and pressed them into slavery. They'd be watching for someone like him.

Baltimore City Police Department—"to protect and serve." Their public site made them seem helpful. Mostly it described how to prevent and report crime. They didn't have enough money to do a lot of patrols or investigation, and even had a donations link where you could "Adopt a Cop."

He couldn't resist. Phineas K. Bottomstuffin promised $1 million to adopt the whole police force to perform at a private striptease party on New Year's Eve. Then he set up a bot to email random "Yo mama" jokes to their complaints department.

After poking around some more, Charles set up sniffers and a traffic analyzer outside their site. He doubted that would help much, so he hunted for communications he could listen to.

Kickin'. The headquarters dispatchers used unencrypted radio. Not only that, the broadcasts were digital, easy to parse.

Charles set up a program to copy and forward all BPD radio traffic to servers he could access anonymously. If the po-boys said "Lee," "break-out," "manhunt," or "Homeland," the program would message him and play back the conversation.

He tested it out. One hit—someone stole a surveillance camera outside his gramma's. The response from HQ, "Write it up, but feds have that location now."

It sounded like he wouldn't see his remaining family for a while. Not that they cared about him anyway.

Fuck it. Charles created a new BetterWorld avatar, this one a Zulu warrior named Iwisa, for the club they used. *Thank you, Compendia.* Their spear, the iklwa, was too hard to pronounce.

He wouldn't hang out at clubs. He'd enter Princess Kiyoko's realm, Yumekuni, and see how to fit in. He had briefly seen her fan site, and a portion of Yumekuni in game mode with a borrowed avatar. But he was still an outsider.

'Course, it would be easier to talk to the living, breathing Kiyoko. She was one room away. He'd definitely do that.

Maybe he'd listen to her music first. And check out some 'How to Game Women' sites.

He wondered how much time he had.

11

Friday

Pelopidas

With Charles wearing the full immersion suit, Pel donned one of the partial game systems—3-D goggles, headset, and gloves—and hooked everything up to Big Red. He started an offline simulation program and entered a featureless void as William Godwin. Charles materialized next, as a Zulu warrior he'd named Iwisa.

Pel spoke in his headset. "Load icons." Dozens of 2-D and 3-D glyphs appeared. He touched one labeled "Map 1," which would display output from Charles's traffic analyzer.

A three dimensional map appeared, with "Celebrate the New Year with the President" in the center, connected to dozens of other Comnet site titles by lines of varying color and thickness. "Not a lot of sites."

"No," Charles/Iwisa said, his feathered headdress and cowhide shield making him hard to take seriously. "Guests probably visit the site once or twice, and most of them might have done that before I put the sniffers out."

"Maybe they'll send out a reminder or something and we'll get all the names then."

"Maybe." Iwisa pointed a short spear at the map. "The thicker the lines, the more data's gone between the sites in the past week. And the darker the color"—the lines ranged from light pink to dark red - "the more individual messages there've been."

The White House Department of Scheduling and Advance had the darkest line to the gala site. They were probably coordinating the event. But V.I.P. Productions, a special events planning subsidiary of MediaCorp, had the thickest line. They must own the Comnet site. "Did you look at the communications from the White House and V.I.P. Productions?"

"I stay away from the White House. They caught too many Collectivistas there. But V.I.P..." He pointed his spear and a second constellation of sites appeared, connected to V.I.P. by lines ranging from pale to midnight blue.

Trouble was, there were hundreds of them. "Can we narrow it down?"

"Yeah. We know from the New Year's site they'll have a DJ."

Pel examined the site. "And a catering company, MC, a string quartet, and a jazz ensemble."

"You're musicians."

"Me and Waylee, anyway. And Kiyoko. But the band members will know each other, and we can't play jazz. Maybe we can get someone to quit. Our former drummer, J-Jay, plays jazz now. Maybe he'd help, if he knows the band."

They narrowed down the V.I.P. connections to caterers, DJs, and musicians near DC, but there were still a lot of connections left.

"So how do we know who got the gig?" Pel asked.

"Snoop around their sites I guess. And see if any of them visit the New Year's site."

Pel felt silly conversing via avatars when in real life, only a few feet separated them. He and Dingo played games without actual eye contact, but that was different. Immersion helped suspend disbelief when fighting invading hordes of zombie Canadians. "Let's take a look at the other connections, and see who some of the guests are. Then I'm gonna have to leave you. Band's playing at Bar Zar tonight, and it takes a good three or four hours to get everything loaded, moved, and set up, and do the sound check."

"All this going on and you're still playing music?" Charles seemed a lot more assertive cloaked in an avatar.

"Gotta buy food," Pel said. *Beer, really.* "And it's the closest we've got to careers. We're playing tomorrow night too, just at a house party up in Towson, though." They needed gigs at big venues opening for major bands, but MediaCorp controlled 93% of the music market, and their gatekeepers frowned on anything "political" or "inaccessible." Dwarf Eats Hippo fell into both categories, plus the worse category of "unreliable."

Iwisa waggled his spear. "I don't understand why musicians would try to break into a presidential fundraiser and dig for secrets—"

"To broadcast them—"

He kept going. "I mean, I could see Tupac pulling some shit like that, but you more like Jay-Z."

Pel made his avatar scowl. "I don't think so."

"I mean, could you see Jay-Z doing James Bond shit like you trying?" Iwisa doubled over laughing. "He'd be all, 'Which jet should we take, and these shoes okay?'"

Pel didn't wait for him to stop laughing. "Well, I wish I had money like him, and I wish people with money like that would put it to good use. But come on, Jay-Z's twice our age and not our genre." He pulled a card out of Godwin's pocket and handed it to Iwisa. "Take a listen." It contained a link to their band site and free samples.

"Music's only part time for us," Pel continued. "At least, unless we break through. It's our outlet, our way to connect. I make my living on the Comnet, and Waylee, she's a journalist, and she wants to change the world. Me too."

Iwisa looked at the card. "I was just bustin' you, no need to grief."

"You know you're talking to the chillest character in B'more."

"Yeah, whatev. You sure a contrast with Waylee, though. I mean, I totally respect her, but she seems a little wired."

Pel debated how much to tell him. "It's just how she is. Part of it's genetics—she's got this incredible energy and brilliance, but with side effects.

And part, well, she had a pretty rough childhood, the type you can never really escape."

Iwisa didn't respond at first. "I know how it is," he finally said. "I was lucky 'til moms passed. She was the greatest. But others, like some of my cousins, they had no one, just a house full of addicts."

"Well, Waylee's a fighter. She never took shit from anyone, her stepdad included. You know anger piles up, gets in your bones and festers there. But she channels hers—into her music, into making the world a better place, whatever she can do."

Iwisa raised a fist. "Props. She sure can preach, that's for sure."

"That's the singer in her. And reader. She's been in the anarchist scene since high school."

"Like throwing bombs and shit?"

Pel shook his avatar's head. "No, that's a media stereotype. Violence usually backfires. She helped Shakti and Bryan Cutler grow the People's Party, behind the scenes so her paper wouldn't find out. And helped bring the neighborhood together, to provide our own food and security. For her, it's all about bottom-up activism, people working together on their own terms to replace greed and subjugation."

Iwisa nodded. "Like the Code, free sharing."

"Yeah. Creative free association improving lives and healing the planet." He felt a familiar surge of admiration for his girlfriend. "And as long as MediaCorp controls information, few will even know they have that choice."

Iwisa glanced at the Dwarf Eats Hippo card again. "She's something on stage. I saw a video on BetterWorld."

He must have visited Kiyoko's site. "Which song?"

"Uh, don't remember. But y'all risking a real future."

"She's been performing over ten years and hasn't gotten anywhere. She doesn't think she has a future in music."

Iwisa stood for a moment. "I assume I can't come see y'all play."

"No, you can't be seen. Dingo'll be here if you have any problems."

He frowned. "That dude's psycho or something."

Not the first time someone's said that. "That's my home skillet you're talking about. He's just a free spirit, that's all."

"'Kay, as long as he ain't gonna come after me with a knife or some shit."

"Don't you remember? He put himself on the line to bust you out."

Iwisa nodded. "Yeah, you're right." He looked at the card again. "You got videos here?"

"Some, yeah."

"Kiyoko's on them?"

"She is our bass player." Charles seemed infatuated with her. *What to say?* "She has a lot of admirers, but she's not the loose type, and not in the mood for romance these days. Shitty ex-boyfriend."

Iwisa shuffled his feet. "She's pretty set up in BetterWorld. Better than I ever was."

"Yeah, she spends a lot of time there. It's a point of contention."

He frowned. "Why's Waylee so down on BetterWorld?"

"She just thinks it's a distraction. You heard her the other day."

"So? The real world sucks."

"Exactly. But you can hide, or you can stand." The sort of brave words Waylee liked to use. But now that they had Homeland Security on their ass, hiding didn't seem like such a bad idea.

* * *

Sunday

Charles

Charles sat in one of the living room chairs, listening to everyone talk about the weekend's shows. He didn't really fit in here. Where would he go after New Year's? Would he ever see his gramma and cousins again? Or would the po-boys watch them all the way to the grave?

Last he saw his gramma, she'd come to wish him a happy seventeenth birthday. They talked at one of them little tables while the other convicts sat with their one allowed visitor, and guards walked up and down, listening to everything they said. That was over a month ago, and she hadn't come again. She must have had too much else to worry about.

He didn't have any real friends in the hood to miss. Maybe at school, but Pel and the others were better. They looked up to him and gave him whatever he needed. 'Cept money, they didn't seem to have much of that.

And there was Princess Kiyoko, sitting on the couch with Waylee and Shakti, talking in her singsong voice. She posed her real hair today—brown with rainbow streaks, bound in silk bows. She looked more beautiful than ever. And from what Pel said, she was single.

"We need a new drummer," Kiyoko told Waylee. "J-Jay had soul, not like those synth tracks that Pel programs."

Across the room, Pel slapped his head with both hands. "Says the bass player. I got a thousand jobs to do. All you have to do is stand there in your cutesy little outfits and play single-note lines."

Waylee put her beer down. "Shut the fuck up, the both of you." She stared at Pel. "You're supposed to be the level-headed one, and here you're bickering like a child."

Pel gave her the finger and stomped into the kitchen. "Dinner's about ready."

Charles's hosts ate dinner together a lot, like family. 'Course Waylee and Kiyoko actually were family, and Pel was long term with Waylee. But Shakti and Dingo seemed just as hooked in.

When his mom was still alive, she made the best lake trout. That shit was the bomb, even if it wasn't actual trout. Crispy batter on the outside, extra tender on the inside, and every last bone pulled out.

She'd pile macaroni salad and collards on the side—though he wasn't fond of the greens. And she cooked sweet potato pie most Sundays.

It was just him and his mom 'til she passed and he had to move in with his gramma and aunt and all them cousins and neighborhood kids who didn't have any place else to go. He heard some crazy ladies collected cats. His gramma collected kids. She could cook too, but you had to fight for a decent portion.

Pel returned to the living room. "Come and get it. Your turn to do the dishes afterward, Dingo."

Dingo groaned.

They stepped to the big wooden table in the dining room and grabbed plates and silverware. Their big-ass dog sat next to it with his tongue out, like he hadn't just been fed ten minutes earlier.

Charles held up when he saw the bowls of green spaghetti and fake meatballs on the table. They never served real meat. At least it was better than the slop in juvie. Charles busted past the others and pulled up a chair next to Kiyoko.

Kiyoko smelled like cherry blossoms. She turned and smiled at him.

His heart stopped beating.

"How's everything going?" she asked, then twirled some green noodles around her fork.

"Uh, good, you know, I mean…" *Should have practiced something to say.*

Kiyoko stuffed the noodles in her mouth. Charles waited for her to finish chewing, but then she turned to her sister. "I came up with a new bass riff for 'Cowed to be an American.'"

Charles decided to butt in. "Did you find anything out about that drone?"

Heads turned.

"Yeah," Kiyoko said. "Thanks for reminding me." She stabbed a meatless ball with her fork, but left it on her plate. "I uploaded the drone video to my social site and some discussion halls, and asked if anyone else had seen one. I tagged it as high priority on the B-Scene."

"What's that?"

Her eyebrows raised. "Baltimore social net. So I got some responses back, and it started a discussion thread."

"And?" Pel said.

"They've been seen all over B'more past few days. And before that, since day one, them BPD mini-copters. Theory on the discussion thread is they're looking for the juvie escapees, and there's more than one drone out there, but no one knows how many."

"Thanks Sis," Waylee said. "That's good news."

Dingo leaned forward. "How is being the target of a massive search good?"

"'Cause they're unfocused. And they may have already cleared our area, which means we're safe."

Charles nodded. Waylee was smart for an amateur.

They returned to eating. Charles turned to Kiyoko. "You sure smacked down that Prince Vostok."

She smiled, one of those real smiles that nice people gave. "Thanks again for your help. It had to be done, and your burning oil played a big part."

"How much money did you win?"

She looked away and pursed her lips. "Well, I had a lot of debts to pay off, and I gave Pel most of the rest. So enough to buy some stuff, but nowhere near what I need to get out of this place or expand my business, hire people or whatever."

Pel's comlink—he didn't wear his data glasses in the house—played some tune. He looked down. "News update."

"I'll catch it when I'm done," Shakti said.

The others filed into the living room and Pel powered up the wall screen.

Same newscaster. "It is now thought that the culprits were wearing masks."

"Geniuses," Dingo said. "Only took them five days."

"One of the culprits was identified as the deceased television entertainer Dick Clark, longtime host of American Bandstand and Dick Clark's New Year's Rockin' Eve." A sidebar appeared with Clark's photo and biography, and links to more information.

"Another culprit's description matched Storm, a fictional character in a superhero series called X-Men, popular in BetterWorld simulations and games. Storm also appeared with the X-Men, a group of so-called mutants, in several movies and in old-time printed comic books." More background info and links appeared.

Pel looked at Dingo and Waylee. "See, you should have worn anonymous masks like me and M-pat."

"The other two have not been identified," the newscaster continued, "but it is suspected they wore masks as well. If you have any information, please contact the police immediately." Voice and text links followed, along with a reminder about the $100,000 reward.

Pel paused the feed. "Charles, anything about this on BPD traffic?"

"I'll check." He didn't have a comlink so would have to jump into the immersion suit later.

Shakti entered and sat next to Waylee. The broadcast resumed. "We have now an interview with one of Lee's prison mates."

Out of all the ape-like ass plugs, they picked the worst—Botis. "Yeah, I knew that boy Charles." Botis swaggered, showing off his grill. "I can't believe you ain't caught that chunky little bedwetter yet."

Charles's skin burned. *Turn it off.*

"Bedwetter?" the interviewer said.

"Yeah, used to cry for his dead mommy and wet his bed every night."

The lies shrank him to the size of a pea. "That's a lie!" He glanced at Kiyoko, afraid she might believe it. "I never..."

Kiyoko looked back, frowning. "I can't believe they'd air something like that."

Pel paused the feed again. "It's just a mindfuck. MediaCorp and the government do it all the time. Don't worry about it."

Charles fought for breath. "Don't worry about it? That's your advice when he lies about me in front of everyone?"

Dingo smacked his right hand with his left fist. "I see a news studio in need of an EMP bomb."

He cared at least.

"Enough with the EMP bombs, Dingo," Waylee said. She looked at Charles. "Pel's right, it's just Authority fucking with you."

Pel forwarded to the end of the interview. It was followed by a link, "Click here for the interview in its entirety."

The broadcaster returned. "What do you think? Is Charles Marvin Lee a threat to America? Or just a harmless child? We'll tabulate the results."

A poll link appeared below.

Waylee shook her head. "The news profession continues its downward slide."

"There's an option to write your own comments," Kiyoko said, looking at her comlink. She swiped her fingers across its screen.

"Maybe we should get people to vote 'harmless child,'" Pel said. "If the feds think he's harmless, maybe they'll spend less time looking for him."

"No way," Dingo said. "Boy's honor's at stake." He turned the backs of his hands toward Charles. The tattooed eyes glared at him. "'Sides, all we've done, you'd better be a stone-hearted bad-ass motherfucker."

Charles couldn't stay in the room. He ran up the stairs, fighting to keep tears from leaking out and embarrassing him further. He bypassed the immersion suit, just throwing on the helmet and gloves.

First thing was to watch the whole interview with Botis, no matter how awful it might be.

The shit-tard douche nozzle bumped himself up, like he was all that, and put down Charles with all kinds of lies. He'd pay for that.

He went to the poll next. It was no doubt a rush job – the comment box had no filter against command sequences. He pasted in codes that broke past the poll's external shell and brought up a files directory. *Sweetness!*

He found some Botis-related files and deleted every one of them. Then he inserted a worm that would go through all the station's files, replicate itself, and delete everything else.

A security program immediately attacked and neutralized the worm.

Underestimated them. He started deleting files manually, anything that might contain Botis video.

A red alert message popped up in front of him. "Intrusion detected."

Fuck. What was he being attacked with? His defense program didn't recognize it.

He tapped the disconnect icon. Nothing happened. He couldn't exit.

Charles cut off the suit power. Blackness and silence. Like he'd killed himself. He pulled off the helmet, disabled the wireless signal, then powered it back on in safe mode.

The intruder program was still there, but at least it couldn't communicate with the outside. He varied his defense parameters to wall it off. A green message popped up. "Threat contained."

Time to assess the damage. He looked and looked, but couldn't find anything wrong. Maybe he was missing something. He generated a core dump so he could examine the virus code, see what it had been doing.

Strange. The virus had essentially self-destructed, maybe when he quarantined it. Sections of memory had been overwritten with random garbage. He examined recent changes to the disk drive and solid state cache. Same thing, small stretches of random bits. He definitely needed a better defense program.

Charles thought about telling Pel and the others, but they'd be disappointed in him. He was supposed to be a pro, but somehow he'd gotten infected. Well, it was gone now, and no damage done.

Still, he picked through the core dump systematically, running a translation and recognition program and hoping the virus had left some trace on one of the threads. *Ah!* He found something alien, something that didn't belong. Something that issued interrupts and called another process.

His defense program hadn't recognized the virus code. Next step would be Comnet searches and the Collective forums. Except that would give him away, saying, "yo, I just got infected with your virus, and here's where you can find me."

Instead, he downloaded the latest update of every virus database out there.

The fragment didn't match anything known. Must be a custom job. Special, just for him.

What if it was the feds, and they'd traced his location? Charles ran a program to display all the information that had been passed to and from his immersion helmet, along with its timestamp.

Nothing after the infection. It looked like his location was still disguised. And no new ports opened. He must have neutralized the virus before it could do its work.

12

Monday

Waylee

"Kiyoko saw a Homeland drone again last night," Pel said from the other side of the dining room table. "One of the Watchers."

Waylee put her coffee down. "And again you didn't tell me?"

He took a bite of jelly-slathered toast and shrugged.

Her stomach clenched, then her fists. "Don't just shrug me off, you rude motherfucker."

Pel put his toast down. His eyes narrowed. "We're on the same side, you know."

Waylee turned away, trying to still the rage that she knew was inappropriate. She focused on the adjacent window, but the drawn curtains, their red color faded, brought gloom rather than peace.

It was just the two of them at the table. As always, Charles was up in the game room, immersed in the Comnet. Shakti had gone to work at the print shop, the weekend over. Dingo only worked part time in the afternoons, but was out backing M-pat on a domestic dispute of some sort.

Domestic dispute. Without M-pat's anger management strategies and communication lessons, she and Pel wouldn't have lasted so long. Truth was, she adored Pel and couldn't imagine surviving without him.

Waylee looked back at her boyfriend. She should defuse the tension. "Sorry. We're not even close to ready for this fundraiser. It's gnawing at me."

He nodded. "I set you off. And I'll wake you up next time."

"So where'd she see the Watcher?"

"Here by the house, when she came home. It flew off when she waved, but didn't go far."

"It was right here?" Now she had a reason to be angry. "And you didn't think that was important?"

He sighed. "I'm telling you now, aren't I?"

Jackass. "I thought they were done snooping around our neighborhood."

"Kiyoko said it must have a thing for her. Joking, I assume, but I can't always tell with her." He gulped the rest of his coffee.

She glanced at her comlink. Ten in the morning. Her sister would be asleep at least two more hours. "What time was that?"

"Kind of early for her. Around three. Said she got bored."

"I'll go wake her up in a few and get the details. I can't believe you two didn't think this was important."

Pel rolled his eyes and resumed eating.

He never gave in, even when he was wrong. "You've got no right to make decisions for me," she said.

He threw down his toast. "Look. These drones can sort of see through walls, but people are just silhouettes. I looked it up. No way they'd recognize Charles. Especially when he's in the game room with the steel sheeting."

"Well, Dr. Knows-it-all, they wouldn't be back without a reason."

From upstairs, Charles shouted, "Hey, anyone here?" He sounded panicked.

Waylee jumped up, knocking her chair to the floor. She ran for the stairs, Pel following. "What is it?"

Charles stumbled down the stairs into the living room, data gloves on and VR helmet tucked under one arm. "Picked up radio traffic—I've been monitoring BPD's radio communications..."

"And?"

"They've got at least ten cars headed to our address from Headquarters and the Southwest District. Plus a group from Homeland, coming from FBI headquarters off the beltway."

Fuck. The colors faded from the room.

"Our address?" Pel said. "You're sure?" His voice sounded distant.

Charles recited their address correctly. "I wasn't sure what your house number was when I was listening, but it sounded bad so I looked it up."

Fuck. Waylee's knees gave out, and her body sagged to the floor. "Pel..."

"Goddamn it, Waylee." He reached under her armpits and yanked her up. "Call Shakti and warn her. Charles, how long 'til they get here?"

Charles seemed to shrink. "Got me. They're trying to arrive all together though."

"Fifteen minutes if we're lucky," Pel said. "Get all your shit together. Everything. Your clothes, your pillow, your toothbrush, everything you've touched. Throw it on your bedsheets and roll it all up in a ball and bring it down here."

"Why?"

"We're getting out of here and so are all traces of you. Keep the gloves on. Give me the helmet."

Charles passed him the helmet and ran back up the stairs.

Waylee fought the anguish descending over her like a fog. *Later. Come back later. I don't have time for you now.*

Pel pulled his comlink out of a front jeans pocket. "Dingo, emergency."

"'Sup, bro?" came Dingo's voice. From the angle, Waylee couldn't tell if he was on video or not.

"Cops are on their way here. Lots of 'em. We're getting out of here."

"On my way over." The volume dropped a little. "Chief, emergency. We've gotta get over to the band house."

"No, no," Pel said. "You should get out of here."

"I'm on the way, bro."

Pel stuffed the comlink back in his pocket. "I'm getting my data cubes and shit." He ran up the stairs.

"Shakti," Waylee told her comlink. It dialed her number.

Shakti's smiling face appeared on the screen. "Hi Waylee. What is it?" Her eyebrows rose. "Something wrong?"

Her face must be broadcasting agony. "Everything's... Shakti, the cops are on their way. Don't come home. Go now, go to our rendezvous spot."

Shakti's eyes widened. "You're... I can't go now, I'm in the middle of work..."

"You've gotta go right now." *Oh no, Kiyoko.* Waylee clicked off and ran up the stairs. She spotted Pel in the game room, throwing stuff into the big canvas duffel bag he'd bought.

Kiyoko's door was unlocked. Inside, she stood trapped in her cylindrical cage, a black phantom waving cyborg arms.

Waylee tripped over something – the damn cat – and sprawled onto the floor. The cat howled, and darted under the bed.

Kiyoko didn't seem to notice. Waylee scrambled to her feet and knocked on her sister's helmet. "Kiyoko! Get out of there!"

Kiyoko put out a hand in a stop gesture.

"It's an emergency!" Waylee looked for a power button. Seeing none, she ran to the wall outlet and yanked out all the electrical cords.

Kiyoko pulled off her helmet, her face furious.

"What the hell is wrong with you, you fucking freak?"

Waylee stifled the urge to slap her. "Cops are coming. We've gotta go."

"What?"

Waylee started releasing the immersion suit from its cage, twisting the quick-release fittings along the arms, legs, and torso. She'd seen Pel and Dingo do it a thousand times. "I told you we might have to run."

"You know, I was in the middle of something."

She had unhooked half the support fibers. They drooped like dead tentacles from the black frame.

"I didn't do anything wrong."

"Harboring a fugitive?"

"Then get him out of here."

"We are. You've gotta come with us." She cast off the last of the tentacles.

"Why?" Kiyoko crossed her arms. "Besides, Princesses don't run."

Waylee fought an overwhelming urge to scream. She only half succeeded. "For fuck's sake, you're not a fucking princess! You're just a deluded little girl who can't deal with real life."

Kiyoko's face morphed from incredulity to sadness to fury. "Get out of my room. I hate you."

"You what?" The fog returned. Kiyoko, her sister, her only family. Pel, he hated her too. They all did. *No. Come back later, and you can destroy me all you like.*

Someone—Kiyoko—pushed her out the door. "Get out, crazy fucking bitch!"

She was back in the hall. The door slammed and she heard it lock.

"Kiyoko!" Tears blurred her vision. She threw her shoulder against the door, but it held—all the doors in this house were solid wood. "Kiyoko!"

Pel grabbed her right hand. Charles stood behind him, holding a bedsheet wadded into a big ball.

"We've gotta go," Pel said. "Right now."

"No, not without my sister." She pounded the door with the side of her fist.

No response.

Pel seized her by the arm. "We've gotta get Charles out of here."

She tried to shake him off, but he wouldn't let go. "Kiyoko won't come."

"She'll be okay, she didn't do anything." Pel pulled her away and led them downstairs.

When they reached the living room she heard screeching tires and car doors opening and closing. Their dog Laelaps—at least it sounded like him —started barking.

It couldn't possibly have been fifteen minutes, could it?

* * *

Dingo

M-pat parked his black Honda across the street from the band house. Dingo threw on his data glasses. Mrs. Lockton had begged them not to leave her alone with her abusive husband. They tossed him out and told her they'd be back as soon as they could.

Two black tire-shaped objects—the ones Pel called Watchers—hovered over the house. The RV was still in the yard. *Bad.*

As soon as they got out of the car, Dingo saw the first police cruisers coming south down the long road into the neighborhood, sirens off but lights flashing. One of BPD's toy helicopters flew overhead. Then from the west, unmarked black SUVs and town cars turned into the cross street, one after the other.

Dingo stood with M-pat in front of the Honda, watching the police arrive. "We gotta delay the po-boys."

M-pat frowned. "How we gonna do that?"

"I don't know, you're the chief." Dingo activated his data glasses. "DG, call Pel."

No answer. Either they'd escaped on foot or they hadn't gotten out yet and were busy scrambling around. Maybe Kiyoko insisted on feeding the cat first.

The lead cop cars and SUVs screeched to a halt alongside the house on both sides of the lot facing streets. The following vehicles, at least a dozen in total, stopped behind them. Doors opened and thugs poured out: men and women in police uniforms, grey suits, or baseball caps and windbreakers with three-letter obscenities like FBI or ATF, new divisions of Homeland Security. Most wore bulletproof jackets and pants and carried shotguns or pistols.

A military-style armored troop carrier pulled up and discharged men in full body armor and helmets. They brandished automatic weapons or sniper rifles and ran to positions on either side of the house. The biggest bullyboy carried a black battering ram with both hands.

"Stay here," M-pat said. "I'll handle this. You'll just make things worse."

"You got it, boss man." He'd never seen Authority this serious, except in broadcasts where they were bombing compounds in Africa or Latin America. He turned up the microphone gain on his data glasses and pointed the voice tube at them.

A middle-aged white man in a suit seemed to be in charge, moving his hands around and talking into a headset mike. M-pat approached him. He was surrounded by police before he got close.

"Name's M'patanishi," he said in a loud, clear voice to the highest ranking badge.

"I'm the chief facilitator of this neighborhood. Can you tell me what's goin' on?"

"Police business. Get lost."

"Excuse me, SIR, but the city council recognizes me as an authority here, so I will not get lost, as you put it."

"Get lost," another police thug said, "or we're arresting you."

Pel's voice sounded in his ear canal. "We're leaving now."

Dingo moved back behind the Honda and scanned the streets with his data glasses, feeding the video to Pel. "You're surrounded. Sort of. They're on both streets by the house but they haven't moved in. You can still get out the alley." A narrow alley ran between the backyards on their block and stretched from one side of the neighborhood to the other. So far, the police hadn't seemed to notice it, or maybe they would hit it on foot once they got positioned.

"Looks grim. Thanks for the tip."

"I'll distract them. Wait for the commotion." He clicked off the connection and walked down the cross street, away from the band house and the cops. Once out of sight, he hopped a short chain link fence into their neighbors' back yard. Home of the Johnsons—husband, wife, three kids. Their mangy golden retriever ran up to him, tail wagging.

"Not now, Killer." He opened his backpack—his bag o' tricks—pulled out the Dick Clark mask, and slipped it on. *Good thing I kept it.* A pair of transparent gloves followed.

As Dick Clark, superhero from beyond death itself, Dingo walked briskly up the narrow side yard, then casually into the front yard. He saw two columns of unattended police cars. Time for a joyride.

A cop cuffed M-pat, who didn't offer any resistance. *He could Krav Maga their asses, why's he being such a pussy?*

Dingo opened the Johnsons' front gate and strolled over to the nearest unattended BPD cruiser. It was empty, key still in the ignition, power still on, no one paying attention. He opened the driver's side door and slipped in, dumping his backpack on the passenger floor.

The control console looked just like a Comnet interface, a big touch-screen with all kinds of graphics displayed—speed, engine status, cameras, communications... Forward/Park/Reverse joystick was obvious, positioned right next to the driver's seat. Dingo took the cruiser out of Park and creeped down the road, away from the band house. The car made no noise—hybrid motor used electric mode at low speeds.

So far, so good. He switched the radio to satellite and downloaded a classic rap anthem, NWA's "Fuck tha Police." He turned into a driveway, then reversed back into the street, facing the band house now.

Some of the Authority thugs stared at him. One of the others held M-pat's Glock, the one he kept in his concealed holster. The high-ranking cop yelled at M-pat. He didn't seem remotely fazed. He had a permit for it, after all, and Baltimore was a pretty dangerous place.

Dingo started the song and swiped the volume slider to max. Drums, bass, and shouted rhymes rattled his brain like the shaker ball in a can of spray paint. Bad ass speakers for a cop car. He drove slowly past the line of police vehicles and officers standing outside, middle finger raised in salute.

Living with musicians and all, Dingo occasionally wrote his own street poetry. He clicked on the mike to the megaphone mounted on the squad car roof, and put it to his lips. Middle finger still extended, he shouted out his own lyrics for "Fuck Tha Police," keeping rhythm with NWA's bass and drums.

Fuck tha police, cuz I sho' ain't a one
To respect fuckin' fascists, cuz they got a badge and gun.
Oinkin' on some donuts, then you come here and harass.
Put them guns away, I'll kick your sorry ass.
Fuck tha police...

The entire contingent stared at him, from street thug to Master Suit himself. They seemed to have no idea what to do. Then, all at once, they reacted, pointing their guns at him, telling him to stop, and jumping in their cars.

Dingo mashed the accelerator down to the floor. The car took off like a rocket.

"Let the game begin!" he screamed over the pounding of the car speakers, houses flying by.

Pelopidas

Pel flipped through the camera views on their living room wall screen. He had retrieved his data glasses, but the cameras were hard-wired to thwart signal jamming.

The alley looked clear, just as Dingo said. Laelaps barked and barked at the intruders outside their side fence.

Waylee was right. They should have taken off last night when the Watcher returned. *We're totally unprepared. How the fuck did they find us?*

Charles stared at him with wide eyes. His data gloves shook. "What do we do? We can't leave Kiyoko."

Waylee glanced back toward the stairs.

"She'll be fine," Pel said. "Let's focus."

Loud rap music blared from the front street, getting closer. *Fuck tha Police.* It had to be Dingo.

Pel switched to the camera covering the front. Dick Clark drove a police cruiser slowly past the assembled cops, blasting defiance, his middle finger extended.

Pel couldn't help but laugh.

Neither could Charles.

Waylee, though, looked about ready to cry. "All our planning for nothing…"

The entire besieging force seemed to forget about the house. Most of the BPD officers ran for their cars. Dick Clark took off with half a dozen police cruisers in pursuit.

Pel switched to the back camera. Still clear. "Let's go. No noise." He put on his data glasses.

He unlocked a window on the side facing their next door neighbor, and pushed it open for the first time in months. The front of the RV lay just beyond. He slung the big duffel bag of gear and data cubes around his neck, then scrambled through the opening.

Charles followed, but got caught on the sill. Pel grabbed his arms and Waylee lifted from behind, and he tumbled to the ground.

Waylee came through last, gripping Charles's bedsheet bundle, her face listless. She handed the sheets to Charles and closed the window behind her. They huddled in front of the RV, invisible from the street—at least for the moment.

Pel peeked around the side. Between the house and the RV, he could only see a narrow sliver of road. No cops there. He motioned with his arm and inched to the front passenger door.

He tried to yank the old fashioned keys out of his jeans, but he'd stuffed his comlink in the same pocket, and his fingers couldn't get past it. *You've gotta be kidding.*

He took a deep breath, then fished out the comlink, then the keys. He glanced at the street again. Still no one visible, but he heard shouting and heavy footsteps.

Hand trembling, he unlocked the door. He jumped inside.

Charles followed, then Waylee. She closed the door, the noise barely audible.

Maybe we should stay here. Maybe the cops wouldn't think to search the RV. *Of course they will.*

Pel climbed into the driver's seat and slipped the key in the ignition. He glanced at Waylee, sitting shotgun.

She looked back, her eyes desperate, then opened the navigation program on her comlink. Charles huddled on the floor between them.

Ok. Here goes. Pel twisted the key to the right. The engine roared to life, loud and obvious.

He heard shouts, but didn't look back. He slammed the accelerator down. In the side mirrors, the rear wheels threw up dirt and dead leaves.

Laelaps barked louder.

With the PowerPack and turbocharger, their RV had twice the torque of a stock model. But still it barely moved, lumbering down the side yard like an elephant. *Come on, you bastard.*

More shouts and barking. He heard gunshots, then a yelp.

Laelaps. I'm so sorry.

"Stop!" not far behind them.

His right foot stayed put. The RV knocked one of their rain barrels off its concrete block platform. It bounced off the front grill ahead of them, trailing hoses that smacked against the windshield like tentacles.

They entered the back yard, which was big by Baltimore standards. He drove right through the vegetable garden, crushing and mangling their winter greens. He aimed for the back fence, between two poles. They were going fast now, hopefully fast enough to get out. Momentum was a function of weight too, and the RV was heavy.

They smacked into the chain link fence and knocked over a big section.

More shouts and gunshots.

They were in the alley now, but he couldn't turn the RV quick enough, and it smashed into their back neighbor's fence, flattening it too.

He hit the brakes, then threw the vehicle into reverse.

"Cops are running after us," Waylee shouted. "Go, goddamn it."

"I'm trying." He shifted into forward, yanked the steering wheel all the way to the left, and stepped on the accelerator again. Fence fragments and vines scraped down the right side as they fishtailed into the alley. "You'll have to repaint," he said to Waylee as he fought to straighten the beast.

Ahead, the alley ran two blocks to the road that would take them out of the neighborhood. It was barely wide enough for the RV. He floored the accelerator and they picked up speed.

More gunshots. He heard smacks against the back of the RV. Charles hugged the floor. Were they crazy, shooting guns like that in a residential neighborhood? He and Waylee had nothing to fire back with, not that either one of them could shoot anyway.

They barreled down the alleyway, bouncing over potholes, no one visible in the yards or houses on either side. A good thing – if someone stepped into the alley, he wouldn't be able to stop in time.

He heard sirens to the left. Cops had gotten back in their cars. He glanced at the outside mirror. A black town car, flashing blue light on the dashboard, had entered the alleyway but gotten hung up in the broken fences. *Hah!*

Returning his eyes ahead, tree branches crossed the alleyway just above eye level. He winced as they collided. Branches bent and snapped and leaves flew everywhere.

The alleyway widened at the next block. Here, people parked their cars on concrete pads in back of their houses. An elderly African-American woman, Mrs. Henson, was hanging up laundry in her backyard. She cast wide eyes at them as they passed.

The alley ended ahead at the street that separated the neighborhood residences from a sprawling complex of warehouses and machine shops to the south. The local Baptist church blocked the view to the left and a two-story apartment building blocked it to the right, but he didn't have time to stop and watch for traffic. He swung the steering wheel to the left and the RV screeched onto the street, tipping off its right wheels. The rear swung out of control. Next to him, Waylee gasped, then the RV plopped down again with a jolt.

No traffic—everyone was at work—but the sirens were closer now. Pel wrestled the RV back into position, then stepped on the gas again. They passed the street their house fronted. Police cruisers—two or three—accelerated toward him, overhead lights flashing and sirens blaring.

Fuck. We'll never outrun those things. "DG, navigation."

A local map appeared in his vision, charting a path through the adjacent industrial park. The plan was to ditch the RV and hoof it, but they'd have to lose the pursuit.

To the right, a featureless warehouse wall rose directly against the street. Ahead, the road sloped down toward the Gwynn's Falls river valley. As soon as he passed the last side street, he pulled a knob hanging a few inches from the cab roof.

The knob released a hook, and a wide tray mounted on the roof sprang up and catapulted a hundred caltrops he'd snipped and bent from sheet metal. They bounced all over the road behind him and pointed razor-sharp edges toward the sky.

He heard two loud pops. In the mirror, a cop car with flashing lights skidded to a halt. The one behind swerved to avoid it, and its tires blew out too. The others slammed on their brakes.

"Fuck yeah!" Their pursuers would have to backtrack over half a mile to get around his trap.

Next to him, Waylee frowned. "One of those drones is following us."

Pel tilted the side mirrors up and saw a Watcher behind and twenty to thirty feet above. He shouted over his shoulder, "Charles, stay out of sight." Nothing to do but keep driving. "Waylee, which way should I go?" He didn't dare look at her again, had to keep his eyes on the road.

"The interstate's only two more blocks."

"Yeah, but there's no on-ramp here. Besides, we can't exactly hide this thing on the interstate."

"We're fucked," she said. "I'm sorry."

"Focus." The road turned abruptly to the right. "How do we lose that Watcher?"

"Underground?" she said.

"What?"

"The storm drains."

* * *

Dingo

Dingo was pretty sure this was the most fun he'd ever had in his life. Better than sex or drugs or both together with a band playing a few feet away. Every cell of his body screamed with the sheer joy of being alive.

He whipped the police cruiser to the right, out of their neighborhood onto U.S. 1. Toward the heart of Baltimore. Maybe it would have been better to go the other way. Too late now.

He switched on the vehicle's cameras—one inside, pointing at him, and two exterior, one pointed forward and the other behind. He wasn't Pel, and definitely not Charles, but he'd picked up enough skills to do what he needed. And the control interface had an audible command mode. Taxpayer dollars well spent.

"Broadcast on Comnet. All cameras and microphones."

Some lights went on. He was live. He linked the communications to the public forums, making sure to include /snarknet, and called out every tag he could think of.

"Listen up, yo-yos," he said then, looking into the interior camera but watching the road sufficiently to dodge cars who were too slow to get out of the way. "This here's Dick Clark, rockin' you out from beyond the grave, broadcasting live from a borrowed BPD car."

The rear camera showed a good half dozen, maybe more, cop cars trying to keep up with him. "Unfortunately, you missed the best part, dear viewers, where I drove by a huge gathering of Authority thugs, and gave them the finger to feast their eyes on and an earful of anthem to rock their sorry world. You, dear viewers, should do the same. Give Authority the finger every chance you get."

The four lane road was pretty empty headed downtown. He sped over Gwynn's Falls and past the MediaCorp billboard he tagged or set on fire whenever he got the chance. Speedometer read 110. *Fuck yeah!*

He slowed a little to let his pursuers get closer, and downloaded the whole Dwarf Eats Hippo catalog from the cloud. BPD sucker had saved his passwords in memory, so he'd pay list price.

"Random play," Dingo told the computer. "Dead Eyes" cued up first.

He addressed the internal camera. "This is the baddest band in B'more, Dwarf Eats Hippo. Check them out, yo. Then buy their songs – they're too poor to serve meat for dinner."

Waylee's voice was almost sweet at first, Pel's electronics mild. Then she wailed hell's bells on the guitar and screeched like a starving banshee.

"Skin stretched

Over empty skull,

Painted for the carnival..."

Damn girl's a firebomb. She's as noisy when she's fucking Pel as she is on stage. How'd she end up with a boring dude like him? Must be a musician thing. Dingo started fantasizing about a trio with him, Waylee, and Kiyoko, what it would be like.

Yuck. Housemates too long, too much like incest.

Someone honked. He'd just blown through a red light. He was driving too fast to daydream. This shit was just like Grand Theft Auto X, except when the game was over, it was over for real.

Traffic picked up. Rundown townhouses crowded either side of the road, people staring from their stoops. He saw more cop cars ahead, approaching with flashing lights.

"Enough of U.S. 1," he told the camera. He swung left onto Monroe Street, another red light but fuck it. The tires screeched, he smelled smoke, and a panicked sedan swerved out of the way.

I should put on the siren so people'll get out of the way. "Computer, siren." Nothing happened.

He scanned the console. *Ah.* He pressed the siren and overhead flashers icons. The *weoo weoo weoo* blended well with the music.

Mother fuck. He'd gone the wrong way down a one-way street. Cars honked and swerved to avoid him.

He glanced at the rear camera display. The cops hadn't followed. *Limp-dicks. Must be planning an ambush.*

Boarded up, crumbling tenements lined the road. Addicts shambled around like zombies.

"Dear viewers," he told the camera, "you'll notice what a shithole this city is. Look around, the whole world's a shithole thanks to the greedy bastards at the top."

He swung to the left at the next intersection, but an approaching car tried the same route and he smashed into its side with a loud crunch. He bounced off and tried to keep the car straight, but it spun out of control, everything a blur.

* * *

Kiyoko

Kiyoko's anger at her sister gave way to fear. Cops were coming? She hoped they'd get Charles well away. He was a nice kid, and nice kids were the ones who suffered the most.

She plugged the power strips back in and put on the helmet. There wasn't anything incriminating there that needed deleting, but she cleared her passwords and everything from the cache. She exited immediately afterward.

She pulled off her suit and dropped it on the treadmill. She just had a nightie underneath. Couldn't get arrested like that. She opened one of her wardrobes, flipped through it, and pulled out a white silk dress. Purity and innocence in Western mythology, but death in Chinese. She threw on the dress and matching slippers and started brushing her hair in the antique mirror nailed to the door.

Laelaps barked furiously outside. She heard shouts, then gunshots. The brush slipped from her fingers.

More shouts and gunshots, and a crashing noise from the back.

Kiyoko started to cry and couldn't stop. *This is undignified.* No, her sister was right, she was nobody, and now even the pathetic life they had was over.

A huge crash came from downstairs, followed by unfamiliar voices shouting in the living room. She dabbed her tears away and breathed deliberately like the samurai did to steady their minds before battle. She opened her door, prepared to face their enemies.

Soldiers in body armor, their faces walled off behind clear plastic, ran up the stairs. Two aimed complicated-looking guns at her, and the rest fanned out, checking the other rooms in pairs.

She tried not to panic. "What are you doing?"

"On your knees, hands on your head," one of the soldiers said, voice muffled by a filter over his mouth.

"I bend my knee to no one." Her courage had returned. "Please don't point those guns at me. I'm unarmed."

A man and woman in FBI windbreakers and caps walked up the stairs. "Cuff her," the woman, no faceplate blocking her pretty features, said. One of the soldiers hurried behind Kiyoko, pulled her wrists together behind her back, and slapped on a pair of metal handcuffs.

"Do you have a warrant to barge into our house like this?" she asked the FBI woman.

Her partner pulled a piece of paper out of an inner pocket and held it in front of her. She couldn't read it. The tears had returned and blurred her vision. "Did you kill my sister?"

The woman moved closer, her eyes soft. "Just your dog, ma'am. And I'm real sorry about that, it attacked us."

"He's never bit anyone. He just barks." She collapsed in tears, unable to wipe them away and unable to see. Her sister was okay, that was the important thing. But nothing would ever be the same again.

The FBI agents lifted her up.

"My cat, what'll happen to my cat?" Nyasuke could starve to death. Or end up on the street or Death Row, like the kitten her evil father took away.

The woman put an arm around her and walked her down the stairs. "Just cooperate with us and this will all be over soon," she said. "I promise."

* * *

Pelopidas

The industrial park near their house was big, but full of dead ends. Waylee hadn't been able to locate a stormwater or sewer map on the Comnet.

"The caltrops only gave us a few minutes," Pel said. "And that Watcher is overhead. Even if we find a manhole around here, how are we gonna pry the cover off and get inside before the cops arrive? And without the Watcher seeing us?"

Waylee swiped her comlink screen. "There's a big factory at the end of the road we're on – that printing company Dingo used to work for. It's right against the river and all those trees."

"Perfect." He knew where that was – Dingo worked there briefly until management fired him for trying to organize an Industrial Workers of the World local. They could follow the river to the nearest stormwater outfall, then take the pipes as far away as they could get.

"Charles," Pel said, keeping his eyes forward. "Get ready to run, we're stopping soon."

No reply.

"Waylee," he said next. "Get the flashlight and tire iron out of the tool kit."

"Tire iron?" Charles said behind him. "Expecting zombies?"

Waylee said nothing as she left her seat.

All the buildings around here were huge and featureless. The printing company was no exception. Pel drove through the parking lot and slammed the RV to a stop right against the main entrance.

"Let's go!" He grabbed the duffel bag lying between the front seats. It was heavy. He hopped out and ran up a short flight of stairs, headed for the glass doors beyond. Waylee followed with the tire iron and flashlight, then Charles, carrying his bundle of sheets and clothes.

Once they were all inside the factory, Pel locked the doors.

A morbidly obese male receptionist stared from behind the front desk. "May I help you? Why'd you lock the doors?"

He heard sirens. Cops would be here soon. *We need some confusion to slow them down.* "Boss fired me so I'm back to blow the place up." He held up the duffel bag. "Get on the intercom and tell everyone to get in their cars and get the hell out of here. The place blows in five minutes. I'd rather not kill anyone."

The receptionist looked at him blankly, as if trying to process what he'd heard. Pel pointed the bag toward his face and screamed, "Now!"

That did it. Eyes wide with fear, he picked up a phone and hit a button. "Uh," the voice on the intercom began, "we have a bomb threat. It's set to go off in five minutes, he said."

He hung up the phone and waddled toward the door, but Pel held up a hand. "This door is staying locked. Go out the loading docks."

The fat man ran off to the left, huffing with exertion. Pel motioned for Waylee and Charles to follow him, and headed for the back of the building. He saw a fire alarm just past the reception desk and pulled it down to emphasize his point. Loud bells rang and white lights strobed in the ceiling.

Past the entry room, the interior was as big as a Wal-Mart. Envelopes, flyers, and magazines ran from digital printing presses down conveyor belts to stuffing machines, sorting machines, and machines whose purpose he didn't have time to guess at. Some of the equipment had been stopped, but most kept churning.

People sprinted past them, some screaming. A balding man shouted, but the bells drowned him out.

A young woman, terror in her eyes, ran up to them and pointed toward the front. "Get out, there's a bomb!" She took off, not waiting for a response.

Waylee grabbed Charles's bundle from him and tossed it in a bin marked "hazardous waste."

"Fitting end to lame-ass clothes," Charles said.

"Don't know why we bothered bringing them," Waylee said.

Pel didn't waste time arguing.

Once they reached the back of the building, now deserted, Pel scanned the walls for an exit sign. *There.* He followed the arrow to an emergency exit. It was plastered with warnings about activating the alarm system, not that it mattered now.

He opened the door and heard police sirens on the other side of the building. Outside, ragged trees and a thick understory of invasive honeysuckle bushes stretched as far as he could see, even overhanging the exit itself. Although it was December, the weather was still fairly warm and most of the leaves hadn't dropped. Great cover, although it'd have been better before the last derecho. And the Watcher might be able to spot them on infrared.

Pel looked up but didn't see any drones. He motioned for Charles and Waylee to follow him. "Hurry."

Waylee shut the door after they exited. "Now where?"

"DG, aerial image." He panned along the translucent map and zoomed in. The river was obvious, not far away, but the tree canopy obscured the banks, and street view didn't cover river beds. There would be a stormwater outlet somewhere, though. "Let's go down to the river and look for a storm drain," he told the others.

They reached a trail just past the first line of trees, but it was partly open overhead, so he kept going, forcing his way through tangled twigs and vines. Just past the trail, the ground sloped sharply downward. Pel slipped and fell hard on his ass. Embarrassed, he jumped back up and continued forward.

Behind him, Charles said, "Ain't there a way 'round this?"

Pel turned and put a finger over his lips. They continued down the slope, grasping tree trunks and branches to keep from falling.

The river—just a wide shallow stream, really—flowed just below them now. It smelled faintly of piss. Trash littered the banks. To their right, an old stone railroad bridge spanned the river. And just beyond the bridge, a concrete pipe jutted above the water, presumably to drain the acres and acres of rooftops and parking lots they'd left.

Pel followed the river but kept under the tree canopy. He shifted the bulky duffel bag to his other shoulder. *If I was a drummer, I'd be in better shape.*

They crossed below the bridge and made their way to the pipe. It was about three feet wide and completely dark inside.

"No way I'm going in that," Charles said.

"You sure as fuck are," Waylee said. "Otherwise we spend the next decade or two in prison."

Pel's data glasses had low light vision but that was useless with no light whatsoever. "Pass me the flashlight."

Waylee handed it to him.

He wondered how long the batteries would last. A couple of hours? Pel strapped the duffel bag to his back and scrambled in.

Three feet was plenty of room to crawl through, but it wouldn't be quick. The inside smelled awful, like petroleum, sulfur, and dead things. The bottom was damp, and soaked his jeans.

Charles followed, then Waylee. "It'd better not rain while we're in here," Waylee said.

"No talking," he whispered back. "Who knows where it'll echo to."

* * *

Dingo

When Dingo's police car stopped spinning, it was on the sidewalk. Nothing felt broken. The console was dark—no power.

A couple of drug zombies, men of indeterminate age, shambled toward him. He heard sirens in the distance.

He hit the power button and the cruiser returned to life. He opened the door, grabbed his backpack, and hopped out.

"Want a ride, yo?" he said to the approaching creatures, who looked like they had the critical thinking skills of mashed potatoes.

"Wuh?"

"Take this car to Moo-Boy at," and he made up an address, "and he'll give you cash for it. But you gotta hurry, before he leaves."

Dingo ushered one of the men into the driver's seat and the other into the passenger. He shifted the car into drive and smacked the new driver in the head. "Get going, yo."

The police cruiser lurched onto the road, leaving the rear bumper behind.

He didn't wait to see more. He spotted an alleyway across the street between two boarded-up buildings, and bolted for it.

He reached the alley and stomped through waist-high weeds and jumbles of fast-food wrappers, plastic vials, and faded lottery tickets. Rats scurried out of the way.

The sirens grew louder. He ducked behind a concrete block wall.

High pitched wailing pierced his ears, then receded.

He peeled off the Dick Clark mask and shoved it in his backpack. Then he opened the navigation app on his data glasses.

Waylee's safehouse was four miles to the northeast. A long ass walk, but best to stay off the buses, which had cameras. Maybe he could take a taxi to Hopkins and walk from there. Except he only had $5 in his wallet, only a mile's worth of fare. *We should have prepared better.*

With Homeland on their ass, he'd have to be extra careful. He switched off the data glasses and removed the battery. He fished through his backpack for his old comlink, which he still used sometimes, and took its battery out too.

He peeked back into the alley. No one there. He started walking north, planning to stick to alleys. *Would be nice if someone tried to jump me in this shithole. All this shit going down, and no Krav Maga yet.*

* * *

Pelopidas

The stormwater pipe sloped gradually upward. The air grew still and humid, and stank of oil, mud, and rotting leaves. Despite the chilly temperature, sweat dripped from Pel's brow and into his eyes.

The pipe's rough concrete jarred his knees. His jeans provided almost no padding. But with only three feet of clearance, especially with that bulky bag on his back, he couldn't move any other way. The cement scraped his palms, but pushing with his forearms banged the elbows. He pulled his flannel sleeves forward to cover his hands, providing some protection at the expense of dexterity.

He heard rapid breathing behind him. Sounded like Waylee. He stopped and turned.

Charles halted, a grimace on his face. Further back, Waylee's lips trembled.

"Waylee," he whispered, "are you okay, love?"

"I... can't see... back here." Tears glistened at the corners of her eyes.

"Take my data glasses." He activated the low light vision app and passed it back to her via Charles. Trouble was, low light seriously hogged the battery. "And pull your sleeves up to protect your hands."

"Thanks, Pel." She sniffled.

The slope leveled off. Muddy, dank-smelling water pooled on the bottom. The pipe continued in the same direction. He kept crawling.

The flashlight revealed an opening in the distance. A maintenance tunnel? They'd be able to walk then.

Pel heard something approaching, a pattering noise. He swiveled the light. Two orbs stared back at him in the semi-dark. He focused the beam on them, revealing a huge rat with long, bacteria-coated incisors.

The flashlight dropped. He rose up, and smacked his head against the top of the pipe. Pain shot down his spine. "God—"

"What is it?" Charles said.

Pel fumbled for the flashlight, teeth gritted. It was still on and just at his knees. He swung it around, searching for the rat.

There it is. The rat turned and scurried off ahead of them. He hoped it wouldn't return with reinforcements.

Pel explored his aching head with his fingers. It felt damp, but maybe from moisture or sweat, not blood. His fingertips didn't look red. "Just me being stupid," he told Charles. Best to keep the rat a secret.

He resumed crawling. Definitely an opening ahead.

He hurried forward and reached an intersection. Unfortunately, with a cross pipe that was smaller, not larger.

Rungs headed up to a manhole cover. At least he could stand and stretch.

Pel let the others enter. They crowded together in the vertical space, their clothes and hands coated with grime.

Waylee looked up. "Can we get out here?"

"No, too close. Still in the factory district."

"I can check." She pulled her comlink out of a pocket, even though she had his data glasses on, which were easy to command. She opened the navigation program and peered at the screen. "No signals."

"Wouldn't think so," he said. "Which is good, that means no one can see us."

"So we keep going straight?" Charles said. "I mean, we're not gonna go down those little pipes, are we?"

A joke rose toward Pel's tongue, but his exhaustion smothered it. "Can I have the tire iron?" he asked Waylee.

"Why?"

"Just 'cause."

Rat defense in hand, he knelt, took a breath, and crawled into the pipe's continuation. He pushed himself, crawling as fast as he could, knees banging against the concrete.

After a few minutes, Charles squeaked, "Wait!"

Pel turned. Charles and Waylee were far behind. *Oops.* He waited for them to catch up, then resumed at a slower pace.

How did Homeland find us? Maybe someone turned them in. But who? Not Waylee, obviously. Not Dingo or M-pat—they did the dirty work, setting off the EMP and knocking out the guards. And they both had records. Kiyoko? She let herself get captured. But she wouldn't turn in her own sister, that just wasn't in her.

That left Shakti, as improbable as it seemed. "Waylee?"

"Yeah?"

"Do you think Shakti could have turned us in?"

She coughed. "Are you fucking kidding me? We might as well ask if you did it. Just get us out of here. Please?"

She was right. One thing at a time. "It wasn't me, obviously, or we'd have stayed at the house and got caught."

"Just shut up."

"Shakti's no snitch," Charles said quietly behind him.

How would you know? He decided not to pursue it, though.

The pipe went on and on, nothing but more dank concrete. Pel lost track of time. He could ask Waylee, but it didn't matter. Maybe they wouldn't find any bigger pipes. Wouldn't the outfall be the biggest one, just like a stream network?

They came to another intersection. He saw a manhole overhead, but this time, the cross pipe was three feet wide, like the one they'd been following.

The manhole cover clanked.

"Car?" Waylee asked.

"Some kind of vehicle."

It clanked again. So they were under a well-traveled street. "Let's take a left here," he said. "This'll take us south of the interstate, maybe somewhere the cops won't be looking."

"And we can pop up and call for a pickup," Waylee said.

"Yeah."

Manholes appeared more frequently above the new pipe, which meant more opportunities to stand and rub their aching knees. It felt like they were making better progress, and could escape this abyss more easily.

The flashlight began to fade. *I should have been counting manholes or something to know where we are.* "Waylee," he whispered. "Flashlight's going. I need the data glasses back."

"Why?"

"I'll bring up a white screen on my comlink and set the brightness to max."

"That's not gonna do much. We should get out of here."

"It'll be enough with the low light app."

"Alright." Waylee passed his data glasses back via Charles.

"We'll save yours to make a call when we go back up."

When the flashlight died, Pel switched to the comlink. It gave out a tenth the brightness at best. With low light vision, he could see, but Waylee and Charles crawled in gloom. Waylee started breathing rapidly again. *Please don't lose control…*

The pipe ran on. Every muscle in his body ached. His knees and hands burned with pain. The stink of dead things and chemicals, the refuse and pollution from Baltimore's streets, settled into his nostrils and deep into his lungs. He could barely breathe, like there was no oxygen down here, only toxic gases. *This was a bad idea. Better to live in prison than die down here. They won't find our bodies until the next storm flushes us into the river.*

He shook his head. *Focus. You're going into hysterics. Waylee and Charles are depending on you.* One good thing about winter, the bacteria would be less active. And they'd made it this far without passing out.

At the next manhole, he glanced at the comlink's power indicator. Half the bars left. "Waylee, want to lead?"

She coughed. "No thanks. I don't want you guys staring at my ass for hours."

He laughed. "You do have a motivating ass."

She sniffled and wiped her eyes. "Get us out of here, Pel."

He looked at Charles, who hadn't spoken for quite a while. "Keep following me, and focus on the light. I won't go any faster than you can."

They both nodded.

He clapped Charles on the shoulder and squeezed Waylee's hand. "Doing good so far. We'll go as far as we can until we run low on power, then we'll have to surface."

He turned right at the next intersection, hoping to find an exit with minimal traffic. Hearing another clank, he turned again two intersections later.

When both the comlink and data glasses had dropped below 10% power, he stopped at the next manhole. "Not sure where we are, but we've been crawling for three hours. We've gotta be pretty far from the river."

Waylee and Charles nodded.

Pel dropped the duffel bag and pocketed his comlink. He clambered up the rusty manhole rungs. At the top, he waited for the sound of cars driving over but didn't hear anything. He pushed up on the cover but it was a lot heavier than he expected. He could barely budge it. *Fuck.*

"Need a hand?" Waylee said, her voice unsteady.

"Yeah, but how?" Only one person could stand on the rung.

She took a deep breath. "Give me the tire iron and I'll stand below you and use that while you push with your hands. Charles, hold my feet so I don't fall."

Pel shrugged. Worth a try.

He placed his palms against the bottom of the cover. Waylee stood on the rung below him, pressed against his body, and jabbed the edge of the cover with the tire iron.

It was too awkward and too dark. The iron slipped and flew toward his face.

He swung his right forearm over and it hit there instead. "Watch it!"

"Sorry. I'm sorry. You alright?"

"Let's try again. Stick the iron in the crack." *That's what she said.* He almost smiled. "Then we'll try to pry it off."

He pushed as hard as he could. A sliver of blinding daylight appeared. Waylee jabbed the flat end of the tire iron there, and shoved it through.

"Okay, now pull down."

As Waylee levered the heavy cover up, he pushed it toward the side. They got it off the inner lip and resting partly on the pavement.

He saw a narrow arc of a two-lane street. A car approached. He ducked.

The car passed to the right of the manhole.

"Okay, we're gonna have to climb out of here as fast as we can." He waited until he couldn't see any more cars, then helped Waylee push the cover to the side. Once he had enough room to stick his torso out of the hole, he had plenty of leverage to shove it the rest of the way off.

He jumped out. They were in a neighborhood of single-family homes. He had no idea where. No one visible. Waylee passed him the duffel bag.

Then he grabbed her wrists and helped her out, and finally Charles.

They used the tire iron to wrestle the cover back in place, then walked briskly down the nearest side street. He led them to a sheltered spot between a garage and a wooden fence.

Waylee looked at her navigation display. "I can't believe we crawled that far."

"Call J-Jay for a pickup," Pel said. "Don't forget to run the ID spoofer, and don't mention any names or…"

Waylee narrowed her eyes at him.

"I know, just being cautious."

As Waylee made her call, he glanced at the street. *What if Shakti told the cops about our hideouts? They could be setting a trap.* Waylee knew her friends, though. She didn't trust people blindly.

He removed the nearly-dead batteries from his data glasses and comlink. He'd installed spoofing software on all their comlinks, but wasn't sure how well it would fool Homeland Security. Best to ditch the links altogether, Waylee's included, before they reached J-Jay and Bess's house.

What to do next, he had no idea. The hideouts were temporary. *What then?*

13

Waylee

Grime cascaded down Waylee's body and circled the drain of her former drummer's shower. J-Jay had played in Dwarf Eats Hippo for three years, and even lived in the band house for a while, before he lost his edge and turned to playing jazz standards. "Chance to make a living at this," he'd claimed.

Picking them up from their tunnel exit more than compensated for selling out, though. Risking arrest instead of collecting a $100,000 reward certainly wasn't selling out.

J-Jay and his girlfriend Bess had given them new clothes and thrown away their storm drain-fouled garments. Bess promised to remake her hair after the shower—replace the red, white and blue cornrows with something more discreet. Waylee didn't know how she'd repay them, but she'd try.

They'd stay in West Baltimore until midnight or so, then J-Jay would drop them off at her friends' townhouse up in Charles Village. It would be safer there. Artesia and Fuera were plugged into the People's Party and its allies, and they had a high-bandwidth Comnet connection – although Pel had been paranoid and wiped their comlinks and data glasses, then thrown the husks down a storm drain.

The shower door opened. Pel stood there, naked and erect. His eyes wandered across her body. "You're so hot."

Normally sights like that set her on fire. But she felt nothing. "Not now."

He entered the shower anyway. He kissed her neck, then cupped her left breast.

She planted a hand against his chest and pushed him away. She started to say something but tears came instead.

He wrapped his hands around hers, his excitement fading. "It's okay. We're safe."

"What about our lives being over forever?"

He hesitated. "I don't know about forever…" He picked up the washcloth from the shower floor and ran it up her arm. "Important thing is, we escaped. We're not in prison."

She pulled her arm away before he could reach her chest again. She didn't want him trying to seduce her.

His face tensed with irritation. "Just trying to help you wash. And I need a shower too. We can save water this way."

Not that tired line again. She turned off the water. "I'm done."

He raised his eyebrows at her. "It doesn't look like it."

"They'll have to clean the house after we leave," she said. "A handful of skin cells, and they'll have our DNA and pin J-Jay and Bess—"

"Yes, I told them how to destroy DNA. So I wanted to tell you, Dingo and Shakti are safe. You've gotta see the video he uploaded."

That was good news at least. "I can't believe you thought my best friend ratted us out."

His face fell. "I was just going through the possibilities…"

"What happened to my sister?"

He stared at his feet. "Don't know yet. The police have M-pat. I assume they're questioning Kiyoko."

"We've gotta help her, she's just a little girl inside."

He looked up. "We will. And she's not just a little girl. Give her some credit."

She turned away, not wanting to cry in front of him. She couldn't hold out much longer.

His voice hardened. "I'm trying to help. None of this was my idea."

Why did he have to say that? She whirled. "Stop being a baby. Just leave me alone."

His eyes narrowed, he muttered something, and stormed out of the bathroom.

Waylee collapsed to the shower floor and lost control, blinded by tears, gulping for air.

* * *

M'patanishi

M-pat sat cuffed in the back seat of a parked BPD car while the feds busted into the band house. Most of the local cops had chased after Dingo.

The boy wasn't right in the head, but sometimes he stood like a giant. He'd disrupted the siege long enough for the others to escape. At least for a while. They'd never lose those drones in an RV.

M-pat leaned back on the hard plastic seat and prayed silently, something he rarely did outside of church. *Lord God, please help my friends escape. They are righteous folk, even if they don't exactly follow Your path. Amen.* He wasn't really a proper Christian either, not like Latisha, though he'd come a long way since his corner days.

He could have escaped too during all the chaos, but there was no point. They'd have to release him anyway. The po-boys didn't seem to suspect he had anything to do with Charles, just cuffing him as an irritant. Baltimore cops never gave more than one warning. And they got extra agitated when they found his Glock.

"Got a permit for that," he'd explained.

He might as well have been parlaying with the moon.

M-pat watched two FBI agents and a pair of armored stormtroopers haul Kiyoko out of the house. They threw her into a black SUV. *Poor girl.*

Two po-boys, both of them rookie age, hopped in the front of the squad car. "They read you your rights?" one asked through the thick glass between them.

"Yeah. Now let's get this nonsense over with."

A few minutes later they arrived at the Southwest District station. It looked like a brick schoolhouse with square concrete columns in front. When they threw up these institutions last century, they must have hired a low-bid architect with one design and no imagination.

M-pat had been here a dozen times as a youth. The booking room hadn't changed, all white and gray and flickering fluorescents. No air flow to speak of, and it smelled like sweat and stale coffee.

His escorts steered him to a familiar booking officer on the other side of a steel grate, then took off the cuffs. The booking officer, probably past retirement now, smirked. "Haven't seen you in a while."

"Been walking the straight path," M-pat said. "This here's uncalled for."

The officer looked unimpressed. "Empty your pockets. You know the drill."

M-pat handed over his wallet and comlink and everything else but his shirt, pants, and socks. They patted him down again, then took digital mug shots and fingerprints.

An overweight detective wearing a Ravens tie met him in Interview Room 2 and read his Miranda rights again.

No, he wasn't willing to answer their questions without an attorney present. "I wanna call a lawyer."

The detective sighed, then led him to a small desk with a landline and a cardboard box full of lawyers' business cards.

M-pat searched through the box but couldn't find the number he wanted. In fact, the selection was pretty limited. "Can I see the city directory?"

"What for?"

"So I can pick my own lawyer rather than the scammers who pay you to put their cards in that box."

The fat detective frowned. "You'd better be careful making an accusation like that."

"You gonna honor my Constitutional rights?"

His eyes narrowed, then he brought over a tablet and opened a search program. "Who are you looking for?"

"Councilman Cutler. He'll straighten this out."

* * *

Charles Village neighborhood, Baltimore

Pelopidas

Pel followed J-Jay, Waylee, and Charles into Artesia and Fuera's well-kept townhouse a few blocks east of Johns Hopkins University, where the two married African-American women worked as sociology post-docs. Dingo and Shakti ran to greet them as soon as they entered.

Pel put down his duffel bag and exchanged West Baltimore handshakes with Dingo. "Nice work. You totally saved our ass."

Dingo grinned. "I sure monkeyed the po-boys this time."

Shakti, wearing the yellow and red sari she'd donned for work, hugged Waylee. "Do I know you?"

J-Jay's girlfriend had replaced Waylee's bright cornrows with jet-black strands that hung straight down and still smelled like peroxide.

"Pretty boring, yeah," she said in a quiet voice. Her eyes were still red and puffy from her crying fit. "Glad you're safe."

Shakti held her tight. "You too."

Pel glanced at her. No cops here to greet them. He felt ashamed for scapegoating Shakti. Truth was, their enemies were just too powerful. They never should have taken them on.

"My video's going viral," Dingo said. "A hundred thousand views and climbing fast."

Pel turned back to him. "I liked the split screen with three camera angles. But it ends with the car spinning, then it's over. If you hadn't messaged me, I might have thought you died."

"Yeah, car lost power when I hit that building. Maybe the second death of Dick Clark explains its appeal."

That. "I thought you burned your mask. The rest of us did."

His eyes dropped. "Nah, I thought it would come in handy." He looked up again. "And it did. Did you like the band plug?"

"Thanks, but that's even more evidence against us. Why don't you give me the mask so I can burn it?" The townhouse was old and had a fireplace.

"Fair enough." He started to pull off his backpack.

Pel threw up a hand. "Later."

Shakti and Waylee ended their long hug. Shakti looked down. "So I got a message from the boss. Dingo and I are fired."

Waylee's eyes drooped. "Sorry. I…"

"Shitty job anyway. Mostly ad design, and no benefits." Her voice turned

Caribbean. "But how am I to register voters when we on the run, and what 'bout our fundraisers we got planned?"

Artesia and Fuera interrupted, taking turns hugging Waylee.

"Thank you so much for putting us up," Waylee said.

Artesia patted her back. "Of course. Least we can do after you hosted our wedding reception."

Waylee waved Charles over. "This is Charles. I hope it's alright if he stays too."

Artesia held out a ring-covered hand. "So you're the so-called cyberterrorist the feds are looking for?"

Charles hesitated, then shook her hand. "It was just a prank. All I did was add a message to the MediaCorp news feed about a zombie outbreak in DC."

"Too bad it was fake," Dingo said. "Would be bad-ass, seeing all them DC lobbyists ripped apart by zombies, then turning and attacking Congress."

Pel shook Artesia's hand. "Thanks for letting us stay. Charles is no terrorist, but he's a computer genius and he's gonna help us get our message out."

Artesia turned to Waylee. "What's all this? You've been awfully vague about why you broke this kid out of jail. I mean, you're one of my dearest friends, and I'm totally down with you, but it would be nice if you filled us in."

"We were still working out the details," Waylee said, "but we were gonna make a video and show it to the biggest audience possible. A video that would wake people up and question what they're told. With MediaCorp's control of the Comnet and news outlets, there's no way the general public will hear an outside voice like mine unless we change the rules of the game."

Artesia crossed her arms. "You know, breaking someone out of jail wasn't such a good move."

Waylee's shoulders drooped. "I..." Her eyes moistened. "I didn't think Homeland would get involved. Everything's ruined now. And poor Kiyoko..."

Pel wanted to hide. "We should have left the night before, Waylee was right. I fucked up."

Fuera frowned. "Will they look for you here?"

"I expect they're stumped," he said, "and we're gonna make them think we split town."

Waylee looked from Artesia to Fuera. "We've gotta stay somewhere, and I trust you two the most. And you can relay messages for us. You know everyone I know."

Artesia scoffed. "Bullshit we do."

"Well you know all the respectable people I know." Waylee turned to Shakti. "I imagine the house's been ransacked by now."

"Maybe by the police, but they'll leave most of it. Scavengers won't move in until the cops are long gone."

"We should call someone and ask them to keep an eye on the place," Pel said. "My cousins would do it, or any of our neighbors." His musclehead cousins volunteered on the Greektown Peltasts, a foot patrol like M-pat's.

Artesia offered drinks. Everyone wanted something. Waylee filled a glass with Jameson. Artesia let Charles have a rum and coke. "You're a criminal already," she said, smiling. "Might as well have a drink."

"I'll have a Wobbly," Dingo said.

Artesia's brow furrowed. "I'm not a mixologist."

Shakti giggled as Dingo explained, even though they'd heard it a million times. "Equal portions Red Label whisky and Black Label beer. Stir vigorously. Share with your comrades in equal portions until all drinking needs are met. And let the People's Happy Hour commence!"

Fuera laughed. Artesia poured him a Natty Boh and Jameson. "Just pretend."

Pel had one too. He choked on the taste. He led a toast to Dingo, "To the craziest but bravest motherfucker in Baltimore."

Waylee then refilled her glass and turned to their hosts. "Can we see the news?"

"Sure." They had a small wall screen nestled between crowded bookcases and above a storage cabinet. Artesia clicked on the power, bypassed a puff piece about the president's kids, and navigated to coverage of the police raid. There weren't enough seats for everyone, so Pel and some of the others stood to the side.

The video began with a military troop carrier and police cruisers parked at the band house. Cops and suits stood in circles or poked through the grass.

Their local newscaster narrated from a popup window. "This is the scene in Baltimore's Wilhelm Park neighborhood this morning, where officers of the Baltimore Police Department and the Department of Homeland Security attempted to seize Charles Marvin Lee, a recent escapee from the

Baltimore Juvenile Correctional Facility, and the possible terrorist cell who helped him escape. Most of the suspects fled the scene, including Lee, if he was there, but one, whose name has not been released yet, was apprehended. Police are confident they'll catch the others soon."

A rotating image of Charles appeared to the right, along with the same slew of information as the last time she saw it. "Here are the other suspects, who live in the house you see here." The screen displayed stills of himself, Dingo, Waylee, and Shakti, with links to additional information.

"If you have any information regarding their whereabouts, there is a $100,000 reward." A link appeared above the video. "Police believe additional people are involved, but have not named further suspects at this time."

"So what we do now?" Pel asked the others. "Stick with the plan? Give up on it and run for Canada?"

Waylee stood. "How do we find out where Kiyoko and M-pat are? We've gotta get them out."

"I'll call one of the People's Party lawyers tomorrow," Fuera said. "If that's cool."

"Francis is probably the best for this," Shakti said.

Pel agreed. He was one of the best attorneys in the city, did a lot of pro bono work, and enjoyed tweaking the authorities.

J-Jay took off. Pel wrapped Dingo's Dick Clark mask with paper towels, doused it with lighter fluid, and burned it in the fireplace. The living room began to reek of burning silicone and Fuera had to set up a fan.

Artesia led everyone downstairs. "We set up the basement."

Just past the stairs, a matching faux-leather couch, love seat, and chair clustered around a glass-topped coffee table and faced a huge wall skin. Beyond them, three double-size air mattresses with pillows and sheets crowded the carpeted floor.

On the far end of the large room, two sets of virtual reality helmets and gloves sat next to plush recliners with built-in fiber-optic sockets. "For BetterWorld," Artesia commented. "But you can use them while you're here. We're too busy most of the time anyway."

"I brought my cleaning spray," Pel said. "And I can make more."

Fuera pointed at the ceiling. "There's a spare bedroom on the second floor if anyone wants that," Fuera said.

"Let Waylee and Pel have it," Shakti said. "They've had a rough day."

Won't argue with that.

"Thanks," Waylee said. Her breath stank of whiskey.

"And when Waylee called us last week," Artesia said, "we picked up some clothes and toiletries. I'll bring them down."

"Can't promise they'll fit," Fuera said, "or that we have the remotest idea about men's fashion."

Pel heard a *plop* behind him. Charles had collapsed onto one of the air mattresses.

Pel's aching knees shook. He'd need a lot more to drink before he could sleep.

* * *

FBI Headquarters, Baltimore County

Kiyoko

Kiyoko sat in a whitewashed room of the drab FBI headquarters just past the Baltimore beltway. She'd been alone for hours, sitting in a folding chair behind a metal table, perhaps forgotten entirely.

The two agents who'd brought her had promised to return right away with tea and donuts. At least they'd removed the handcuffs. The woman had introduced herself as Agent Harrison, and the man, Agent Recelito.

Everyone else had escaped. Good for them. She hoped they had the sense to get out of the country. Then they could all move to Tokyo or Shanghai, turn disaster into opportunity. She just hoped Prince Vostok wouldn't stir up more trouble in BetterWorld while she was stuck in this room.

The door opened. Agents Harrison and Recelito entered. *Took you long enough.*

Harrison set down three plastic cups of tea and a half-filled box of Mistah D donuts. The agents sat on the opposite side of the table and unrolled flexible data tablets, bending the screens vertical so she couldn't see the displays.

Kiyoko plucked a cinnamon twist out of the box and sipped her tea. Neither was much good, but breakfast was breakfast. Especially when it was hours overdue.

"Sorry it took so long," Harrison said, and blew on her tea.

Kiyoko nodded, most of her attention on the sugary cinnamon twist.

Recelito scrolled through something on his tablet. "So, your name is Kiyoko Pingyang."

Kiyoko assumed they were recording her, even if she couldn't see the cameras or microphones. "Yes. I go by Kiyoko." Japanese for spiritually clean child. Her surname was important too. One of the greatest heroes of ancient China, Princess Pingyang raised an army and overthrew the evil Sui Dynasty.

"But that's not your birth name."

"If you met my parents you'd know why. When we got to Baltimore, Waylee had our names changed, but it's all legal. It's on my driver's license."

"You and your sister are close," Harrison said.

Kiyoko shrugged. "We tolerate each other most of the time."

"And she's your legal guardian?"

"I'm an adult now, nineteen, almost twenty." She finished the twist.

"Was your legal guardian."

"Yeah. She's a lot older than me. Different father – he went crazy and killed himself before I was born."

The agents stared at each other. Harrison continued, "So you ran away from your parents… when?"

"Uh, twelve years ago. I was just a kid." She fished through the box and picked a blueberry cruller. The "blueberries" were tasteless little smudges of blue dye.

"And you never thought about returning?"

Philly was a blur of shouts and slaps and bruises. And fear. Fear that rose and fell but never ended. "My mother never really liked us. And Feng, my father, was a monster." *From the blackest pits of hell.*

Her father, mother, and sister had screamed at each other almost daily. And with alcohol or meth addling his brain, Feng escalated to slaps and punches. And later her mother would pass the abuse on to Kiyoko, the one in the house least able to defend herself.

Kiyoko's parents didn't care for her, said she was a pain in the ass. But they hated Waylee, 'cause when she wasn't in her depressed state, she fought back, unintimidated by the fifty pounds and two decades of fight experience Feng had on her. And she called the cops as soon as she could get to a phone.

The police would arrest Feng or her mother would throw him out, and Kiyoko would thank the starry heavens. But he always came back. He'd be all nice and apologetic at first, but he could only pretend for so long. Then the monster emerged.

Eventually Waylee exploded.

It was about an hour after dinner. Her mother had passed out in the bedroom, Feng hadn't come home from work, and her sister had cooked one of those Hamburger Helpers.

Feng stumbled in, stinking drunk, and cast lecherous eyes at Waylee. Said she was a whore and he knew she wanted it. He grabbed her by the arm, threw her down on the old sofa, and started pawing at her clothes.

Waylee clutched his face and thrust her thumbs in his eyes. He shook his head but she wouldn't let go. Her thumbs went in to the knuckles and blood dripped out. He screamed.

She kept gouging, ignoring his flailing hands. His right eye popped out of its socket and hung by fibers, bright red blood squirting from his skull and stinking of bad pennies.

The screams were surely enough to summon all the legions of hell. Feng kicked and thrashed, his eye swinging back and forth along his cheek and the socket gaping like a cave, vomiting a river of blood. Kiyoko wet herself in terror.

Somehow Waylee got her out of there.

Of course they could never go back - the suggestion was ludicrous. She sometimes wondered what happened to her parents, if her father lost both eyes or just one, if he ended up killing her mother, if she killed him, if the cops searched for Waylee or they decided Feng got what he deserved.

Best to forget it and move on...

"Are you okay?" Agent Harrison asked, leaning forward.

"If it weren't for Waylee," Kiyoko said, "I'd be dead by now."

Harrison and Recelito glanced at each other.

"Feng would have killed us both." Kiyoko felt the shame that accompanied every remembrance of her parents, that she should come from such evil stock.

Harrison typed something on her tablet.

I should shut up. "Can I see a lawyer?"

"Just a few more questions," she said.

"You live at," and Recelito stated her address.

Why ask something they know the answer to? "Yes." Kiyoko finished the cruller and picked a jelly donut.

"For how long?"

"Four years, more or less." The red jelly inside was perfectly homogenous, and tasted only vaguely of strawberry. It reminded her of Feng's eye and she fought not to throw up her food.

"And before that?"

She traded the jelly donut for a chocolate glazed. "Here and there. Wherever Waylee went, different hoods around Baltimore. College Park for a couple of years when she was in journalism school."

Harrison tapped a cadence on her tablet and peered at something Kiyoko couldn't see. "Just a couple of years?"

"Yeah, at first she took the train from Baltimore. Two hours each way including the buses at both ends." Then the state tried to put her in a foster home. Said Waylee was an unfit guardian, that she was always gone and mentally unstable. "That didn't work out so well, so we moved to College Park, different places around there."

Harrison consulted her computer again. "And then she got a job back in Baltimore when she graduated?"

"Yeah, at the *Herald*. So we moved back, but then she got uh... downsized."

"And she hasn't been employed since?" Recelito said.

"She freelances when she can. And we have the band, we're pretty popular, in B'more at least. Dwarf Eats Hippo, you should check us out."

Harrison looked her in the eyes and smiled. "I will. Is that what your costumes are for? You have an amazing wardrobe."

"I made them myself. I wear some on stage, but they're for contests too, and sometimes I get paid to model." She took another bite of chocolate glazed. "Why'd you go poking through my clothes?"

"We're combing your house for leads. Nothing personal, it's just we've got a fugitive to catch."

Kiyoko finished her donut. Slim pickings now, all plains, but she hadn't eaten since yesterday, and she and Waylee had ridiculously high metabolisms. "How long do you plan to hold me here?"

"This is an important investigation," Harrison said. "I was hoping you could tell us about Charles. Why was he staying at your house?"

Kiyoko finished her tea. "I'd like to see a lawyer before I say anything else."

Harrison frowned. "I was really hoping we could wrap this up and get you home soon."

"Am I under arrest?"

"It's in your interest to cooperate voluntarily," Recelito said. "You're not our preferred target, but the fact is, you aided and abetted a known fugitive."

"If I'm not under arrest, then I'm free to go, right?"

"I'm afraid not. Because of the type of weapon used to free Mr. Lee, and because he's in an organization of cyberterrorists called the Collective, this has been deemed a national security case. That gives us wide latitude to do pretty much whatever we want, miss."

"I'm not a terrorist or a national security threat. I have stuff to do. I need to feed my cat." Kiyoko stood and walked toward the door.

The agents jumped out of their chairs and cut her off, blocking the exit. "Sit down, miss," Recelito said, his voice cold.

She stood in place. She was a Princess, not someone who could be ordered around. "Let me go. I no longer consent to this interview."

"According to the Homeland Security Consolidation Act of 2022, we can detain you 72 hours," Harrison said. "If you cooperate voluntarily, you'll be back home a lot sooner than that. If not, we'll hold you for 72 hours, then arrest you on charges of aiding escape of a prisoner. That's a ten year sentence."

Kiyoko breathed in deeply. She wouldn't cry.

"We'll be back tomorrow." They picked everything up and left.

Kiyoko tried the door. It wouldn't budge. Was she locked in this room with no light switch, no bed, no toilet, and no Comnet access for 72 hours? Would she be stuck someplace like this for ten years? Or someplace worse, where she'd be beaten and raped? Her hands shook and shook and wouldn't stop.

14

Tuesday

Pelopidas

Pel sat at the tiny kitchen table with Artesia and sipped extra-strong coffee. Drawn curtains kept out the sunlight, promising a day of enforced gloom.

Artesia spoke to Francis on her comlink. "Thank you. We appreciate it."

Pel felt gelded without his link, but Homeland must have brought in cyber specialists to find them, and they were as good as anyone in the Collective, maybe better.

Artesia ended the connection. "Francis says he'll help. He'll call back as soon as he finds out where Kiyoko and M'patanishi are."

"Good news. Thanks for staying home today." Artesia had called in sick while her wife went to work.

"Of course. Everyone else still asleep? I can make more coffee, and there's fresh bagels from Eddie's."

"Waylee's still out, and I haven't checked the basement." He'd tried to coax Waylee out of bed. She claimed to have a hangover, but her listless expression meant she'd lost her battle with the cyclothymia. This was why their band had a reputation for unreliability – she was utterly useless when this happened. Maybe there were some drugs out there they hadn't tried, some meditation technique.

"Is she alright?" Artesia asked.

He decided not to lie. "No. Except for a few blips, she was in superhero mode for months – the longest she's ever been there – and now she's paying the price. You know her as well as anyone. Do you have any advice?"

"Love conquers all." She smiled. "And a nice breakfast. I'll put something together."

Pel went down to the basement. All three were still asleep. He kicked the air mattress Dingo and Shakti were sleeping on. "Wakey wakey."

Dingo threw aside the cover sheet. He and Shakti were naked beneath it, and didn't bother hiding anything as they got up and stretched.

"Dudes, show some decorum," Pel said, casting eyes toward Charles, also awake now, and staring at them.

"Turn around, yo," Dingo said to Charles. He wrapped the sheet around Shakti, attempting to duplicate her saris. "M'lady."

Waylee was more difficult to rouse, but the smell of frying eggs helped. As they ate in the dining room, birds chirped on Artesia's comlink.

"It's Francis," Artesia said, looking at the screen. After a few "yeahs" and a "just a minute," she passed her comlink over. "He wants to talk to you."

Francis was on voice-only. Pel pressed a thumb over the camera lens anyway. "Thanks for your help."

"I have some news. M'patanishi's being held at the Southwest station.

Councilman Cutler got him a lawyer. He's being charged with obstruction of justice."

Pel chuckled. "That's ironic."

"No concealed weapon charge. He has a permit. So the next step is he goes before a judge for arraignment, probably by video. He pleads not guilty, they set a hearing date, then his lawyer argues for release. Obstruction of justice is just a misdemeanor, and even though he's got priors, he's a pillar of the community with a lot of connections. I'd be surprised if he even has to post bail."

"So he'll be out soon."

"Yeah, and unless they're pricks about it, they'll drop the charges – not worth their time."

"Great." Pel repeated the news to the others.

"What about Kiyoko?" Waylee asked.

Pel relayed the question.

"That, it seems, is more problematic. The FBI have her. I called them up but they said her case falls under national security and they wouldn't say any more."

Shit. "Can you get her out?"

"I'll try. National security is a bullshit excuse that's way overused. Plenty of case law to back me up."

After Pel clicked off, he looked up his friend Marcio. They'd grown up in Greektown together, although Marcio was actually Salvadoran. Good times, playing Little League and video games, then graduating to weed and girls. Like most of his friends, Marcio still lived in the neighborhood, but the place had plenty of jobs and minimal crime. Pel usually looked him up when he visited.

Pel turned off the camera and GPS on Artesia's comlink, then loaded a location spoofer and ID spoofer from one of his data sticks. He picked a location in south Chicago, and device and subscriber IDs typical for burners. Then he typed his friend's number.

"Who's this?" Marcio answered, voice only. "How'd you get this number?"

"It's Pel, you rude motherfucker. I'm on a burner."

"Pel! 'Sup, bro?"

"Seen the news?"

"I fucking hate the news."

"You sound like Waylee. Okay, she and I are in a bit of legal trouble."

Better not say anything incriminating. "Cops are after us though I'm not clear why."

"*Vea?* You don't know why?"

"They think we were harboring a fugitive. We had to skip town. That's why I'm calling, I need a favor."

"You were harboring a fugitive?"

"No, they just think that, and I'm not sure why. Anyway, I need you to go see my cousins and ask them to keep an eye on our house before it gets ransacked."

"Why don't you call them yourself?"

Was Marcio deliberately being irritating? "Because their phones might be tapped. You're not an obvious connection, though."

"*Vaya pues.* I'll tell them."

"My dad has keys and the alarm code. Tell my parents not to worry, I'll clear this mess up, and in the meantime, I always wanted to see the world anyway."

"Where you going?"

"Tell you what, I'll send you a postcard."

Pel asked how everyone in Greektown was doing, told him to say hi to everyone, then said goodbye. Since this was a misdirect, he didn't warn Marcio to delete the call record or clear the cache. Word would spread that he'd skipped town and might have left the country.

* * *

Kiyoko

Laying on a plastic-encased foam mattress that stank of other people's sweat, Princess Kiyoko didn't know why the gods chose to be so cruel. Perhaps it wasn't a choice. Perhaps it was the nature of gods to be cruel, or at least indifferent to suffering.

Kiyoko was a good person, a creature of the light. Yet she'd been taken away and imprisoned in this awful place. Her captors had moved her to a tiny concrete cell with this narrow cot and a cold steel toilet, which no doubt had a camera trained on it. She saw no chance of rescue, and had soaked both sides of her thin pillow with tears.

The latch on the solid white door scraped and clanked. She rolled on her side and cast aside the scratchy grey blanket.

The two minions of darkness entered, carrying folded metal chairs and a small cardboard box with no top. They set the box on the bare floor next to the cot.

She sat up and looked inside. A baloney and processed cheese sandwich huddled next to a little cup of apple sauce and plastic bottle of Happy Deer Spring Water.

Her tormentors unfolded the chairs, sat down, and spoke in the guttural language of the underworld.

At first, she strained to understand, then she realized they were casting a spell on her. A spell to transform her, make her one of them, follow the biddings of their masters.

No. Kiyoko threw her hands against her ears and recited the mantra of protection, the one she'd discovered as a child to ward off her parents' iron hands.

Stars above,
Stars so bright,
Fill the world
With silver light.
Protect me with
Your magic rays
And drive the evil
Here away.

The mantra worked, even without BetterWorld *qi*. The creatures argued with each other.

She kept repeating it until they left her alone again.

She lay back down on the smelly mattress and pleaded with the gods. "Release me, or send me a champion. Do not forsake me in my time of need."

The gods did not answer.

* * *

Charles

"Think it's safe to go back into the Comnet?" Charles asked Pel, admiring Artesia and Fuera's immersion gear.

It was just the two of them in the main part of the basement. Shakti and Dingo were washing and sorting clothes in the adjacent laundry closet. Pel had dumped all his stuff on the white carpet and sat on the floor, sorting through it. Besides the VR helmet, he'd packed two sets of 3-D goggles, headsets, and gloves, plus his homebuilt supercomputer, data cubes, and memory sticks, and all sorts of cables, signal processors, and tools. *Too bad he left the suit.*

Pel looked up. "It's more a matter of procedures than timing."

Charles wanted to punch himself. The government hackers, or maybe MediaCorp's, outsmarted him, transmitting his location and hiding the fact. He should have told the others right away. Shouldn't have assumed he could crack anything thrown at him.

It was his fault the authorities had found them. His fault they didn't take off before the raid. His fault Kiyoko, the beautiful angel from BetterWorld, was in custody. His fault Waylee, their leader, had broken down. "What's gonna happen to Kiyoko? What can I do to help?"

"Nothing you can do for her," Pel said. "It's up to our lawyer."

"So is Waylee still in charge?" All she did was sleep now.

Pel glanced at the ceiling for a second. "No one's in charge. That's the point. Everyone should be free and equal, like the media says America's all about, but then goes into fits whenever someone tries to make it real."

"I'm down. Code of the Collective. No leaders, freedom of information, freedom to do what you want."

Pel stood up. "I've been thinking about our plan to sneak into that fundraiser. Maybe it's not a good idea now."

They can't just give up. "We've done all that work. You went to so much trouble for me. Shouldn't we go through with it?"

Pel looked down. "I don't know how we can. We can't go back to the house. We've gotta focus on helping Kiyoko. And Waylee's a mess."

"We've got this place." Charles pointed to the piles of immersion gear.

Pel stared at his VR helmet on the carpet. "We didn't count on Homeland Security getting involved, and being so, uh, capable. We should have thought things through better."

Charles wanted to admit it was his fault, but the words wouldn't come out. "You know Homeland's got some of the best hackers in the business. They give out money and prime gear and official approval to do all kinds of spy shit. They go out and catch hackers and give them a choice – work for us or go to prison."

"Would you work for them if they offered?"

"They made an example of me last time."

"'Cause you embarrassed MediaCorp. They'd have you executed live if they could."

"Yeah, fuck them. Anything I can do 'gainst them, I'm down with."

Pel examined their hosts' immersion setups. "We need to know how Homeland found us, and how to avoid them in the future."

The virus from the news station, most likely custom designed. "I'll be more careful."

Pel looked at him. "I don't think that BetterWorld trap gave them more than a citywide location. Otherwise they would have moved in sooner. You got out of that pretty well."

He's got no clue. Charles tried to decide what to say. Like a chump, he'd fallen for two traps, not just one. He couldn't seem to stop making bad choices. "If we're careful, though… I mean… we can't just give up."

Pel examined his reflection in a helmet faceplate. "We could use a passive rather than active approach."

"Huh?"

"Keep gathering the info we need, but no intrusions. And nothing that might point to us. Use Artesia and Fuera's gear until we're sure mine is safe. I'm ditching William Godwin and staying away from the Collective."

Pel had changed his mind about quitting. Charles felt like cheering, like maybe he hadn't ruined everything after all. "What about that broker you gotta deal with?"

His face clenched. "Shit. Yeah, we need to pay the balance. I promised some wireless keys. I was hoping you could help with that."

That ain't exactly easy. Charles eased onto one of the recliners. He wouldn't be able to walk or run around, but it was definitely comfortable. "We should check the New Year's traffic programs."

"Yeah, maybe the White House sent a message to the attendees since we last looked, and maybe we can figure out who the caterers and musicians are."

Artesia's—or Fuera's—immersion helmet smelled like perfume. Shakti flashed into his mind. She wasn't beautiful like Kiyoko, but it was his first time seeing a girl totally naked, and it was a good long view, dark nipples and curly pubes. Unfortunately it came with Dingo's trouser hose, which ruined the whole image.

Pel brought him back. "First thing, look around and see if Homeland knows what we're up to."

"Yeah, let's go in, and do everything systematic." *I've gotta step up my game.*

Pel sat in the recliner next to him and put on the gloves and helmet. Charles did the same.

* * *

Kiyoko

Princess Kiyoko stared in the metal mirror over the steel washbasin. She wasn't sure how long she'd been imprisoned. Her dress looked rumpled, her hair tangled and greasy, her face tired and dull. She yearned for a shower and change of clothes. And she could kill for a box of Pocky. The food here was awful.

She repeated the protection mantra. She would endure.

Her cell door opened. Two grim-faced men with buzz cuts entered, wearing white collared shirts with black ties. "Lawyer's here," one said.

The other handcuffed her wrists behind her.

"You don't need to cuff me."

"Procedure, ma'am."

They led her by the arms to a small fluorescent-lit room with white brick walls, a plastic table and two metal framed chairs with vinyl padding. A dark man wearing a navy blue suit sat in one of the chairs behind a stretched-out data pad. He rose as one of the guards removed her handcuffs.

"Kiyoko Pingyang?" His eyes were relaxed and sympathetic. Her champion?

"Yes, that is I."

He stepped forward and held out a hand. "I'm Francis Jones. I'm your lawyer."

Kiyoko hurried to her champion and wrapped her hands around his. It felt warm.

The guards left, shutting and locking the door behind them.

"I'm here to get you out," her champion said.

She hugged him, tears of joy blurring her vision.

He wriggled out of her grasp. "You, uh…"

Did I do something wrong? "I'm sorry."

"No, don't be." He gestured toward the chairs. They sat. She wiped her eyes.

He swiped fingers on his data pad. She couldn't see the screen. "We can speak in confidence," he said. "They're not allowed to listen in or watch us."

"Okay."

"First, let me tell you what's going on with your case. The FBI is going to press charges of aiding escape of a prisoner."

"They said that's ten years in prison."

"That's the maximum. It's never applied. Realistically, since you've got no record, we're probably just looking at probation. And that's if you're convicted. The government's case is weak." He glanced at his screen. "They'd have to prove this so-called fugitive was living at your house, that you knew he was living there, and that you knew that he was a wanted fugitive. So far, they have disclosed no physical evidence of any of that."

She wanted to hug him again.

"Some more good news," he continued. "No more of this national security bullshit. I've got the ACLU behind me, and we'll make sure your rights are respected, and you go through the normal judicial system. Which means you get a bail hearing, and we'll plead financial hardship since you have no family—"

"My sister and her boyfriend are family."

"No family with means, and you have no income to speak of."

She had some income but mostly off the books. Certainly she wouldn't argue the point.

He continued. "So I'll argue for release on your own recognizance. The charges are relatively minor, they have no real evidence against you, you've never been arrested before, and you're not a risk to anyone. You'll have to stay in town and appear in court, assuming they don't drop the charges entirely, and there's a chance they'll put on a tracking bracelet, but you'll get to go home."

"Please don't let them put a bracelet on me. I don't want the cops following me everywhere I go."

"Oh. Well it depends on whether the judge considers you a flight risk. Since your sister fled, and no one knows where she is, the judge may well assume you'll skip town to join her."

"But I didn't flee. I stayed put when the cops arrived."

"Yes, that's true. I'll be sure to bring that up."

"So how's my sister? Have you heard anything?"

He nodded. "She's out there, but that's all I know. I'll let you know if I hear more."

Hope she made it to Canada.

"Alright," he said, "now let's go over what happened. Everything you say will be confidential, but I need to know all the details so I can prepare your case."

It seemed like she could trust Francis Jones, but Kiyoko decided to omit as much as possible. She'd tell him Charles was staying at their house, but not say how he got there or why he was there. Or anything about her sister's crazy ambitions to break into a presidential fundraiser and bring down America's rulers.

15

Thursday

Waylee

Waylee had never seen such a big crowd. Faces, mostly young, stretched from the stage all the way back into darkness. To either side, they crowded the stadium benches up into dimly lit firmaments. The fans screamed with excitement, jumping up and down.

She glanced to her right. Kiyoko, wearing a frilly pink dress spattered with cat silhouettes and ribbons, patted her bass and smiled. To the left, Pel, costumed as a Borg, set up rhythm and background loops on a huge touchscreen. Waylee switched on her guitar, fingered an F power chord, lifted her pick high in the air, and swiped it down against the strings.

Nothing happened. No sound but the faint clicks of unamplified strings.

God damn it. She checked the guitar's active electronics and wireless system, and her amp. All on. She motioned for Shakti to bring out another guitar, then grabbed the mike. "We're Dwarf Eats Hippo, and…"

Nothing from the mike. She tapped on it. Nothing.

The fans stopped gyrating and stared at her. Where was Shakti? And Kiyoko? She was gone too. And Pel, he'd disappeared from his station. The crowd turned and started for the exits.

"Wait, hold on," she shouted. "We—"

She couldn't hear her voice now. She screamed, a deep lungful of air behind it, forcing out that energy she was so famous for. But nothing came out.

Someone was shaking her, shaking her shoulders.

The emptying stadium disappeared into fog.

"Wake up, damn it." Pel.

Just another stupid dream she couldn't afford to have analyzed. She wanted to ask Pel what he wanted, but her face buried itself in the pillow. Song lyrics composed themselves.

One sour day,
With malicious glee
God took a dump
And created me.

"Kiyoko's being released," Pel said.

Waylee sat up and stared at him, noting the little flecks in his brown eyes, the hairs and pores on his olive skin, and the light shadows across his chiseled face, all of which were too detailed and non-ephemeral for a dream.

"She's going home today. No bail, no tracer, and Francis thinks they'll drop the case entirely. They don't have any real evidence and they're just using her to fish for us. Worst case, she'll get probation. No prison."

Waylee opened her arms. He climbed on the bed and embraced her.

"You're so kick ass, it hurts," she said.

He kissed her, but when his tongue ventured out, she disengaged. "How do we get in touch with my sister without getting caught?"

"Through Francis, I assume."

"You're assuming Homeland Security and their army of rogues respect the law and aren't monitoring him."

"Yeah, I thought about that. That's why I haven't told him much. I have another idea."

"Which is?"

Pel sat back against the pillows. "Charles volunteered to contact her in BetterWorld. He has a new avatar. No one knows it's him. We tested it."

"How?"

He glanced toward the bedroom window, its curtains drawn since their arrival. "We gave him an address down the street, and we've been keeping an eye out. No visitors. Nothing going on there at all."

Waylee's fists clenched. "That was fucking stupid, to bring those assholes right here where we are."

Pel frowned and got off the bed. "There was no reason to think anyone would know about it. We were just testing."

"Well, we should have discussed it first."

"With you? When you won't even get out of bed?"

Waylee felt overpowering shame. "I… Pel, you know my brain fucks me up the ass every chance it gets." She thrust out a hand.

Pel clasped it and she pulled herself off the bed. The fog had dissipated a little. "The worst is over. I can feel it. I'm coming back, I'll do my share."

He smiled. "I've got some more good news."

"What's that?"

"We're making progress on the fundraiser. We have a guest list and know who's staffing."

The fog lifted even more. "So it's still a go."

He rubbed his beard. "We don't have the equipment yet. And we don't have a way in. But… we're working on it."

* * *

Charles

"We ain't got time to look for wireless keys," Charles told Pel.

Pel's lips pressed together. Beyond, Dingo paced the basement like a caged zoo animal. Waylee wasn't the only one going wack.

"It's harder than exploiting a firewall. To get passwords like that, you gotta physically break in someplace, take the social engineering tack, or use brute force, trying random combinations. It ain't a quick game."

Pel clenched a fist, but didn't throw a punch. "I'll talk to the broker. I have other valuables. My gaming gear, our wall screen, maybe some band equipment. Kiyoko'd have to sell the stuff at the house, then wire the money."

"I can mention it when I talk to her," Charles said. "I should do that now. Let her know everyone's safe."

"She's probably being watched."

"Yeah, I'm taking precautions. I got a plan."

"Which is?"

"I got scripts that can do all manner of runarounds in BetterWorld." He picked up the immersion helmet. "I can look up the New Year's attendees and staff, see if any of them have avatars. I told you 'bout those vampire bots."

Pel waved his hands. "Don't hack anyone associated with the fundraiser. The White House and Homeland Security might suspect something's up, and they'll nab us when we try to get in."

"Yeah, you right." *No more retard shit.*

Pel twisted the corner of his mouth. "But who knows… you could just look them up and maybe we can use the info somehow."

Charles donned his helmet and gloves, and returned to the Comnet. He entered BetterWorld as the Zulu warrior Iwisa, bought a canoe, and teleported to Trout Lake with it. The admins had deleted his Dr. Doom avatar. But a few of his vampire bots were still out there, sleeping in trees or underwater. The biggest nest was at the bottom of Trout Lake.

Iwisa took the canoe far from shore. The paddle threw up a slightly different splash pattern with each stroke, a nice randomization feature. Some of the drops landed on his bare arms but without a full immersion suit, he didn't feel them.

Near the middle of the lake, he stopped and sent out his activation code.

Three men and three women poked their heads above the water. He pointed at one of the women, the one with normal-sized breasts. "Come with me. The rest of you, go back underwater and wait for my next command."

The fembot climbed into the canoe, dripping water. She was young and beautiful, almost rivaling Kiyoko. She smiled and tilted her head forward.

"I'm giving you a new identity when we get to shore," he said. He closed his virtual eyes and brought up a Comnet portal.

He scoured Collective sites for useful Qualia programs to load into the fembot. The good thing about eight billion people on Earth was that pretty much everything had already been thought of. You just had to find what you wanted and apply it.

Then he'd let Princess Kiyoko know they were safe, sort of. And being BetterWorld elite and all, maybe she could help.

* * *

Waylee

"Are you crazy?" J-Jay shouted over the prepaid comlink Artesia had bought them.

Emotions spilled through Waylee's brain, too fast to label. "We'll figure out how to displace the current drummer. All you have to do is contact the band manager and apply. You're a jazz drummer, after all."

"So why would they want me? They've gotta have at least one backup they already know. Get real. I did y'all a solid shelterin' you the other day. That wasn't nothin'."

"You can convince them, audition and get on their list. We can do it. We have to do it. We have to wake people up, end MediaCorp's destruction of free thought—"

"Tryin' to bug the president usin' a drummer the band doesn't know? You gotta ask yourself, is that really doable, or is that Waylee lost deep, deep in Crazy Land?"

Waylee hurled the comlink against the bedroom wall, where it shattered. *Coward.*

After a while, Waylee tromped down to the basement and sat next to Pel on the faux-leather sofa. His computer, Big Red, perched on the coffee table, and he pulled the keypad closer.

Shakti blew her a kiss from the adjacent love seat. Dingo threw up a clenched fist. On the other side of the room, Charles removed his black immersion helmet and gloves.

The solidarity felt good. "J-Jay won't help," she announced.

No one's eyes widened with surprise. "It is a lot to ask," Pel said.

"It's not a suicide mission. But whatever." She looked from face to face. Quiet defeatism never benefitted anyone. "The fundraiser is only two weeks away. How are we going to get in?"

"Can we stay here that long?" Shakti asked. "Fuera seems a little tense."

"They said we could stay as long as we want. Consider it karma for the hundreds of guests we've put up. But we should help clean and cook—"

"We have been," Pel said, maybe a hint aimed at her.

"And clear out at the first hint of cops," she said. "I'll make sure they know that."

Charles plopped into the chair opposite the love seat. His eyes were puffy, like he hadn't been sleeping.

"So let's get back to the fundraiser," Waylee said. "Maybe just Pel and I should go. The more people, the greater the chance of getting caught. Pel and I are performers, the next best thing to actors."

Dingo's lips pinched in disappointment, but Shakti breathed relief. Pel looked away.

Waylee touched her boyfriend's arm. "I need you there. I'll do the interviewing, since I've done hundreds of them, but I need a wingman."

Pel checked a cable attached to Big Red. "Your suggestion sounds, uh, sensible." He tapped his keypad and the big wall skin brandished neat rows of icons and windows.

He brought up a gallery of photos, each with a name beneath. "Two hundred guests attending and forty staff, plus aides, bodyguards, and entertainers. No press—"

"Not that they practice journalism," Waylee said, "but who will be there from MediaCorpse?"

Pel narrowed an eye at her. "We know who the guests are, thanks to a reminder the White House Department of Scheduling and Advance sent out."

They went through the list, which included the President and First Lady, high-ranking Congressmen, three Supreme Court justices, and some of the wealthiest people in America, each paying half a million apiece for two tickets. The CEO and half the board of MediaCorp would be there.

Just what I hoped for. "That's what a military spokesman would call a target-rich environment. We're bound to get some interesting material."

Shakti leaned forward. "How are you gonna get in? As staff?"

"Trouble is," Pel said, "they've all been cleared already. We'd have to find jobs with the catering company or whoever, replace someone who's working on New Year's Eve – and no one would give up a gig like that voluntarily – and get clearance from the Secret Service. All in two weeks."

Shakti shook her head. "This was a bad idea. We should just cut our losses."

Waylee's stomach tightened. Why did she think this would work? Was it just her hypomanic cycle, as bad in its own way as the depression she was climbing out of? "I don't suppose we could sneak in? Hide in the building the day before, then come out with catering uniforms on?"

"I've been studying Secret Service procedures." Pel said. "They're pretty thorough. They'll comb the Castle with terahertz scanners before the event and detect any signs of life."

"Can we go in beforehand and leave a door or window unlocked?"

Pel shook his head.

"Is there a way to fool their scanners?"

Pel's eyebrows lifted. "Trouble is, we don't know exactly what kind of equipment they have. I did a lot of research on the Watchers, though. They emit different frequencies that can penetrate concrete, plastics, clothing, flesh... They can detect any kind of motion, even breathing, and see everything you're carrying, even if it's something you've swallowed."

"So the Watchers could see everything we were doing?" Shakti asked.

"If you're on the other side of a wall, they have to use microwaves and can only see your outline."

"Can they see through metal?" Waylee asked.

Pel brought up a search engine on the wall skin and flew through articles, finally settling on a security manual on how to interpret scanner imagery. "Most frequencies can't penetrate metal. X-rays can see through most metals except for lead. And anything that dense would set off alarms could be uranium."

"Do they have suits of armor in the Smithsonian?" Dingo said. "You could sneak inside one. Or mummies—you can wrap yourselves up as mummies."

Outlandish, but maybe worth looking into. Waylee turned to Pel.

"The Castle isn't used as a museum anymore," he said. "It might have some stuff in storage, though."

"Have you been there?" Charles asked him.

"Yeah, as a kid. The museums were all free then. The Castle used to be open to the public, but it's just offices and private event space now."

"The current administration equates anything public with socialist," Shakti said. "No doubt they plan to transfer the entire Smithsonian and all its contents to some multinational corporation."

"I looked it up," Waylee said. "The Smithsonian's a self-sufficient non-profit, so they're out of the president's reach." She turned back to Pel. "Let's go back to the guest list. Sneaking in as caterers runs the risk of supervisors not knowing who you are. But guests could be anyone."

Pel returned to the gallery of faces and scrolled down. "What about the DJ? I looked him up, he's a douchebag who specializes in crappy music. But it's just one person. Waylee's right, catering staff and musicians will know each other."

"Maybe we can get this DJ to cancel," Waylee said. "Then send a fake replacement recommendation from him to V.I.P."

"I can DJ in my sleep," Pel said. "But how do we get him to cancel? Who'd give up a chance to entertain the president and a bunch of billionaires?"

Dingo thrust out a finger. "How about getting him a gig at a porn star party?"

Pel lit up. "Dude, that's brilliant."

He beamed. "It doesn't even have to be a real party. Or it could be real but we fake the invite."

"Alright," Waylee said. "Let's put that on the list of possibilities."

Shakti leaned forward. She always got excited when brainstorming. "What about pretending to be someone on the MediaCorp board who's usually impossible to get hold of—"

"Like on a private space flight?" Pel said.

"Uh, that's a long shot."

Dingo hit an imaginary snare and cymbal with imaginary drumsticks, and said, "Bud-a-boom!"

Shakti rolled her eyes. "Unintended." She looked around. "Maybe call up someone at V.I.P. and pretend to be a MediaCorp big shot and say you've got this nephew or niece who wants to DJ for the president and they'd better damn well give them the gig."

Pel tapped one of his Jack Sparrow braids. "Doesn't sound true. Big Shot families don't usually contain professional DJs."

"Big Shot might want admission tickets for family though."

"There we go," Waylee said. "If we don't have to DJ, we can spend all our time mingling and picking up material. And if we're fellow elites, the guests are more likely to talk to us."

Charles peered at her. "How are you supposed to pass as a rich person?"

"Easy. Just need the clothes and a back story. *Herald* nightlife sent me to VIP events all the time. If there's one thing I know how to do, it's connecting with people."

"Okay," Pel said, "so we either find someone on the invite list who cancels—"

Dingo jumped in. "Or we make someone cancel—"

"And send 'family' in his place."

Waylee's heart raced. "Or we contact V.I.P. as this Big Shot, say he has relatives who want to hang with the president on New Year's, and ask how much. Cost's no object, he'll pay whatever it takes. Christmas present."

"And how do we pay for that?" Pel asked.

"We don't," Waylee said. "Just promise to pay."

Charles threw up a hand. "I'll get what you need. Big Shot, back story, maybe even some money."

16

Kiyoko

The cops hadn't bothered cleaning up after ransacking the band house. They took all the electronics, including her immersion suit, the downstairs Genki-san, and their band computers. At least M-pat's wife fed her cat. The neighbors and Pel's cousins kept scavengers away. And the neighbors across the street buried poor Laelaps.

One of Pel's cousins offered to move into the house "to keep her safe," but the way he leered, she sent him away. She called some of her cosplay friends who were happy to stay over a while. Their martial skills were limited, but they made the place look occupied. M-pat promised to keep an eye on the place too, even with only one deputy left.

Then her champion, Francis Jones, arrived with three assistants, returning everything taken by the police. "None of it's legitimate evidence. BPD likes to confiscate stuff for their own use or to sell, but case law says they can't unless it was used to commit a crime or was acquired through crime."

Kiyoko didn't tell him the Genki-san was Pel's and he never bought anything legally, a practice she long ago gave up chiding him about. Her stuff, though, was all legit, and she had receipts.

One of the assistants, a heavyset grandmother type, went through the house with a small box that she called a signal detector. She found remote cameras and microphones in almost every room, including Kiyoko's bedroom and the bathroom. She plucked them all out and put them in a metallic bag.

"Thanks," Kiyoko said. "Someone'll be here from now on, so they can't put new ones in."

"They can still monitor you from outside the house," the woman said.

"Like the Watchers? I'm used to them."

When Francis Jones and his assistants left, and with her friends immersed in a Dungeons & Dragons game in the dining room, Kiyoko returned to BetterWorld. Maybe she'd join their game later, but she found the rules tedious. BetterWorld calculated all that stuff for you.

Yumekuni survived her absence. But Prince Vostok had appealed his defeat. *Uh oh.* He insisted she couldn't have made her army invisible without cheating.

Kiyoko had recorded the entire battle. She sent the admins a full accounting of her *qi* storages and transformations. Vostok had just erred in attacking a realm with huge energy deposits and a ruler who could channel them. She omitted any mention of Charles and his tweaks to her stocks of oil.

She checked her messages next. Mostly fan mail and spam. She searched for something from Waylee or Pel/William Godwin, but found nothing. Her prioritization algorithm gave the top ranking to a recent message from someone called Iwisa, based on the sender being a legitimate avatar and the keywords "Dwarf Eats Hippo," "agent," and "audience."

Kiyoko opened the link. A handsome coal-black man wearing a Victorian suit and top hat appeared in the message portal. He stood on the bridge of a formal Japanese garden, leaning on a silver-tipped walking stick. Odd combination of elements. She started the video.

In vivid three dimensions, the man tipped his hat. "Greetings. I am Iwisa. I am a big fan of your band, Dwarf Eats Hippo. As it happens, I am a professional music agent with a lot of connections, and I would like to help broaden your audience. We should meet at your earliest convenience. I promise it will be worth your time."

She looked him up. Yes, he was indeed a registered agent. In BetterWorld, anyway. He didn't list an outside name.

Kiyoko replied. "Thank you for your message. You may meet me in my realm of Yumekuni at any time. The teleport coordinates to my palace entrance are X3875977, Y0569656. Password noh8rz. I will provide an escort from there. I look forward to our meeting."

Iwisa arrived at Kiyoko's high ceilinged, silk festooned throne room less than an hour later. He was accompanied by two of her armored bot guards and a striking brunette wearing a leather half top and miniskirt, cast iron arm bands, and brass goggles perched on the crown of her head.

Kiyoko rose from her golden throne. "I am Princess Kiyoko, ruler of Yumekuni, the loveliest realm in BetterWorld."

"Indeed it is," Iwisa said. "Rivaled only by your personal loveliness."

"You are a gentleman." She held out her hand, palm down.

He kissed it, then gazed in her eyes. "I am Iwisa." He gestured toward the girl. "This is Steampunk Girl."

"That's Grrl with two R's and no I," his companion said.

"I see." *An interesting couple.* "And you're both in the music business?"

"Yes." Iwisa passed her a large envelope, secured by red twine. "I have a proposal for you."

Kiyoko unraveled the twine and opened the envelope. Text appeared in a popup portal. "Only you can see this message. I am here on Waylee and Pel's behalf. Sorry about the false pretense. I can get you away from the people monitoring you on the Comnet, and tell you more about your sister, but you must be willing to change avatars temporarily. Please say 'it's a wonderful idea' if you agree."

Kiyoko wasn't sure if she was disappointed or grateful. "It's a wonderful idea."

"Great," Iwisa said. "I will come back with more details."

Was he leaving, then?

Steampunk Grrl extended a hand. "It was nice to meet you."

Kiyoko shook her hand… and all of a sudden she was staring at her own porcelain features, whimsical smile, pink locks cascading past her shoulders.

She peered down. Cast iron bands now twined around her forearms. A leather half top cupped her breasts. She looked at Iwisa.

"Shall we go?" he said.

At first, she wasn't sure. "Yes," she decided. Her voice sounded pleasant but alien.

Kiyoko and Iwisa teleported to the largely unused Western Continent, then boarded a bullet transport. The four-seat capsule flew through a transparent tube faster than the speed of sound. These transports didn't exist on the Fantasy Continent, but were common elsewhere.

"Can we talk here?" she asked.

Iwisa held up a hand, then brought up a navigation map. "We get out here." He pointed to a dot marked "Horse trails."

The trail stop was deserted. Two horses stood next to a communications interface mounted on a metal pole. A woodland stretched in all directions, trees spaced far apart and grass growing between.

They mounted their horses and she followed Iwisa into the woods. The grass looked green and uniform, not brown and weedy like her yard in

Baltimore. The horses seemed to know where they were going, or maybe Iwisa was directing them.

"We can talk now," he said.

"So what happened to me? I'm not into steampunk, by the way."

"You look different, that's the point. Steampunk Grrl is a bot. Before you switched, I mean. She runs on the best AI scripts out there, but follows my commands. She jumped over to your princess avatar when you shook hands, and moved you over to her body. And to anyone monitoring you, you're still in your palace."

Kiyoko didn't know that was possible. "Can't the admins still follow my data packets?"

"Nope. You're going through a totally different server now and the bot is ghosting I/O through your login server."

Interesting. "Are you a bot?"

"No, I'm real."

"So what's this bot gonna do as me?"

"Whatever you want her to. You can tell her what to do just by sending a message, but you have to be really specific. She doesn't have much imagination. She has access to all your avatar files, though – how you move, what your voice sounds like—"

"That's all the same as the real me."

Iwisa looked over at her. "That's 'cause most people want to be more attractive in BetterWorld, but you don't need to. You're like an angel."

"Your flattery is noted and appreciated."

He bowed.

"So you're real," she said, "and you know me outside."

"Yeah."

"Are you Francis Jones, or do you work for him?"

"Who?"

"My lawyer." *My champion.* "He saved me from imprisonment."

"Everyone's happy you're out."

"Especially me. So where are Waylee and Pel? How are they doing?"

Iwisa stopped his horse. Hers did the same. "They want you to know they're safe and doing fine. They're nearby, and they're going through with the New Year's plan."

It took a while for that to register. "Are they total retards? I thought they'd be in Canada by now."

"Maybe after they pull this off they'll go to Canada. Never thought to ask."

"I doubt Waylee's planned that far ahead. Tell her to get out and seek asylum someplace the government isn't bombing, then I'll join her and we can move to Tokyo or someplace where our band'll break to the top."

"I'll tell her."

Kiyoko sent a message to her possessed avatar. "Retire from public interactions until further notice, practice all my avatar's skills and build them up."

"Understood," it replied.

Iwisa maneuvered his horse until they were close enough to kiss if they wanted. "Pel needs your help. He might want to sell the immersion suit, wall skin and band equipment."

She sidled her horse away. "He can sell his gaming stuff and the Genki-san, but no way is he selling our band equipment. We make decisions together, and I say no."

Iwisa sat on his horse, face blank. "I'll tell him."

"And tell him he's an idiot."

"He's not an idiot."

"You're not Pel, are you?"

He shook his head. "No, I'm not Pel."

He must be Charles, then. Dingo didn't have the skills. Best not to mention it, though, since Homeland was after him.

They rode on, Kiyoko furious at her sister and everyone else, but also unable to get those words out of her mind, 'you're just a deluded little girl who can't deal with real life.'

Iwisa turned to her again. "There's other ways you can help too."

"How? I'm not a hacker like you."

"How can you tell?"

She rolled her eyes and pointed at her face.

"Think that's a good trick? You ain't seen nothing yet."

"Can you teach me some of these tricks?" All this time in the Comnet, and she was practically helpless.

"It's like anything else, you gotta put in a lot of hours – 10,000 they say – to be elite. I started little, spending afternoons and weekends in the library. I'd love to spend the time with you, though."

Another pickup line. "So what do you want my help with?"

Iwisa nudged his horse forward again. "Like I said, I'm with Waylee and Pel. I... I've made some bad mistakes on my own. I thought with you along, that wouldn't happen. You know BetterWorld and people here, and you won't turn us in, and you can tell me if an idea sounds bad. Or good."

"So what'll we be doing?"

"A lot. Mainly, find some MediaCorp execs or board members. Pel and I looked at MediaCorp's public site. Thirteen directors on the board. We're hoping one will be unreachable soon, so Pel and Waylee can be spoiled relatives."

"That sounds risky."

He shrugged. "We'll see. But first we need to find some programmers or administrators. The only way to get god powers in BetterWorld is to have programmer privileges."

"God powers?"

"To do whatever you want. Like teleport wherever you want, or fill your bank account. And use BetterWorld as a platform to hit outside targets. I was thinking we could get into MediaCorp's databases that way. Unlikely we'll find their directors on BetterWorld, but they'll be in the corporate intranet."

She turned her horse around. "We could look, maybe some of them do have avatars."

"Even if they do, we can't own them. Pel said it would tip them off. We gotta be indirect."

"Well, let's start looking. I know where all the admin types hang out, the ones who have avatars anyway." She just had to remember she wasn't Princess Kiyoko if she met anyone she knew.

Kiyoko would try to talk Waylee out of this mission of hers, but her sister almost never listened to her. If she didn't, she'd try to help her.

* * *

Pelopidas

In the shuttered living room, Fuera handed Pel the flat rectangular boxes he'd been expecting. They were addressed to a fake name at a townhouse down the street, and Fuera had picked them up as soon as the delivery man drove away. The "From" label listed "Pandora Productions" in New York.

"Christmas presents?" she said.

He decided not to open them there. "Something we paid for." Besides Kiyoko's credits, he had traded all his VR gear. He'd never give Big Red away, though.

"You celebrating Christmas with your family, or you still gonna be hiding here?"

Was that a hint to move on? "My family's Eastern Orthodox. They celebrate Christmas on the Julian calendar. January 7 on the modern calendar." He'd been bringing Waylee and Kiyoko to the Christmas Eve feasts, one of the ways he tried to mitigate their horrific childhoods. Kiyoko even attended mass with his family, saying she loved the spirituality and pageantry, although Waylee always refused.

"We'll be gone by then," Pel said, "but I thought Waylee told you we'd like to stay 'til the end of December."

She frowned. "Sure, I'm just hoping you have a long-term plan."

"We do."

"We're taking an awful risk, you know."

"No one knows we're here. And we'll leave soon." Pel picked up the cardboard boxes and returned to the basement, where they spent most of their time. Watchers could see through walls but not through the ground.

He laid the boxes on the coffee table. "Got our gear." Waylee, Dingo, and Shakti crowded around as he cut open the first box with his Leatherman blade. Beneath a layer of bubble wrap, a transparent vacuum pack compressed layers of black and white fabric. "This one's mine."

He opened the pack and unfolded a single-breasted dinner jacket, matching cummerbund and trousers, white shirt, cufflinks, and bow tie. He tried on the jacket. A perfect fit. He held up the bow tie. "Anyone know how to tie one of these?"

"So that's your gear?" Dingo said. "A tux? I admit, you've got that James Bond swank thing going on, but…"

Pel pointed to the top shirt button. "I halved the size of our equipment order and applied the savings to embed it into our clothes. That button is actually a nonreflective fish eye lens. Optic software corrects on the fly to create a normal image, which is stored in memory chips embedded in the seams."

The ghost snares – amplifiers, processors, and carbon nanotube antennae – had been woven into the jacket. Indeed, the whole jacket was one big passive electronics array, none of it detectable. A small plastic bag in one of the pockets contained a memory wafer that presumably housed the decryption software.

Pel gave the other box to Waylee. "This one's yours. I hope you like it."

She tore it open, ripped apart the bubble wrap and vacuum packing, and unfurled a long silver dress full of ruffles and embroidery—ideal for hiding her spyware. "This is beautiful, Pel. I… wow."

"Everything's here," Pel said. "I have to test it all."

"We need shoes and accessories," Waylee said.

"They're coming. This broker's the epitome of refined taste, so everything will match and pass the snoot test."

"And more importantly, we need ID's. Kiyoko has a friend that makes fake ID's for underage students."

He thought about it. "I think I'll go through M-pat." *Assuming he's not done with us.* "Less likely they'll talk. Out of state driver's licenses would work best."

Dingo flashed the eyes on the backs of his hands. "Yo. I should go get those drugs you wanted. Maybe there's a cheaper source than Rosemont."

"You just want to get out of the house," Shakti said. Charles was the only one not going crazy from the confinement, but he lived in the Comnet, surfacing only when forced by bodily functions.

Waylee stood. "We all want to rejoin the world. It won't be long now."

"Where you gonna go?" Pel asked Dingo. "You don't know anyone around here, and someone'll turn you in if you show up in West Baltimore."

"Can M-pat search for us?" Waylee asked.

"He already did," Pel said. "Too expensive, and too late now."

Shakti squinted her eyes. "I don't even know why you need those drugs. It's a New Year's party. Everyone'll be drinking."

"Yeah, that's one of the reasons I picked this event," Waylee said. "I guess we'll have to do this the old-fashioned way." She folded her hands. "And I've been thinking, we shouldn't be supporting the drug gangs anyway. I know Kiyoko'd frown on it."

"Kiyoko doesn't want us to do this at all," Pel said.

Shakti nodded. "Me neither."

Waylee's eyes shifted. "Yeah, yeah." She glanced at Charles, oblivious in his immersion helmet. "My sister's right about one thing. When we're done collecting our material and broadcasting it, we'll have to skip the country."

Pel's chest tightened. He didn't want to leave Baltimore, leave his family and friends forever. "The government can kidnap or kill people anywhere in the world. They do it all the time. We'll have to change our identities or we'll never be safe, no matter where we go."

17

Charles

Charles/Iwisa and Kiyoko/Steampunk Grrl stood together on the fore-deck of a sailing ship. A cloth air cylinder filled the space overhead. Houses and farms passed below. Iwisa held Steampunk Grrl's hand. Charles could feel the touch of Kiyoko's palm, the grasp of her fingers, all the way across Baltimore.

They had rented an airship to take them to Club Elite, a huge structure that defied the laws of gravity and floated around with the clouds. Most BetterWorld residents couldn't see it, nor knew it existed. But as a V.I.P. with her own realm, Kiyoko could visit whenever she wanted.

"I model my costumes there sometimes," she told Charles, "and jam with other musicians. I've made some good connections there."

She had asked for the club's current coordinates and entry password. Like his old club, Swagspeare's, anyone could enter once they had the pass-word. Steampunk Grrl and Iwisa, for instance.

Charles hoped Kiyoko would find the success she and her sister and Pel deserved. He still hadn't revealed his outside identity, although she probably suspected. She'd been nice to him at the band house, but hadn't shown any signs of interest. He was underage and overweight. At least here, he had a chance. And BetterWorld romances spilled outside all the time. He just had to be patient.

"So how we gonna find the admins?" he said. They were alone except for the pilot and crew, all bots. And a hold full of vampires.

She looked back at him. "I was hoping you'd know. But I have an idea."

"What's that?"

"If they have god powers, we just have to get them to show off somehow."

"How do we do that?"

"I've noticed hackers can be brilliant on one hand, but suckers for sex, money, or technical challenges."

He thought about it. She was probably dead on. "So what's your plan then?"

"I thought I'd go for the technical challenge. A scavenger hunt. Like my palace, Club Elite has one fixed teleport site, a pad at the air dock. So anyone who teleports from inside the club is likely to be a programmer."

"What's a scavenger hunt?"

She stared at him. "And I thought *my* childhood was deprived."

"Is it like hunting for Easter eggs?"

"Kind of. The organizer—me in this case—gives the participants—everyone at the club hopefully—a list of things to retrieve, and the first one who comes back with all the items wins."

"So the ones who can teleport wherever they want, and can search through BetterWorld's databases, will have a big advantage."

She smiled. "Exactly."

"After the contest, I'll send the vampires after their avatars. They'll take them over and I'll have access to their computers. 'Course, you know, we can only do this once, because the admins will go on a vendetta and destroy all the vampires and close the exploit. And cybermercs will converge as soon as they figure out what's going on."

"Cybermercs?"

"Hired hackers."

"Then we should surprise our targets, and strike them all at once." She winked. "I learned a lot fighting Prince Vostok."

The airship slipped into a berth along others of its type and everything from biplanes to flying saucers. Steampunk Grrl led him down a walkway toward a nine-story pyramid. A wide platform, held up by black columns, ringed the third floor.

The walkway ended at a fancy looking gate. Two bling-covered gorillas, just like the one at Swagspeare's, stood in front, arms crossed and faces frowning.

Steampunk Grrl gave them the entry code. The gorillas uncrossed their arms and stood aside. The gate swung open and she strolled in.

Iwisa followed her into a giant room vibrating to dance music. Smart-dressed people and half-animal creatures danced amidst pulsing lights. Some posted texts while dancing, which scrolled by on a sidebar. Too loud for vocals.

A private message popped up from Steampunk Grrl. "This club has nine levels. We can message all nine if the club manager thinks it's interesting enough."

Kiyoko seemed to know where she was going. He followed her into an elevator. She pressed the top button, and seconds later, it opened to a lounge. People sat on couches or at small tables, the music quiet enough for conversation. Open sky blazed through glass walls.

Steampunk Grrl sat at a table. He joined her. She pulled a piece of paper and thick pen from her leather pouch, and started a list. "An orange. A pearl. A bottle of Juyondai sake. The head of Alfredo Garcia…"

When she finished, she called over a server, a beefy man in black leather. She leaned toward him. "Could we see the manager on duty? I have a fun idea for the club."

"What'll you have?" he said.

A bot, and not even a smart one. Charles wondered why people even ordered drinks. You couldn't taste them and they wouldn't get you drunk.

Steampunk Grrl stood. "Never mind." She walked over to the female bartender standing behind a long counter, and repeated her question.

"What sort of fun idea?"

"A scavenger hunt." She showed the bartender the list. "Winner gets an airship and a slot in a system-wide contest with a million credit pool of prizes."

A jewelry-covered Indian woman, midriff bare like Steampunk Grrl, appeared next to the bartender. She'd teleported there – either a programmer or a special bot. "I'm Priyanka. I'm the manager."

"Steampunk Grrl." She bowed from the shoulders.

Priyanka returned the bow, then scanned the list. "Who are you with?"

"Chaoji-Mao Entertainment. Out of Shanghai. We're prototyping a game for MediaCorp."

Priyanka nodded.

"What do you think? All you have to do is let me message everyone, and whoever's interested can meet me on the Level 3 terrace."

Priyanka ran a hand through her long hair. "Sounds interesting. Give me your text and I'll send it for you."

Access to the com system must be restricted, Charles thought. He followed Steampunk Grrl back to the elevator.

The terrace was big, with lots of pools, tiki huts, and palm trees. Bikini-wearing honeys chatted with athletic-looking men in swimming trunks. A dolphin leaped from pool to pool.

Iwisa followed Steampunk Grrl onto a wooden performance stage in the center. She posted the list of items as a grab file, certified by club management as virus free.

One or two at a time, people and creatures gathered from other parts of the club. He'd never seen so many tails and wings on avatars. Except on the Fantasy Continent, you couldn't even get a non-human avatar normally. But they had to be users—a bot wouldn't show interest in a scavenger hunt.

Steampunk Grrl waited until people stopped showing, then addressed the crowd. She described the scavenger hunt, list of items, and the prizes. Charles scanned the avatars, storing the video for later analysis. "Everyone'll get a participation prize," she said, "and we're throwing a party here, so be sure to come back. Good luck."

Angels and demons flew off, followed by a guy with a rocket pack and a goofy looking kid with a helicopter beanie. Other avatars disappeared, no doubt teleporting. The rest ran or walked for the exit, headed for the designated teleport pad or an aircraft. Those ones probably weren't bothering with.

Charles stored images of the flying and teleporting avatars. "I'll wait back at the airship," he private messaged Steampunk Grrl.

"I'm staying to greet the winner. I'll meet you there when I'm done."

On the airship, Charles loaded the hit list to the vampires. They wouldn't be able to get into the club without invites. But there were plenty of guests coming and going.

May need help with this. He sent Pel an encrypted message. "You in the Comnet?"

"Yeah, doing research."

"Got a big op underway, and I need backup." *Time to test his gaming skills.*

"Where are you?"

Charles sent him a file, also encrypted. "Activate this script and you'll pop into one of my vampires." *I'll put him in Mordoch.* He looked a well-dressed young executive, but had the best defenses.

Mordoch messaged him a few minutes later. "It's Pel. This is weird. Where am I?"

"Airship hold. Get used to Mordoch, try him out. I armed all my vamps before we left. Yours I built guns into both arms. Your suit is bulletproof. We move as soon as Kiyoko gives the word."

"Kiyoko?"

"Yeah, she got me here. She's in disguise though."

"Why am I armed? What do you want me to do?"

"Take out any guards or cybermercs who show up."

"Won't they have god powers?"

"The cybermercs maybe, but we've got surprise on our side." He'd never actually seen a cybermerc in BetterWorld before. Would they even bother with avatars?

"Okay," Pel messaged. "How do I use the guns? What do they do?"

"Just point and shoot. The targeting software'll do the rest. Game rules apply otherwise, but you've got lethal ammo." If he hit a bot or avatar, he'd probably kill it. Bots would turn to corpses, avatars would disappear and the user knocked offline. They'd have to log back to their normal starting point. "I'll send in backup."

"Who's the backup?"

"Whatever vampires aren't busy." The next ask was hard. "If security shows up, make sure you kill Kiyoko too."

"What?"

"Her Steampunk Grrl avatar I mean." He sent a picture. "She'll get bounced out. Can't get sniffed by cybermercs that way, and no one will guess she's involved."

An hour after the contest's start, Steampunk Grrl messaged him. "First one teleported back. I'm feeding you the video."

A mostly naked girl with purple hair and balloon-like breasts emptied a sack on the stage.

"Well congratulations, uh…"

"Violetta," she said.

"Violetta," Steampunk Grrl said. "Everything's here, and you're the first one back. I expected it to take longer."

A humanoid with tiger features appeared to the right of Violetta. It carried a wooden treasure chest. The tigerman glanced at Violetta, then placed the chest at Steampunk Grrl's feet and opened it. All the items were arranged inside.

Steampunk Grrl looked at Tigerman, then Violetta. "Am I to believe that Alfredo Garcia had two heads?"

Another avatar appeared, also with a full bag, and everyone began arguing. Steampunk Grrl messaged all the contestants, asking them to return.

"Time to go," Charles messaged Pel. He released his vampire bots, all thirty of them.

The bots fanned across the aircraft berths and the teleport pad and searched for arriving guests. When able, they touched guests' avatars and took control of them, then entered the club.

They'd have to act fast. Someone would complain that their avatar had been hacked and then the cybermercs would come in. He ordered his vampires to enter the club in groups of two to four, one a hacked avatar and the others not. Once they got inside, each would approach a potential programmer and attack.

* * *

Pelopidas

Pel/Mordoch joined a hacked female avatar and one of Charles's male bots. They recited the password to two gorilla guards and entered the nine story ziggurat that housed the club. The huge dance floor inside was mostly empty.

"Where am I going?" he messaged Charles.

A 3-D map of the club opened in front of him, his avatar depicted on the entry floor. Two levels higher, "Level 3 Terrace" was shaded red. Bat icons, presumably representing the vampires, advanced in that direction.

Pel decreased the opacity of the map until he could see through it easily. He climbed two sets of stairs and exited onto a sprawling patio of pools, palm trees, and tiki huts. People in swimsuits and club wear congregated around a stage. Some looked human, if unrealistically endowed, some were human-animal hybrids, and some went further, like the pillar of flame and the double helix. Steampunk Grrl—Kiyoko—knelt on the stage.

"We're going to have to re-do this without any cheating," she said.

"How can it be cheating if you didn't state the rules?" an overdeveloped violet-haired girl said.

Charles's platoon of vampires entered the crowd. They approached some of the avatars, mostly non-human ones, brushed against them, bumped into them, or placed a hand on their back. The touched avatars froze in place. No one seemed to notice.

Mordoch sat down at a thatch-covered tiki bar by the stage, where he could see everything but not present an obvious target.

Behind the bamboo counter, the bartender, a shirtless buff-boy with long blond hair, sidled up. "What'll ya have, brah?"

Pel ignored him.

"Something's going on," a tiger-faced man by Steampunk Grrl said.

The purple-haired girl turned. "What?"

A dark-skinned woman, one of Charles's, clamped a hand on Purple's right breast. She stopped moving, lips parted in mid-sentence.

The tiger furry disappeared. Teleported away.

Another avatar vanished. And one, a burly looking man, drew a gun.

Mordoch jumped off his bar stool and pointed his arms at the burly guy. His palms dropped and a barrel protruded from each wrist. Flechettes flew out in a blur, and thwacked into the man's neck. He shook spastically, then disappeared.

The vampires ran from one target to another. Avatars shouted and scattered in panic. A crimson demon unfurled bat wings and bounded into the air. Mordoch fired another pair of fletchettes. Both hit. It spiraled downward and splashed into a pool.

Club doors flew open. Men and women in guard uniforms rushed out, guns drawn. Others materialized on the patio.

Sorry, Kiyoko. Mordoch put his guns on full auto and shot into the crowd, making sure to hit Steampunk Grrl. She shook violently and vanished. He hit a guard too, who disappeared. And a couple of dudes in swimtrunks, who just dropped and lay bleeding. *Those must be bots.*

Several guards fired at him. Some of the rounds hit, but his suit absorbed the damage. How much it could take, he had no idea.

He vaulted over the bar counter, bullets whizzing by. Once on the other side, he grabbed the buff-bot by the hair and held him in front as a shield.

Buff-bot twitched and spasmed as bullets struck his chest and head.

Mordoch whipped his arms under Buff-bot's armpits to hold him in place. He fired at every guard in sight, again full auto. Some of the guards shook and disappeared and others collapsed to the ground.

Both his magazines were empty. It didn't look like he had refills. *Crap.*

A sphere appeared in front of him, with a single rheumy cat eye above a gaping mouth of needle sharp teeth, and waving tentacles on top. It swiveled all the tentacles toward him.

Mordoch dove out the other side of the tiki hut, hearing a high-pitched screech behind him. Another cat-eyed sphere appeared to his right.

He kept running, and reached the edge of the patio. It was a long drop, but not necessarily a fatal one. He decided to ensure that it was. Mordoch vaulted over the railing into the air, then jackknifed so his head pointed down.

The pavement rushed toward him. He should have felt wind in his face, but that was one of the subtle effects BetterWorld still lacked.

Everything flashed red. Red switched to utter blackness.

Green reboot messages and hexadecimal addresses scrolled up, beeping softly as they passed. Not a normal BetterWorld death, where he'd appear at his login point. But no doubt this was safer.

* * *

Charles

The beholders had to be cybermerc avatars or bots. They seemed impervious to his vampires' weapons and infections, and brushed aside the "Word of God" spam attacks that he griefed the regular guards with. They went after Pel first, then counterattacked his vampires. One by one, his bots died or froze.

Then the entire patio and everyone on it stopped moving. Only now did he realize the palm fronds had been swaying in the breeze.

Charles activated the self-destructs on all thirty bots. The vampires disappeared.

Time to focus on the spoils. He'd infected over fifty computers, more than half operated by BetterWorld employees. The viruses sent him avatar parameters, user profiles, and network addresses, created back doors on their computers, and then deleted themselves.

Violetta had won the scavenger hunt, presumably exploiting god privileges. Charles opened the back door to her computer. First, he gave himself root access, then activated a script to erase his footprints as he explored. He couldn't find her real identity, but it wasn't important. She had access to the entire BetterWorld infrastructure. He copied all her scripts and passwords, including the ability to bypass BetterWorld's laws of physics and security restrictions.

Using Violetta's passwords, Charles unlocked a series of firewalls and entered the network of BetterWorld servers. They said the Milky Way galaxy contained billions of stars. The BetterWorld network looked bigger.

He set up more back doors and downloaded code and passwords that looked interesting, but couldn't find a network map or search engine. Where was the bank? Where were the portals to other MediaCorp networks?

He could empty the accounts of the fifty elites he'd hacked. That's why he created the vamps in the first place. But none had admin access to the credit bank. Probably it would be full of traps and cybermercs anyway.

No matter. Violetta and others had the address and passwords to the central MediaCorp intranet. The rest could wait, this was what Pel and Waylee really wanted.

He logged on the intranet. He didn't have root access, at least not at the moment. But Violetta's password let him into remote applications, financial databases, personnel files... even webmail and chat rooms. He found a list of the corporation's Board of Directors and executives, and looked at their bios and resumes.

The directors and officers were all active in business and government, there seeming no real distinction. Some had professorships too. Several had children around Pel's age. No doubt their extended families would have more.

Here's a good one. Richard T. Shafer wrote on a Board of Directors forum, "For those of you attending the New Year's fundraiser: If you get a chance, please pass along my regrets to the president that I couldn't attend, and that he has my full support. I've had this Angola trip scheduled for over a year, and frankly, need the time away. I have a list of trophies to bag before they're all gone, rhino for example. I'll bring back something for everyone."

Pel could take it from here. Charles sent him login instructions, plus a video clip of a pirate swinging by rope onto a Spanish galleon.

18

December 31
Washington, D.C.

Waylee

"Here we are," the taxi driver said in a Slavic accent, stopping in front of the Smithsonian Castle at 1000 Jefferson Drive SW. Secret Service agents and DC police stood everywhere. *I should tell him to keep driving.*

The moment of terror passed. Waylee gave the driver $50. "Keep the change."

"Thank you. You will be wanting a ride back to Greenbelt?"

"Perhaps."

"I am Jurgis." He handed her a card. "You call me when you want ride."

Pel opened the back door and they stepped out. Cold air seeped through Waylee's dress, but they had no budget for fancy coats, and wouldn't be outside long.

She didn't even recognize Pel with his executive haircut, bare chin, and tux. She'd been equally transformed: blue-eye contacts, face made up like a model's, hair dyed blonde and arranged in a bun, dress long and silver and full of ruffles and embroidery. She'd never worn high heels before and had taken days to practice in them. Learning her new persona had been even harder.

"You are a vision, Estelle," Pel said.

"And you, Greg."

Greg was the nephew of MediaCorp Director Richard T. Shafer, currently on safari in Angola to kill endangered animals. V.I.P. Productions had been happy to fit Greg Wilson and his fiancée Estelle Cosimo, both actual people, into the New Year's gala. Huge bribes of BetterWorld credits, courtesy of Charles, had helped "compensate for the inconvenience." Their fake messages from Mr. Shafer promised to pay the entry fee "with interest" as soon as he returned. "Cost is no object when it comes to re-electing our president."

The taxi drove off. *This is it.* Pel, normally so stalwart, had been terrified that morning, and his jitters had been contagious. She told him, it's just another show, no big deal. But they split two minis of liquid courage – Jack Daniels and Captain Morgan—in the taxi.

Waylee/Estelle and Pel/Greg handed their tickets to a young, blue-suited White House staffer, one of several stationed beneath the red stone entry arch. He slid them one at a time in a portable reader, which announced their authenticity with a green light and a beep.

He gave the tickets back. "Welcome, Mr. Wilson, Miss Cosimo."

Waylee ignored him as she assumed Miss Cosimo would do, and strode up a set of stairs arm in arm with her fiancé. The key to success was to act confident, act like they belonged.

It was easy. Except for the damn high heels. She stumbled on the second step. She clutched Pel's arm and caught her balance, but heard a gasp from behind. Miss Cosimo was ridiculously awesome, though, so she continued up the stairs as if nothing had happened.

Just outside the front door, two burly Secret Service men, wearing dark suits and the latest in multispectral glasses and earpieces, checked their IDs and scanned them with portable X-ray machines. She'd doused herself with sex pheromones, not that she'd ever needed such things, but the agents showed no sign they noticed.

Their driver's licenses looked official. And their cameras and signal detectors were well shielded and disguised, just some buttons and threads in their clothes. Security wouldn't be looking for anything that small anyway, Pel had promised.

"May I see your purse, ma'am?" one asked in a deep voice. He'd shaved his head, probably to disguise early male pattern baldness.

Waylee handed Bald Eagle her pearl-colored handbag, which contained only a temporary comlink and a confusion of makeup supplies.

He inserted a perforated plastic rod inside, waved it around, then passed the purse back. "Enjoy yourselves." He smiled with his mouth but not his eyes.

And they were in. Lacking coats, they bypassed the checkers on either side of the entryway. More Secret Service agents, clean cut men in tuxes and women wearing long dresses and flat shoes, eyed them. Waylee and Pel passed two roped off staircases and entered the lower main hall, the castle's biggest interior space.

A string quartet stationed near the entrance played something Bach-like. Two rows of multifaceted marble columns subdivided the big room. Velvet drapes occluded tall windows along the walls.

A handful of guests filled plates at scattered food and drink stations, the men uniformed in nearly identical tuxedos and bow ties, the women draped in floor-length gowns. Some sat together at round tables. At the far end of the room, a stage with a piano and drum kit overlooked rows of red padded chairs.

They were unfashionably early. Less than a third of the two hundred guests had arrived. To the left of the stage, the DJ fiddled with his computer and sound gear. Waylee thought about requesting Motörhead's "Eat the Rich," but Miss Cosimo would certainly not approve.

Pel seemed entranced by the rows of silver buffet dishes, their colorful morsels displayed like works of art. "Should we get some food?"

The aromas included seared meats, which, thanks to Shakti's vegan crusade, Waylee found repulsive. And Miss Cosimo didn't attend parties to eat. "There's plenty of wait staff wandering," she said, adding a huff for emphasis. "They can fetch our food for us. Let's mingle." They had studied the guest list and memorized faces as best they could.

Pel headed toward the curly haired Chair of the House Natural Resources Committee, busy conversing with the CEO of a multinational mining company. Waylee followed. Their 'ghost snares' could intercept any trace of comlink activity, but had a limited range, especially with overlapping signals to contend with. After the party, they'd sync the signal timestamps with those from their video cameras so they'd know whose comlinks were whose.

The Congressman had a guard of his own, who trained data glasses on them. *Guards are just servants with guns, Estelle would think.* Their disguises held, although of course they'd submitted their own "recent photos" to the event organizers.

"So you understand our concerns," the CEO told the Congressman as Waylee reached earshot. "I thought those EPA bureaucrats had been emasculated."

The Congressman shifted his feet. "We can block the regs. But we should coordinate with the president. He'll be here soon, and he can fix things more quickly. It's actually on the agenda to get rid of the EPA altogether. They're hard to control sometimes."

If Shakti was here, she'd lose it. Waylee waited for a chance to butt into the conversation.

From behind her, a cultivated female voice said, "So, you're Dick's nephew." Waylee turned.

An auburn-haired woman in her sixties, a MediaCorp director named Beatrice Baddelats, glared at Pel/Greg. She wore a sapphire blue gown and large golden earrings. A nearly empty martini glass swayed from one hand. "I can't believe the bastard—if you'll pardon my French—is off shooting animals in Africa and missing the biggest event of the year."

"My uncle likes to get away," Pel said. The CEO and Congressman moved off.

"Yes, he does. It's a wonder he's done so well for himself."

Pel shrugged, and introduced Waylee/Estelle.

Ms. Baddelats had a strong grip. "You don't look like your Comnet pictures."

Waylee froze. She bore a vague resemblance to Estelle, and did her best with contacts and dyes. But she'd assumed no one at the gala would actually know her.

The woman squinted. "You've got nose and lip piercings too that you're trying to hide."

Waylee had put liquid latex and foundation over the holes but it wasn't perfect. "Teen angst. Over it."

Ms. Baddelats looked skeptical.

"Pictures don't do my fiancée justice," Pel said. "Isn't she beautiful?"

"I suppose so."

"Well it was nice to meet you," Waylee said, impaling Ms. Baddelats with all the negative energy she could muster. Miss Cosimo wouldn't put up with "I suppose so," so she turned and headed for the nearest food table. Pel followed.

The remaining guests arrived. As advertised, no press. Her main target, MediaCorp Chairman and CEO Robert Luxmore, entered around 9:30 with his surgically enhanced trophy wife. He was shorter than Waylee expected, grey haired, and beady eyed.

We meet at last.

The string quartet stopped their tedious screeching. "Ruffles and Flourishes" played over the speakers mounted throughout the big room. The seated guests stood, and everyone looked toward the entrance. "Ladies and gentlemen," a man on the stage announced, "the President of the United States."

President Albert Rand and the First Lady strode into the room, flanked by aides, military officers, and Secret Service agents. The president was tall and dark haired, young for someone so powerful.

The DJ played "Hail to the Chief." Waylee composed lyrics on the fly.

Hail to the Thief,

He's a puppet and a bastard.

If you're not rich then

Your voice shall not be heard...

She caught Pel's eyes. "Let's move closer."

Too many others had the same idea, and she couldn't get within twenty feet.

A twenty-something blonde aide glanced at her watch and said something to the president. He nodded and strode toward the stage.

Waylee acted before the other guests and claimed a center seat in the front row. Pel roamed the periphery, presumably to collect more comlink data.

President Rand approached the microphone, confident like a rock star. "Well, thanks for coming. I'll be brief. I'll be done well before midnight."

A lot of people laughed. Waylee forced herself to chuckle.

President Rand's eyes settled on her for a full two seconds before moving on. "First off, I'd like to thank my good friend Bob Luxmore and V.I.P. Productions for putting this little shindig together."

Standing to the right of the stage, Luxmore put up a hand and smiled to applause.

"Second, I'd like to introduce my lovely wife, for those of you who haven't met her. Come on up, honey."

Mrs. Rand, an athletic-looking woman with overdone makeup, walked onto the stage and waved, then stood well to the side.

Problems on the marital front?

"Afraid this is too late for the kids," he said. "We'll have to do a day event sometime and everyone can bring their kids and grandkids. Great-great-grandkids, in the case of Senator Reichenbach there."

Even the senator laughed.

The president scanned the crowd. "It looks like we've got more wealth gathered here than the rest of the country put together. So I hope the food doesn't give you gas—it might crash the stock market."

More laughter. Waylee struggled to smirk. Until she realized he wasn't guarding his words.

"No, I've been assured this is top-notch fare. Just stay away from the Mexican stuff."

A few chuckles. Miss Cosimo would fantasize about bedding the president, so when he glanced at her again, Waylee sighed and smiled.

"This is an intimate gathering we have here," President Rand said, "so I'd like to hear from all of you, listen to advice you might have."

Her skin tingled with anticipation.

"Maybe you have campaign ideas," he continued, "or maybe just general advice, but I'm looking to get your perspectives. I'll be circulating; you don't have to stand in line. I'll get to everyone. And don't hold back, tell me what you really think."

"Who's your opponent going to be?" a man called out.

"Well," the president said, "there's no front runner yet, and it's premature to speculate. But with your help, we'll mop the floor with whoever they come up with, so it doesn't really matter. You know I won in a landslide last time, and I hope to win even bigger this time. And just as important, expand our party's margin in Congress, consolidate all the way down to city dogcatcher."

Applause all around.

"We won't concede a single state or a single race." He held up a finger. "Except maybe Vermont."

"Can't fight the kook factor," one of the guests said.

"So we can talk about the election and we can talk about policy. You know I made my fortune in the investment world, so I have a pretty good idea what makes our economy tick. I balanced the budget—"

Applause.

"And everyone here has prospered during my first term. Am I right?"

Nodding heads and affirming murmurs.

"And when you prosper, the country prospers. A rising tide lifts all boats. So my administration, with the help of our friends in Congress, has been expanding opportunities. Removing obstacles like high taxes and unnecessary regulations. Transferring assets like BLM land and national forests to those who'll put them to good use. Negotiating free trade agreements with the rest of the world. Encouraging new markets, like the explosion we've seen on the Comnet."

Vigorous applause.

Waylee wished she had a bomb underneath her dress, one that would take out the whole room. Except of course it would only turn these assholes into martyrs and accelerate the march toward a police state. No, she had to discredit them instead.

"Because as we know," the president continued, "growth only happens in the private sector. Government has one job—to maintain the peace and defend the country. Everything else is best left to the market."

Yet another round of applause.

"Of course, that's an ideal world I'm describing, where the individual is king and there's no need for government. We're in a state of transition now."

I don't see anyone in my neighborhood transitioning to prosperity.

"In a global economy, Americans have to work harder and smarter to compete. That's why I've focused so much on job training and encouraging placement services. We're working with schools to teach useful skills like computer programming and business, and give kids role models to follow. Even prisoners are learning work skills, given the chance to be productive, instead of just sitting in their cells and returning to a life of crime when they get out."

Privatizing schools, indoctrinating kids, and using prisons for cheap labor.

The president finished his speech, took a few questions, then stepped down from the stage. The blonde aide, a heavyset Asian woman wearing oversized goggles, and two Secret Servicemen ringed him. Next to the stage, he shook hands with Luxmore, first citizen on the social pyramid.

A picket of bigwigs and aides blocked Waylee's approach to the president. She couldn't get through without throwing an elbow. But her video needed face time, that was the whole point of being here.

She waved Pel over, then a caterer carrying a tray of martinis. Crowds always parted for pregnant women and alcohol. Plus, lips needed loosening.

Waylee led the caterer, a young brunette with flawless features, through the crowd. "Excuse me, pardon me." Pel followed.

They reached the inner circle. One of the Secret Servicemen peered at the martinis through his data glasses and stuck a small wand in each one. He nodded.

The president and Luxmore grabbed drinks and took long sips. They didn't bother thanking or acknowledging the caterer, and she wandered off to serve others. Waylee remained drinkless, but filled the vacated spot.

"Good speech, by the way," Luxmore told the president.

"Thanks, Bob. I assume I can count on your continued support?"

"Of course. You've been a good friend, Al. We've come a long way, but there's still so much more to do."

The president took another deep gulp of vodka or whatever it was. "I admire what you're doing with the free immersion units. All America should admire it. I'm going to mention it in the next State of the Union."

Waylee moved within kicking distance. "Free immersion units?"

Luxmore and the president turned toward her. The president smiled invitingly.

"This is the greatest honor of my life, Mr. President," she said.

"The honor is mine, Miss…"

"Cosimo. Estelle Cosimo. You can call me Estelle."

"Pleased to meet you, Estelle. You can call me Al." He thrust out a hand.

The chubby Asian woman pointed her big eye lenses at them as Waylee accepted the president's handshake.

"We'll send you a link to download your stills," the other aide, the blonde, said.

Waylee didn't want to be photographed, but Estelle would relish it. She smiled as the president's hand lingered in hers, then brushed the presidential thumb and batted her fake eyelashes at him.

Waylee pulled Pel forward with her eyes. "This is my fiancé, Greg Wilson."

Pel shook the president's hand, also smiling for the official camera. "It's an honor, sir. My uncle's Richard Shafer."

Luxmore's eyebrows raised.

"A big supporter of mine," President Al said. "It's too bad he couldn't come."

"He sends his regrets."

"Don't worry about the free immersion systems," Luxmore told Pel/Greg. "Tell your uncle not to fret. They'll be pared down, ultra-cheap, made with robots and prison labor."

"Bob's reaching out to the underserved," the president said. "MediaCorp is performing another great service, just as they did creating the Comnet and increasing transmission speeds over a thousandfold."

"Didn't the government pay for all the optic lines?" Waylee asked.

The president raised an eyebrow. "A partnership. MediaCorp developed the software and built the server facilities."

Luxmore scowled at Waylee and addressed Pel. "We're still working out the details, but there'll be a presentation before the board in a couple of months. We'll more than make our money back analyzing user activity and directing tailored ads. If you buy the equipment and software, you can opt out of the ads, of course."

"Good incentive to buy," Pel said. "And I assume you have advertisers lined up?"

"We have some preliminary handshakes. Details are a little too in the trenches for me."

The president peered at Waylee's hand. "It looks like your fiancé neglected to give you a ring."

Waylee mentally slapped herself. "It's being resized."

Pel leaned forward. "To tell you the truth, Mr. President, her first ring wasn't quite what she deserves. I'm having a show-stopper custom made. It was supposed to be a surprise."

Waylee gave him an appreciative look.

"Well this would have been the place to show it off," the president said. "It's a pity you didn't time it better." He finished his martini and handed the empty glass to his assistant.

Waylee wished for a martini or twelve. "Enough about my ring. You're the star of the show here, Al, if I really can call you that."

"Of course you can." He smiled.

"So it sounds like you're pretty confident about the election."

He looked at her and raised an eyebrow. "But you have reservations?"

This would be dangerous, but her video needed material. "Like you said in your speech, your policies benefit those of us here."

The president nodded and his lips parted.

Waylee plowed forward before he could interrupt. "But we're such a tiny fraction of the electorate. What about the people who work long hours but can't buy a house, can't send their kids to college, or can't even see a doctor when they get sick? There are a lot more of them than there are of us, and you're doing *nothing* for them. How are you going to get *their* votes?"

The president frowned. "You sound like an agitator, one of those People's Party socialists."

Luxmore's scowl deepened. Pel retreated a step.

I'm more of an anarcho-syncretist, but good guess. "You said not to hold back. I just wonder why you're so confident."

The president stared at her, then turned and waved over a short man with boyish features. "Estelle here is worried about my chances. Thinks the masses will blame their problems on me."

The man pulled a card out of a coat pocket and handed it to her. "Rick Mustel. Special Advisor to the President for the Media."

"Estelle Cosimo." She shook his hand. It felt clammy.

Pel didn't introduce himself. He wasn't staying in character very well.

Special Advisor Mustel waved his hands as he spoke. "We've got a strategy for that. People are surprisingly easy to influence once you know how their minds work. For starters, people make most decisions using their guts, not logic. That's just the way we operate."

Rationalism keeps fascism at bay. Emotion and logic have to work together in a positive framework...

Waylee couldn't articulate her argument without breaking character, and Mustel continued. "Back in the 1980s, psychologists studied how news anchors changed their facial expressions when mentioning presidential candidates, and how these subtle cues influenced voters. Peter Jennings, an anchor for ABC News, was downright enthusiastic about Ronald Reagan. You could see it in his face. And his viewers voted overwhelmingly for Reagan, much more so than viewers of other news programs. That was forty years ago. We've learned and refined since then, and know exactly how to push emotional buttons so people will do whatever we want without having the slightest clue about it."

"So you see," the president said, "we've got a handle on that."

Luxmore stepped forward. "People are generally stupid," he said. "That's why they need ones like us to tell them what to do. It's been that way since the day humans first gathered together in villages."

"Men of gold," Mustel said.

"What?" Pel said.

Waylee started to explain, but Luxmore was quicker. "Plato's philosopher-kings. Bred and educated to make the right decisions."

"Exactly," the president said. "Most people don't know what's in their best interest. Anyone can get ahead if they work hard, but America has been lulled into dependency by ninety years of socialism, the growth of a nanny state. I'm trying to change that, encourage people to better themselves. People's lives get better, the economy grows, revenues grow and we keep the deficit under control."

Is that his golden rule? Waylee directed her response to both Luxmore and the president. "What about all men and women being created equal? That governments should consent to the will of the governed?"

Luxmore ignored her. Mustel's eyes widened. The president laughed and shook his head. "Well, Jefferson was certainly a great man, but what does that have to do with what we're talking about?"

A thousand angry hornets buzzed inside her skull. "Excuse me?"

Pel gave her the cease and desist look. She fought for control.

The president's smile disappeared. He glanced at Mustel, then back

copied her tactic, lifting a spoonful of whipped cream and a couple of blueberries into her mouth. It tasted surprisingly fresh. "So now, if you're an independent content provider...."

Ms. Baddelats waved her spoon like a metronome. "If you're not affiliated with MediaCorp, and you want your movie shown or your game played or your article read, you rent the bandwidth, buy ads, and try to pass the costs to your customers. If you're too cheap to pay, there's still some old Internet routes, but good luck finding anyone willing to wait hours for your material to load. Brilliant business model, they say." She dove back into the parfait.

Waylee suppressed her anger. "So it seems. I assume the free immersion suits are also a long-term strategy?"

She looked up. "I asked him about that, right after your little argument, actually. Why President Rand knew about this planned suit giveaway but the company board didn't. Bob downplayed the short-term costs, talked about targeted ads to the users, but the real goal is to move more people onto BetterWorld."

"Makes sense, MediaCorp even controls the currency there."

"Yes, but I have to admit, I've never taken a shine to it. I have been fighting to put age restrictions on BetterWorld, time restrictions too, but unfortunately I'm in the minority. How is the next generation going to manage the world if they've grown up in a womb of make believe?"

You are my new best friend. "You are so right. But I assume Luxmore wants the whole planet immersed in BetterWorld?"

Ms. Baddelats shuffled her feet. "As soon as we make it more hacker-proof, he said. Apparently it has security issues."

Charles. She fought not to smile. "He's pretty involved in politics."

"Perhaps overly so." Ms. Baddelats poked her spoon between the remaining berries to reach the ice cream beneath.

"Do you think he'll run for president after Rand's next term?" She knew the answer, but wanted video comments.

Ms. Baddelats looked up from her parfait and snorted. "Oh, heavens no. What an enormous waste of time that would be. No, he's content to pull strings behind the scenes to get his way. That's the real reason I don't like him. The man scares me. You wouldn't believe the influence he has."

Waylee started to ask for details, but the woman was on a roll. "He's both CEO and Chairman of the Board, plus the largest stockholder. That's really too much control, considering we're now the biggest company in the world. At the very least, he should step down as Chairman. But 'you don't put shackles on visionaries,' he says if someone dares suggest it. Balderdash, I say. If you ask me, the man's got a Napoleon complex. You ought to hear him in the boardroom, talking about bettering humanity. His version, mind you, not mine, which is more about being a decent Christian."

She hooked her fingers into quote marks, somehow managing not to drop anything. "'We can create a world where those with ability can do anything they imagine. We must work with politicians to ensure that moochers, obstructionists, and naysayers don't get in the way of progress.' How is that a core business model? How does that help starving children?"

Ms. Baddelats seemed done with her tirade, so Waylee asked, "Can you force him out?"

"If there's a way." She patted Waylee on the shoulder. "Wish me luck. Now if you'll excuse me."

She handed the remnants of her parfait to another server and took careful steps toward two of her colleagues.

Holy crap, I might have a friend in high places.

The music stopped and the president returned to the stage. "I've been given the honor of counting down the last seconds of an exceptional year and bringing in an even better one." He peered at his watch. "Ok... ready?" and he began counting.

"Three... Two... One... Happy New Year!"

The jazz band played "Auld Lang Syne" and guests drank and cheered and blew on noisemakers.

Waylee didn't pay attention because she was kissing Pel. Without him, she wouldn't be here. She'd probably have killed herself by now. Their kiss lingered and lingered, heat rushed through her veins, and she wanted him right there in front of everyone.

She realized people were staring. Including President Al. "Mingle some more, darling," she whispered, and kissed Pel's earlobe. "Back to work."

As the band pounded out some sort of zoot suit leg-shaker, Waylee fixed her eyes on the president and strode over. She slithered past a blockade of irritated guests, then the president dispersed the circle around him and waved her the rest of the way in.

President Al smiled when she arrived. "That was quite a kiss." He teetered a little on his feet.

Waylee decided to exaggerate her buzz. "I'm drunk."

He drew closer. "You're allowed. It's New Year's." She could smell the alcohol on his breath.

"I believe you promised me a toast." Estelle would want a dance, but of course that would be scandalous.

"Didn't you hear me?"

"I meant… uh, something more personal."

From somewhere inside, man-neurons widened his eyes and lifted his eyebrows. He shooed his photographer away and raised two fingers to the young blonde aide.

The aide turned to a small table and hurried over with two glasses of ice and a half-full bottle, "Glenmorangie" at the top of the elegant label, "30" beneath. She poured them each a drink.

President Al peered at the amber liquid in the glass, then sniffed it. "This Glenmorangie was sitting in a cask before you were born, waiting patiently for this very moment."

"To America," Waylee proposed.

"America."

They clinked glasses and drank, Waylee fighting her instincts and sipping, President Al gulping half the contents. Smoke turned to honey and lingered on her tongue.

Where to begin? "So how can I best help your campaign?"

His eyes roved across her body, just for an instant. "What do you want to do?"

She gave him the coy Estelle smile. "Well, I'm definitely a people person." She wasn't lying there.

He took another sip, eyes fixed on her. The aide pretended to look away.

"And I love video. Your media advisor seems quite an expert."

President Al snorted. "I'm surrounded by so-called experts." He sipped again. "It's refreshing to talk to someone real."

Estelle would beam at a compliment from the president, so Waylee gave her warmest smile. "Thank you."

"I tell you, the toughest part of this job is looking in a camera and spouting out a bunch of B.S. to keep my poll numbers up."

"Then why do you do it? Why not just say what you think?"

The aide stared at her, as if she wanted her to move along but didn't dare say so.

President Al finished his Scotch. "Are you kidding?" He held up his glass and shook it. "First thing they teach you in politics—control the message."

The aide refilled their glasses.

Time for more material. "And that must be easier with Bob Luxmore on your side."

He nodded, then frowned. "I heard about that little outburst earlier."

Uh oh.

"He does have a temper sometimes," he continued. "I hope you'll excuse him." He didn't wait for her to respond. "Fact is, our country wouldn't be where it is today without Bob Luxmore and people like him. He's a pioneer, like the old railroad builders and industrialists."

"And he's been your number one supporter."

He swirled his glass, the ice jostling together and plowing aside the liquid. "It takes more than one person to win an election."

He wasn't exactly forthcoming with the sound bites. "Yes," she said, "but MediaCorp does what you want, covers what you want. That's a pretty big advantage, considering they control the entire Comnet."

He raised an eyebrow but nodded. "We just happen to agree on a lot, share a common vision. I don't sit on the board like your fiancé's uncle. I don't tell their anchors what to say."

Two possible tacks. She picked the first. "What's the common vision?"

His eyes sparkled. "A golden age where personal rights are respected, and great men—and women—are free to create wealth that lifts the economy and benefits everyone." He drank again.

"Like the Comnet?"

"Yes, the Comnet's a great example. Sure, the previous administration paid for the lines in exchange for free government access. But mostly it's been a private venture, and my administration hasn't interfered." He glanced at his watch.

You can't go yet. "But you share information, right?"

"As a matter of national security, of course. Their resources are incredible. You should know that."

"Like how incredible? My fiancé never tells me anything."

He smirked. "Let me put it this way, we're headed toward a world where MediaCorp knows everything about everyone. It's inevitable. Everyone's on the Comnet except an Appalachian mountain man or two." He laughed.

Waylee felt sick. "And the free immersion suits will help, I assume."

He nodded. "And wait until they perfect neural implants."

What?

"So of course we've got to work together, ferret out terrorists and criminals." He looked at his watch again.

Waylee licked her lips to keep his attention. She decided to boil the water. "But aren't you worried? How sure are you Luxmore's not playing both sides? You know, sharing information with your opponents to hedge his bets?"

The aide tensed. President Al's eyes narrowed. "I understand you're mad at him, but we're on the same side. We help each other out."

He admits it at last!

"Luxmore works for you, then?"

He threw his shoulders back. "He's a smart man, and I'm probably the closest he has to a friend."

"So MediaCorp persuades the public to support you…"

"Staying on message, we call it."

She suppressed her anger. "And like you said, they've got the world's biggest database. Luxmore must know everything about you. What if he leaked something damaging?"

"About me?" He shook his head. "He wouldn't. Which is good —he can turn anything into a public issue. Name a person alive who doesn't have skeletons in their closet."

Her stomach churned. "Sounds like quite a partnership. The sky's the limit, it sounds like."

He finished his drink. "Like I said, maybe he has some anger issues, probably his first wife's fault, but yes, I consider him a good and loyal friend."

The First Lady stomped over and grabbed her husband's arm. "There you are." She cast suspicious eyes toward Waylee/Estelle. "And who is this?"

President Al introduced her, then said, "I'm afraid I have more mingling to do. Thank you for coming, Estelle, and please give your information to my campaign manager."

The First Lady glared at her as they left. Everyone else seemed to glare at her too.

If only she could keep this persona, the things she could do. By tomorrow, though, word of tonight's antics would get to the real Estelle and the gig would be over.

19

January 1
St. Mary's County, Maryland

Pelopidas

We did it! In the back seat of an electric SUV, Pelopidas squeezed Waylee's hand. She squeezed back, harder.

Their taxi driver had dropped them off at a house in Greenbelt, and an elderly couple, friends of Shakti, picked them up on the next block to transport them to their next temporary digs, a cooperative farm in St. Mary's County. Shakti, Dingo, and Charles had already moved there.

The old man, Peter, wore actual suspenders and sported a long white beard. Sunshine, the woman, had grey hair and a plaid house dress that might have been fashionable a hundred years ago in rural Iowa. She volunteered that she and Peter were not in fact a couple, but "got along well enough."

Waylee leaned forward. "So you're activists in the People's Party?"

Sunshine, riding shotgun, turned and smiled. "Maybe not activists like Shakti. But we do what we can to promote a more peaceful and sustainable world."

Waylee nodded. "Sweetchious."

Peter, behind the wheel, spoke when they hit the interstate. "Was it worth the risk?"

"It was fucking incredible," Waylee shouted. Her breath reeked of bourbon or whatever she'd been drinking.

Sunshine frowned.

"Sorry," she said in a quieter voice. "Pardon my French, as my new best friend Betty Battleaxe says."

"Waylee's had a lot to drink," Pel said. *More likely, her hypomania's peaking.*

Waylee slapped the back of Sunshine's seat. "President Al admitted he's a corrupt son of a bitch and MediaCorp pulls the strings. We've got it all on video."

Sunshine didn't share her excitement. "Those people make me sick."

Waylee tugged Pel's jacket.

"What is it?"

"President Al said MediaCorp's developing neural interfaces. Can they do that, hook your brain up directly to the Comnet?"

He laughed. "That's decades away, even if it's possible at all. I mean, we've come a long way with artificial limbs and eyes and whatnot, but they can't replicate reality or read your thoughts. The brain's just too complicated."

Waylee sat back. "Well that's good to know."

Pel turned to Sunshine. "So Shakti said you have an optic line?"

She nodded. "High capacity. So we can connect to the rest of the world and share our experiences."

Waylee raised her voice again. "That's fucking perfect. You're perfect, all of you." She turned to Pel. "Remind me to make sweet love to Shakti when we get there."

"I will not," Pel said. She was joking, of course. Waylee had never been interested in women, nor shown any sign she'd cheat on him.

Maybe we should get married when this is all over. His family didn't like Waylee yet, but at least they'd given up trying to get him back with Audrey. He'd have to buy a ring, maybe not up to Greg and Estelle's standards, but something nice.

Pel massaged Waylee's hand, warming his fingers with hers. "I love you."

She turned and kissed him. "Love you too. Thanks for making this possible."

They exited the interstate onto State Road 5, then drove south past dark forests and fields.

"We're still in Maryland?" Waylee asked.

"It's not all developed yet," Sunshine said. "Just most of it."

Several turns later, they arrived at an LED-illuminated sign labeled "Welcome to Friendship Farm." Underneath, "An intentional community."

"Here we are," Peter said.

An unpaved road took them past fields, solar panels, wooden buildings, and silos. They parked in front of a well-lit two-story house with mismatched wings. Smaller houses nestled among bare trees beyond. Someone strummed a guitar inside the main building.

The front door opened into a big living room full of people. It smelled like stewed tomatoes and incense. Shakti, her wide face beaming, hugged Waylee, then Pel. "It's a good thing you ignored my skepticism," she told Waylee. "I'm so in awe of you."

Dingo smacked fists with them. Charles did the same. Over two dozen others greeted them, ranging from ancients to infants. Everyone wanted to know everything.

"Can we trust all these people?" Pel whispered to Shakti.

"Of course. They think you're heroes. That's why all the kids are up past their bedtimes."

He didn't feel like a hero. They still had a lot more work to do.

Waylee pulled the clips out of her bun and shook her hair into chaos. "Got anything to drink here?"

"We make wine and mead," a thirtyish woman said.

"And grow the best pot in Maryland," a brown-bearded man said, putting aside a guitar.

Dingo threw up a fist. "Break that shit out."

Pel began unhooking the micro-cameras from his suit and Waylee's dress. He'd start with the ghost snares tomorrow.

The brown-bearded man shooed a group of kids off a solid-looking wall bench, removed the seat cover, and tapped numbers on a keypad. "A lot of folk prefer them synthdrugs, but this is better for you. All natural, 100% organic." He lifted back the seat and pulled out a large glass canister half filled with green and orange buds.

Waylee settled into a chair with a bottle labeled "Friendship Farm 100% Organic Mead." Bongs passed around the room, bypassing the kids.

Charles leaned toward Pel. "I saw this huge rat before you got here. Shit, I thought the ones in B'more were big, they ain't got nothin' on this one."

Pel kept working, but Peter spoke. "We don't have any rats here, just mice."

"Weren't no mouse. Thing was size of a cat. Ran under the front porch."

Peter laughed. "That's a possum, son. He lives there." Others joined the laughter.

Waylee struggled to her feet. "I just want to thank you all for putting us up. We're going to make history."

The thirtyish woman frowned. "How long will you be here?"

Peter spoke at the same time. "No one can know Friendship Farm's involved."

Waylee thrust up her mead bottle and bounced the top against her forehead. "Our secret."

Ignoring a familiar half embarrassment, half pride in his girlfriend, Pel plugged one of the micro-cameras into an interface. "Let's take a look at the video." He switched on the room's outdated wall screen.

Video and audio quality were as good as the practice runs. Pel forwarded past the dull parts, and paused when his audience burst into discussion or howls of outrage, which was often.

Between the two cameras, they had twelve hours of footage. Way too much for one sitting. The residents with kids drifted away first, then others followed. Pel ended the show after a couple of hours, too tired to stay up any longer.

"So now what?" Dingo said.

"Tomorrow we start working on the comlink signals." He turned to Charles. "And getting on the MediaCorp feed."

Charles looked away and said, "Gotta sleep."

Had he had even thought about how to get their video on the air? They hadn't talked about it.

They also hadn't really talked about their future prospects. They couldn't stay long at the farm, or anywhere else he could think of. They might be hunted the rest of their lives, especially if Homeland identified them as Greg and Estelle. Hunted until they were caught or dropped dead from the stress.

Sunshine led Pel and Waylee upstairs to a small wallpapered room with two single beds, an upholstered chair, and a wooden dresser. "Good night."

Waylee pushed the beds together, strutted over to him, and ran a hand down his shirt and into his pants.

"It's almost dawn, Waylee."

"Estelle. You're gonna fuck me 'til I'm sore, President Al. I know you want to." She unbuckled his belt and removed it. "And then I'm gonna punish you for being bad." She snapped the belt with a crack.

January 1
Afternoon

Shakti

Digesting a late lunch, Shakti sat in a wicker egg chair in the main house's spacious sun room. Rain pattered against the glass roof panes. Dingo lay in a Brazilian hammock, smoking pungent Friendship's Finest from a pipe.

"It's the middle of winter," she said. "It used to snow this time of year."

Dingo glanced over and shrugged.

Shakti closed her eyes, the symphony of raindrops calming her spirit. She'd known Sunshine and most of the others at Friendship Farm long enough to trust them. Since Maryland legalized marijuana a few years back, they'd planted twenty acres of designer strains. They traded for most of their needs, creating a virtual currency, and donated most of their dollar income to the People's Party and its associated charities. The party's state coordinating council and committees met at the farm occasionally. She always attended those meetings and stayed the night. A chance to get away from The Gritty City. And get high as the jet stream.

She opened her eyes again. Maybe they could stay here permanently. She'd have to buy more clothes. "This would be such a great place to live. Maybe it's a blessing we've been exiled from Baltimore."

Dingo sat up, his never-combed hair squished on one side. "Do I look like a mother fuckin' farmer? I'm thinking New York or Montreal."

Why were they even a couple? *The boy's so damn selfish.* "Well g'long t' New York or Montreal, see's I care, but I nah go with you!" Her skin flushed; she'd shouted and slipped into Guyanese.

Dingo's eyes widened for a second. He emptied the pipe ashes into a small bowl on an adjacent pub table. "Whatever, do what you want. I'm not gonna tell you what to do, but no way am I living someplace where the idea of fun is watching plants grow and weaving underwear from corn husks. This is the 21st century A.D., not B.C."

Was he making fun of her? "This is the real world right here, not your concrete monstrosities. New York, Montreal." She spat. "How long would all those city people last without farms, forests, and oceans puttin' food in their mouths and oxygen in their lungs? Humans, we's a part of nature, part of the whole, and when you forget that, you tapin' dirty socks over your eyes and stumblin' around like a damn fool, stompin' all over the garden that keeps you alive, and then walkin' off the nearest cliff."

Dingo flinched. "Damn, girl. I'm just sayin', this ain't my thing."

"Why can't you try something new for once? Your feet are too small, that's your problem." He wasn't a BetterWorld addict like Kiyoko and Charles, but he wasn't far above.

Waylee and Pel entered the room, hand in hand. They'd been even louder than usual last night until Shakti got up and banged on their door and told them there were kids in nearby houses.

"There you are," Waylee said. She looked more like herself, wearing jeans and a music festival T-shirt, and her jewelry back in. Without his beard, Pel still looked like a stranger.

Shakti abandoned the wicker chair and hugged her friend and hero, the agitation with Dingo under control. "Slept all day?" The sun was already sinking toward the horizon.

"Needed it." Waylee withdrew from the hug. "Got a lot to do now. Do you mind helping me ditch the blonde hair?"

"Sure. What'll it be?"

"Orange and red waves, like fire."

Dingo plopped out of the hammock. "So when are we getting this footage out?"

"I have to edit it," Waylee said, "and Pel and Charles have to analyze the comlink data."

"Which'll take a while," Pel said.

"And we gotta stick around here in the meantime?" Dingo said. "Shakti and I should take off. You don't need us anymore."

"I'm staying," Shakti said. "Dingo, don't go." He made life interesting, helped her forget the world was dying, helped keep her sane.

Waylee stared at Dingo. "Where are you going?"

Dingo shrugged.

"Then you're not in a hurry. Let's talk to Charles and work out a timeline."

Waylee

Waylee led Shakti and Pel into the adjacent living room. They found Charles at a desk in a small alcove. His fingers flew across the glassy touch pad and virtual keyboard of an interface unit, one of several in the house. It looked like the Genki-san in the band house but with a big popup screen attached. Thick headphones covered Charles's ears, and a microphone perched in front of his mouth.

The screen showed a familiar pink-haired girl sitting on a low bed, surrounded by hanging silks. Her sister.

"Hey, it's Kiyoko!" Shakti said. "Can she see us?"

Charles didn't respond.

Waylee tapped on his shoulder.

He pulled off the headphones. His face knotted with irritation. "What?"

"Can Kiyoko see us?" Waylee said. *What's up with the décor?* "Where is she?"

Charles pointed to a piece of black electrical tape on the monitor. "First thing I did when I got here was tape over all the cameras. I customed the firewalls to keep other hackers out, but best to keep the tape on while we're here."

"How's she doing? This is BetterWorld, right?"

"Yeah, but your peeps got no immersion unit, not even goggles," he said. He turned to Pel. "You shouldn't have traded your gaming gear away."

Pel huffed. "No choice. Those ghost snares were expensive, and Kiyoko's BetterWorld credits didn't cover everything."

Waylee pointed at the screen. "So are you almost done here?"

"We're trying to decide when to broadcast Waylee's mashup," Pel said.

"Just figure it out. I'm busy here." Charles put the headphones back on.

Pel's face contorted, as if he might go postal on the boy.

Waylee touched his arm. "We can talk to him later. It'll take me days to put the video together."

The door to the dining hall was open. She walked over and peeked inside. The long tables were unoccupied, but conversation and chopping noises leaked from the adjoining kitchen.

She closed the door for privacy and returned to Pel, Shakti, and Dingo. "I'm going to assume Charles can get us onto MediaCorp. We need a feed with maximum viewership."

"Super Bowl's coming up," Dingo said.

Waylee almost jumped out of her shoes. "When is it?"

"Month from now," Pel said. "February 4th. Miami Dolphins vs. New York Giants. It's being held in Atlanta."

"At last your sports trivia comes in handy." Waylee bounded over to another interface unit and powered it on. She opened a search program and spoke, "Number of super bowl viewers."

She followed a link. 210 million viewers last year, two-thirds of them Americans. The most watched event in U.S. history, well over the critical mass she needed.

She kept digging. Pundits expected this year's Super Bowl to be even bigger.

* * *

Pelopidas

Charles was still on the Comnet when Pel returned from dinner. He was losing weight, whether from healthier food or skimpier portions, but skipping meals altogether might make him sick.

Charles turned and removed his headphones. "When are we bailing the country?"

"Another message from Kiyoko?"

"Gotta admit, freedom beats jail."

"We're okay for now," Pel said. "We've still got a lot to do."

His lips pinched together.

"You know, there's still plenty of food left in the kitchen. I can make you a plate."

Charles shrugged. Then his eyebrows raised. "Can I help with the decryption?"

"Sure, but getting into MediaCorp should be your top priority. You're the only one who knows how to do it."

He looked away. "I've got god powers on BetterWorld now. I had passwords to some other MediaCorp sites, but most of them don't work anymore."

Hard to stay ahead in this game. "They must have identified all the people you owned and cancelled their access."

"Yeah. All their avatars were deleted too. Good thing is, some of the backdoors I set up still work. Rest, I think the computers were wiped. And we can still get on the central intranet, no problem there."

"Watch for traps."

"I'm real careful now. But check this out." Charles led him to the Comnet interface he'd been using. "A hundred gigabits per second, yo."

"Not bad for a farm." Although they had a profitable crop.

Charles brought up a long discussion thread on one of the restricted Collective forums. Their owning of the BetterWorld programmers had been voted "Op of the Year." Speculation varied about who was behind it, but one Collectivista wrote, "the vampire bot technique is classic Dr. Doom. The BetterWorld exploiter who hoaxed MediaCorp, busted out of prison, and laughed at Authority on his way to freedom. If it's you, Dr. Doom, hats off to you."

Pel smacked fists with him. "You, sir, are a legend in the making." *It means Homeland will up the search, though.*

Pel loaded the data from the ghost snares onto Big Red, the home-built supercomputer he'd brought from the band house. The data was too sensitive for the Comnet, no matter how secure his cloud partitions might be. Then he inserted the memory wafer with the decryption software and copied the files.

Sure, they'd recorded some interesting video at the gala, but the comlinks were the real treasure. If they cracked the signals, they should be able to access messages, documents, even spy on the users through their cameras and microphones. The whole world could learn the elite's most embarrassing secrets.

Pel started the decryption program, which loaded a Pandora Productions banner on the top. He pointed to the first data file and hit the "Visualize raw data" tab. A three dimensional graph of peaks and troughs appeared. "Those are digital 1s and 0s leaking from comlink processors. The higher the peak, the stronger the signal. When I figure out how to sync the timestamp on this data with the video timestamp, the strongest signals will correspond to the people closest to me."

Charles nodded.

"The hard part will be deciphering all these signals. There'll be more than one from each comlink. I've been researching it, though. The comlink displays have characteristic frequencies. We can read what shows up on the screen."

"They aren't shielded?"

"They are, but not perfectly. Our ghost snares could pick up the tiniest traces. And there's the net transmissions, which are strong but encoded."

Charles rolled his eyes. "Everyone knows that."

"But one of the faint signals will come from the processor's encryption calculations, and we can use that to identify the key, decipher all the Comnet transmissions, and even impersonate the owner."

Charles threw him a bro fist. "Hoist the Jolly Roger."

Pel explored the software options. One tab tested different cryptographic algorithms to identify the comlink's key. He could also adjust the parameters to determine target frequencies, adjust the signal to noise ratios, discriminate between different sources, and a lot more. But mostly you had to write scripts, and none of it was intuitive.

He scrolled through the documentation. It was full of matrix algebra, differential equations, and obscure terms like "Kronecker delta function." Without an electrical engineering degree, how the hell would he make sense of it?

His stomach clenched. *Did we ruin our lives for nothing?*

21

January 4

Waylee

The Friendship Farm residents loaned Waylee a clunky-looking laptop. Like all the farm computers, it had been custom built by techies in Takoma Park, a DC suburb governed by the People's Party, and ran an Ectoplasm GUI over ArchDruid Linux. It had a standalone roll-up screen she could clip to a frame or tack to a wall, kind of like Pel's computer. Waylee brought a small wooden table into the room, set up the equipment, and confined herself there. The first thing she did was wipe the hard drive and reinstall Linux, then all the other programs she needed, so the computer couldn't be traced back to the farm.

She had to sort through twelve hours of New Year's footage, add background material, and compose narratives and music. She'd structure the video like a breaking news story, where you had to grab the viewer and summarize the most important information in the first thirty seconds, and then add increasing layers of detail. Trouble was, Pel wasn't making much progress with the comlink data and she needed that to decide where to focus.

Pel opened the bedroom door, as if she'd summoned him. He started to say something, then stopped.

"What?"

He closed the door behind him and sat on the joined beds, pushing aside the rumpled sheets. "I have some good news and some bad news."

"Can't you speak without clichés?"

His eyes narrowed. "Yeah, well I can do some things you haven't a clue about. Like, I found some video tutorials on signal processing, and it's making more sense now. That's the good news."

He's a techie. Why does he need video tutorials? "And the bad news?"

He smirked. "Will you whip me with my belt again?"

"If you're talking about our roles as Estelle and President Al, those were just love smacks. Lucky for you I respect your boundaries." She locked eyes with him. "Actually, I'm sorry I did it at all. Too much to drink."

He leaned back. "And if I really were the president?"

"I'd have been…. Uh, less restrained." She slid her bulky chair away from the computer table, scraping the wooden floor in the process. *Oops.* "So what's this sort of bad news? Obviously it's not catastrophic or you'd have come out and said so."

"Homeland thinks Charles was behind that BetterWorld op, where he hacked into their system."

"Well he was, wasn't he?"

"Yeah, but they figured it out, or guessed it, and the FBI's offering a million dollar reward. And a hundred thousand each for me, you, Dingo, and Shakti. Broadcast all over the Comnet."

Waylee relaxed. "That's it? That means they don't know we were Estelle and Greg."

Pel leaned forward. "Yeah, they'd be pretty panicked about that. But Charles had to delete his avatar."

She shrugged. "So he'll create a new one."

"Yeah, I don't think he can go a day without seeing Kiyoko."

Waylee bolted from her chair. "What do you mean see? He's barely seventeen."

"It's just BetterWorld." Pel stroked his chin, now rough with stubble. "She probably doesn't know it's Charles."

I don't have time to babysit long distance.

"Pel, can you straighten that out? I don't want anyone, Charles included, messing with my little sister. Remember how long she cried after her last boyfriend?"

"Yeah, but he was an asshole, slept with two of her friends."

True. Which was why Waylee smacked him on the side of the head with a bottle of gin, and while he was out cold on the floor of the club, took a sharpie and drew a dick on his forehead. "I'm not saying Charles isn't a nice kid. But one or both of them are likely to get hurt, and I can't deal with the extra drama."

Pel gave her the ironic eyebrow.

She ignored it. "You've got a rapport with him. I'll just piss him off and we need him."

"I'm sure it's all harmless." He stood.

Men always stick together. The bro code. "Well Kiyoko's my sister, don't forget. And we can't have Charles moping around with a broken heart."

She glanced at the door. "I'll talk to Shakti. Someone here could make a fortune by ratting us out."

Shakti wasn't in her bedroom. They walked downstairs, then Pel headed back to his computer.

She heard Shakti in the sun room arguing with Dingo. Her voice sounded distinctly Caribbean, which only happened under stress.

The two stopped and stared when she entered.

"Something wrong?" Waylee asked.

"Nah," Dingo said. "She's just being bossy, probably taking after you."

Waylee didn't bother editing her thoughts. "Grow the fuck up."

Shakti, who was still wearing the saffron sari she fled her workplace in, strode over and nudged her into the living room. "Dingo wants to leave. Boy says he can steal a car and sneak into Canada. Good riddance I say."

"Come on, you can't mean that. Sure he's an ass sometimes, but he's good at the core."

Shakti crossed her arms. "So what do you want?"

I bet real revolutionaries aren't distracted by personal drama. She led Shakti up to her bedroom and shut the door. "Did you know the FBI issued a huge reward for us?"

Shakti's arms unfolded. "How huge?"

"One million for Charles, a hundred thousand for the rest of us."

"How come he's worth ten times the rest of us?"

Waylee shrugged. "Our price may rise. But you know these people better than I do. Would anyone turn us in?"

"I don't think so. Your footage really riled them up. Peter and Sunshine watched all twelve hours."

"So, no worries?"

Shakti pressed her lips together. "It is a lot of money…"

Waylee's optimism evaporated. "Can you find out? On the sly?"

She looked down at her feet. "Yeah."

* * *

January 5

Dingo

"Smell you later, bitches!" Dingo hopped into the trash-filled cab of an old pickup truck. A pungent Rastafarian named Raustis sat behind the wheel.

Nobody looked happy. Shakti looked about to cry.

Sorry. But he had to do what he had to do. Time to move on. "You got my new Comnet ID, stay in touch. I'll let you know where I settle." He blew Shakti a kiss. "'Til next we meet."

Raustis threw the truck into gear and off they drove down the dirt road. "I'll take you up to Baltimore, but can't take you any further."

"Thanks bro. I'd have said DC, but that place got cameras everywhere."

They exited the farm and drove north. Dingo had shaved his head and changed piercings to disguise himself. He had his bag o' tricks, some clothes and shit, his stun gun, a new comlink, and an empty wallet. No gas money. He'd refused to borrow anything from Shakti – she was near broke herself. Pel, Waylee, and Charles – none of them had a cent left. Hard way to televise the revolution.

Raustis switched on the truck's sound system and tapped a playlist link on the display. Heavy dub bass boomed through the cabin. "Where in Baltimore are you going?" he shouted over the music.

"Putty Hill. Need to earn some money off the grid so I can get to Montreal." *Paulo said he'd throw some work my way.*

"Where's Putty Hill? Never heard of it."

"Northeast suburbs."

Raustis frowned. "That's a two hour drive."

"Just take me to a bus stop then."

"Buses and trains all got cameras."

"Yeah," Dingo said, "but I look different now."

"Not that different. And how you gonna pay the fare? No, I take you, then check up on our distributors, make sure they not cutting our product or other such mischief."

"Need backup? I know Krav Maga like most people know breathing." He threw a couple of quick punches to the air.

"Near tempting, but a man with a price on his head bring about bad vibrations."

22

January 6

Charles

Charles abandoned his fruitless work on the Comnet and joined Pel in the humid cellar beneath the big house. Bottles of homemade wine and mead filled wall racks floor to ceiling. Barrels crowded the concrete floor. Pel sat at a table made from unfinished planks, staring at Big Red's clip-up screen.

A million dollar reward. Biggest price on a hacker ever. He must have owned some big players. The downside was, he lost an awesome avatar. He'd put a lot of work into Iwisa. But with all the uproar over his vampire attack, he had to delete it. No more horse rides with Princess Kiyoko.

Pel pushed back his wooden chair. His eyes were red. "Can't get anything useable from the government comlinks. The president, the Congressmen, their staff, all seem to have special shielding and encryption. No detectable processor signals, and our program can't decipher the screen or transmission signals. Must be state of the art NSA stuff."

"What about the others?"

"That's the good news. Luxmore and his wife have NSA tech, but the others we can crack. Including the MediaCorp board members. It'll just take a while."

Pel didn't have a Comnet connection down here. He seemed to get more paranoid by the day. Wouldn't be long before he wore aluminum foil on his head. Trouble was, that shit was contagious. "Should we tell Waylee?"

"Yeah." He locked his supercomputer—even Charles didn't know the password. "How's the Super Bowl feed coming?"

"Uh…" Charles wondered the best way to confess.

"Well, we've got plenty of time. Come on." They climbed two sets of stairs to the guest rooms.

In the bedroom she shared with Pel, Waylee sat at a desk staring at her computer screen, moving video clips with an editing program. "Hi guys," she said without turning.

"Pretty sure I can get some material from the comlinks," Pel said, "except for the government ones. They're levels ahead."

Waylee turned and smiled. "Got anything good yet?"

"Working on it."

"Any progress on the Super Bowl?"

Charles thought about turning and running, but stood his ground. "About that. It's impossible to do remotely. You need an insider."

Waylee froze like ice.

"But you did it before," Pel said. "Put that zombie message on the news ticker."

"I wanted to tell you, an insider helped me. An engineer most likely, but a closet Collectivista. We're everywhere."

Waylee just sat there.

"This engineer," Pel said, "can you get in touch with him or her?"

"I don't know for sure he's an engineer. I'm just guessing."

Pel stared at him.

"I don't know who he is. I thought about taking over the news feed this one day when my gramma was watching it and they said this stupid shit how the Collective might be spies from Kazakhstan."

"I remember that."

"So I started a thread on one of the Collective boards, asking for leads. And this user disgruntld1, he posts a lot of anti-Authority stuff on snarknet, set up a backdoor and sent me a network map and instructions. Then he looked the other way when my text went out."

Pel glanced at Waylee and back. "I'm guessing the backdoor's gone now?"

"Yeah, sorry. I checked a couple weeks ago. And I had to erase all my old files."

Pel's mouth opened but nothing came out.

"I've been researching. No pinging though. Haven't found another way in."

At the desk, Waylee shut her computer down.

"I was gonna contact him, but thought you'd frown on bringing in an outsider."

Pel's face reddened. "Then you should have mentioned it earlier. We can take precautions."

"You know, taking over the whole feed is way harder than adding some text. They monitor it as it goes out. They can just flip a switch if they don't like what they see. You might have to take over the control room."

Pel turned to Waylee. "He's probably right. I should have thought of that."

"We should just get out of here," Charles said. "Give your video to some journalists in Korea or someplace."

Waylee jumped out of her chair. "No one will see it, that's the whole problem!" She screamed.

He felt like running for the stairs.

She slapped her head. "MediaCorp controls the entire Comnet, and they'll squash it. Sure it'll pass around the marginal wonk crowd, freaks like me and Shakti, but it won't hit the mainstream. Not enough people will see it to change anything." She pointed at him, her eyes murderous. "We ruined our lives breaking you out, Charles, and now you say it's all for nothing."

"Wasn't for nothing, I…"

But she stomped out of the room, tears streaming down her face.

Pel started to follow, then threw up his hands. He turned to Charles, fists clenched. "Why the fuck didn't you say that a long time ago? Like when Waylee first contacted you?"

Charles burned with shame. He felt like a child, like he should hide somewhere. "I…" Words wouldn't come. Although really, social engineering was an accepted hacking technique. People did it all the time.

Pel shook his head. "I can't believe how stupid I was, thinking you were this great hacker when really you're just another lame-ass kid."

* * *

Shakti

Except for the watchman on duty, who guarded the ganja fields with the aid of half a dozen German shepherds and a whole heap of electronics, most of the farm residents gathered in the main house's dining hall each night for dinner. They lined up and served themselves from steaming pots and buffet trays. Some talented cooks lived here, and used fresh ingredients, often picked that day.

Shakti dished a plate of veggie enchiladas and rice, the onion and cilantro aroma making her mouth water. She took a random spot at one of the long tables, hoping to make some more friends and consign Dingo to the past. *Men are such bastards.*

Amy, a thin sixteen-year-old redhead, sat next to her. Shakti didn't know her well; she kind of kept to herself.

"Hi, Amy," Shakti said.

Amy turned and smiled. "Hi."

"So how's everything with you?"

Amy's eyes widened in surprise. "Uh, okay." She started poking at her food.

Shakti cut off a bit of enchilada, rewarding her taste buds with peppery squash and mushrooms. "Where's your mom?" Amy's mother took care of the chickens and kept the tractors and other equipment running.

Amy jerked a thumb toward the neighboring table, where her fortyish mother flirted with Carl, the brown-bearded man. "I can't wait to get out of here," Amy said. "This place is so lame."

"Are you kidding? This is heaven compared to Baltimore. Ever been there?"

Amy squinted. "The Inner Harbor once. Seemed okay. But I've been to DC a bunch of times. That's where I want to live. There's stuff to do there."

Shakti ate a forkful of tomato-filled rice. "Community's important. What you have here on the farm, the People's Party is working to build in city neighborhoods, but it's a struggle against lifetimes of indoctrinated anonymity." She paraphrased Councilman Cutler. "Without community, we're each lonely, desperate creatures, impoverished of possibilities, alienated from our humanity and defenseless against those who hold power."

Pel and Charles shuffled in and picked separate tables. Shakti looked around but didn't see Waylee. "Excuse me," she said to Amy. "I'll be back."

She walked over to Pel's table and sat across from him. "Where's Waylee?"

Pel shrugged. "Moping. I wish she was normal. I don't have the patience for this shit anymore."

Her muscles tightened. "Just want to be there for the good times?"

He smacked his fork against the table. "You don't know how much I gave up. Or don't care." He pointed at Charles, lost in his meal. "We had a good life before we made the mistake of trusting ourselves to a teenager."

He threw up his arms. "And now what? How are we supposed to cross the border and find a place to settle and not get extradited or kidnapped or wasted by a drone? The government doesn't like thorns in their side, and neither forgets nor forgives." He picked up his plate and stormed off, not waiting for a reply.

When Waylee still hadn't appeared by the end of dinner, Shakti took some food up to her room. She wasn't there. Nor in the shared bathroom.

Shakti returned downstairs. Some people had left, but most were cleaning and chatting. "Anyone seen Waylee?" she shouted.

No one had.

"Anyone wanna help me find her?"

Pretty much everyone but Pel and Charles volunteered. "She's just moping somewhere," Pel said. "She'll come back when she gets hungry."

"Don't be an asshole," Shakti said. "She needs you."

"She's right," Charles said to him. "You her man."

Pel scowled. "What the fuck do you know about it?"

"Basta," Shakti said. "Chill. You're both helping and that's that. We're a team."

Everyone threw on jackets or fleeces. Sunshine and Amy passed out LED flashlights. "We'll fan out in pairs," Sunshine said.

Pel waved an arm. "Just don't yell out her name, 'kay? We're trying to keep a low profile."

Shakti paired up with Amy and walked down one of the dirt roads, exhaling clouds of fog. She swept her flashlight back and forth, bathing small spots of trees, fields, and buildings in brilliant white, the spots sometimes unblemished circles or ellipses, other times pierced by the jagged shadows of senescent branches. Something crawled from the pit of her stomach, but she forced it back down, knowing at least they were in friendly territory.

"We'll find her," Amy said. "Farm's not that big. Only takes fifteen minutes to walk from one end to the other."

Dead leaves crackled beneath Shakti's feet. Beams of other searchers criss-crossed the farm, brightening and dimming like fireflies as they swept across her line of sight. She turned to the teen. "Do you have any Diazepam, Percocet, anything like that?"

She shrugged. "I'm sure someone here does."

"Waylee has a… condition. Meds don't cure it, but we can at least reduce the anxiety a little."

Amy didn't respond. She glanced back over her shoulder. "Hope she stays away from the fields. Dogs aren't big on strangers."

They hadn't heard any barking, so she must not have gone that way. They headed for a cluster of wooden outbuildings. Equipment storage and repair shops, if she remembered right.

Flood lights flashed on as they approached. Shakti's eyes fought to adjust.

"Motion detector," Amy said, as if they were some uncommon marvel.

They found Waylee in a wide three-walled shed, huddled on the wood chip floor between a tractor and some sort of tilling attachment. She wasn't moving.

Shakti knelt by her friend, brushed her fire red hair aside, and massaged her shoulders. "Waylee, hon."

No response. At least she was breathing.

"Come on, let's go to bed. Things'll be better in the morning."

Waylee turned a blank face toward her. Black riverbeds of eye shadow ran down her cheeks. Wood chips and dirt adhered to one side.

Shakti brushed off the debris. Her skin felt ice cold. She only had a flannel shirt and jeans on, but the temperature had dropped into the forties.

"Come on." She grasped her friend by the armpits and lifted. Amy grabbed an arm and pulled.

Once on her feet, Waylee stood like a wax statue. Shakti unzipped her jacket and put it on her, then pulled up the hood and tightened it.

They led her back toward the main house, each holding a hand. Waylee gazed at the ground as she shuffled along.

Shakti shivered from the cold. "I've never seen her quite this bad."

Amy peered at her. "This happens a lot?"

"Not a lot, but she's really stressed."

"We got a whole field of herbal stress reduction. Maybe she should give it a try."

"Everyone's right," Waylee muttered. "That was stupid, thinking we could take over the Super Bowl broadcast."

Amy stopped, forcing a halt. "Say what?"

23

January 8
Baltimore

Kiyoko

Kiyoko refused to be a vampire.

"But it's a vampire role-playing game," one of her new housemates said, baring fangs as he spoke. "You have to play a vampire."

The talk of vampires invoked memories of Iwisa. She hoped he'd return to BetterWorld, maybe in some other form. She'd learned so much from him, and he was her only connection to her sister. And she'd come to enjoy his company, their conversations.

"Can't I be a werecat?" she said.

Someone knocked on the door. The half dozen costumed vampires in the living room turned to look.

Kiyoko got up from the couch and peered through the peephole. M-pat. And behind him, her lawyer Francis Jones in his blue suit and the chubby grandmother with the bug detector. She carried an aluminum case in one hand.

Kiyoko unlocked the three deadbolts and opened the door. "Come in."

M-pat halted at the threshold. "Da fuck?"

"We're playing a game," Kiyoko said. "They're all vampires but I'm a real live human. Like you." She ushered him in, then Francis and the grandmother. "Don't worry, they won't bite."

"That's what you think," her quasi-friend Absinthe said, baring fangs and twirling her long emerald green hair. Absinthe had been her first and last goth lover, a hundred years ago it seemed. She could do amazing things with her tongue, but scoffed at the concept of loyalty. Worse, she worshipped darkness and liked to play rough, even knowing how awful Kiyoko's childhood had been.

Kiyoko introduced everyone. "Tea?"

She got no takers. M-pat smiled. "So how you been?"

"A little anxious, but happy to sleep in my bed. What's going on?"

The grandmother pointed to a large fly, maybe a deerfly, clinging to the outside corner of a living room window. Kiyoko looked closer. It was clearly made of plastic, and lacked details like leg hairs. The antennae were a lot bigger than a fly's. The eyes were tiny camera lenses.

The woman returned to the center of the room, set her aluminum case on the table, and opened it. She pulled out a cylinder like a big flashlight but with metal on the end.

She walked over to the window, placed the end against the glass opposite the artificial fly, and pressed a button on the side. The fly dropped to the ground. "That's one down."

"Is it legal to destroy those?" Kiyoko asked.

M-pat looked out the window. "A better question, is it legal for the gov'ment to put them there."

"Unfortunately," Francis said, "they probably have a warrant. However, you certainly have a right to dispose of unwanted trash on your property. Anyway, we need to talk."

"Follow me," Kiyoko said. She led them down to the basement, which not only lacked windows, but because it was their practice room, had been soundproofed with padding made from recycled denim.

Francis tapped a finger against a directional mike jutting from one of the flexible floor stands. "You set everything up again."

Kiyoko and some musician friends, her sister's friends really, had repaired the mess the cops left, and reassembled the equipment at one end of the basement. They'd jammed together a couple of times, but her heart wasn't in it.

The grandmother walked around with her bug detector. "Clean," she said.

"Who owns this house?" Francis asked.

"We all do." She paused. "Actually, Pel's parents have the title. It was a foreclosure fixer-upper. Pel didn't have any credit to show for the loan."

"That's good, that means the government can't seize it. I'd fight them anyway, but I'd have a stronger case if it's owned by someone uninvolved with any alleged crimes. Now what about all this band equipment, and the rest of the stuff in the house?"

"I own some of it. Some, uh, doesn't have paperwork or anything."

"I'd get rid of that. So here's what's happening. Your sister and her boyfriend did something to really piss off the government, and Homeland Security is going to come down hard on anyone associated with them. I don't know what they did, but this morning they and Charles Lee were placed on the FBI's ten most wanted list. The reward's a million dollars each."

Kiyoko shivered. Top of the FBI's most wanted? A million dollars? Iwisa said Waylee's infiltration of the New Year's gala had been a huge success. The White House must have figured it out.

M-pat cast his eyes back and forth. "Props that they scored and got away, but I'm glad I ain't part of it." He stared at her. "Same for you, you ain't suited for prison."

"So what's gonna happen?" Kiyoko said.

"They've been officially designated as terrorists. Under the expanded USA PATRIOT Act, constitutional rights are thereby thrown out the window. You could be detained indefinitely as a person of interest. We'd fight it of course, but we're talking fighting the whole U.S. government."

Kiyoko sat on the stool behind the mixing computer. She wouldn't cry. "The FBI told me I can't leave town." Her voice sounded cracked. "What should I do? It's not fair…"

M-pat walked over and squeezed her hand. "Girl, you gotta keep a Positive Mental Attitude. A whole lot of people could get shit on, but you most of all. But we can beat this. I know you strong. Pack a suitcase and let's talk options."

* * *

St. Mary's County

Charles

Charles trudged down the stairs to the cellar. He was used to being ignored, but not having everyone hate him like this.

He'd tried apologizing to Waylee. He should have been straight about the engineer who'd helped him broadcast the zombie ticker. He wasn't trying to play her or anything. And besides, it didn't matter. Broadcasting a video was a whole other level.

Waylee had refused to reply. Girl was wack. Shakti had been sitting in the room with her, said she had a fever from lying outside in the cold, and told him to go away.

Entering the basement, he saw Pel at the wooden table, swiping fingers over a Comnet interface. He'd run an optic cable from a new hole in the ceiling. Big Red sat to his right, still running algorithms to decrypt data from the New Year's party. Pel glanced at Charles, then returned to his screen.

Charles eyed the bottle racks on the walls. All this wine down here, maybe they should open a bottle or two. He'd never had wine before, but rich people liked it, so it had to be good. He walked closer. "Ever drunk any of this wine?"

Pel turned and frowned.

"Just wanted to say I'm sorry," Charles said.

Pel pointed at his interface screen. "Take a look at this."

The center portal contained the FBI's Ten Most Wanted list. The first three thumbnail photos showed him, Pel, and Waylee, with their names underneath. Clicking on the photos, the FBI was offering a million dollar reward for each of them.

Pel turned his chair and stared at him. "Well now you're not the only one with a million dollar price on your head."

Guess I'm not top dog anymore, just tied for it.

"The White House must have figured out that Greg and Estelle were me and Waylee. And obviously they're pissed."

Charles took a step back. "I thought you had good disguises."

Pel sighed. "Me too. But Homeland was after us, so once someone talked to the real Greg and Estelle about New Year's, it would just be a matter of comparing images from the president's photographer to Homeland's database and applying facial recognition algorithms."

"So what now?" He pointed at Big Red. "It looks like you're still cracking comlinks."

Pel nodded. "I like to finish what I've started. I guess I'm as stubborn as Waylee. And who knows what we'll find. Maybe even bank access, money to change our identities and keep away from Homeland."

That sounded good. "How long we staying here?"

He rubbed his facial scruff. "This seems like a safe haven. But three million dollars is a strong incentive to turn us in. There's twenty people living on this farm old enough to use a comlink." He slid his chair over and crunched some numbers on Big Red. "Even if each person is 90% trustworthy, that gives an overall 88% chance that someone will turn us in." He sighed. "And Waylee blabbed about taking over the Super Bowl broadcast. I wish..."

Charles waited, but he didn't finish. "Then we gotta go?"

Pel wagged a finger. "Better idea. All the comlinks and interfaces are in the Friendship Farm network. Can we disable them all but see who tries to call the authorities?"

"If they all use the Comnet router here in the house, sure. Easy to get on the server and shut down outgoing signals. Or I could put up a wall to gov'ment destinations and have it call me when someone tries to go there. They got a Mexican kid here, looks about twelve, who does all the IT. Easy to chump."

"Isadora. She's actually fourteen and from Honduras, and pretty smart. I'll keep her busy helping me decrypt the New Year's comlink signals."

"Sure that's wise?"

Pel put his chin in his hand, then nodded. "Shakti said she seemed okay. Besides, I can keep an eye on her this way."

Makes sense. He looked at Pel, who was so forgiving, and had done so much for him. As good a friend as he'd ever had. *Might as well come clean on my other bad too.* Charles tried to find the words.

Pel stared at him. "Something wrong?"

"Uh, I gotta fess up on somethin'. From a while back."

Pel crossed his arms. "Let me guess—it's your fault the cops raided the band house?"

His heart raced. "You knew?"

"No, but I should have. Now I do. I've been wondering how they found us."

Should have told them right away. "When them news 'tards set Botis lyin' on me, I got in their system to delete the videos, and my suit got infected. I thought I cleaned it up, no damage done, but authorities musta got a fix on me."

His eyes narrowed. "Why didn't you tell us? If you'd told us right away, we'd have been long gone when the cops arrived."

"Thought it was taken care of. And 'shamed, I guess."

"Pride is your worst enemy. The ancient Greeks, my ancestors, called it hubris. It was their heroes' downfall. And it dragged down those around them too. Remember that."

"Yeah, I know."

Pel threw up his arms. "Of course that broadcast was a trap. You told me yourself how Homeland catches hackers and puts them to work to stay out of jail. They're a scary fucking enemy and you have to watch your step."

"I know, I wasn't thinkin'."

"Well you almost landed us in prison, and now we've got no home." His face calmed a little. "But one good thing."

"What's that?"

"Homeland isn't all powerful. If we don't make any more mistakes, maybe we can stay hidden."

"Know that."

Pel jabbed a finger at him. "Yeah, know that. Come to me any time you sense trouble. Don't keep it to yourself."

"I already figured all that. That's why I axed you and Kiyoko to help with the Club Elite op. I learned."

"Yeah, that was a brilliant bit of work."

"So we good, then?"

Pel nodded. "Still need your help. Nothing's changed there. And we've still got lots of options."

"Waylee won't speak to me."

Pel sighed. "Me neither, and I didn't even do anything. But she's not just depressed, she's got some sort of infection. You should stay out of her room."

Once Pel had Isadora occupied, Charles moved his Comnet interface up to his bedroom. He navigated to the farm's central server. He'd already given himself administrator privileges and explored the system.

He built a list of police and Homeland voice numbers and Comnet addresses, then added news outlets. He created a filter that would block any transmissions to them. A linked script would send him the betrayer's user name. He executed the scripts. *Done!*

Would be good to know where the betrayer was too. He wrote another script that would access the GPS in their comlink and send him its location. And 'cause the caller or sender would know something was wrong if they couldn't get through – unless they were dense as a rock – he rewrote the first script to shut down external transmissions altogether until he gave it the word. Password `judas_owned`. The Bible reference made him miss his gramma and rue the times he busted on her God talk. *I'm a better person now I hope.*

He checked the time. 6:15. The GPS script had taken way too long to test and debug. But he'd put the Comnet filter up right away, and no one had tripped it.

What about before that? He opened the past logs and ran a search for the numbers and addresses he'd blocked. Nothing since they'd arrived. Maybe they could trust these peeps and Pel was just wack. Or maybe not everyone knew about the reward.

I should see how Kiyoko's doing. With cybermercs on the prowl, he browsed the Compendia for a new avatar concept. He settled on Touissant, named after François-Dominique Toussaint Louverture, the leader of the Haitian Revolution and Scourge of Slavery.

He decided to ignore the grumbling in his stomach and skip dinner. Kiyoko needed a replacement avatar too. As awesome as Steampunk Grrl was, she wasn't safe anymore. He copied her AI programs to a starter model girl. Kiyoko could change it later and add her own outfits.

Charles started writing a speech for their next meetup. Then he changed his mind and deleted it. He'd just be himself.

January 9
Baltimore

Kiyoko

Kiyoko/Cat Girl clung to her horse as it galloped through the woodland, Touissant following. The good thing about virtual horses is they never got tired.

Touissant—formerly Iwisa—had brought a replacement for Steampunk Grrl. Beautiful features but bland. As before, Kiyoko switched avatars, leaving any surveillance behind. Once away from Yumekuni, she added silver hair, a Victorian dress, and cat ears. No tail. Ears could fasten to a headband, but a tail smacked of code tampering.

"Thanks for coming back," she shouted. "BetterWorld isn't the same without you."

"Nor you," he shouted back. "Sorry if I seem a little clunky, but I don't have an immersion suit here, and Touissant's face is on autopilot."

"You're fine." BetterWorld had pretty amazing AI.

They eased their horses to a trot, leagues from the bullet capsule stop. Touissant sidled his horse next to hers and spoke in a normal voice. "You heard about the bounty?"

"Yes. I don't know whether to be mad at my sister or proud of her."

"You should be proud. She owned the most powerful people in the world."

Cat Girl shot a spray of stars from her fingers, a trick Kiyoko learned herself.

"The thing is," Touissant said, "she had one of those breakdowns. And it's my fault."

Kiyoko's muscles tensed. Her immersion suit translated that as a leg squeeze, and her horse accelerated into a gallop. She pulled back the reins and halted it. "Stupid horse."

Touissant caught up. "You okay?"

"What happened to my sister?"

"'Kay, since this place isn't monitored, first thing I should say, is..."

"Yes?"

"I'm Charles on the outside."

Thanks, Captain Obvious. "I know."

He paused for several seconds, his avatar motionless, then he said, "You do?"

"Well, who else?"

"I guess it's pretty obvious," he said. "I wasn't trying to hide anything."

"So what happened to Waylee?"

"Well, she's got the flu or something, but they're giving her medicine."

She never gets sick. "What about the breakdown?"

"She thought I could take over the Super Bowl broadcast and show her video. But of course it's impossible. You'd have to be in the control room and the satellite uplink and who knows where else."

Kiyoko didn't know what to say. *I thought Charles could do anything.*

"She won't see anyone or talk to anyone now," he said.

"Look, Charles. My sister can be a bitch sometimes, but she's got this condition she can't control. If you set it off, it's your responsibility to bring her back."

"That's Pel's job."

Anger boiled through her veins. "How dare you put this on him when it's your fault."

Touissant sat on his saddle without replying.

208 ◆ T.C. Weber

"We all thought you could break into MediaCorp, me included, and you never told us otherwise until now." She felt betrayed. "We're going through deep shit for busting you out of jail. Our music career's probably over, and that's my life. At least you can try to make it mean something."

Touissant spoke at last. "I'm sorry."

"Isn't there anything you can do?"

"I've been doing everything I can. They wouldn't have gotten into the Smithsonian without me."

Poor boy's probably cowering. "I know. All I'm asking is, please try."

"I will. I'm totally down with you."

Her sister always meant well. She saved her from Feng, raised her, even beat up her shitty ex-boyfriend. *And what have I done in return?* "I'll help. Whatever I can do. Although I may have to run for it soon. Homeland's on a rampage."

"Come join us. Waylee would joy out. And I..." He paused.

"Yes?" She was still mad at him, but there was too much else to worry about.

"I love you."

He didn't trace a heart or anything cheesy like that. He meant it. Kiyoko considered all the possible responses. But none of them would work.

* * *

St. Mary's County

Shakti

Wearing borrowed hiking clothes, Shakti jogged next to Pel toward a small house nestled in an orchard, a chicken coop on one side and goat pen on the other.

She couldn't believe Amy would betray them. But Charles had alerted them that she tried to call Homeland Security's reward hotline. He cut all communications, and gave Pel a comlink that tracked her GPS coordinates. They had to act before she left the farm.

Pel gazed at the comlink. "Target's still in the house. Hasn't moved much."

They approached the door and slowed. Pel pulled his stun gun out of a pocket.

"I don't think you need that," Shakti said.

"Three million dollars is an awful lot of money."

"Yeah, but…" Shakti knocked on the door.

"It's probably unlocked," Pel said.

"Who is it?" A woman's voice, but not the one they were after.

"Is Amy there? It's Shakti."

"Target's on the move," Pel said, looking at his screen. "Out the back door."

"Oh joy."

Pel took off around the right side of the house.

Shakti took the left.

In her peripheral vision, she saw the front door open. She glanced back and saw Amy's mother peering out.

Shakti kept going. Chickens scattered out of her way, some flapping their wings in a vain attempt to get airborne. She almost chuckled. Just like running through alleys in Guyana as a child.

Behind the house, Amy darted between dormant fruit trees. She was fast.

Pel wasn't far behind, but with her short legs, Shakti would never catch up.

"Stop or I'll shoot," Pel yelled.

Amy accelerated in response and entered the mid-aged forest that covered the southwest portion of the property.

"Please stop," Shakti shouted. "We just want to talk." If they didn't catch her, Amy could hop onto another network and call the police. And she'd almost certainly lose them in these woods.

Shakti fell further behind.

Ahead, Pel stumbled over a downed branch. He stopped and aimed his stun gun at Amy. It clicked.

She faltered, apparently hit.

He kept pointing it.

She dropped, crashing face first into a spicebush thicket.

Pel ran to the prone body ahead and checked her pulse.

Shakti arrived. "Is she alright?"

"Amy!" Her mother's voice sounded behind them, accompanied by footfalls and the snapping of twigs. "God, Amy! You people, what have you done?"

Shit. Shakti turned the teen over. Her face was scratched from falling into the shrubs, but she was breathing.

"She's okay," Pel said.

Her mother grabbed Pel by the shoulders and shoved him aside. She knelt next to her motionless daughter and cradled her face. "Amy. Amy!"

"She's just stunned," Pel said. He found Amy's comlink on the ground and pocketed it.

"We're really sorry," Shakti said, "but she tried to turn us in to Homeland Security. Let's bring her back to the house."

"She wouldn't do that," her mother said.

"Well she did," Pel said. "For the reward I assume."

"How long will she be out?" Shakti asked him.

"Not long. She'll be conscious in a few minutes, and able to walk in half an hour or so."

"How much is this reward?" the mother asked.

"Doesn't matter," Pel said. "We've disabled all communications. We thought we could trust you, but obviously we were wrong."

Anger burned behind the woman's eyes. "Get off our farm."

January 10

Waylee

Her fever under control, Waylee sat on the front porch of the main house with a borrowed guitar, refining the chord pattern of a song she'd just written.

The spiders gather,
A world to drain,
Entangling the living
In nets and chains.
Sally forth,
Quixotic rube,
Do your best,
But know you'll lose.

Shakti, her sari smelling a little ripe, peered at her from the adjacent seat. She'd never been a big fan of Waylee's music, preferring lighter stuff like Thievery Corporation or Arcade Fire. Which was cool, they had just as much to say, and were much better musicians.

"Why don't you write something upbeat," Shakti said, "something in a major key?"

"I play what I feel."

"Reverse that and feel what you play."

Waylee looked at her brilliant friend. "Sure, why not."

She launched into a briefly popular #M-Power Girlz song, an up-tempo affirmation in D major, full of bright keyboards and hand clapping. Not her style of music—but why should she hunker behind style walls? Even stripped down on guitar, it did cast the blues away, especially when she and Shakti sang together and swung their heads in unison.

Tha corner boyz, they keepin' you down,
Don't cop their shit or hide in a frown.
Ain't got time to play them dumb games,
You got a brain and places to go.
Hear the news, don't throw up your hands,
Use that energy and do something now...

"Again," Shakti insisted when she finished the song.

Just beating the flu and four days of sleep had lifted her brain out of the abyss. Playing #M-Power Girlz helped even more. *I can't believe I never thought of this.*

Keep on striving, climb to the top,
Give it everything that you've got!

"So how are you doing with Dingo gone?" Waylee asked after the second time through.

Shakti's shoulders drooped. "Maybe he'll return, or we'll meet up later." She shook her head. "We've got other things to worry about."

The front door opened. Waylee turned and saw Sunshine. "You can come in now."

All fourteen adult residents sat in the big living room. Amy too. They had deliberated for six hours, trying to reach a consensus—exile Waylee and her friends, or not.

None smiled at her. A bad sign. *We have nowhere else to go.*

"Please, sit." Sunshine motioned to an empty sofa. Waylee followed her suggestion, Shakti too.

Sunshine peered at her. "How are you feeling?"

"I'm on the mend. Thanks for the antibiotics."

"All the kids here, we keep a supply handy. You can keep the bottle, make sure you finish the whole thing." She exhaled and looked around at the others.

Pel emerged from the stairwell, followed by Charles. They joined her on the couch.

"How's it going down there?" she asked.

"We've keyed eighteen comlinks so far. No transmissions of interest, just users checking the time or sending Happy New Year messages."

"That's it?"

Pel patted her hand. "Wait until we actually replicate the comlinks. That's when the fun begins."

Waylee leaned past him, toward Charles.

He inched away.

"We've all been fucking up," she told him. "But we're still a team. Let's move forward, however we can." She offered a fist to bump.

His eyes relaxed. He leaned toward her and tapped her fist. "Like I said, I'm sorry. I promised Kiyoko I'd help you, and I will, whatever's needed."

Sunshine cleared her throat. "First things first." She turned. "Amy?"

The thin teenager stood. "I'm sorry I tried to turn you in. It's so much money, and I wasn't thinking. How it wouldn't just affect you, but everyone here. Aiding and abetting fugitives, everyone'd go to jail. I thought maybe I could work some kind of deal, but everyone thinks the feds are all frowny on pot legalization, and can't be trusted."

Sunshine folded her hands. "Thank you, Amy. There's also principles to consider. These people are our guests, and extending kindness to guests is one of the oldest precepts of humanity. Furthermore, you have everything you need here, and we're disappointed that you would succumb to greed."

Amy looked down. "I know."

Sunshine turned back to Waylee's couch with a 'your turn' expression on her face.

Shakti stood. "We're sorry we chased you and used a stun gun on you."

Pel remained seated.

"Thanks." Amy sat back down.

One of the younger men stood. "Like Amy says, everyone here could go to prison for aiding you. The farm confiscated. She said you plan to break into the Super Bowl?"

My scumbag brain did it again... "The broadcast, not the stadium," Waylee said. "But it looks like we can't." *We've still got the video and data, we'll figure something out.*

One of the older men shook his head. "That's a relief. It'd be way too dangerous."

"And don't forget," Sunshine said, "this farm is the main source of funding for the Maryland People's Party and its charities."

"We know," Waylee said. "We shouldn't have come."

Amy stood again. "I wanted to know, what happened to my comlink? I couldn't find it. I'm not allowed Comnet access for six months now, but still, do one of you have it?"

"I opened it up and threw it in one of the ponds," Pel said, not looking the least bit contrite.

Everyone stared at him.

"Look, I don't want anyone going to prison."

Sunshine waved a hand. "We've made a decision. Apologies have been made, and are much appreciated. But the fact is, your presence is too stressful for our community."

"I'm sorry about that," Waylee said. "But we have no vehicle, and no place to go."

"We'll walk you to the front gate," the brown-bearded man said, "and you can hoof it from there."

Several people nodded.

"If we had a car," Pel said, "we could make for the border. Canada's only nine hours away, but Mexico's an option too."

"What about the wall?" Waylee said. "La Gran Muralla? We can't get through the checkpoints, and the rest is impenetrable."

"So Canada, then."

"We can't give you a vehicle that might be traced back to the farm," Peter, the white-bearded man who'd given them a ride from DC, said. "Even if we had one to spare."

"You've got plenty of money," Pel said.

The residents impaled him with angry stares.

"We'll give you a day to come up with a plan," Sunshine said. "How's that?"

"How about two? And keep the Comnet filters on until we're long gone."

The residents discussed Pel's counteroffer but some wanted them gone immediately. Sunshine announced the consensus. "One day, but we'll maintain the Comnet filters for a week afterward. Of course if someone wanted to, they could just walk to the next farm and call the police."

"Too bad we lost the RV," Waylee said. "We could have stayed anywhere."

Peter buried a hand in his bushy beard. "I think I've got an idea."

* * *

Baltimore

M'patanishi

"So all I'm sayin' is, Dolphins gonna toss them long balls and burn their ass, yo," M-pat said to his friend Phinehas, sitting in the chair next to him on his townhouse porch.

Phinehas opened the cooler in front of them and pulled out another Natty Boh. "My ass." He popped the top off and took a swig. "Giants got that pass rush, know what I'm sayin'? 'Kay, Fins got a decent line. But Giants just gotta rush four, maybe throw in some blitzes, and Armstrong's gonna be running for his life. And you know being young and all, he got a tendency to act dumb under pressure."

"You full of shit, yo. Armstrong don't get to no Super Bowl by being a fizzle."

"Whoa, change of topic, yo. That fly shorty up the street's comin' this way."

Kiyoko strolled down the sidewalk toward them. She had silver robes on and a long, light blue wig that fluttered in the breeze.

"What's up there, cutiecakes?" Phinehas said when she arrived. "You are looking especially fine today."

Kiyoko ignored him and leaned toward M-pat. "Can we talk in private?"

"Yeah, sure." He pointed to the cooler. "Leave me one at least," he told Phinehas.

Inside, his wife was in the kitchen starting dinner, his son upstairs napping. "'Sup?" he said.

"This place been swept?"

"Just like yours was."

Kiyoko placed her blue-nailed hands together in a prayer position. "You've been looking out for us since the day we moved here."

He shrugged. "Ujamaa. Goes both ways. Waylee helped me organize the neighborhood, then Shakti moved in and brought money from the People's Party, set up the patrols, the community garden, all the cleanups."

"You always made me feel safe," she continued. "You're a good man."

She obviously wanted something. "What do you need?"

"I'm ready to go. Got some suitcases packed. Everything else'll be looked after, shipped once I settle. The lighter stuff anyway. I got a plan to lose the surveillance. It's just drones so it won't be that hard. So all I need is a car. The cops confiscated our RV."

"A'ight. Where you goin'?"

"First, southern Maryland."

"Huh?"

"Charles said they're staying on a farm, friends of Shakti's. I'll go pick them up, then drive up to Vermont. I got contacts there who'll help us cross into Canada. They know this smuggler."

"Well, the hood won't be the same without y'all. But they catch your sister, she doin' time. So I guess what it come down to, how we get you a car?"

Kiyoko shuffled her feet. "I thought maybe I could rent one off the books? Borrow from someone and reimburse them?"

M-pat stifled a laugh. "We talkin' one-way trip, no return."

Kiyoko nodded. "Yeah, and I don't wanna get anyone in trouble."

"We could check with Paulo. He got cars if you got money."

Kiyoko frowned. "I don't have much cash. And I don't like supporting criminals. How'd you like it if someone stole your car?"

"I'd find the motherfucker and break their kneecaps."

Kiyoko averted her eyes.

"Look," M-pat said, "I'm gonna help you. Whatever it takes."

She looked at him and smiled.

"It's part my fault you're in this shit," he said.

"How's that?"

"I let Waylee do most of the planning. She did good, but she ain't no pro, know what I'm sayin'?"

Kiyoko cocked her pretty head and scrunched her face.

"What I'm sayin' is, we shoulda been better prepared for that smack-down. Anyway, what we gonna do to get you safe?"

"Maybe I could trade for a clunker," she said, "but one that'll still make it to Vermont. We've got band equipment and house stuff, if Waylee and Pel are ok with it."

"You need somethin' off the record. You buy from someone 'round here, word gonna spread. Dingo and I got those vans last month. I could get you another one. We surrounded by factories and wrecking yards, no lack of choices."

"So steal something?"

Why she gotta be so difficult? "Not from someone who'll miss it. We talkin' spare inventory, somethin' that won't be missed for a while, from some company that'll just write it off and collect the insurance."

Kiyoko nodded. "Okay." Then she hugged him. "You're the best." Her hair smelled like flowers.

Movement caught his eye. His wife, frowning at them from the kitchen doorway.

He pulled out of Kiyoko's embrace and eyed his wife. "Business, baby."

Kiyoko waved. "Hi Latisha."

"Hello Kiyoko." Her voice was cold, even though M-pat had not once cheated on her since Baraka's birth.

"Thanks again for feeding my cat while I was locked up."

Latisha relaxed. "Weren't no thing. Couldn't see one of God's creatures go and starve."

Kiyoko smiled. "M-pat's a lucky man." She turned back to him. "Can you get something tonight?"

"No, gimme a day to scout."

"Send me a message when you're ready, and where you want to meet. I'll have a friend bring my stuff."

M-pat started rolling through the possibilities in his head. "Whatever I get, I'll bring it by Paulo's first and get it painted. I'll owe him."

She shook her blue hair. "No need to owe him. You can have my immersion suit, and I'll see what else."

He nodded. He hoped he could find something on such short notice.

26

January 11
Cedarville State Forest, Maryland

Waylee

"We're here," Peter announced from the driver's seat of the converted school bus.

Sitting in one of the upholstered seats behind him, Waylee wedged apart two of the slats blocking the adjacent window. Pel had insisted on closing all the blinds.

They were driving down a two-lane paved road past a dense expanse of trees. Cedarville State Forest, twenty miles north of the farm, back toward DC.

"Never seen so many trees," Waylee said.

Across the bolted-down table from her, Shakti joined her at the window. "Pines, probably loblolly. The dormant trees are mostly oaks. The ones with the spiky balls are sweetgums."

Thanks, nature girl. Waylee was more interested in what the hell they were going to do next.

Peter had borrowed the bus from a neighbor, saying he wanted to take it camping in northern Virginia. It needed new tires and an engine overhaul, and couldn't get them to Canada. Even if Pel fixed it up, the owner wouldn't allow it.

But it made a decent shelter. The owner had replaced the original benches with couches and chairs, tables, bunks, a bathroom, kitchen, and all the other necessities of home. And they'd packed it with camping gear and food before they left the farm.

They passed a pair of whitetail does browsing at the forest edge, something Waylee rarely saw in Baltimore. The deer snapped their heads up and stared at the bus, their ears and nostrils flared.

Shakti pressed her hands together, palms touching and fingers pointed upward. "Namaste."

They pulled into a small parking lot and stopped. Waylee saw a peak-roofed visitor center through the windshield.

Peter looked back at her, Shakti, Pel, and Charles. "Okay, kids. After watching those arrogant bastards at the Smithsonian, I wanna help you however I can. First thing is to check in with the staff."

"Why do we have to do that?" Waylee asked.

"Cause if we don't, we'll get evicted. Can't hardly hide a school bus. Now the reason I suggested this place is first, it's empty this time of year, but second, I used to volunteer here and know everyone who's survived the yearly cutbacks."

Pel leaned forward. "You're not gonna say we're in here, are you?"

Peter crossed his arms. "Son, I was born before your dad was even a sperm." He pulled the door lever and stepped out.

Waylee turned to Pel. "I want to finish what we started."

He nodded. "We can finish decrypting the comlinks and see what else we get."

"I'd like to contact Ms. Baddelats. Maybe we can work together."

He frowned. "We should be careful. We have to keep our location secret."

"I know. I'm not stupid."

Peter returned about fifteen minutes later, holding a map and some brochures. "Two weeks, off the books, no charge."

"Thank you so much," Shakti said.

He closed the door and passed out the brochures. "In case you're interested, hiking trails, bird lists and whatnot. Woodpeckers are still around. Saw a red-bellied at the feeder."

Shakti opened a window and took a deep breath. "I love the air."

It smelled like pine, not the gasoline and old sock stench Waylee was used to in West Baltimore.

"We need electricity," Pel said. "And Comnet access." Peter had brought the computers Waylee and Charles had been using, although they couldn't keep them.

"We'll have an electric hookup," Peter said. "You may be out of luck as far as the Comnet goes."

Charles frowned. "Then why we here?"

"It's just temporary," Waylee said.

Peter returned to the driver's seat and they continued down the road. He turned into an empty campground, gravel pads and picnic benches nestled amidst the trees, and pulled into one of the spots near the bath house. "Here we are. Home sweet home. For the time being."

"How often do the rangers or whoever come by?" Pel asked.

"Not often, especially since the grounds are closed until spring. But you might want to stay out of sight weekdays between nine and five. Other than that, you're fine."

"I can put one of our cameras outside the campground entrance," Pel said, "and have Big Red warn us if someone comes."

Peter ran a cable to an electrical outlet, then untied a tent from the roof rack and tossed it down by the picnic table. Instead of setting it up, he came back inside. "Okay, here's the plan. We hang in the bus 'til sunset, around five o'clock, then we can start getting dinner ready and whatnot. I'm sleeping outside tonight. No rain forecast." He winked at Shakti. "You're welcome to join me."

She wrinkled her nose.

"It's the middle of winter," Waylee said. Even though year to year temperatures were climbing, it had still been pretty damn cold the past few nights.

Peter chuckled. "Goose down bags I got are rated to fifteen degrees. Ain't forecast to get much below freezing. But you can stay on the bus. There's four bunks in the back, and electric heaters."

"If you've got an extra sleeping bag," Shakti said, "I'll sleep under the stars."

Pel plugged in Big Red and the other two computers. "I'm gonna finish processing that comlink data. Waylee, how far are you on the video?"

"I need your comlink treasure."

Shakti caught her eyes. "Let's go for a walk. There's something primeval about forests that brings life to your soul." She had the trail map in one hand.

Pel stared at her. "That's not staying out of sight. Besides, we have work to do."

He waved Peter over. Waylee edged closer.

"We had to ditch our comlinks," Pel told him. "Can we borrow yours? I was thinking I'd convert it to a wireless hotspot, and our computers could access the Comnet through it. You'd still be able to use it."

"Sure." Peter pulled his comlink, a new Samsung, out of his jacket pocket. He looked at the display. "No signal."

Pel held out his hand. "Can I see it?"

He passed the comlink over and Pel fiddled with the screen. "Wi-Fi piggybacking's out of the question," he said. "We're surrounded by forest. Looks like 4G LTE's our best bet—there's a tower just out of range. Slower than 5G but better than nothing."

"At least a thousand times slower than fiber," Charles said behind them.

Pel turned in his direction. "Yeah, well, that's not an option at the moment." He trudged back to the closet, just forward of the bunks, and pulled open the twin doors. He plucked wire hangers off the bar and dropped the clothes on the closet floor.

Peter hurried back there. "Hey, hey, that's my stuff."

"Sorry."

"What are you doing?"

Pel counted up the hangers in his hand. "This should be enough. I assume you've got clippers somewhere. Need the metal for a Yagi antenna."

"And what's a Yagi antenna?"

"Directional antenna so we can boost the gain of your comlink and get a decent signal. I'll need PVC pipe or something for the boom…"

"I don' t know about PVC," Peter said, "but we've got tent poles, awning poles…"

Pel nodded. "And we can use a tree as the mast. The leaves are off. I assume there's a toolbox on board."

"This bus is a work in progress, so yeah. Boxes of parts too."

Pel flashed a thumbs up. "I've got everything else in my duffel bag— solder gun, multimeter, connectors… I'll have to start with a 2-element, which will give us five dB gain—they're real easy to build. Once we get a minimal signal, I can download instructions to add more elements, if we need them."

Pel looked excited. He loved fiddling with tech, which was why their music had so many layers and why the band house was so tricked out with electronics.

She hoped he succeeded. They had no place to go, no way to get her video on the air, and at best, two weeks to figure something out. Ms. Baddelats might be their only hope.

27

January 12
Baltimore

Kiyoko

Kiyoko/Cat Girl's horse trotted through the woodland, Charles/Touissant astride the horse to her right. His body was rigid as a statue, the price of a "ridiculously slow connection."

"What did Waylee and Pel say about selling our house stuff and band equipment?" she asked.

Touissant swiveled his head. "Waylee was surprised you asked, said do what you need to. Wants to sell the whole house to fund her next steps, but Pel ain't down."

Kiyoko thought about her virtual realm. "Can MediaCorp or the government confiscate everything I have on BetterWorld? Or delete it?"

"They did it to me. They can do whatever they want."

She examined her friend. Touissant wore a navy blue jacket with scarlet trim and gold epaulettes, white pants, black leather boots, and a sabre. Very Napoleonic, decidedly pre-steampunk.

"I need a matching persona. What did Haitian women wear during your General's time?"

Touissant smiled. "We can look it up."

They crossed a stream. Water rushed over rounded pebbles, drowning their horse clops with thousands of miniature echoes. "My life on the outside is ruined," she said. "Now my life here could be ruined."

"Back everything up so you can restore it. I'll help."

"I did that. I'm not totally useless. But if MediaCorp takes Yumekuni away and gives it to someone else, Prince Vostok for example, how can I get it back?"

"We'll raise hell," Touissant said. "You've got a lot of fans who wouldn't put up with it."

"You're right." Rather than continue, she halted her horse. *Better get this over with.* "I've been thinking about what you said the other day."

Touissant halted beside her. "Yes? Damn this slow connection. Sorry."

"You know I can't date someone who's underage."

His face didn't react. "Why not? Who cares what the government thinks?"

Good point. "And we're very different."

"Not really."

"I do consider you a really good friend."

His face drooped. "Welcome to Friendzone, population me."

I hate that term! "Are you saying you don't value me as a friend? Do you know what it's like to get hit on all the time just 'cause you're pretty and people want to stick their... whatever in your... whatever?"

Touissant cringed. "I didn't mean it that way. Talking to you is the only thing I ever have to look forward to."

Her anger diminished. "We're being cliché. I'll see you soon and we can discuss it in person."

From somewhere beyond the sky, she heard faint thumps, like an arrhythmic heart. She focused on the sound. A noise from outside. Someone pounding on her bedroom door.

"I've got to go," she said. "Someone's banging on my door."

Kiyoko pulled off her immersion helmet. "Hold on!" She hadn't showered or dressed yet - should have done that when she woke up.

Absinthe stood outside the door, hands on hips, a scowl on her face. She never went anywhere before noon, and must have spent the night. Absinthe's expression softened into seductive. "Well, you look adorably edible in that nightie." She stepped forward and settled a hand on Kiyoko's left breast, index finger rubbing the nipple. "I almost forgot how nice those are."

Kiyoko felt only the vaguest stirring. "Is that why you interrupted me? Still hopping from bed to bed?"

Absinthe snatched her hand back. "You've got feds downstairs, and they're getting restless."

Her heart stopped. Why had she wasted her morning in BetterWorld? Today was supposed to be her escape day, and now it was too late. "Tell... tell them I'm not decent and have to put some clothes on. Maybe you could make them tea or something?"

"You want me to play housemaid?"

"Just tell them I'll be down soon."

Kiyoko shut the door and relocked it. She should have left last night, even if her ride wasn't ready. She peeked between the wooden slats of her window blind. A uniformed cop stood outside just below and locked eyes with her. She closed the slats and started picking through her wardrobe.

She stopped and went to her night stand and fished for her comlink. "Francis Jones," she told it. Francis claimed to have a secure line, but according to Pel, there was no such thing where Homeland was concerned.

"Hello Kiyoko," her lawyer answered.

"FBI's here. At my house. Can you come?"

"Absolutely. Don't say anything until I get there."

"When will that be?"

"Let's see… Half an hour?"

"Please hurry." She terminated the connection and returned to her wardrobe.

Kiyoko settled on a red silk dress circled by an embroidered gold dragon, high heels, and a matching wig. Power, vitality, and luck. She threw them on and sat at her cramped makeup station.

Someone knocked on her door. "Kiyoko?" Voice of Harrison, the female FBI agent. "FBI. We need to speak with you."

Kiyoko shouted at the closed door. "Just a minute. I'm putting clothes on."

"You've got five minutes or you're under arrest."

That meant they weren't here to arrest her. "I'm hurrying."

The knocking resumed in exactly five minutes. Kiyoko breathed deeply, filled her lungs with power, and opened the door. "How are you, Ms. Harrison?"

The agent's eyes narrowed. "Couldn't you have just put on a T-shirt and jeans?"

"I don't own T-shirts or jeans."

Agent Harrison gestured for Kiyoko to follow her downstairs. The other bedroom doors were ajar.

In the living room, Agent Recelito stood next to Waylee's recliner, sipping coffee. Kiyoko's temporary roommates and the friends who'd stayed the night sat in the chairs and sofa.

"Well, if it isn't Princess Kiyoko," Agent Recelito said. "We have a schedule to keep, you know."

"Your friends here have been filling us in as best they can," Agent Harrison said.

What?

"Unfortunately," Agent Recelito said, "they don't know anything useful about your sister and her boyfriend."

"They say you're not involved in politics like the fugitives," Agent Harrison said.

"I vote," Kiyoko said, "but that's about it."

Agent Harrison nodded. "And you've followed the judge's orders about not leaving the city."

Agent Recelito handed her a sheet of paper. "This is for you."

Kiyoko scanned it. An itemized bill for $123,811.44. "This is a joke, right?"

"That's what you owe the government for destroying those monitoring devices."

Kiyoko folded the bill in half and handed it to Absinthe. "My assistant will take care of it."

Absinthe scowled.

Agent Harrison glanced at the comlink strapped to the back of her wrist. "Okay, everyone, clear out. Everyone but Ms. Pingyang."

Her friends looked relieved. Some went upstairs. Most exited the front door. Kiyoko sat on the sofa. Where was Francis? It had been more than half an hour.

The FBI agents pulled up chairs across from her. Agent Recelito spoke. "Why don't we try doing this the easy way."

"Doing what?"

"Where's your sister?"

"Long gone. Beyond your reach. Next question?"

Recelito's mouth opened, but nothing came out.

"Where'd they go?" Agent Harrison asked.

Kiyoko leaned back against the cushions. "I decline to answer any more questions."

Agent Harrison sighed. "I don't understand why you're willing to go to prison for a sister who could care less about you."

Kiyoko didn't respond to her trick.

"She abandoned you. You're going to prison while she's sitting on a beach somewhere drinking mai tais and laughing. Is that fair?"

Waylee on a beach. There's the laugh. "What's a mai tai?"

The door opened. Francis Jones. Her champion. Late but not too late.

"This interview is over," he said.

The agents stood. Agent Recelito stared at Kiyoko. "You want to play that game? Your sister and her comrades are designated terrorists. That means your case is now federal, with a mandatory prison term. We know you helped shelter them and hide their activities from the authorities. We know you helped finance their operations with BetterWorld credits. We have everything we need to put you away."

Kiyoko's knees shook as they left.

* * *

Cedarville State Forest

Charles

Kiyoko was right. He had duped everyone about owning the MediaCorp news feed, even if he didn't mean to, and it was on him to make things right. He had to redeem himself. And even if Kiyoko friendzoned him, so what? Kiyoko, Pel, Waylee, and the rest were his brothers and sisters now. A Collective within the Collective.

4G was off the scale slow, but he was stuck with it. Sitting in his narrow bunk with his interface unit and popup screen, he looked up disgruntld1, the Collectivista in MediaCorp who'd helped him what seemed a century ago.

The account still existed. He called Pel over.

"Be extra careful," he said. "In case it's a trap. But let's see if he can help."

Charles created a new account, FreedomDoctor, visible only on the Collective network. Using Collective Router encryption, he sent disgruntld1 some choice video clips of his boss of bosses, Robert Luxmore. He added text, "Greetings from a fellow Collectivista. Want to get this and better on air. Have access codes and scripts to trade and glory to share. Contact me ASAP."

He waited, but received no response.

28

January 13
Cedarville State Forest

Charles

The next day, as Charles worked alone at the smaller of the two tables, FreedomDoctor received a message.

`disgruntld1: Your offer sounds tempting.`

Charles set up a chat box with disgruntld1 and called Pel and Waylee over. "This is that engineer, or whatever, who helped me with my zombie message."

Waylee jumped up and down. "Charles!" She leaned in to stare at the screen, her breath hot on his cheek. "Tell me it's true!"

Pel edged in front of Waylee. "So is he an engineer or not?"

Charles typed.

`FreedomDoctor: Are u an engineer?`
`disgruntld1: Certified broadcast engineer ☺`

"How do we know this is the same person?" Pel said. "How can we trust him?"

Good question.

`FreedomDoctor: Tell me something Authority wouldn't know.`

"Authority could know anything," Pel said.

"Shut up," Waylee said behind them. "Let him dialogue."

```
disgruntld1: Trollface McTroll on snarknet is actually
a bot.
```

"That's useless," Pel said. "Ask him about your ticker op."

```
FreedomDoctor: What password did u give Dr. Doom?
disgruntld1: How do I know ur not Authority?
FreedomDoctor: I'm Dr. Doom.
```

Pel threw up his hands. "Why the fuck?"
Charles ignored him.

```
disgruntld1: Righteous if true.
```

"Looks like an impasse," Pel said.

```
disgruntld1: Which pw?
FreedomDoctor: studio subnet News.US.R3.textsys
disgruntld1: Little bird sez password was Ay2ENTg8
```

"That's right," Charles told Pel. He had a good memory for passwords.

```
FreedomDoctor: Great op, but nothing compared to next
one.
disgruntld1: What's up with yr piddly bandwidth?
FreedomDoctor: Camping. Living primitive.
```

"So will he help or not?" Waylee asked.

```
FreedomDoctor: r u in?
disgruntld1: Luxmore's a royal douche and so is rest of
company. But what's the op?
```

Waylee clapped her hands. "Ask him if he'll broadcast a video for us during the Super Bowl. Five to fifteen minutes, preferably closer to fifteen."

```
FreedomDoctor: Here's the ask. Want to broadcast 5-15
minute video during Super Bowl.
```

No immediate answer. Then,

```
disgruntld1: :D
FreedomDoctor: ☻
disgruntld1: :O
disgruntld1: u serious?
FreedomDoctor: yes
disgruntld1: U have to send from MediaCorp main control
studio. I do IT there, I know the system.
```

"So we don't have to break into the Georgia Dome?" Pel asked.

```
FreedomDoctor: what about Jorja Dome?
disgruntld1: lern to spel
FreedomDoctor: f u
```

"Don't piss him off," Waylee said.

```
FreedomDoctor: ☺
disgruntld1: Here's how sports events work.
disgruntld1: The broadcast director works out of a
trailer in stadium parking lot and decides which cam-
eras & mics to use. They patch in graphics as needed.
Then the signal goes by high-capacity optic cable from
stadium to MediaCorp main campus in northern Virginia,
where commercials & other content are inserted, and fi-
nal signal uploaded to satellites and Comnet.
disgruntld1: The studio crew can override anything com-
ing in from remote sites before it gets aired. But from
main control there's no override except at the individ-
ual receiving stations, & there's thousands of those.
disgruntld1: Therefore u would have to take over main
control studio at game time to transmit your video.
disgruntld1: QED.
```

"Snotty little bastard, isn't he?" Pel said.

```
FreedomDoctor: Can u do it if we send u the video?
disgruntld1: By myself? R u high?
disgruntld1: U need someone @ control studio, @ server
console, @ Comnet router, and @ uplink station, all
different locations. Maybe someone @ power station too.
disgruntld1: And there's security, lots of it.
FreedomDoctor: Can u get help?
disgruntld1: Co-workers R all douchebags. U want to do
it, u bring people.
disgruntld1: I can send u schematics & manuals. 100,000+
pages, have fun.
FreedomDoctor: That's what search is for.
```

"This doesn't seem very doable," Pel said.

"I don't know," Waylee said. "He listed four places, and there's four of us here. And I bet we can recruit more."

* * *

Baltimore

Kiyoko

Kiyoko organized a big outing to Club Kuro Neko, recruiting Absinthe and a bunch of other goths and cosplayers. She created a special costume for the occasion, a samurai cat girl, complete with armor, ears and tail.

Absinthe volunteered her black hearse for transport. Samurai helmet in hand, Kiyoko spotted the Watcher high overhead, betrayed by clear skies and moonlight. She pretended to ignore it, and waited until last to pile into the back of the hearse. Before getting in, she donned the helmet and cat ears and carefully adjusted her costume in the outside mirror.

Absinthe rolled down the driver's window. "Hurry the fuck up. You can do that on the way."

"No mirror." Kiyoko checked her plastic sword, then clambered in. She set her comlink video to low-light magnification, aimed it out the back window, and watched the Watcher follow them. Tears blurred her vision. She'd never see her home again.

Absinthe pulled into the parking lot. Club Kuro Neko had sprouted inside a long-abandoned granite-block church. Its bell tower collapsed during a derecho a few years back, leaving an ugly scar on the southeast corner.

The bouncers waved Kiyoko through. She'd never once paid cover at a Baltimore club.

Inside, bubbly J-pop echoed off the vaulted ceiling, shook her feet, and drove her sadness away. A whiff of sweat mixed with flowery incense and spilled beer. She strode past costumed regulars gathered around wall screen anime, game stations, and tall lotus-like tables. Beyond the crowded dance floor ahead, an animated furry quintet played on a screen mounted between a multihued rose window and the altar.

Friends, quasi-friends, and pseudo-friends accosted her every other step.

"Righteous costume."

"Meow."

"When's your band playing again?"

Normally she lived for this shit, but she had a mission to focus on. She found her friend Jayna at one of the bar counters, dressed as a slutty elf warrior, more skin than not. A lit-boy in wire spectacles and a floor-length scarf talked to her cleavage.

Kiyoko shooed the boy away. "Jayna, what the fuck?" They were both the same height, with Eastern faces, but Jayna had extra-fleshy breasts and hips.

"You told me to dress up. Just said, make sure it includes a wig." Which was blonde.

"Please tell me you have a cloak or something."

She shrugged and sipped from a technicolored drink.

"Right. Plan's off." *I wish I had M-pat's knack for planning.* She glanced around for someone else to switch with.

"I brought a coat," Jayna said. "It's over on the rack."

"Well why didn't you say so? Go to the basement supply room and I'll meet you in an hour. Bring your coat."

Kiyoko told her ride and quasi-roommates, "I'm meeting this totally hot guy later. I'm feeling lucky, so don't wait up."

"Okay, ho," was the gist of the typical reply, sometimes accompanied by a look of surprise.

When an hour had passed, Kiyoko descended the stairs to the basement bar, passed the bathrooms and a smooching couple in the hallway, and into an unconverted old classroom.

Inside next to the blackboard, Jayna huffed. "Took you long enough. Had to fend off a couple of live-at-homes who wanted the space."

"Sorry." She locked the door and pulled off her helmet. The costume exchange took a while to get everything properly fitted. "You make a cute samurai cat," she told Jayna when they looked presentable.

"And you are one hot warrior elf," Jayna said.

"Thanks. I don't usually play blondes."

Kiyoko called a taxi. "Driver'll meet you in the parking lot," she told Jayna after she switched off. "Take the back door."

"Okay."

"Sorry you have to leave early. And that you sacrificed a costume."

Jayna tilted her mouth into a 'meh,' then hugged her. "Good luck, Princess Kiyoko."

Kiyoko put on Jayna's trenchcoat and waited half an hour. She took the side exit and followed the cracked sidewalk north. No sign of the Watcher. *Hope Jayna doesn't get in trouble.*

It was still early, and cars streamed by. But a couple of dark-clothed predators eyed her from across the street. Her blood turned to cold sludge.

Kiyoko felt through her purse and found the pepper spray Waylee insisted she carry. M-pat had taught her some vicious self-defense moves too, but these men were pretty big. She walked faster.

The predators matched her pace, and cast glances in her direction. At some point they'd cross the street and make their move.

Kiyoko pivoted toward them and whipped out her comlink. "I'm calling the police, assholes," she shouted. She pretended to type a number and put the comlink to her mouth.

The men turned and walked off.

An approaching car, an ancient Chrysler, slowed. It stopped beside her. The passenger window opened, and the male driver leaned toward it. Too dark to see his features. "Hey girl, goin' my way?"

She recognized the voice. M-pat. He cracked open the door.

She hopped in. "Does your wife know you're out picking up elf maidens?"

He laughed and off they went.

"You weren't followed, were you?" Kiyoko asked as they turned onto U.S. 1, headed to Paulo's chop shop in Putty Hill.

"Girl, please."

One of the garage doors opened when they arrived. They drove inside, then Paulo hit a button and it closed behind them. He waved, and they got out. She kept Jayna's coat fastened.

M-pat's black electric Honda sat to the right, and beyond that, a 17-foot cargo truck with Boroborinsky Brothers Moving and Shipping decals. "That's your ride," M-pat said. "I took out the GPS, retagged it, and had it painted and decaled."

A shaven-headed punk ran out of the office. He looked familiar. It was Dingo, sans hair! He bowed and twirled his fingers. "Princess Kiyoko. I tremble in your exalted presence."

"You may rise, knave."

They hugged. "You have elf ears," he said. "And what's with the trench-coat?"

Kiyoko pulled off the ears and shoved them in a coat pocket. "What are you doing here?"

"Prepping your ride. Like it?"

"If it'll make it to the border, I love it."

"It was in pretty sad shape when M-pat brought it here, but now it'll take you wherever you wanna go. And I did the decals. Like 'em?"

Boroborinsky Brothers? "Why are you still in Baltimore?"

"It's temporary. Saving up for my exodus north."

"Is Shakti here too?"

His eyes drifted down. "We... uh... had a falling out. A differing of life strategies, if you will."

"That's too bad. You'll never find another catch like her, you know."

"Yeah, I know. Hold on, I got somethin' for you." He ran back into the office and returned with a stuffed black garbage bag.

"Garbage? How thoughtful."

"No, for real." He untied the top. The bag was full of clothes and shoes. "Goodwill throwaways. Normally you're about as incognito as a peacock among pigeons."

She hugged him again. "Why Dingo, I believe you actually just compli-mented me."

M-pat opened the hatch of his Honda and rolled back the security cover. "Got all your stuff here. Guaranteed it's more than you need."

One of the duffel bags contained her immersion suit, minus the frame and treadmill. "I thought you were selling this."

M-pat pointed a thumb at Dingo. "No need. Your ride prep was free."

Awesome. "Where's Nyasuke?"

He pulled a cat carrier out of the back seat.

Kiyoko ran over and unlatched the carrier gate. Her soulmate poked his head out and meowed. She pulled him the rest of the way out and held him close. "Oh, I missed you too, my little nyan-nyan." She turned to M-pat. "How long as he been in there?"

He looked about to laugh. "Oh, he fine."

Kiyoko went into the bathroom and changed out of Jayna's slutty elf costume, donning a yellow gown and golden wig from her bags. The color of Imperial China, prestigious, beautiful, and auspicious.

Paulo and Dingo whistled when she emerged.

She curtsied.

Paulo brought out a bottle labeled "Cachaça 51" and passed out small paper cups. He poured a shot of clear liquid into each one. It smelled like turpentine.

"I don't drink," Kiyoko said.

Paulo looked at her as if she were an alien. "Then one cup is all you need."

Sure, whatever. Kiyoko lifted her cup, preparing herself. *Hope I don't get in a wreck, or worse, end up sleeping with Dingo.*

Paulo raised his cup. "Boa sorte. Good luck."

The cachaça tasted as bad as it smelled.

January 14
Cedarville State Forest

Waylee

In the back of the converted school bus, Waylee awoke in silent darkness before dawn, too excited to sleep. Charles had recruited an engineer at MediaCorp to help them get their message on the air. They could make this work. She could feel it.

She couldn't believe how quiet this place was at night. The stillness of winter, Shakti called it. The air in the bus was stuffy, with undertones of oil and dust. Waylee slid out of her bunk and threw on the nearest clothes that resembled hers.

Pel stirred in the bunk above and rolled over. She'd ravaged him in the bath house last night until the shower water turned cold and the winter air chilled their flesh. In the lower opposite bunk, Charles lay motionless beneath his blanket and sheet, face planted in his pillow.

Waylee tiptoed to the front of the bus and eased onto the forward-facing couch. Her computer sat on the faux-wood table. She turned the power on.

Next to it, Big Red hummed softly and displayed a black and white image of a narrow, leaf-covered road enveloped by tall trees and dense shrubs. Pel had placed an infrared camera at the campground entrance and set up a motion detector program to warn them if vehicles or people approached.

Waylee opened her video program, looking forward to another editing session. It was like combining journalism and music, objectivity and art.

Charles had set up an "asymmetric backdoor" to the MediaCorp intranet, which he claimed was virtually undetectable. With a little help from Pel, she dug up some more gems. The company recorded all their board meetings. During one of his bombastic orations, Luxmore told the others, "MediaCorp is about more than just moving electrons around, providing information for its own sake. We're about providing the right information, information that will shape the world."

That's definitely going in.

Waylee opened a Comnet portal on the computer and ran a search for Beatrice Baddelats. She'd make a great ally. The more she knew about the woman, the better.

She tagged a few articles for later reading, related to genealogy and charity work with a children's hospital. The good stuff wouldn't be public, though, so she moved her search to intranet forums.

Her diaphragm seized in mid-exhale. Yesterday, the board impeached Ms. Baddelats "for interacting poorly with others and failing in her fiduciary responsibilities."

Waylee checked the video recording.

Ms. Baddelats thanked Bob Luxmore for his long service, but said it was time for him to focus on his CEO duties, and let someone else take the chair. Shoulders back with confidence, she nominated one of her fellow board members, Morris Rodriguez, for the position.

"I decline the nomination," he said.

Her jaw dropped. She looked around the table, but no one would make eye contact. Chairman Luxmore motioned that Beatrice Baddelats be removed from the board, effective immediately. The vote to impeach was, except for Ms. Baddelats, unanimous.

Big Red beeped. Pel's motion alarm. Waylee swiped a finger against the black screen perched on top.

The screen woke up and displayed the campground entrance in grainy black and white. Something big and light gray passed out of the frame.

Pel shot out of his bunk, grabbed jeans and a flannel, and dashed forward, eyes wide with panic. "Someone's coming."

Dawn had yet to arrive. Not likely a ranger or forester. Pel threw on his jeans and backed up the camera footage. Looked like a moving truck.

Weird, but better weird than police cars.

A pair of amped-up headlights roamed the campground, bright white LEDs cutting through the skeletal trees. Cold sweat oozed from her skin. "I'm waking Peter," she said.

She hurried out the bus door. Frigid air tore at her skin. A few feet away, Peter's tent door unzipped. In the trees beyond, Shakti remained a lump in her Brazilian hammock.

"Expecting someone?" Waylee asked Peter as he emerged.

His lips trembled. "No. We should hide."

The headlights caught their bus. Too late.

The truck paused, then entered their loop.

Pel exited the bus, stun gun in shaking hand. Shakti poked her head above the rim of her hammock.

Waylee sprinted into the bus and shook Charles until his eyes opened. "Wha?"

"Someone's coming. Can you upload all our video to a Collective site?"

He blinked. "Are you kidding? This connection, it'll take hours."

She should have known that. "I've gotta hide it then." Pel had been backing everything up—he always did that—but where did he keep the data cubes? They weren't hooked up to the computers. He must have put them away somewhere. She dashed back outside. "Pel. Where's—"

The truck pulled into their campground site, the headlights blinding her like twin suns. Her fists clenched.

Peter approached it, feet moving in slow motion. Pel hung back. Maybe he had a good hiding place for the data.

The engine stopped but the lights stayed on. Someone hopped out, silhouette of a girl in a trenchcoat, details drowned by the backlight. Waylee blocked the lights with her hand, but still couldn't see.

"Pel? Waylee, is that you?" Kiyoko's voice.

Waylee ran toward the silhouette. It brightened into her sister, red-eyed but smiling, wearing a golden wig.

She squeezed Kiyoko to her chest, wanting never to let go. She smelled like faint sweat and alcohol, no hint of the cherry blossom perfume she loved.

"Good to see you too," Kiyoko said, and hugged her back.

Still entwined, Waylee gazed in her sister's eyes, just inches away. So much behind them. "Last time I saw you... I didn't mean what I said. You're not a deluded little girl."

"Thank you." Kiyoko kissed her cheek. And you know I don't hate you. I love you."

Tears blurred Waylee's vision.

"You've always been there for me," Kiyoko said, "the only one. That's why I'm here for you."

Waylee brushed the tears out of her eyes. "What do you—?"

Pel thrust his face in her periphery and addressed her sister. "Can you turn those damn lights off?"

Kiyoko let go. "Sure." She climbed back into the truck cab. The lights shut off, leaving floating bright glows in their wake.

When she exited again, Pel asked, "Why are you here? How'd you know where to find us?"

"You're not glad to see her?" Waylee said.

"I am, but she's probably been followed, and they'll be on us any second."

"I'm not being followed. We - M-pat and I - planned this carefully."

"How, how do you know? You have no idea how good Homeland is at finding people, the resources they have. Not to mention how tempting a $3 million bounty is. You can't trust anyone."

"You've sure turned paranoid."

"That's because people really are out to get me."

"Oh, quit harassing her," Waylee said. She introduced Peter and summarized their saga since they fled the band house.

Kiyoko nodded. "Charles has been filling me in." She turned to Shakti. "I saw Dingo. He was actually nice to me."

Shakti bounced on her feet. "How's he doing? Did he say anything about me?"

"I think he misses you. He said no one else can compare, more or less."

The campsite began to brighten. Sunrise.

"That truck's gotta be out of the state forest before the staff arrive," Peter said. He examined his comlink. "Early birds could be here in half an hour."

"Well let's go, then," Kiyoko said. "We drive to Vermont, then we cross into Canada."

Shakti smiled. "So I guess this is it. I have relatives in Toronto. They'd be happy to put us up for a while. Dingo can meet us there."

"Can someone else drive first shift? I was up all night and I'm about to pass out." She did look less animated than usual.

Waylee waved her arms. "Hold on. Let's discuss this first. Charles contacted someone who'll help us take over the Super Bowl feed. It's too big an opportunity to pass up, but we have to do it from MediaCorp's broadcast center in Virginia."

Kiyoko's jaw dropped. "I thought... Are you crazy? Sorry, I mean..."

"We can do it," Waylee said.

"Won't be long before the FBI starts looking for me."

Peter made a "T" gesture with his hands, one of those football things. "Whoa there. We can talk about this later. We gotta get that truck out of here, pronto. I gotta place on the farm we can stash it. Kiyoko, that's your name?"

She curtsied.

He grinned. "Follow me." He cupped his hands around his mouth. "Everyone else on the bus. Leave the tent and all, I'll come back for it."

* * *

St. Mary's County

Peter stopped the bus outside a dilapidated wooden barn on Friendship Farm and hopped out. He pulled open the barn's double doors and waved Kiyoko forward. Her truck barely cleared the doorway.

Kiyoko strolled out of the barn, cat in her arms. Peter closed the doors, ushered her onto the bus, and followed her on.

Waylee, Pel, and Shakti faced each other on the short couches in the front, computer gear covering the table. Charles sat in one of the two chairs across the aisle.

Kiyoko took the chair opposite Charles. They smiled at each other.

Peter stood next to the driver's seat. "You can't stay here at the farm, obviously. So we head back to Cedarville or you hop in Kiyoko's truck and we say goodbye."

Waylee slid out of her couch and stood in the aisle, scanning the others' eyes. "We can worry about leaving the country later. Right now, we've got a chance to finish our mission."

Pel's mouth opened, but Waylee continued. "Betty Battleaxe stood up to Luxmore and yesterday the Board of Directors impeached her. Even the elite can't stray from the script."

Eyes widened.

"...And elections, insiders have an overwhelming advantage. Rand's not even worried. Same thing with information. MediaCorp's made it impossible for people like me to reach a significant audience. Like I said when we started this, we can't win a fixed game. Nothing's changed. We've gotta kick over the table." Her fist smacked against the table top.

"Jeez, careful," Pel said, eyes on the computers.

They're fine. "And even if no one wants to help, I'm doing it."

Pel threw up his hands. "Waylee..."

She stared in his tense eyes. "What? What happened to you? When'd you turn so scared of everything?"

He half rose from his seat. "What? Smart is more like it."

Her stomach tightened. "Look, we got Charles out and we collected some great material in the most exclusive gathering of the decade. We can do this, too."

Pel shook his head. "That's just your manic phase talking. Just because you think you can take on the world doesn't mean you actually can."

Domineering asshole...

She thrust a finger toward him. "Fuck you, Pel. You're a real prick sometimes."

He leapt up. "After all I've done for you? Thrown my whole life away? How dare you! Well, crash and burn on your own." He stormed toward the door.

Waylee straddled the aisle with arms out, blocking his exit. "No way are you running off."

He thrust his face inches from hers. "Out of my way." His eyes promised murder.

"Go ahead, hit me," she said. "Try it. I'll beat your fucking ass, coward, and you know it."

Kiyoko jumped up and clapped her hands over her ears. The cat dove under the table. "Stop it! Stop it! What's wrong with you two?"

Waylee stared at her sister. An alarm rang beneath the waves of fury. "Sorry. I didn't mean what I said. My stupid brain..." She shut her eyes and started playing "Home" by Edward Sharpe & The Magnetic Zeros in her head, the happiest love song she could come up with at the moment.

"What are you doing?" Pel said beyond the darkness, his voice still edgy.

The song continued.

I'm not thinking straight either," he muttered. "Maybe no one does, they just think they do." He spoke louder. "How long did you say before the feds start looking for you?"

"A day or two, I'd guess," Kiyoko said. "We can be in Vermont by then, maybe Canada."

Waylee opened her eyes. Everyone was sitting. "Will it make a difference if we wait?"

Kiyoko pulled her cat from its hiding spot. "What if they put extra patrols on the border?"

"They're probably already there," Waylee said. "In case Pel and I show up. We might be better off waiting to try it. There's gonna be less heat up there if we wait."

Pel pursed his lips. "Maybe."

She addressed Charles. "Do you think we can get into the MediaCorp complex?"

He glanced at Pel. "Don't know enough yet."

"Then let's look at the plans," she said, "get some help, and see what we can do."

"That sounds reasonable," Shakti said, facing Pel.

"You always side with Waylee," Pel replied.

Anger poked tentacles through Waylee's brain. She closed her eyes again and resumed playing "Home," but wrote new lyrics on the fly. *Home. We lost our home. But I'll always have a home when I'm with you...*

"Even if we can get in," Pel's voice said, "the bully boys will come down hard. How would we get out?"

Waylee stopped her internal song and opened her eyes. "All part of the planning." She caught her friends' eyes. "So do we have consensus, to at least spend a few days putting a plan together?" *Go quiet into Luxmore's night? Never!*

"What about Canada?" Kiyoko said.

Shakti leaned forward. "Waylee had a good point. Homeland's probably already watching the border."

"They always watch the border," Waylee said. "But they want us pretty bad, so they'll wait in force. And there's that $3 million motivation for so-called friends to turn us in."

Kiyoko looked distressed. "Then what do we do? Are we stuck here 'til they find us?"

Waylee crouched next to her sister. "We'll figure that out too."

Kiyoko ran fingers through her rainbow-streaked hair. "I want to know what Pel thinks." She cast pleading eyes at him. "What should we do?"

Waylee stood and stared at him.

"I'm tempted to turn myself in," he said. "See if Francis can get me a decent plea bargain."

"No!" Waylee reached over and grabbed him by the shirt. "No, you can't do that!"

Pel knocked her hands aside. "Then Canada. Or go somewhere by boat."

"Let's compromise," she said.

Heads tilted and eyebrows raised.

She looked from face to face. "Have some faith in me, and I'll have faith in you. Let's look at our options. If you honestly think we can't get into MediaCorp, I'll respect that."

Pel sat silently for a while, then returned her gaze. "Even if you don't always make the best decisions, you can see opportunities like no one else."

That's progress, I suppose.

"I don't know how we can pull it off and escape," he said, "and I don't trust this engineer. But like Charles said, we haven't really looked into it yet."

Peter crossed his arms. "Sounds like you're not ready to take off yet. Back to Cedarville, then?"

"If that's what we're doing," Kiyoko shouted, "I need my stuff out of the truck."

"Of course."

She lowered her voice. "And will the truck be safe there?"

Peter smiled. "I have a padlock. And no one uses that barn but me; that's why I had you park there."

Waylee peered through the windshield at Peter's cabin just beyond. It was small, but he lived by himself.

"Do you have high speed Comnet access?" she asked him. "Like they have at the main house?"

Peter narrowed his eyes. "Yeah. Why?"

Waylee paused to edit her thoughts. "If we kept a low profile, it would be a lot easier researching our options with a decent link."

Charles leaned out of his chair. "Yeah. Props to Pel for making that 4G antenna and all, but it's as slow as my old gym teacher's brain."

Peter chuckled. "You kids are just spoiled. Back in my day—"

Everyone groaned and looked away.

He kept going. "—there wasn't even an Internet. If you wanted information, you had to go to a library. And use a thing called a card catalog. No mobile phones either. Telephones had to be plugged into the wall, weighed a ton, with rotary dials…" He finally noticed the lack of interest. "Anyway, you can't stay on the farm. Remember we decided you should leave?"

"No one will know…" She stopped, seeing frustration build on Peter's face. He'd done so much for them, so had the other residents, and here she was disrespecting their will, trying to exploit them just like a Bob Luxmore would do. She threw up her hands. "You're right."

Charles scowled.

"You made your decision," she said, "and it's not for me to undermine it. I'm an outsider here."

Shakti nodded.

Waylee asked Pel, "Can you research from the campsite?"

He looked at Charles, whose mouth drooped.

"Everything will take longer," Pel said. "But we can deal with it." His eyes widened. "We'll have to upload all our video and data at some point, which isn't really feasible on 4G. Should have done that before we left the farm. I just was busy and didn't think of it."

He turned to Peter. "Could we at least do that, as long as we're here?"

"How long will it take?"

He shrugged. "Gonna have to find good homes for it all, and make lots of copies. Probably a while."

"Are we close enough for Wi-Fi?" Waylee asked. "We could do it from the bus."

Pel nodded. "Yes, yes. Not as fast as their landline, but a lot faster than cell."

Peter agreed and wrote his code on a piece of paper.

"Don't worry," Pel said, "we'll cover our tracks."

30

January 15
Cedarville State Forest

Charles

Kiyoko sat next to Charles on the forward couch, staring at the Canadian border on his interface screen and nibbling strawberry Pocky she'd brought from B'more. She wore a denim jacket, a scary looking Dwarf Eats Hippo T-shirt, and baggy jeans at least two sizes too big. Goodwill gifts from Dingo, she'd explained. Not very Princess-like, but why bother dressing up when they were hiding in the sticks?

Last night he watched Kiyoko walk to the campground bath house. He'd imagined her stepping inside the shower stall, closing the plastic curtain, then stripping off her clothes, first that trenchcoat, then her shoes and stockings, her yellow wig and dress, finally her bra and underwear. She'd fold them neatly on the wooden bench inside the stall, and enter the shower, her naked body the most beautiful thing in creation. She'd run water through her rainbow streaked hair, then take the soap and lather her upturned breasts and pointy nipples, then move down her firm stomach and circle her thighs. Then she'd slip her fingers between her thighs and start rubbing…

Charles suddenly felt uncomfortable. He had a severe stiffy. Kiyoko was practically touching him—she'd know for sure. And Pel and Waylee sat right across from them, busy on their computers. Waylee got rabid sometimes, and might freak if she thought he was hitting on her sister.

No privacy on this bus. Peter hung outside, but the rest were stuck in here most of the day. "Can't wait to get out of here," he said to Kiyoko.

She cast those exotic eyes on him. "Think of it as a vacation."

"What, on a bus in the woods? BetterWorld's way more interesting."

Kiyoko nodded. "True, but you need a fast connection. My immersion gear won't work at all here." She frowned. "I can't use my account anyway, with the FBI looking for me."

Waylee glared at them. "I can't believe you two. BetterWorld's just a distraction from real life, from making the real world a better place. Worse, MediaCorp's using it to take over the global economy, and then we might as well anoint Bob Luxmore as the One True God."

Maybe she's right. Besides, Kiyoko was sitting next to him, their legs touching now. Who needed BetterWorld? Charles looked back at his screen and searched for blog entries about surveillance drones on the Vermont-Canada border.

"Do you miss your grandma?" Kiyoko said.

Charles thought about it. "Maybe a little. But I doubt she notices I'm gone, what with all them kids and drunk-ass aunt and all the other people that hang out there."

Kiyoko poked him in the side. "Of course she'd notice. You're not exactly an average person."

Charles poked her back. She giggled.

"I was in juvie for months," he said. "They weren't expecting me out for another year."

Pel unclipped Big Red's monitor screen from its stand and rolled it up. "Some of us are trying to work." He rolled up the keyboard next, unplugged everything, and marched to the back of the bus, pushing through the curtain to the bunks.

Charles stared at the curtain. Maybe he could clear the room. Shakti was out wandering, so only one left.

"Hey Waylee," he said.

She looked up from her computer screen. "Yeah?"

"Something up with Pel? Maybe you should go check on him."

She narrowed her eyes. "He's stressed. But he's right that we have work to do. I thought you two were helping."

"We are, just..."

"Well alright then." She returned to her screen.

That didn't work. I'll just wait for her to use the bathroom or something.

Kiyoko pointed at one of the articles she'd been reading. "There's cameras and motion detectors all along the border." She moved her finger to a blog entry. "And people are saying there's a lot more drones and Homeland agents from Maine to New York than usual."

"You said you knew people who could get us across?"

She turned to him. "Yeah, sort of. It's a friend of a friend of a friend kind of thing."

Charles nodded.

Kiyoko frowned. "Waylee's right, a $3 million reward is awfully tempting, and the actual smuggler, I don't know anything about him."

"Maybe we could disguise ourselves. Like with those masks everyone wore breaking me out of juvie."

She smiled. "Of course. We could do that, if we could get the masks. It's one of the longest borders in the world. There's gotta be a way."

An alert message popped up on the screen: 'Package arrived.'

About time. He pulled the computer over a little. "Gotta check something."

"What is it?" Kiyoko asked.

"We'll see." Charles navigated to the anonymous cloud compartment he'd set up for the MediaCorp engineer. It had a long list of new documents and a readme file, presumably from disgruntld1. Charles checked the files for malware, confirmed they were clean, then downloaded them to his computer.

As promised, the files contained details and schematics about Media-Corp's broadcast and computer networks. It would probably take days to digest. The readme file included a backdoor address and password, but warned that most of the network was unreachable from outside the building.

Charles copied the files onto a memory wafer. "Waylee?"

She looked up again. "Yes?"

He handed her the wafer. "Got a bunch of documents from our engineer friend. Can you give this to Pel and take a look?"

She grinned. "Awesome. I knew we could count on you." She bounded down the aisle and through the back curtain into the bunk room.

So it is possible to outsmart her. He was finally alone with Kiyoko.

Kiyoko looked a little worried. "We're not going to break into Media-Corp if we'll get caught, will we?"

"Of course not. That's part of the deal, we only do what we know we can do."

No telling how long the room would stay empty. Charles decided to make his move. He leaned against Kiyoko and targeted his lips toward hers.

She turned her head and the kiss landed on her cheek. Disappointment rose inside him, followed by embarrassment.

Kiyoko slid away and blushed.

He'd failed. He'd told her he loved her, but she just wanted to be friends. *Of course.*

"Charles," she said, looking down. "I'm sorry, this isn't the time." She looked up and spoke softly. "I told you, I can't date you, you need someone your own age."

"Waylee's older than Pel."

"Not by much. And they're both adults, legally I mean."

I'm an adult. No one takes care of me.

She sidled closer. "I'm sorry." She covered his right hand with hers, her warmth spreading through his veins. "It's not personal. We just can't do this. Please respect me when I say that, okay?"

The disappointment grew. "Yeah, it's just..."

Kiyoko peeked down the aisle. "'Kay," she whispered in his ear. "Just one kiss, but that's it, and it doesn't mean we're going out or anything."

He looked at her, his heart pounding.

Her eyes darted around and her fingers fidgeted. "It's just 'cause you are pretty awesome and it's been a while since I've kissed anyone, and I should just shut up..."

She placed her hands on his cheeks and kissed him. Her lips were soft and moist and warm. The cherry blossom smell of her hair and neck wafted through his nostrils. It was heaven, like being jolted with electricity, way better than he'd imagined.

He'd never actually kissed a girl before so he tried to duplicate the way she moved her lips. But then she pulled away, and it was over.

She blushed again. "Okay, it's clear you need some practice. Here..." She positioned his arms around her waist, his hands on the small of her back, then put her hands around his neck, her face inches from his. "Now kiss me, put some passion in it, but no slobber or anything. And no tongue." Her eyes sparkled. "Merge your soul with mine."

They kissed again, pressing tighter than before. Their mouths opened together, their breath merged. She tasted like strawberry sugar. His hands moved up and down her back. Then he disappeared in her, like an immersion suit. *Princess Kiyoko. I'm the luckiest man in the world.*

Kiyoko let go of his neck and ended the kiss. "That was nice." She pulled his hands off her back. "I'm a little out of practice myself. My last boyfriend, last summer and fall, wasn't a real boyfriend at all, he was just a player and I still feel stupid for giving myself to him."

"I'm not like that."

"I know. Not everyone's like that, I know." She held his hand. "Remember what I said, though. We're not dating or anything. We should get back to helping Waylee and finding a way to safety."

"Ok." No point disrespecting her and ruining what they'd built. She was nice and wouldn't do anything to hurt him. And who knew what the future might bring. Ten more months and he'd be eighteen. He'd work out and learn Krav Maga and be a king like M-pat.

Kiyoko put a finger to her lips. "Waylee can't know. She wouldn't understand."

"Yeah, our secret."

31

January 16

Waylee

Waylee hardly slept. A hypomania symptom, but a good one. Sleep wasted valuable time.

While Charles and Kiyoko researched MediaCorp's broadcast system, she refined her video. Knowing she tended to miss details, she ran each version by Shakti for feedback.

Waylee also decided to contact Beatrice Baddelats. Even though she'd been ousted from MediaCorp's Board of Directors, she still had sway.

She borrowed Peter's comlink and disabled the camera. Charles routed it through one of the Collective's anonymous exchanges, creating a fake callback number, one that didn't belong to anyone.

Ms. Baddelats answered after three rings. She scowled. "Who is this?"

Waylee thought about using Estelle Cosimo's voice, but settled on her own. "Hi. Beatrice Baddelats?"

"Yes? Why are you audio only?"

"We spoke at the New Year's party. Estelle Cosimo."

Ms. Baddelats snorted. "You're a fraud. You were impersonating her. Did you know you're on the FBI's Most Wanted list?"

"That's a travesty. That list should be for murderers and financial scammers. And CEO's who fix elections and try to control the world."

Her eyes narrowed. "What do you want from me? How did you get my number?"

Waylee focused on the first question. "I want to help you bring down Bob Luxmore."

"You're wasting your time. The board loves him. They set me up and stabbed me in the back."

"Forget the board, we—"

"Homeland Security's onto you, Waylee Freid, born Emily Smith. I looked you up. You're just some socialist punk from Baltimore—"

"I'm not a socialist. I'm—"

"I don't want anything to do with you. Do yourself a favor and turn yourself in. Don't call me again." The screen returned to the dial pad.

Bitch. Waylee felt betrayed; her only outside ally had turned on her. Of course, she and Ms. Battleaxe never were allies except in the land of over-optimism.

She shuffled into the back of the camper and curled up beneath her musty blanket. She breathed in and out, trying to stave off depression. The world faded away.

Pel shook her shoulder. "Finished decoding the comlink data." It was the first time he'd touched her since their argument two days ago.

Waylee threw off the blanket. She still felt energetic, still in the upper half of her quasi-sine curve. She lifted her arms to hug him, but he hurried away, ushering everyone to the forward couches and chairs.

Waylee plopped down next to Shakti on one of the couches. Her sari smelled worse every day, or maybe it was her underwear. *Not that mine is any better.*

Pel and Charles sat on the other side of the table, facing Big Red and an interface unit. Peter and Kiyoko took the chairs across the aisle. Kiyoko pinched her nose and waved the air. "Pee-yew! Who hasn't been showering?"

Charles and Shakti cringed.

"We can't wash clothes," Waylee said, "that's the issue. No detergent."

Kiyoko said, "Well Dingo gave me a whole bag of clothes. You all can split them up. And you can use my soap, I left it in the shower."

Pel focused on his screen. He looked excited and smug, the way he always did after solving a problem. "Been working on this since the day after New Year's. Got as much as I can. Props to Charles for his help."

Charles shrugged. "You did ninety percent of it."

Pel glanced around. "Anyway, we pulled the IDs and encryption keys from eighty nine comlinks, and Comnet access passwords from sixty two."

Waylee led the applause. That many comlinks, they were bound to find something useful.

He nodded. "Every time a link accesses the Comnet, which happens more often than you'd think, it sends the user name and password, along with a signature identifying the comlink. The wireless signals were encrypted but our analysis program identified the keys from processor echoes."

"English, please," Waylee said.

He hesitated. "Details aren't important. What's important is that we've got a bunch of digital comlink signatures and the user names and passwords. We can pretend to be the users and access their accounts. And we can load scripts on their actual comlinks and cause all manner of mischief."

"Can we do that from here?"

He stroked his growing beard. "It's too much for us," he said. "I'd like to distribute these codes to elites in the Collective and encourage them to run with it."

"After the Super Bowl," she suggested.

"No, better do it now, before the guests are notified and they change their passwords or buy new comlinks. Besides, it'll be a good distraction; Homeland will think that's what we were after."

Makes sense. "Anything that will help us get into MediaCorp?"

"Maybe." He turned to Charles. "Ready to hoist the Jolly Roger?"

Charles smiled. "Aye aye, Cap'n."

"We've got no captains here," Waylee said, "but… mind if I look over your shoulder? I should learn this stuff."

Pel nodded. She abandoned Shakti and crowded next to him and Charles. He inched away when their legs touched.

Face blank, Pel swiped Big Red's keyboard mat and woke it up. He opened some windows on the fabric-thin screen clipped to its foldout metal frame. One of the windows displayed a spreadsheet of names, Comnet IDs, passwords, and random-looking text. "We should be careful with Ms. Baddelats since she's on to us."

The name pierced her like a dagger. "Yeah. She might have some dirt on Luxmore, though."

"Okay. But let's start with… Wilfred Pickford, another MediaCorp board member. He and his wife were next to us at midnight."

Waylee remembered their New Year's kiss, how she'd wanted Pel right there in the midst of America's elite. She gazed at her boyfriend's handsome features and hoped she hadn't ruined things between them.

Pickford and his matronly wife had also kissed at midnight. Even the people's enemies were still human beings and capable of love and compassion. Too bad their focus was so narrow.

Pel ran his location spoofer and logged onto the Comnet with one of his fake IDs. He downloaded a program, from one of the hidden Collective sites it looked like, and checked it for malware. Finding none, he opened it.

A blank window appeared, with menus on the top and icons underneath. "It'll figure out what kind of comlinks our targets have from the digital signatures," he said, "and display replicas on our monitor."

Charles craned his neck to get a closer look.

Pel brought up fields labeled "User ID," "Password," and "Signature," and swiped over data from the spreadsheet. The blank window transformed into a Comnet screen with sparse factory defaults. "The Comnet now thinks we're accessing from Pickford's link. We don't know what's on his real comlink yet, though."

"We got his other passwords?" Charles asked.

"Not for Pickford." Pel tapped on his name in the spreadsheet, which brought up another window with blue text. "He didn't check his mail or anything, but his comlink ran some updates at midnight."

"So computers celebrate New Year's too," Waylee joked.

Pel smiled. "They update software and back up data every day unless you tell them otherwise. Sometimes it's irritating."

Charles peered at the screen. "So we gotta get on his comlink to get his files and shit?"

"Yeah, and once you have the signature, it's easy." Pel opened a menu above the virtual comlink and tapped an option called "Sync." A yin-yang symbol filled the display and spun clockwise. "His comlink's on, which is good. He won't notice what we're doing; it's all in the background."

The yin-yang rotated for a while, then disappeared, replaced by a slate-gray screen with the MediaCorp logo and rows of icons. "Voilá. We now have an exact duplicate of Pickford's comlink, with all his programs and data."

"Can we go the other way?" Charles asked.

Pel nodded. "Yep. The Comnet thinks we're Pickford. It's like doing a cloud backup and install." He slid the keypad and display over. "Wanna drive?"

"No doubt." Charles clicked the maximize button, and Pickford's comlink filled the screen. He pressed the 'Comnet' icon. "So I'm some rich old white guy now?" He navigated from site to site and downloaded programs, not saying anything.

"What are you doing?" Waylee asked.

Charles kept his eyes on the screen. "Loading worms and rootkits."

Pel turned to her. "We can access all his data now—emails, voice mails, you name it. All his passwords are saved in files we have on our duplicate here. But we can also take control of his comlink, turn on the camera, microphone, and GPS, and spy on him 24/7 without any indicator lights or listable processes." He returned to the screen. "The rootkits will hide our tampering and modify his anti-malware program to let us do what we want. We'll install backdoors in case he changes his Comnet password."

"We can sync to his other computers too," Charles said. "Get whatever's there."

Pel nodded. "And send viruses to his contacts to take over their comlinks, although we have to be careful—likely someone will notice."

"We need a strategy," Waylee said, "before you tip people off and they replace all the comlinks you hacked."

"I agree. And like I said before, we need help. It's more work than we can handle by ourselves."

"Can we see Scott Overmann's emails?"

He squinted. "Who's that?"

"MediaCorp News Director. A.k.a. Minister of Propaganda."

Charles turned. "We can send him a document from Pickford, maybe as a reply to something, and encode a virus in it."

"What about his security software?"

"I'll write something special, custom encrypted. Like Homeland did to me. My defense program didn't recognize it because it was brand new." He scanned the display. "This guy can make us stinkin' rich."

"You can access his bank accounts?" Waylee said.

"Old people and IT don't mix." He grinned at Pel. "No offense, old man."

"Who hacked all these comlinks, you snot-nosed brat?" He smiled to let Charles know he was kidding.

If Pel's old at 26, I'm ancient at 28. "We can use money," Waylee said, "but the Super Bowl broadcast is our top priority."

Charles's face fell. "We can do both."

"You said you can get on other comlinks and activate their cameras, mikes, and GPS?"

"Yeah," Pel said, tilting his eyebrows at her.

"If we get to the right people, we can map out the broadcast center that way. Especially if they've got data glasses like you used to have."

Pel's eyebrows relaxed. "I miss those."

"And don't forget we have disgruntld1. He sent us those network schematics—"

"Without any interpretation."

Always interrupting. "And I bet there's more he can do."

He frowned. "Assuming we can trust him."

* * *

January 17

Waylee searched through her copy of News Director Overmann's emails. *Thank you, Charles.*

Rick Mustel, the president's Special Advisor for the Media, emailed Overmann every night at 1 AM with a list of stories like "Check the new study (link here) showing how private schools outperform public schools. Be sure to blame teachers unions for public school failures."

The next morning, Overmann, a former political media strategist himself, incorporated Mustel's suggestions into executive memos that he sent to all the news staff, addressing what stories should be covered and how they should be covered.

Waylee ran some comparisons. Mustel's talking points were remarkably similar to the news that day. So when the president told her, "I don't tell their anchors what to say," he was lying.

More damning, Overmann sent information the other way. "Justice Consiglio quite naughty – check out these live sex sites he frequents. Cover or no?"

Mustel's response: "Hold off. Our team thinks he'll play ball."

The individual pixels seemed to pop out of the screen at her, flashing different colors. Conspiracy to blackmail a Supreme Court justice couldn't possibly be legal. *Jackpot!* Except of course her evidence was collected illegally and therefore inadmissible.

What was the president's agenda for the Supreme Court anyway? Waylee slogged through three years of communiqués.

Uphold private property rights…

She kept looking.

No anti-trust enforcement, especially regarding MediaCorp…

Of course.

Support the administration's initiatives against "cyberterrorism." These included a new guideline recommending life imprisonment for anyone committing crimes linked to the Collective.

That's us. She should probably be afraid. She should probably call off any attempt to air her video.

Fuck them. Fear keeps them in power. Fear keeps us down. She'd just have to make sure no one besides her got caught.

January 18

Waylee

Sitting on her narrow cot in the back of the bus, Waylee watched her video. Finished at last.

It began with an annoying emergency tone and a blue screen with the Presidential Seal. The tone gave way to Pel's voice, modulated to sound official, saying, "This is an emergency message from the President of the United States. We apologize for the interruption. Please stand by. You must take immediate action following the end of this broadcast."

From there, the president and Luxmore did most of the talking. Her favorite clip: "We help each other out." She had laid a track of tense, dissonant music beneath, the volume just audible enough to provide continuity over the camera cuts, and set the viewers' brains on edge.

Waylee copied the video to a data wafer and handed it to Pel, who was working with Charles and Kiyoko on the forward table. "Ready for broadcast."

Pel plugged the wafer into Big Red and swiped the touch pad. "What's the run time?" he asked over his shoulder.

"Whole thing? Fifteen minutes. But it's breaking news format. Five minutes should be enough to get our message across and hook people. The video will reach at least a third of the country, and then everyone will talk about it. After that, if you know social network theory, if only ten percent of Americans speak against the president and MediaCorp, the majority will follow." She slapped the table. "Luxmore and Rand are doomed."

He half-turned his head and raised an eyebrow. "Don't forget they have ample chance for rebuttal."

"Doesn't matter. The stain will be permanent. So how are we distributing the rest of our data, all the files and emails?"

"I stored it on a bunch of darknet servers. I'm adding your video to it." He opened a window with lines of alphanumerics in black and purple fonts. "After the Super Bowl, this script will post most of the links on Collective discussion boards, from which they can be distributed across the Comnet. I'm keeping some copies hidden. Just in case."

She stared at his screen. The Collective discussion boards weren't exactly public. "We should publish links in the video."

On the other side of the table, Charles leaned forward. "Winning strat. And our Collectivistas can keep them solid."

"What do you mean?"

"Keep the mirrors moving and block spam attacks. I can code that, easy." He nodded in agreement with himself. "And we should set up bots to boost your trend."

"So the Collective's gonna help?" *Awesome.*

Still staring at the screen, Pel said, "We picked sixty-four inner circle hackers with top notch creds. They have to pass a Neumann-Heinzinger trust test first, and rate a random sample of others. And rate disgruntld1 - I want to see what people think of him."

What the hell is a Neumann-Heinzinger trust test? "There's still some honest journalists out there. We should send them the files too."

Pel turned. "Why don't we just do that now and be done with it? Then we don't have to risk life in prison."

Not this again. "I thought we were going to research the possibilities first."

He sighed. "I did say that."

"Nothing we uncovered will see an audience unless we make it impossible to ignore. And we need thirty percent."

Pel scratched his ear. "If you type up their addresses, I'll write another notification program."

"Thank you." She leaned over to kiss him.

He flinched.

He still hadn't forgiven her? "Can we talk?" She flipped a thumb toward the door. It was after five and park staff would be gone.

Pel's shoulders drooped. He got up and threw on a jacket and followed her out of the bus into the forest.

The setting sun cast long shadows from the bare trees. Dry sticks and leaves crunched under her feet as they walked away from the campsite. She hadn't bothered with a coat and immediately regretted it. *Better skip the preliminaries.*

She turned to Pel, her heart afraid to beat. "Pel, are you not in love with me anymore?"

He averted his eyes. "Waylee—look, this isn't the time for talks like that. And I don't want to fight and send you into a rage or depression."

She played an upbeat love song in her head, then stepped forward and twined her fingers into his. "You're not my enemy. MediaCorp and Homeland are all the enemies I can handle."

He didn't pull away. "Have you thought about what will happen if you go to prison? About your mind? You've already had two major depressive episodes in the past month, which technically means you've transitioned to bipolar II."

"When exactly did you get your medical degree? I must have missed the graduation ceremony."

He pulled his fingers out of her hands. "Just info on the Comnet, you know that. But I worry about you."

Waylee's knees threatened to stop holding her up. *He's right, I'm falling apart. Thrown into the world with cast iron shackles.* "We won't get caught." She turned up the internal volume of her love ditty. "Pel, I'm so sorry I threatened you and called you a coward. Can't you forgive me?"

He exhaled a cloud her way. "I know you can't help it."

"I didn't mean to ruin your life." Tears emerged from their hiding places, threatening another descent into hell.

He gripped her hands, transferring heat to them. "Don't go there. I can't not love you. It's impossible."

"I don't know how you put up with me."

"It is hard sometimes." His eyes softened. "But you're a part of me. Leave you, I might as well cut my limbs off."

She threw her arms around him and her song echoed through the trees.

"I know you need me," he said, "and I'm here for you."

She kissed him. His lips pressed hard against hers and they held each other tight. The cold disappeared.

They stayed there even as dusk gave way to darkness.

* * *

January 19

Sitting together on the bus, Waylee and Pel examined aerial imagery of the MediaCorp complex. It contained thirteen different buildings, massive parking lots, and a field full of satellite dishes for transmitting and receiving. Concrete vehicle barriers circled the perimeter, along with electric fences topped by coils of razor wire. Manned steel gates blocked the two entrances. The place resembled a fortress.

Waylee looked on as Pel and Charles struggled through disgruntld1's files describing MediaCorp's broadcast and computer networks. Between the engineer's backdoor address and comlinks hacked at the New Year's gala, Charles entered more sections of the MediaCorp intranet. They learned how the signals were processed and where the guard stations were. And Charles discovered an employee manual and security procedures for their Virginia campus. He kept looking and found technical manuals and training books for their equipment.

Breaking in would be challenging. At the entrance, employees and visitors had to stop at the guard station. Employees could enter with an electronic badge, but cameras scanned them with facial recognition software. Visitors had to show IDs and fill out paperwork. Terahertz scanners examined all vehicles for anomalies.

Once on campus, all building and room access was controlled by electronic badges, retinal scanners, and thumbprint readers. All the badges were personalized and contained beacons, and computers tracked the owners' location. If more than one person entered a door at once, alarms sounded. Multiband cameras were everywhere, monitored by artificial intelligence analytics that alerted security staff if someone appeared in the wrong place at the wrong time.

"This is hopeless," Pel said. "Maybe at least the guards are hacks."

They combed through the corporate intranet.

"More bad news," Pel concluded. "MediaCorp has a professional security division of former cops and special forces. In a pinch, they can summon local police or Homeland Security."

She refused to give in. "Still, there must be weaknesses. Let's keep looking."

Pel sighed. "Okay. But first, we've gotta find out who disgruntld1 is."

"He's an engineer and member of the Collective," she said.

He smacked his hands together. "But we don't know who he is. No way in hell we're going anywhere near the MediaCorp campus if it's a trap."

Pel and Charles searched personnel data for broadcast engineers at the Virginia headquarters that worked in IT, had been there a while, but hadn't been promoted recently. Over four thousand people worked at the Virginia campus. Eleven—nine men and two women—might be disgruntld1.

The chat messages reeked of male nerd. Charles set up a data mining program to find everything available about all eleven possibilities, though.

33

January 20

Pelopidas

Pel received trust survey responses from 37 Collectivistas. No one gave disgruntld1 a "don't trust" rating, but no one gave him a "trust with life" either.

He picked the twenty with the highest total scores, and sent them invites to a virtual room in the Collective's Emporium. `Have treasure to share. Request help exploiting it.`

Sixteen hackers, including the silver-haired gentleman who'd sold him the microcameras and ghost snares, showed up at William Godwin's eighteenth century library. Pel wasn't sure if Godwin even had a library, but doubted anyone would care. He dedicated one of the bookcases to most of the comlinks he'd decrypted, each represented by a leather-bound book with random numbers on the spine. He'd decided the owners' names should be need-to-know, distributed in tandem with their comlink profile.

Charles had passed along AI programs to make his avatar move realistically with minimal control. Charles, Waylee, and Kiyoko looked over his shoulder at the monitor.

"Thank you for coming," Pel/William began. "First things first. This meeting and the op I'm about to describe are as secret as it gets. If you disclose anything to anyone, the rest of us come down hard on you."

Everyone agreed.

"You're here because you've got rockets in your asses, and because I can trust you." *I think.* He gestured toward the bookcase. "Here in my possession, I have access to the comlinks of some of the richest and most powerful people in America." He explained the ghost snares and how he deciphered the signals, but in general terms, no mention of the Smithsonian.

The gathered avatars stared at the book spines. "And who is 887713?" one asked.

"You'll find out if that's one you pick."

"And you're selling them?" the silver-haired broker asked.

"Not exactly. I have a lot of targets here and a very limited time window. As soon as the owners realize they're compromised, they'll get new comlinks and change all their passwords. So what I propose is a combined strike. We'll share the spoils."

An avatar resembling a Na'vi from the *Avatar* movie and video game spoke. "So do we each get 4.88235 comlinks?"

Wise ass. "No. I propose dividing up the tasks according to your skills."

The Na'vi pointed at a hip-looking teen. "Then what about Hopper there? He's got no skills."

Hopper extended a middle finger.

Pel waved his hands. "I've already done the hard stuff." He pointed at the books. "You'll be those users as far as the Comnet can tell, and you'll have access to all their data." He swung his finger toward a bookcase on the opposite wall. "And I've provided all the worms, rootkits, etc. you need for control." *Thanks to Charles.* "If you've got your own 'ware you prefer, that's cool."

Some of the Collectivistas nodded.

"The first thing we need to do is to install the software we need, set up backdoors, and get on their other computers. Then we scour through their contacts, their contacts' contacts, and so on. Anyone who works for MediaCorp, I want to access their comlinks. Especially if they're a sys admin. Same goes for MediaCorp computers, especially servers. I want on."

"Why MediaCorp?" Hopper asked.

"Why do you think? They're enemy #1 of information freedom. We're going to change that."

"How?" a black-clad ninja asked.

"Long-term operation. We'll penetrate every nook and cranny of that organization, and when all is ready, tear it down."

A Japanese lolita spun her frilly umbrella. "Awesome."

"Now the next thing, and don't wet yourself when I say this, is bank transactions. We'll empty their bank accounts and split the loot."

They all knew bank security was nearly impossible to crack, but no one would admit that in front of their peers. A Yosemite Sam avatar jumped up and down, shooting pistols in the air. Another displayed dollar signs in his eyes.

"Some other things. Download everything you find, emails, documents, video, whatever. Here's the storage link." An address, only accessible using the Collective Router program, appeared before them in glowing letters. It would copy all incoming data and redirect it to multiple anonymous servers. "You can share your findings here also."

"Will we publish it?" the lolita asked.

"When we've sorted through everything, and the time is right."

She spun her umbrella again.

"We're also going to activate their cameras, mics, and GPS's," Pel said, "and see if our targets do anything interesting."

"Like porn?" a bronze-skinned Amazon said.

Pel sighed. "No, we just want to know what they're up to, and look for opportunities to expand our reach." He scanned the gathered faces, even though you couldn't really tell what people were thinking by looking at their avatar. "I want everyone to set up their ops and execute at the same time. As soon as our targets figure out what we're up to, game's over. So I'm giving you all 24 hours, starting right now, to secure your comlinks and prep. We'll hit our 'go' buttons all at once."

The avatars regaled him with nods, bows, and thumbs up.

"Now," he said, "who's gonna do what?"

34

January 21

Waylee

The most likely candidate for disgruntld1, they all decided, was Hubert Stebbens, a broadcast engineer for MediaCorp for eight years. According to Charles's research, he was 34, single, lived in an apartment near the corporate campus, had at least one BetterWorld avatar with god-like powers, and liked to kill newbies in war games and take their stuff.

Hubert's personnel file acknowledged impressive technical skills. His performance reviews never exceeded standards, though, giving low scores for dependability, teamwork, and communication. He had never been promoted, and received disciplinary letters for insubordination, chronic lateness, and misuse of equipment.

Waylee gathered the others to discuss their options. Pel settled behind Big Red on the front couch. He slid over to let her in. Charles and Kiyoko sat opposite them with the other computers. They smelled fresh as flowers. Arriving last, Shakti took one of the chairs across the aisle.

Peter climbed on board and waved a hand before they could start.

"Something up?" Waylee asked.

He cleared his throat. "I've been calling folks at the farm every day. Just to stay in touch, farm business and whatnot."

Pel interrupted. "And?"

Peter frowned. "I just wanted to let you know that people are still talking about you. Amy in particular."

The teenage girl who tried to sell them out.

Pel peered at him. "That's kind of vague. What do you mean, talking about us?"

Peter ran a thumb through his long white beard. "Well, should they have turned you in, that sort of thing."

Heart pounding, Waylee sprang into the aisle and faced him. "What?" Everyone tensed.

Peter held up a hand. "Whoa. No need to panic. I told them you're long gone and I'm coming back soon. And besides, one doesn't betray their guests, especially if they're fellow People's Party activists. That's just completely wrong."

"So how did they respond?"

"They agreed that yes, the concept of hospitality is as old as humanity itself, and it's bad karma to violate it."

Waylee rested a hand on the table. "Amy too?"

"I just talked to Sunshine actually, but I assume so." He scratched his head. "They want the computers back. They figured out I'm helping you and took the computers and said they can be traced back to the farm."

"We need them, and we wiped them before we took them." Charles said.

"Start looking for replacements. And another thing."

"Yes?" Waylee asked.

"If you go ahead with this mission of yours, you'll need to find alternate transportation. The bus stays here. Actually, I should return it."

She hadn't thought of that. "We'll build that into the plan." She sat back down, thinking of Kiyoko's truck.

Peter walked to the kitchenette and opened the white cabinet doors over the stove. "I'll see what kind of lunch I can slap together."

Kiyoko stumbled out of the sofa, bit her lip and turned toward Waylee. "I want to go with you." She looked serious.

"What?"

"I can drive," she said. "Help you get in and out. Or do whatever."

"Well, that's nice of you to offer, but…"

Kiyoko crossed her arms. "I'm not a child anymore."

"Did I say you were?"

"Obviously I don't want to get caught. But I don't want anyone to get caught. We're family. I wanna help." She spread her hands. "And I was thinking, maybe our band isn't done. Once we're safe somewhere, we can admit what we did and we'll be famous."

Waylee had forgotten all about the band. It seemed so irrelevant now. "Maybe there's ways you could help. We don't all have to enter the campus."

Across the table, Charles nodded. "Yeah, she's good crew, you'll see."

Kiyoko smiled. She plopped down at the small table across from Shakti.

"We've got the moving truck, but we'll need at least one other vehicle..."

At the computer-covered table, Pel looked at Charles, then Waylee. "Let's get back to our engineer friend. Hubert Stebbens. I'm 99% sure he's our guy."

"Can we trust him?" Waylee asked.

Charles jumped in. "I trust him. He helped me before."

Pel's eyes narrowed. "That was three million dollars ago."

"But we don't have any reason not to trust him, do we?" Waylee said. It was fine to be cautious, but if no one saw her video, what was the point of all they went through?

"You saw his personnel file," Pel said. "Doesn't work well with others."

"I'm sure my supervisor at the paper wrote similar things," she said. "Shall we move forward with the plan, but move carefully?"

His face tightened. "We should pay him a visit."

Waylee heard chopping noises coming from the kitchenette behind her. She decided to change the subject. "As far as getting in, can we masquerade as employees?"

"And then what? Even if we figure out what equipment to use and how to use it, what do we do about all the real employees who'll stick their nose in our business?"

"Gas the building?" Charles said. "Use knockout gas?"

Pel scoffed. "That only works in comic books."

"Pel's right," Waylee said. "Sleeping gas isn't instantaneous. They'd call for help and reroute the broadcast."

Charles hung his head.

"It was worth considering." She looked at Pel. "Can you show me the broadcast diagram again?"

"Sure." Pel brought up a simplified version on his screen.

The signal from the stadium in Atlanta traveled to the central control studio in Virginia by optic cable. The broadcast director inserted commercials and other content, and the final feed went to the servers and packet switches in the data center, housed in the building's basement. From there, it proceeded to the uplink station and satellite dishes and also to a second data center on campus, where it was routed to the Comnet.

She pointed a finger. "What are those dashed lines?"

"Verifications that the signal's propagating without errors," Pel said. "If anything goes wrong, they know it immediately in control."

"Could we fake the verifications?"

Pel glanced at Charles, who looked back at Waylee.

"Everything passes through the first data center," she said. Her skin tingled. "That's the weak link. I don't think Disgruntled Hubert gave us very good advice. We don't have to infiltrate four or five buildings, only one."

Pel nodded. "So we have to reprogram the data servers to pretend the Super Bowl transmission is going out okay, but actually send out our own video."

"Yes!"

"Eventually an affiliate or someone will call in and ask what's going on, but if the control monitors show the game going out as normal, they won't think it's a problem on their end. The affiliates could show them our video broadcast, though, and say that's what's coming from the studio."

Waylee smelled cabbage boiling. *Yuck.* She squeezed Pel's arm. "How long do you think it'll take MediaCorp to figure all that out and stop our transmission?"

He shrugged.

Staring at his computer screen across the table, Charles made a "hah!" sound and swiped fingers along his touch pad.

"What?" Waylee asked.

He looked up. "One of my schemes to shut down kiddie cops in Better-World was to grief 'em with Word of God attacks."

"I have no idea what you're talking about."

"You don't want people calling the control room, right?"

"Yeah."

"Same principle. Bandwidth overload. We'll clog their lines—the whole campus—with a DDoS attack."

"DDoS?"

Pel glanced over. "Distributed denial of service. We'd use botnets - networks of infected computers with spoofed IDs - to make so many calls to the MediaCorp lines that no one could get through."

Charles pointed at him. "Perfect project for the Collective. We don't have to say what we're up to, just that it's a Super Bowl prank. We'll attack all their lines and ports, clog everything up."

Waylee slapped the table. "I love you, Charles!"

He flinched away.

"How long can you—the Collective I mean—keep anyone from getting through?"

He squinted. "Hmm, I know the Collective does this all the time against gov'ments or companies they got a thing 'gainst. Usually it holds several hours or such."

Pel raised an eyebrow.

Charles nodded. "But MediaCorp, they own the Comnet. Ten minutes probably the best we can do."

"I'll take ten minutes," Waylee said.

Pel drummed fingers against the plastic tabletop. "All that aside, what about MediaCorp security? We can't just fiddle with their computers without being noticed."

"I know just the person who can help with that," she said.

35

January 23

M'patanishi

M-pat had never been to southern Maryland before. Next to him in the "requisitioned" cargo van, though, Dingo spoke directions from his new comlink. "Keep following Maryland 5 for three more miles, then turn left onto Cedarville Road."

Trees and subdivision turnoffs flew by in the dark. *Damn Waylee.* Sister could talk him into anything. But wait 'til he told Latisha about their new house.

Waylee had contacted him two days ago via Francis. They'd chatted on one of those anonymous video connections normally used by porn addicts. She played the video she wanted to broadcast, then clips showing President Rand and the MediaCorp CEO bragging about turning the world into a 21st century slave plantation.

He thought about Latisha and Baraka. What kind of future did his son have? As Waylee put it, the world was sliding to hell with a banana peel on its ass. You could see that shit everywhere you looked, especially in B'more.

Still, life in prison was life in prison. That's when Waylee offered up the band house in return. Six bedrooms, big yard, all kinds of electronics and security. "We'll work out the details when you come," she said.

So he had agreed, with conditions. And Waylee promised they would follow his advice when he arrived.

Following Dingo's directions, M-pat turned at a faded wooden sign marked "Cedarville State Forest." He drove past dense trees until they reached a campsite with a repainted school bus, lights on behind closed blinds. An old white man with a long white beard stood out front.

M-pat parked on the loop road and got out. Dingo hopped out the passenger door.

The old man held out a hand. "Peter. You must be Mahpotonashee."

"M'patanishi." He shook Peter's hand - the vanilla handshake that county types preferred. "Most folks just say M-pat." He waved Dingo over. "This here's Dingo."

"What Waylee's planning is way too bad ass for me to miss out on," he said. "I can use my Krav Maga." He threw a couple of fast punches to the air.

Peter flinched.

Waylee, Shakti, and Kiyoko sprinted toward them from the back of the campsite. Pel and Charles strolled behind them.

Shakti passed the others and leapt into Dingo's arms. "M-pat said he was bringing someone," she said. "But he didn't say it would be you."

"Missed you, babe." They locked mouths.

Waylee wrapped her arms around M-pat and squeezed. Kiyoko followed.

Pel smacked fists with him. "I feel a lot more confident now you're here."

"Yeah, thanks. Be assured we do this, we do it right."

Waylee's smile disappeared. "We can't kill anyone, though. Otherwise, that'll be the whole story."

"Not to mention the death penalty," Pel said.

M-pat nodded, then pointed a thumb toward the van. "Got a whole lot o' shit in there. We owe Paulo and a bunch of other people. But there's still more we gotta get."

Pel stared at the van. "You took the GPS out, right?"

Dumb ass question. "What do you think?"

"What'd you tell your wife?" Kiyoko said, her exotic eyes warming his skin.

"That I was going camping with some fine ass bitches."

Dingo pulled his tongue out of Shakti's mouth. "He wishes he could strut like that."

"'Kay, said I gotta go to DC to teach a Krav Maga course. Said it'll pay well."

Waylee's eyes shone. "We succeed, payoff'll be incredible." Heads turned her way. "Not in dollar terms, maybe. But we'll set the elites' whole narrative on fire, set history on a new course."

"Shit, in dollar terms too," M-pat said. "Never thought I'd have a real house."

Waylee looked at Pel. "Someone's gotta live there, or it'll just turn into a drug squat. Obviously we can't move back."

Pel nodded. "Like I said, though, my parents will want a profit."

M-pat felt played. "How the fuck am I gonna do that?"

Waylee moved her hands in circles. "Easy. It was a fixer-upper when they bought it."

"Sell your townhouse and rent rooms," Pel said. "You can rent out the attic and basement and pay your whole mortgage that way."

It would mean less space, but still a lot more than the row house. And with no mortgage, they could support more kids.

Kiyoko's mouth opened. "How come no one told me about this? My friends are staying there."

Pel turned. "Who's staying there?"

"They can stay if they pay," M-pat said. "As long as Latisha's okay with them."

Waylee motioned everyone inside the school bus. "Let's talk inside."

True, they shouldn't be talking out in the open. And this abandoned campground, all them leafless trees in the dead of night, gave M-pat the creeps. He patted the Glock in its shoulder holster, hoping it could take out any machete-wielding maniac with a hockey mask out there.

36

January 24

Pelopidas

In the stuffy, cluttered bunk room, Pel packed up Big Red and some of his other gear, arranging it in his big duffel bag and padding it with dirty clothes. He heard Waylee near the front of the bus, thanking Peter for all his help.

M-pat had insisted they change locations, saying they'd stayed too long in one place and were too far from the MediaCorp campus. As soon as it got dark again, they would drive his van and Kiyoko's moving truck across the Potomac into Virginia.

Assuming they didn't get caught, M-pat would return home after the Super Bowl, but Pel might be leaving Maryland forever. Sure, Baltimore was falling apart, but it had been his family's home for three generations.

On the other hand, it was like going to war for a just cause. Like fighting fascists in World War II or the Spanish Civil War. And who knows, maybe they could settle in Greece and his family could visit. One thing for sure, he wouldn't miss being shut in this smelly camper with all the blinds drawn.

When he finished packing, Pel settled at the forward table with the computer Waylee had been using. As usual, Charles was hard at work on the other one.

"We have to wipe the farm's computers before we leave," Pel said.

Charles looked up. "We should just buy 'em new ones."

"Yeah, that would be better, but we don't have any money yet." Pel had to see how their Collectivista comrades had fared with the comlinks.

* * *

Charles

Charles had never organized a denial of service attack before. But it wasn't as challenging as owning BetterWorld admins or hacking comlinks. Mostly it was a lot of looking up data ports and phone lines, setting up botnets, and coordinating a big Collective crew.

Hubert and a Collectivista called Hopper were a big help hacking data glasses. And of course Hubert had his own. Charles forwarded Pel a link to the first video dump.

Across the table, Pel actually smiled. "Thanks, Charles."

Charles returned to his screen. MediaCorp had tremendous bandwidth, and their switches, even the voice lines, had all kinds of traffic defenses. Might need a million computers or more to overwhelm them, and some amplification routines. They should attack the local cell networks too. MediaCorp didn't use cells, but some of the employees might.

Pel rose and pumped a fist. "Our Collectivista comrades really came through." He waved Waylee over. "You'll like this."

Waylee was slim when Charles first met her, but now she needed a belt to keep her jeans up, and it seemed like her breasts had shrunk. No one had been eating much since they left the farm, and before that she was sick. She grinned at Pel like there were no worries in the world, though.

"We got a lot of good stuff from those comlinks," Pel said. "Petabytes of files and emails. Enough to keep a journalist busy for decades."

"I love you guys!" Waylee kissed the top of Pel's head, then rubbed Charles's shoulder.

"Any money?" Charles asked Pel.

"Well, you know banks are pretty distrustful these days. They ask all sorts of security questions that have to be researched—"

Waylee traced circles with her index finger, too impatient for details. "Did they get anything or not?"

Pel's smile disappeared. "Low success rate, but we had a lot of comlinks to work with, and recordings to fake the voice verifications, so still enough to be worth the trouble."

"How much is our share?" Charles asked.

"Enough for data glasses and masks, and whatever else we need, and enough to cover M-pat's expenses and make our engineer happy."

Charles leaned toward him. "My gramma's got all them kids to take care of, and no money. Gov'ment keeps cutting back assistance."

Pel sighed. "I see what you're saying. We could move something from Hubert's cut. Nowhere else to take from. Waylee and I don't get anything out of this."

"Sorry, I won't either, y'know. And it might not be a good idea to give Hubert money. He might think it's FBI entrapment. I know his type, he dogs for the lulz and glory."

Pel nodded. "You might be right. I don't know how we'd get your grand-ma the money, though. The feds are gonna watch her forever."

"I'll talk to M-pat," Waylee said. "We'll figure something out."

Charles locked eyes with her. *She's got an answer for everything.*

"Thanks."

On reflection, he added, "I appreciate it."

Waylee nodded. "We're all family here."

He pointed at Pel. "Yo, we should check out the spy vids."

Pel brought up Hubert's video first, and moved his screen so every-one could see. He smiled at Waylee. "Per your suggestion, Hubert's been wearing his data glasses in the broadcast studio building, recording video and audio with position and time tags. He only has access to a few areas, though."

On the screen, Hubert got out of a car and entered a huge building with no windows.

"We need him to wear his glasses at the gate," Waylee said, "or at least put them on the dashboard."

Hubert walked down a hallway and got in a big elevator full of dressed up people, mostly white. They got out and entered a giant circular room full of interface units with see-through popup screens. All along the curving wall, video skins played news, sports, sitcoms, all the MediaCorp dreck. Hubert sat at a console and didn't do much of interest.

"We gotta check out the other vid." Charles looked up at Waylee. "I asked Hubert to install spyware on guards' glasses, but he said no way. So I did it myself, with a few tips from Hubert and Hopper. Pel helped me pick out the target."

Pel brought up a picture of Clint Pickens, a white 22-year-old wearing a MediaCorp Security hat. "This guy's a newbie on campus," he said, "fresh out of the Marines. Infantry, never advanced past E-3, grew up near the broadcast campus. Dumb as a post as far as I can tell."

"I sent Clint a fake software update for his data glasses," Charles said. "All the guards wear them on patrol. He accepted it."

Pel smirked. "Typical musclehead."

"And we can see through them now?" Waylee asked.

"Not real time." Pel brought up the Clint video. "It uploads the data when he's at home asleep."

In stop-motion frames, the guard crossed a parking lot and entered a low concrete building marked 'Security.' "It only takes a still every three seconds when he's moving and every minute when he's not," Pel explained. "Otherwise we'd eat up too much memory."

Waylee fixed her eyes on the screen. "Let's hope he goes inside the broadcast building."

Pel fast forwarded through the video. Clint patrolled the entire campus with another guard, sometimes in a police-type car packed with electronics, and sometimes on foot. He didn't enter any buildings other than security headquarters.

"It's a start," Waylee said. "We can watch their security procedures, and also figure out who patrols the broadcast building and find another target."

"A lot of guards to choose from," Charles said. "Campus operates 24/7."

Waylee smirked. "MediaCorp's bullshit never rests."

Pel rubbed fingers through his beard. "So are you ready for the bad news?"

Her face fell. "What bad news?"

Pel brought up an email sent by the White House Department of Scheduling and Advance to all attendees of the fundraiser.

```
Subject: Important Information: Your Comlink May Be
Compromised

It appears that cybercriminals infiltrated the New
Year's gala at the Smithsonian and gained illegal ac-
cess to many of the guests' comlinks. They are using
this access to commit further crimes, including theft
from bank accounts and credit cards. You may or may not
be affected, but we strongly urge you to replace your
comlink, immediately change all your passwords, and
contact your banks. Any computer that syncs with your
comlink might also be infected. A cybersecurity spe-
cialist will personally be in touch with you to assess
and repair any potential damage.

We sincerely apologize for any inconvenience this at-
tack may have caused. Rest assured that the FBI is mak-
ing every effort to apprehend the criminals.
```

"So that's it for the comlinks," Charles said.

Waylee drummed her fingers on the table. "At least they think we're just after money. Just goes to show, money's all they think anyone cares about."

37

February 3
Loudoun County, Virginia

Waylee

Waylee examined her new face in the bathroom mirror. Thirty-year-old Tania Peart, a systems analyst at MediaCorp's broadcast data center, stared back.

They had been moving around, sleeping in Kiyoko's truck or squatting in abandoned buildings. They spent the past two days in a small house for sale with twenty acres of pasture and woods. No furniture, but it had well water, electricity from a wind turbine, and an old satellite dish that Pel hooked up to a high-speed modem to access the Comnet.

Once again, Kiyoko's friends at Baltimore Transformations had produced a photo-realistic masterpiece, and Kiyoko matched Tania's makeup. Only problem was, the cheeks quivered when Waylee moved her head.

Tania was a brunette close to Waylee's height, but a little on the heavy side. Waylee had been stuffing down gallons of peanut butter and ice cream, and would wear undergarment padding. But it wasn't enough.

Waylee peeled off the mask. It didn't look like her face had gained any weight yet. She needed a snug fit.

Yesterday morning, she'd fixated on the crow's feet at the corners of her eyes, convinced their mission would fail. But with assaults of upbeat music and the constant presence of friends, people who loved her, she fought off the downturn. She was on the upswing now, but she wouldn't let it turn into a speeding train. *Focus. I can control this thing.*

Waylee peeked in the master bedroom. Inflatable mattresses and sleeping bags covered the floor. On one of the mattresses, wearing her crimson dress with the gold dragon, Kiyoko touched up masks and clothes, trying to match photographs on a computer screen.

"Great job," Waylee said.

Her sister turned and smiled. "My friends did the hard part."

"It's too loose, though."

Kiyoko huffed. "Hand it over. I'll see if I can pad the inside a little more."

Waylee tossed her the mask. "I'm glad you're here."

Sitting on the garment-strewn carpet next to Kiyoko, Charles typed programming lines on Big Red. *If he were older, they'd make a cute couple.*

"Hubert's set," Charles said without looking up. Besides passing along schematics and protocols, their engineer friend had volunteered to knock out the building's internal communications, which the Collective's DDoS attack wouldn't affect.

More proof they could trust him. Waylee and Pel had surveilled Hubert for four days. The chubby engineer lived alone in Building 1780 of Media Village, a sprawling townhouse and apartment complex near MediaCorp's Virginia campus. After a lot of arguing, they decided not to approach him, which might scare him off; or break into his apartment, in case he had nanny cams or motion detectors. Instead, they intercepted a package and implanted voice-activated microphones, flash memory, and ghost snares in the corrugated cardboard, slipping them into the top flaps and resealing the box. They watched his apartment with microcameras and retrieved their gear and data when he threw the box out with the recycling. They also tracked his car with a tiny GPS fixed behind his license plate.

While the microphones were in Hubert's apartment, he had no visitors, nor made any calls other than to a taqueria delivery and a sister in Richmond. He didn't drive anywhere other than work, and spent all his free time on the Comnet, mostly gaming. He showed no signs of betrayal.

Still, Pel had claimed it was impossible to be sure.

Waylee heard thuds and grunts down the hall. In the empty living room, Dingo and M-pat threw kicks and jabs at each other. Practicing, releasing aggression, or both. No sign of Pel and Shakti; they were probably still in the adjacent garage fiddling with the stolen Mustang.

M-pat swept a leg behind Dingo's ankles and pushed him. Dingo fell backwards onto the faded red carpet. "Bastard!"

"Do you think we're ready?" Waylee asked M-pat.

The big man wiped sweat off his brow. "They've got ex-special forces and a line to Homeland. All we've got is surprise."

"Then let's surprise them."

After sunset, they ate dinner on the varnished wood floor of what was probably the dining room. Pel had covered the window with plywood so wandering deer or whatever wouldn't see their solar camping lanterns. Dinner hadn't changed for a week—peanut butter and jelly sandwiches, carrots, and bottled water.

Kiyoko, her lucky red wig on, frowned at her sandwich. "How come Waylee gets all the ice cream?"

"I'm trying to pass as someone thirty pounds heavier," she said.

Kiyoko rolled her eyes. "Oh, how convenient."

"You're right, it's not helping much anyway." She looked around. "You all can split what's left."

Kiyoko bounded into the other room and returned with the last gallon of Neapolitan. She opened it and frowned. "Of course you ate all the strawberry."

Sitting on the floor, M-pat shook his PBJ at her. "Motherfuckin' strawberry ice cream's the least of our worries, girl. Fort Knox ain't shit compared to the place we about to break into."

The others stopped eating and stared at M-pat.

Waylee's knees shook. *I'm even scared.*

She stood and held out her bottle of water. Anger barreled over the fear and crushed it beneath relentless wheels. Drums inside her skull pounded *allegro* 4/4 beats, and turbo-distorted guitars churned out metallic riffs. She turned down the internal volume. "I'd like to propose a toast."

Pel gave her the ironic eyebrow. "Are you planning to turn our water into wine?"

Anger fell away. A chuckle escaped her throat. "I wasn't born with those kinds of powers."

Around the small bare room, Shakti, Charles, Kiyoko, Pel, Dingo, and M-pat rose from the floor and held up their plastic bottles. Some eyes darted, some drifted, some focused.

"My friends, my family," Waylee began. Drifting eyes fixed on her. "I can't thank you enough for being here by my side."

She pointed her water bottle at M-pat. "Without you, we'd have no wheels and no chance against the plutocracy's bully boys. Charles would still be in jail and we'd never have started this."

He nodded. "Prob'ly don't seem like it, but I'm actually enjoyin' this shit. Like the old days as a turf soldier, only for somethin' that matters. You right, we gotta take down the overlords if we want a better future."

Waylee looked at Dingo. He thrust his shoulders back.

"Dingo," she said, "you've inspired me for years. You don't sit on your ass complaining. You act. And your complete lack of fear, that's the edge that saved us when the band house was raided."

Dingo raised a fist.

"Shakti, my best friend," she continued. "You are the best of humanity. You keep me going. And you arranged our base after New Year's."

Shakti blew a kiss. "Let's get 'em tomorrow."

"Kiyoko, my sweet, quirky sister."

Kiyoko scrunched an eyebrow. "Quirky?"

Waylee kept going. "We wouldn't have the masks without you."

"Let's not get caught tomorrow."

"We won't, as long as we're careful." *I hope.* She gazed in her sister's brown eyes. "I'm sorry we've had our differences. But you mean the world to me."

Waylee turned to Charles. "And Charles. Captain Nemo of the Comnet."

His forehead furrowed at the reference.

"You're the reason we're here. No one else could do what you've done."

He grinned, then bit his lip. "I'm not gonna have to fight anyone, am I?"

"No, of course not."

He glanced at Kiyoko. "'Cause I haven't started learning Krav Maga yet."

Waylee was pretty rusty herself. Maybe they needed a practice session. "Everything will be under control by the time you enter," she said.

Kiyoko shook her water bottle. "We should make a sacrifice."

"Huh?"

"To the gods, to ensure their favor."

Across the small room, M-pat sighed. "There's only one God. We should pray. Ain't gotta sacrifice no goat."

Kiyoko glared at him. "I wouldn't kill a cute little goat. Why—"

Waylee waved her free hand. "Let's finish the toast, shall we?" She faced her boyfriend. "Most of all, I'd like to thank Pel, the love of my life."

His eyes softened.

"You've been there through five years of ups and downs," she said. "You can solve any problem. And you keep me from being stupid."

"I try." He smirked, then inched forward. "But seriously, I'd be walking dead without you kickstarting my life. Probably working retail like my friends in Greektown, letting the world die and not even noticing."

"Can we sit now?" Charles asked.

"Almost done." Waylee scanned the six pairs of eyes facing her. Seven if she counted the ones tattooed on Dingo's hands.

"Tomorrow," she said, "we infiltrate the most powerful corporation that ever existed. We'll use their own facilities against them. We'll expose the manipulations and conspiracies that keep a tiny elite in control of everyone else. We'll yank the mask off the plutocracy and show America the ugly reptile beneath. We'll be so outrageous, the people won't fail to act. Tomorrow, my friends, let's kick Authority so hard in the nuts, even a Canadian boy band could finish them off."

Pel led the laughter.

Waylee held her bottle high, then gulped lukewarm water that she'd replace with beer or whiskey tomorrow night.

Her friends did the same.

"Let's make history," Pel said.

More thoughts erupted. "I'd die for any one of you."

Kiyoko shifted on her feet. "Please don't."

February 4
Super Bowl Sunday
5:15 A.M.

M'patanishi

M-pat pulled the van into Media Village, headlights cutting through the dark and betraying their presence. They'd be even more suspicious with lights out, though.

"Take your first right," Dingo said from the shotgun seat, following the route on his new data glasses.

"All set back here," Pel said behind him, voice shaky.

All three wore slam-real masks and hands Kiyoko's friends had shipped to a vacant house, and over those, data glasses with low light vision. They had a second set of masks that matched their targets.

Before they could upload Waylee's video, M-pat, Dingo, and Pel had to take over the building's security room. And to get to the security room, they had to seem legit employees – had to look like them, have their access cards, their cars, even their eyes and thumbprints.

Ideally, they'd replace the entire security team, but even three was pushing it. M-pat and Dingo would become guards. Pel would replace an IT technician in the data center. They'd sifted through personnel data and picked their targets carefully.

Like Hubert Stebbens, their first target lived alone in Media Village. Luke Annlote had M-pat's brawn, though, and had fought in the Middle East before joining MediaCorp security. Surprise was essential.

"Over there." Dingo pointed to Building 1860.

"That's his car." A black Mazda hybrid sat in its designated parking spot. Above, his apartment lights were off.

M-pat parked in an empty spot. "No fuckups," he told the others. "What we about to do, we talkin' ten years minimum if we get caught." *Life, if they want to call it terrorism.*

Baraka and Latisha flashed in his mind. He shouldn't have agreed to this shit. But no way could he pussy out. And maybe they'd turn things around in this country.

They got out, Pel carrying a mostly empty duffel bag. All three wore jackets with deep pockets.

The front door had an electronic keycard slot, but it had a mechanical override in case of malfunction, and these were easy to pick with his lock gun. The door popped open and they entered.

Annlote's apartment had the same kind of lock as the building entrance. M-pat put a finger to his lips, pulled the stun gun out of his jacket pocket, and opened the door.

It was dark inside. He had an LED flashlight in his pocket, but his glasses adjusted to the dimness, revealing the room in shades of grey. He motioned for Dingo to take the left. He took the right.

Pel lagged near the door. He and Dingo crossed the living room, over to the bedroom beyond. M-pat eased open the bedroom door. Someone slept under the covers of the king-sized bed. Possibly two people; it was hard to tell in the greyness.

A man's head separated from a pillow. Looked like Annlote. "Who's there?"

Light sleeping must be one of those post-combat things. A second head popped up next to him. A girl. They hadn't planned on company.

Dingo fired his stun gun at the man. His head fell back against the pillow.

M-pat shot at the girl before she could scream. Her head dropped back down.

They rushed toward the bed, pulling rolls of duct tape out of jacket pockets. Annlote rolled out of the bed, naked, and reached for the nightstand.

"You supposed to stay down." M-pat kicked his arm away from the nightstand.

Annlote responded with a kick of his own, catching M-pat hard in the right thigh. He almost buckled, but thrust a palm heel toward the man's chin.

Sweeping a forearm counterclockwise, Annlote knocked his arm down and away, and countered with a punch toward the face. M-pat batted the punch aside, swiveled, and stomped a boot against the shoeless insole of the man's foot. He howled in pain.

And dropped to the ground.

M-pat turned. Pel stood behind and to the side, stun gun aimed at Annlote.

"I had him, fool," M-pat said. "You coulda hit me too."

"Well I didn't."

"Shut the fuck up, bitches," Dingo said, "and help me tape these chumps up." He threw aside the bedsheets. The girl was petite but model-quality fine, with perfect tits and toned thighs.

Dingo whistled, then picked up the hottie and placed her on the carpet by the foot of the bed.

M-pat dragged Annlote to the same spot, ignoring the pain in his thigh.

First thing was to tape their wrists and ankles together, then stick socks in their mouths and tape them in place. Then hogtie the wrists to the ankles and run tape around and around the arms and legs for reinforcement.

The naked girl's eyes opened as Dingo taped her wrists. He held a finger to his lips. "Shhh."

She swung her foot directly into his nuts. Grimacing, he dropped the tape and grabbed his groin.

Damn fool. M-pat turned to Pel. "Shoot her, yo." He finished taping Annlotes's wrists.

Pel fumbled with his stun gun. Wrists bound, the girl leapt to her feet, then threw a high kick to Dingo's face. His head snapped back, a lens popped out of his data glasses, and he dropped.

She ain't no bar pickup. Girl got game. M-pat whipped his Glock out of its shoulder holster and stuck its barrel against Annlote's forehead. He was still out. "Yo, naked bitch. Siddown or I ice yo man."

She looked over, eyes wide with fear.

"You dig?" he said.

"You'll kill us anyway."

"Bullshit we will. This just a simple robbery, 'less you give cause otherwise."

The girl stiffened and dropped. Pel had shot her at last.

"'Bout fuckin' time." M-pat finished taping up Annlote and his karate hottie, then went to check on Dingo, still on the floor. "You operational?"

He sat up, clutching his groin. His data glasses were bent, with one lens missing.

"You just got your ass kicked by a little girl with taped wrists."

He pocketed the ruined glasses and rubbed his jaw. "Caught me by surprise, that's all."

Annlote and his girl regained consciousness and started to squirm, but the duct tape was way too strong to break. Muffled shouts echoed from their sinuses.

M-pat waved his Glock. "Chill the fuck out, yo. I'm a patient man but you are tryin' me."

They glared, but quieted down. Pel had the duffel bag so M-pat sent him to the walk-in closet to get the uniforms and look around for all the other security gear.

M-pat walked to the nightstand and turned on the lamp. Hand comlink and immersion goggles rested on top. He found Annlote's access badge and a .45 combat pistol in the drawer. No car keys.

Clothes lay scattered on the floor. M-pat found Annlote's wallet in the back pocket of his pants. Not much cash.

The girl's bag had fifty bucks. Driver's license said Rose Matapang. One of her keycards was labeled Ultimate Fight School. *Just our luck.*

Pel finished stuffing the uniforms and other gear in the bag. He held up a high-tech Armatix pistol.

"In the bag too."

Pel placed the gun inside and zipped it shut. He swiped fingers along the wide temple arms of his data glasses. "May need your help holding him still."

M-pat grabbed Annlote by the head and faced him forward. He stuck the Glock barrel against his nutsack. "Don't even twitch. I got a nervous trigger finger."

Pel knelt in front of the man until his data glasses were inches from the man's eyes. He tapped the side of the glasses frame. He frowned. "Need more light."

Dingo hobbled toward the bedroom light switch.

M-pat almost shouted. "Leave that off." He pulled out his mini-light and shone it in Annlote's face.

"Not right in his eyes."

M-pat moved the beam. Pel tapped the frame again and kept still. Then he smiled and swiped fingers against the temple arms again. The lenses turned opaque, then displayed a set of eyes. Annlote's eyes. The pupils were crisscrossed with bloody lines.

"Worked," Dingo said. "As good as we practiced."

"Only problem is, it's hard to see now." Pel dispelled Annlote's eyes from the glasses. "Okay, let's do the thumbs."

Annlote mumbled something through the sock.

"Didn't I tell you to shut up?" M-pat flipped him over.

Pel fished a handheld comlink out of a pants pocket, entered his code, and started an app. He pressed its glassy front against Annlote's right thumb, which poked through a web of tape.

When he pulled it away, a perfect replica remained on the screen. He brought up a menu, tapped something, and the thumb replica reversed. "It was a mirror image before," he said. "Let's do the other one just in case."

When they finished the retina and thumb captures, M-pat looked at Dingo. "We need to secure them, real good."

"You got it, boss." Dingo removed a second roll of duct tape from a jacket pocket, but Pel held up a hand, rummaged through the duffel bag, and pulled out Annlote's handcuffs. He tossed them to Dingo.

Dingo placed their captives back to back, snapped one cuff on Annlote, ran it through the bed frame, and put the other cuff on his girl. "Now there's a way to keep a couple together."

Pel set up a microcamera to keep an eye on them.

Where were the car keys?

M-pat found them on the dining room table, along with the apartment key, black-framed comlink glasses, and an open bottle of Jameson. He took them all, bottle included.

He returned to the bedroom and drew a horizontal circle with his finger. Annlote's eyes promised vengeance.

"Sorry about this," M-pat told their captives. "Be thankful you alive. You been stupider, coulda gone the other way. So just relax, sit tight. We'll send someone to let you go, you just gotta be patient."

After they exited, M-pat pointed to the door lock.

Dingo reached into a jacket pocket and pulled out a tube of Gorilla Glue. He squirted it into the card reader and a little into the backup mechanical lock.

One down, two to go.

40

3:55 P.M.
1 hour and 35 minutes to kickoff

Dingo

Guised as security guard unextraordinaire Alvaro Jimenez, including the man's data glasses, Dingo sat shotgun in Luke Annlote's black Mazda.

"Thought a rebel like you would have no problem riding a chopper," M-pat/Luke said from the driver's seat.

"Yeah, laugh it up, Skywanker. How's I supposed to know Alvaro'd have a 'cycle? Lucky I can even drive a car."

"Even that's a bold claim."

Luke Annlote (now M-pat), Alvaro Jimenez (Dingo), and Nick Smith (Pel) had the 4 p.m. to midnight shift at the broadcast data center. Pel was five minutes behind them. Annlote and Jimenez worked as guards, but Smith was a computer guy. Pel definitely made a better techie than a guard. He couldn't fight, and having a rock star girlfriend was the only thing preventing his coronation as King of the Nerds.

The MediaCorp campus rose from the barren trees ahead. The place looked like a fortress. Or a prison.

A double row of tall chain link fences stretched as far as he could see, razor wire on top, concrete pilings in front. A thick-barred gate blocked the road, with a bladed tire trap just beyond. To the left of the gate, a guard watched from inside a reinforced steel bunker, bulletproof windows all around. Cameras and scanners pointed ahead and to the side. Douchebags even had a red stop light at the entrance, as if the rest weren't enough of a hint.

"Yo ho, yo ho, it's off to work we go." Inside, Dingo felt uneasy. Not 'cause he was scared per se. But this was the big time and everything had to go perfect.

The guard in the bunker looked bored as they pulled up, but smiled when they stopped next to the side window. His head was bald as a baseball. "Hey, Luke," his voice came from a speaker. "When you setting me up with Rose's sister?"

M-pat shrugged. He'd said they shouldn't talk much. He held his electronic badge in front of the shoebox-sized card reader.

A small LED lit green. He looked up at the camera above the reader.

Baldy peered into the Mazda. "You too, buddy," the speaker said.

Dingo passed M-pat his badge.

He held it up to the reader and Dingo/Alvaro leaned over his lap and stared at the camera.

The stop light turned green and the gate slid to the side.

"Ride sharing, huh?" Baldy said.

What would a gearhead like Pel say? "Transmission's shot on the bike."

Baldy turned back to M-pat/Luke. "So, Rose's sister?"

M-pat nodded, then pulled the car through the open gateway. In the rearview monitor on the dashboard, Baldy muttered something resembling "what the fuck?"

Dingo put his data glasses back on. Directional arrows and distances appeared over the roads. *M-pat should have said something. Hope we didn't blow it.*

The broadcast building, six stories of featureless concrete atop a slight hill, was just ahead, to the left. A huge parking lot sprawled in front, less than half full. "Over there," he pointed.

M-pat parked as close to the building as he could. He switched off the ignition button and looked at Dingo. "Follow my lead, 'kay?"

"You got it, chief." He had to admit, M-pat had a knack for this stuff.

They hopped out and headed for the only break in the concrete—a plastiglass protrusion with two revolving doors in front and a MediaCorp sign above.

Inside, a trio of receptionists crowded around a monitor behind the front desk, glued to the Super Bowl pre-game show. "...This year's commercials promise to be the best ever," an announcer prattled.

Dingo/Alvaro farted as he passed them, silent but deadly. With luck they'd blame each other.

M-pat/Luke stiffened but kept walking toward the employee entrance. He stuck his badge against the electronic card reader next to the twin metal doors, then looked in the camera lens above it. No biometrics here—would cause a traffic jam. The doors slid to either side and M-pat walked through.

The doors flew back together. Dingo held up his badge, stared in the camera, and they opened again.

The guard room was in the center of the ground floor. The data center was one floor below, filling the entire first basement. They passed employees in the hallway but no one spoke.

M-pat ducked into the men's room. Dingo followed.

The bathroom looked deserted. M-pat entered the first stall.

Dingo looked in the mirror first and admired Kiyoko's friends' craftsmanship and Kiyoko's touchups. *I am Alvaro Jimenez, right down to the eyebrow hair.*

He entered the stall at the far end. No cameras in here. He pulled a small oval piece of latex out of his pocket. It had an ultra-detailed thumbprint on one side, and adhesive on the other. Pel had created them on a portable 3-D printer and trimmed them with scissors.

He peeled off the backing and threw it in the toilet. He took a leak, pretending the floating paper was an enemy aircraft carrier and he was sinking it. "Face the wrath of the Flying Spaghetti Monster."

The toilet flushed as soon as he backed away from it. He admired his mask in the mirror again, then joined M-pat in the hall. M-pat stretched his fake face into a frown, but resumed the march to the security office.

The security room had a plastiglass window to the hallway. Inside, the walls were covered by ceiling to floor display skins showing hundreds of camera feeds and status graphs. Three guards sat at consoles. Two of the three sipped burnt-smelling coffee out of mugs and watched the pre-game show. A middle-aged man he recognized as the shift supervisor paced back and forth in front of the wall skin. It included a view of the hallway by the security room door.

"They got the entrance monitored, yo," he told M-pat as quiet as he could.

"They lookin' at it?"

"Supervisor's throwin' glances." He'd likely see them putting data glasses against the retinal scanner.

"Fuck."

"Go on ahead, I'm gonna say hi."

M-pat passed the window but stopped short of the door and its biometric controls and cameras.

Dingo waited for the hallway to clear, then knocked out a beat on the window.

Everyone turned around. He waved.

The supervisor stared at Dingo and jerked his thumb toward the door.

Dingo glanced at the camera feeds on the wall. He saw M-pat looking into the retinal scanner with data glasses on, the fake eyes as obvious as a clown on Christmas. He couldn't see the fake thumb print, at least.

The door opened. Dingo left the window.

Still in the hall, M-pat pocketed the glasses and thumb printout. He stepped into the security room.

"You're late," a man's voice said inside the room.

Dingo threw his data glasses on, assuming M-pat would provide a distraction. He tapped the side of the temple frame and the hallway dimmed to twilight, overlaid by huge brown eyes set in swarthy sockets, a network of blood vessels in the center.

He hurried to the door, held his badge against the reader, then stared into the twin lenses above it. A green light began blinking.

And kept blinking.

He moved closer, until his eyes were inches away from the lenses.

The light stayed green.

He found the thumb scanner and placed his printout-covered thumb against it. The door clicked.

He shoved the glasses in his pants pocket, then peeled off the thumb printout. It slipped out of his hand.

Fuck. He looked down but it wasn't on the carpet. It should have landed right at his feet, but it disappeared. He scanned the floor further and further away but couldn't see it anywhere.

Then he saw it stuck on the top of his shoe. *You bastard.* He bent down and pocketed it, then went to the door. The handle wouldn't move.

Da fuck? It had worked fine for M-pat.

He tried jiggling it. It wouldn't budge more than a millimeter in either direction.

They must have seen him searching for the thumb sticker. A shitstorm of guards could be on their way.

The door swung inward. M-pat had opened it from the other side. "Problems?"

"I got the green lights." He pushed his way past M-pat into the room, not knowing what else to do.

"You took too long," the shift supervisor said. "Just like you took too long getting here."

They didn't see. "Transmission's shot on the bike," Dingo said for the second time. "Luke had to pick me up."

"Yeah, well I'm noting it in your file."

Asshole.

"You sound different," one of the seated guards said, eyebrows raised. Recalling the personnel files, he looked like Frank, a veteran here.

"Yo mama's cootch must have rotted my tongue." *What does Jimenez sound like, then?*

Frank pounced up from his console.

"Siddown," the supervisor said. He glared at Dingo and M-pat. "You two, get to work."

M-pat sat down at the furthest console.

Dingo parked in the swivel chair at the console next to him. The display, keyboard, everything, was virtual, like the Genki-San at the band house, only fitted over a C-shaped table with a screen all along the back. Power was off. Where was the button? He tried to remember the diagram Pel had shown them.

There. The power button. He pressed it.

A confusing jumble of video images, icons, and keyboards popped up on the back display and table surface. *Where do I start?*

He got up and walked to the coffee maker on top of one of the file cabinets on the far wall. It couldn't be that hard. He used computers all the time, even if it was mostly for gaming. He was pretty damn good at that. And they'd gone over all the security and equipment manuals Charles had downloaded.

Not much coffee left. He didn't drink the stuff anyway, but they had two and half hours to kill before game time. He emptied the remnants of the pot into a ceramic MediaCorp cup and hurried back to his console before someone asked him to make more, something he had even less expertise in.

Once in his chair, he leaned back and sipped the coffee. It tasted like toilet water. *I can't believe people drink this shit.*

He looked over at M-pat, who was moving icons around on his table skin. First thing they had to do was disable all the cameras in this room, find yesterday's footage, and use it to replace the live feed. Easier said than done, even with Pel and Charles's best guesses.

"Jimenez." Frank's voice.

Dingo swiveled his chair around and saw him standing a few feet away, one of the other guards just behind.

"I swear, your voice is different."

* * *

Pelopidas

When the MediaCorp entrance gate appeared ahead, Pel almost stopped Nick Smith's electric Volkswagen and turned around. His hands shook against the steering wheel. *Relax. I look just like Smith, know what he sounds like, I've got his access card. Just be Nick Smith.* He'd passed as Greg Wilson at the Smithsonian fundraiser. And had played hundreds of characters in video games.

The entrance guard barely glanced at Pel as he held Smith's electronic badge to the reader and looked into the camera. The gate slid open and he drove inside, parking the Volkswagen two rows from M-pat/Luke's hybrid Mazda.

His hands started shaking again. He wished Waylee was there to say everything would work out, but she couldn't get in until they owned the security system. Which he hoped M-pat and Dingo could pull off. They had stun guns, could fight, and they'd have surprise. But they were up against pros.

Pel put on his data glasses and opened the car door. *Here we go.* They had studied the campus thoroughly and watched days of footage from Hubert and hacked guards. He tapped the side of his glasses. "DG, call data center office."

A Chinese woman appeared in a popup box. "Data center shift supervisor." *Damn, what was her name again?* He brought up the employee database loaded in memory and ran the facial recognition algorithm. Hu Kwong. *Yes, that's it.*

"Hi, this is Nick. I'm running late, but I've just arrived. Awfully sorry."

"You always late, Nick Smith. You have big problems in review."

"I'll work late. I'll work an extra shift. I'll be there soon."

"First shift already go home. You get here right away."

Pel terminated the connection and entered the building's plastiglass lobby.

Inside, three receptionists argued about which one ripped a noxious fart.

Pel ignored the stink and placed his badge against the reader by the employee doors. He looked in the camera and the doors parted. First stop was the bathroom, where he donned the fake thumbprint.

Nick Smith, older than Pel but the same general size, worked as an IT technician in the building's data center. Pel had chosen him carefully. He was a loner, with no family or roommates to complicate his replacement. More importantly, he monitored transmissions and had administrator access. And with M-pat's pistol held against his crotch, he had been 110% cooperative, telling Pel everything he wanted to know.

Nick was late, but Pel needed the go-ahead from M-pat before displaying eyes and retinas on his data glasses. He swished the right temple arm and sent a one character message: "?"

No answer. *Come on.*

Pel walked to the security room and peeked in the plastiglass window.

Everyone was staring at Dingo, who was seated at a console. One of the guards, standing just to his side, slid his hand toward a holstered pistol.

Fuck. Hoping to distract them, Pel knocked on the window.

* * *

M'patanishi

The guards were on to them. Dingo, anyway. Even though he was mostly Hispanic, Dingo had a generic Ballmer street accent. Maybe Alvarez sounded like an immigrant. M-pat had heard Luke Annlote speak, and when necessary, tried to copy his voice. But Alvarez had gone down without a fight, and they'd gagged him before he could say anything. *That was dumb, should have made him talk first. Too much shit to think about.*

M-pat switched off the security room cameras, making them invisible to external monitors. He couldn't find yesterday's footage, though. Big, big problem.

Someone knocked on the window to the hallway. Pel. The guards turned.

Gonna have to advance the schedule. M-pat whipped his stun gun out of its shoulder holster and fired at the supervisor. His eyes widened and he crumpled to the floor.

Dingo leapt out of his chair. Frank and the guard behind him went for their sidearms. Dingo swung his boot full force into Frank's nuts. As he doubled over, Dingo pushed him into the guard behind him. Frank sprawled backward to the floor and the other guard flailed to keep his balance.

The third guard rose from his console. M-pat fired the stun gun at him, last of its two charges. The guard's knees buckled, he fell onto the chair arm, and both crashed to the ground.

Dingo pulled out his stun gun and shot the guard behind Frank. He dropped to the ground and hit with a *crack*.

The supervisor lifted his head from the floor. He'd only been out a few seconds.

M-pat jumped up and bolted toward him. In his periphery, he saw Frank pull out his pistol.

Dingo fired at Frank with the stun gun and kicked the pistol from his fingers. It flew along the floor into the middle of the room.

The supervisor was still rising from the floor when M-pat reached him. "Goddamn stun guns. Why the hell won't you people stay down?" He planted his left foot and kicked with the right, landing just under the man's ear. His head snapped to the side and his eyes shut.

M-pat grabbed the supervisor's gun and comlink headset, then pulled the handcuffs off the man's belt and snapped them around his wrists.

Frank looked unconscious. Dingo knelt and handcuffed him, then took his comlink and utility belt. He did the same with the guard behind him, and thrust his gun in his belt.

The final guard rose to his feet. He fumbled for his gun, looking a little groggy.

M-pat charged. The guard raised his pistol.

Shit. M-pat reached him just in time and locked a hand around the man's wrist. He twisted the wrist and pulled him forward, off balance. With his other hand he grabbed the pistol by the barrel and snatched it away.

The guard flared with anger. He threw a left jab.

M-pat thrust up his left arm and knocked the punch away. Not having the pistol in a firing hold, and hoping not to kill anyone, he aimed an elbow at his head.

The guard blocked the elbow and countered with a hammer fist.

M-pat blocked the fist with his forearm, but the blow was a feint, and the man kicked him in the knee.

Pain shot through his leg. "Bitch ass punk!" He shifted his stance and jabbed with his left fist.

The guard blocked it.

Broiling with fury, M-pat swung his right hand, the gun still in it. The butt smacked his opponent in the left ear. "Straight to school, bitch!"

The man yelped, but kicked at his other knee.

This time M-pat was ready, and dodged. He swept his right leg under the guard's and pushed against his torso. The man fell hard to the ground.

M-pat twirled the gun in his right hand and pointed it at the guard as he tried to get up. "Game over, chump. Lie down on your face now."

The guard stared in his eyes, then complied. *Motherfucker knows a man who means business.* M-pat felt the rage dissipate. He motioned Dingo over, who slapped handcuffs on.

41

Pelopidas

The security room door opened. "Come in," M-pat/Luke said. "We need you."

"Everything okay?"

M-pat nodded, then limped toward a guard prone on the floor, the man's wrists cuffed together. "Hopefully no one else heard."

Dingo lowered the window blinds. He looked over and tossed a roll of duct tape to Pel. It didn't come close, and rolled underneath one of the consoles.

"I hope you've got more of that," Pel said.

"Plenty."

M-pat pointed to one of the other consoles. "I turned the cameras off in here, but I couldn't figure out the stuff with the old footage."

"On it."

M-pat and Dingo began gagging the four handcuffed guards.

"Nice work," Pel said. He sat at the console.

"Hate them stun guns," M-pat said while he worked. "Near useless."

"Everyone's tolerance is different."

"Wasn't expectin' to act this soon. Hope we can hold out."

"You're the bosses here. Just keep the other guards busy elsewhere. Have them patrol the other side of campus or something."

Pel examined the console. M-pat had indeed switched off the room's cameras. He opened a Unix shell, navigated to the stored data from yesterday, and copied the files to the buffer directory. The data was all well organized and clearly named. "You know, I loaded instructions on your data glasses."

"Too busy trying not to get shot," M-pat said as he emptied the guards' pockets.

"No one else was wearing data glasses in here," Dingo said. "Not like the ones on patrol. Had enough trouble blending in as it was."

Pel found the camera directories. He renamed the copied data from yesterday to resemble raw camera output, and ran a script to give it a current timestamp. Then he changed some pointers in the camera feeds to draw from these files instead of the actual cameras. *Done.*

He heard scraping noises. M-pat and Dingo dragged the three guards into the corner by the door, out of view of the window if they reopened the blinds. They arranged them in a pile with their feet facing, and taped them together.

"There's a lot worse positions you could be in," Dingo said as he wound tape from one ankle to another. "'Course, some of you might enjoy that."

Pel scanned the wall monitors to see what was happening elsewhere. From the security room, they could spy on everyone in the building.

Several panoramic videos showed the circular control room dominating the fourth and fifth floors, where all of MediaCorp's broadcasts and Comnet feeds could be overseen. Pel didn't even know how many channels and backchannels they had, and doubted even most MediaCorp employees knew, since the number of channels increased each day. Today's focus was clearly the Super Bowl, with some 250 million expected viewers and advertisements exceeding $10 million per minute. Much of the high circular wall displayed the pre-game show and associated standby cameras.

Pel flipped through camera feeds on his console, looking for Hubert. He wouldn't know who was entering the MediaCorp campus, what they looked like, or where they were going. But he did know they were coming, and probably knew they were worth $3 million if captured. So Pel still didn't trust him.

Between the giant wall displays, consoles were arranged in tightly packed concentric circles, hundreds of technicians in headgear or immersion suits sitting behind virtual keyboards and mixing boards, and glass video panes curving up like windshields. The producer and director sat in command chairs on a dais in the center. All this Death Star bridge needed was a Sith Lord like Robert Luxmore.

Speak of the devil. All the stadium cameras were on. Two of the wall videos showed Luxmore and his trophy wife in a private stadium booth, chatting with President Rand. The president never missed a Super Bowl, and the broadcasts indulged him with plenty of face time.

Pel zoomed in on one of the monitors. Both men sipped from glasses of gold-tinted whiskey. At least a dozen other VIPs milled about the intimate suite, wearing suits or dresses that seemed incongruous at a football game. Secret Service agents in data glasses stood like animatrons or talked into wraparound mics.

Wonder what they're talking about? Pel followed directions he'd stored on his data glasses, and used Hubert's backdoor to access the feed directory. He found the stadium booth cameras and brought them up on his console. He switched on the sound and turned up the gain.

"I'm telling you, Al," Luxmore said, shooing his wife away. "You've got to improve security in this country."

Might be good material. One of the console displays contained thumbnails of all the open feeds, so you could manipulate window placement. Pel ran links from the stadium booth cameras to console storage, copying the video to a file.

"When terrorists sneak into your own private party," Luxmore continued, "and steal data that's used to ruin my board and embarrass everyone..."

Rand narrowed his eyes. "Shit happens, Bob. If your comlinks were more secure, they wouldn't have been compromised. Secret Service assures me they couldn't get anything off the comlinks NSA designed."

"I knew that girl you were flirting with was trouble, Al. You've got to stop letting the little head think for the big one."

Pel plucked a two-inch data stick out of an inside shirt pocket and plugged it into a console port. He opened another Unix shell and set the camera video to copy to the data stick. He could see Waylee tattooing Luxmore's remark on her ass.

In the stadium booth, a Secret Service flunky refilled their glasses. Rand threw his back and swallowed half the contents. "We plugged the leaks. The new scheduling director assures me it won't happen again. And we're all set for the terrorists' next move. I wouldn't be here if I didn't have full confidence."

Luxmore wagged a finger. "One good thing."

Rand raised an eyebrow.

"This fiasco is just the thing we need to crack down on cybercrime. I need a more secure Comnet and BetterWorld. We need stronger laws and better enforcement and need full access to the users, so we can keep a handle on things."

A Supreme Court justice, one of two Rand had appointed, approached, but the president waved him off. "Anyone Homeland catches," he said, "if they're good, typically we put them to work."

Luxmore leaned forward. "I wouldn't mind a piece of that."

Rand rattled the ice in his glass. "We need to roll up the whole Collective, the People's Party, the other troublemakers. You know, back in 2001, 9-11 gave the second Bush cover to do all sorts of things. I'd love that kind of leeway."

Luxmore nodded. "We need Total Information Awareness. For real, not just what we have now. The more we know, the better decisions we can make. Uncertainty is a leader's deadliest enemy."

A chill swept through Pel and rattled his fingers. Their video might strengthen their enemies, not weaken them.

"The immersion suits will expand our reach," Luxmore continued, "but wait until the neural interfaces hit the market. With that kind of technology, we can monitor *thoughts* if we need to."

The color drained from Rand's face. "Careful what you say. No one wants to hear things like that. Besides, I thought the brain implants were more than a decade away."

"Mostly it's FDA regulations in the way. That's what's really slowing us down."

I should have known not to underestimate them.

Rand nodded. "Well you know my administration is committed to reducing burdensome regulations. Especially where national security's at stake. We'll talk more later." He waved the Supreme Court justice over. Luxmore walked off, presumably to stalk other prey.

"'Sup?" Dingo's voice came from behind. Pel turned. They'd finished taping the security guards together.

Pel pointed to the camera feeds from the stadium booth. "Rand and Luxmore will use our hacking as an excuse for further repression."

Dingo shrugged. "Fascism 101."

"Well I was hoping for the opposite. And Waylee was right about the brain interface research." He hated to risk it, but... "DG, call 42." Waylee's new link, audio only.

"What's up?" She sounded peppy.

She wouldn't be en route just yet. They hadn't planned on taking the guard station so soon. In low tones, he summarized Rand and Luxmore's conversation. "What if our video backfires? What if instead of stopping the march toward totalitarianism, we accelerate it?"

Waylee responded immediately. "We're going to wake people up. People need to know about their schemes, and can act to stop them."

He tried to reply but she kept going. "It's too late to second guess now. We're committed."

That was pretty much true.

"Radical change is always messy," she said. "But if Rand and Luxmore overreact, even more people will turn against them, some passionately so."

More Waylees? Pel checked the time. "Well you'd better get going. We had to advance the schedule a bit."

"On my way." She disconnected.

Pel returned to the search for Hubert. There he was, at a console in one of the outer rings, staring at scripts and moving graphs. He switched to the camera on Hubert's console. Beads of sweat clung to the engineer's forehead.

He fed the camera video to Hubert's display, showing the engineer's nervous face in a popup window.

Hubert mouthed "all good."

He'd forgotten to switch on the audio but that was okay. Pel closed the camera video on Hubert's display and turned to Dingo. "I'm like so late now I'm probably fired. Our friend's on the monitor here. Keep an eye on him."

"You got it, chief."

He pointed to the data stick and spoke loud enough for M-pat to hear. "Take this with you when you leave. Don't forget."

"You say jump, I say how high."

Pel shook his head and moved to another console. It would be nice if he could give himself full access to the security systems from remote terminals. Unfortunately, it looked like they were self-contained and isolated from external commands.

He motioned M-pat over and brought up a 3-D map of locks and cameras, then opened a help program. After querying it, he said, "Just tap on the camera symbol and the feed'll pop up in a window."

It took longer to figure out how to override the door locks, but the system was designed for muscleheads and was user friendly.

"Think I got it," M-pat said.

"If in doubt about anything, ask the help program. In an emergency, contact me, and I'll run up from the basement."

Pel waited until the hallway was clear, then left the security room. He took the stairs down instead of the elevator.

The first door, marked "Authorized Personnel Only," was four flights down. Biometric scanners were mounted next to it. The stairs continued downward, to a utility and storage sub-basement.

He donned his data glasses and displayed Nick Smith's eyes. A retinal scan, thumb scan, badge read, and facial recognition later, the door slid open.

Inside, a megalopolis of blue-lit server racks sprawled toward a dim horizon. Red and green indicator lights, some blinking, dotted the homogenous facades like tiny windows. Fans hummed in the walls and the ceiling far overhead, carrying away the heat.

He shivered. It was the most terrifyingly beautiful thing he'd ever seen. Countless thousands of machines, each one anonymous, but together, in this blue twilight, shaping the thoughts of the world.

Pel wandered down one of the cyber canyons. Each computer and hybrid storage drive was connected to a power strip and neat bundle of optic lines running up the stack to horizontal arteries. According to the floor plans, the data center office, parts room, and other support facilities lay somewhere beyond.

The rows terminated at glowing blue cuboids of plastiglass, power panels enclosed inside. Beyond that was a wall punctuated by doors.

The glass door to the office was propped open. Through windows on either side, Pel saw three people sitting at consoles and one looking toward the door. Hu Kwong. She spotted him approaching and scowled.

"Sorry I'm late," Pel/Nick said as he entered.

"You said that over an hour ago. Where the hell you been?"

Had it been that long? "Got a call. Family emergency."

Everyone turned to look. "Everything okay?" Hu said. "You sound weird."

Pel coughed. "Feels like I've got a cold or something."

Hu backed up, then edged around him to the door. "I have to make the rounds. You get to work."

One of the technicians, a heavyset blonde, glared at Pel/Nick, eyebrows knotted. She logged off her console, threw on her purse, and stomped out of the room.

Pel started to feel guilty about arriving late, but reminded himself the woman was lucky to have a job to complain about. Half his graduating class were unemployed, partly from outsourcing, but mostly because increasingly autonomic systems reduced the need for IT personnel.

He sat at the empty console furthest from the remaining two techs. It had a real keyboard, with springs under the letters. *Let's see if Nick lied to us. I've got Hubert's info as a backup.* He entered Nick's console password. It worked, unleashing a tropical beach photo and a universe of icons on the glass display.

He opened the network monitoring programs and a command line interface. *I'm now a network administrator for the most powerful corporation in the world.* Time to prep things for Waylee and Charles. He typed another password and logged into the root account.

* * *

Dingo

"At least we'll catch the second half," M-pat said from his console, where he watched for Waylee. "All goes well, anyway." He had directed the two guards patrolling their building up to the top floor, as far away as possible.

"This is way more fun than watching a stupid football game," Dingo said.

Pel had asked him to keep an eye on Hubert in broadcast control. All he did was stare at diagrams and squiggly lines, though. Boring.

The stadium booth feeds were more interesting. He expanded both windows and watched the Sith Lords, Master Luxmore and Apprentice Rand, strut among their toadies.

Too bad he'd been cut out of the New Year's op. Waylee had owned them to their bastard faces. Wait 'til they saw her video of them go out to 200 million people, with no way to stop it.

Not far from camera *PresBooth1*, Luxmore clapped President Rand on the shoulder. "Care to make a wager on the game, Al?"

"Now you know as president I have to stay impartial."

The shitsacks laughed the laugh of sadists. Their game had nothing to do with football.

A middle-aged man with flattop hair, a government-issue suit, and data glasses entered the booth. Rand waved him over. "Anything?"

"Not yet, sir."

Rand huffed. "You're sure your intel's solid? I mean, the tip's from a teen-age farm girl, for God's sake."

Flattop fidgeted. "Well, sir, she claimed to know them. The terrorists' leader, who's apparently unstable, personally told this girl about their plan."

Farm girl? Who's he talking about?

Luxmore's trophy wife walked up, umbrella drink in hand. "What's going on?"

"Nothing," Luxmore huffed.

Rand turned to Mrs. Luxmore, scoping her cleavage before answering. "Remember that couple who broke into the New Year's party?"

Shit. Someone definitely sold us out.

"Oh," she said, "the girl who threatened to cut off—"

Luxmore waved a hand. "Yes, yes, those two."

Why would Waylee tell some farm girl about our plan?

Rand sighed. "They're working with that cyberterrorist Charles Lee, and apparently hope to disrupt the Super Bowl somehow. Secret Service wanted me to stay home." He scoffed. "It's my presidential duty to watch this game." He stared at Flattop. "These people are irritants, nothing more. Certainly not assassins, or they'd have set off a bomb or something on New Year's."

"We're ready for anything," Flattop said. "Homeland Security's on full alert. And we've got choppers on site just in case."

Dingo looked over at M-pat. "Yo, uh, Luke."

"'Sup?"

"Someone sold us out. Some farm girl."

M-pat jumped out of his seat. "What? Who?"

"Relax—they think we're in Atlanta. Not here."

M-pat looked from screen to screen on the wall, breath bursting in and out. "Should we cancel?"

Never seen him so agitated. "Dude, it's like ten minutes to kickoff. Let's finish the job and then get out of here."

M-pat sat back down, stinking of sweat. "You sure they focusing on Atlanta?"

He wasn't sure, actually. "Lemme call Pel."

"'Kay, you take care of it." His voice trembled. "I gotta lot to do. Lemme know what he says."

* * *

Kiyoko

Kiyoko sat on one of the mattresses in the back of the Boroborinski Brothers moving truck, immersion helmet and gloves on, and a blanket pulled over her legs. The day was cold, but the 'scrubber fans' Pel installed in the truck to keep them from suffocating made it even colder. At least it didn't bother Nyasuke, comfortable in his fur coat.

Kiyoko had parked the truck in the sprawling lot of a shopping mall near the MediaCorp campus. Waylee and the others would park on the opposite side, change masks, and cross through the mall to get to her. Then they'd head south. Word on the Comnet was, Homeland had an army of Watchers and agents on the Canadian border.

That morning, Charles had tied the suit into a Wi-Fi signal from the mall and disguised her location. She had a lot to keep track of, and put some of it, like the model plane and chatboxes, on standby.

On the right side of her vision, the Super Bowl feed showed pre-game yammering. *Boring.* Along the bottom, she monitored the rotating micro-camera on top of the truck that gave a panoramic view of the parking lot. Equally boring. But she reserved a transparent portion on the left to watch Nyasuke sleep and stretch on the mattress. *Yay cat!*

The number 69 flashed red in front of her. That would be Dingo. *As if.* She touched the number with a virtual finger.

Her decryption program gave her a thumbs up. "Moshi moshi," she answered. In the old days she might have added *bakatare* to greet Dingo, falsely saying it was a term of endearment. But mere morons didn't risk their lives for others or come through when you really needed them.

"Someone sold us out," Dingo's disembodied voice announced.

Kiyoko lurched up, startling her cat into attention. "What?"

"Girl named Amy, apparently. Must have called the reward hotline and told them about the Super Bowl op. Homeland's on alert, waiting for us in Atlanta."

"So they think we're in Atlanta?"

"I talked to Pel and Waylee. You know how to fake your location, right?"

She sighed. "Yes, I know all that." She'd learned a fair bit from Charles, and everyone's coms had caller ID spoofers that routed through anonymous servers and added a fake origin.

"Can you call in a tip saying we're in Atlanta?"

"Sure, I'm on it." She'd make up some burner number and pick a base station there as the origin. *Charles will be proud of me.*

"Thanks. We're all slammed here."

Uh oh. "Everything okay?"

"Yeah, so far. Smell ya later, girly girl." He ended the call.

Kiyoko navigated to the "Select by Map" option of her spoofing program and picked a 5G cell tower near the Georgia Dome. She let the program generate a burner number, then dialed the reward hotline.

"U.S. Department of Homeland Security," a pleasant male voice answered. "How may we help you?"

Her instincts told her to hang up. But she soldiered on. "I'm calling about the reward for Waylee Freid, Pelopidas Demopoulos, and Charles Marvin Lee. I'm looking at all three of them right now."

"Can you tell me where you are?"

She brought up a map display. "I'm at the Vine City MARTA Station. They came out with some others and they're standing there talking... oh, they're all separating now, going different directions."

After a pause, she heard, "Can you tell me your name, please?"

Her brain froze. "Kelly. Kelly Green." *Oh, what a stupid name.*

"Well, Ms. Green, please stay where you are. We'll have officers there shortly. Could you describe yourself, please?"

Crap. "What about the reward? When do I get the reward?"

"When they're apprehended. Now, what do you look like?"

What's totally anonymous? "I've got brown hair, brown eyes. I'm 5 foot 3, dress size 4. I've got a Giants shirt on."

"Well, thank you, Ms. Green. Someone will be there shortly."

Kiyoko hung up, hoping she hadn't botched the call too badly. What would Homeland do when they arrived and couldn't find Kelly Green?

42

Game time

Waylee

Tania Peart disguise on, Waylee pulled her supercharged Mustang GT up to the MediaCorp gate and stopped the music playlist. She'd been supercharging herself with Dwarf Eats Hippo's most energetic tracks, plus some old Rage Against the Machine and Orange 9mm. No pot necessary, although it might have reduced the hurt she felt from Amy's betrayal.

The car didn't look that fancy on the outside. After M-pat and Dingo stole it a few days ago, they'd painted it boring blue. But the engine was something else, the pride and joy of a redneck street racer. Pel thought she could get 220 miles per hour on it, a lot faster than anything the cops had.

She had a big leather purse between her legs, stuffed with guns, a radio, handcuffs, duct tape, and other employee protocol violations. Pel had installed a satellite repeater in the trunk. Charles, disguised as a 22-year-old IT technician named Rodrick Boxer, sat beside her. *Ironic we need masks to unmask the plutocracy.*

Both Tania and Rodrick had the day off, but worked in the broadcast data center. Waylee had received a ☺ message on her data glasses from M-pat, signifying she could go wherever she pleased as long as he could see her through a camera.

"Wasn't expecting anyone else to come in 'til after the game," the unsmiling bald guard at the gate said.

Waylee/Tania pressed her fake badge against the card reader. Since they could go anywhere once they controlled the security room, it was just a piece of plastic with a photo and text laminated on top, no electronics inside. The indicator LED turned green anyway. *Thanks, M-pat.*

"I'm not a football fan," she said. "I am a double pay overtime fan, though."

Behind the plexiglass, the guard pointed at Charles/Rodrick. "And what about him? Why are so many people ride sharing today?"

Waylee shrugged. "He's working too."

Charles nodded and passed his badge. Waylee held it to the reader. "I'm not his supervisor or anything so it's cool if we fraternize, right?"

The guard smirked. "You mean bump uglies?"

Charles posed for the camera. "Shit."

Waylee turned to look at him. The masks concealed some of the subtler emotional cues, but his eyes were wide, staring out the windshield and up toward the sky.

The traffic light turned green and the gate slid to the side.

She kept her foot on the brake. "What's up?" she asked him.

"Watcher."

Here? Fuck you, Amy. She scanned the sky ahead.

A dark wheel-shaped object studded with antennae flew a slow circle about a hundred feet above the buildings.

Other than that, the campus seemed quiet, though. No guard vehicles with flashing lights or snipers pointing rifles from the rooftops.

She patted his hand. She'd gotten the smiley face. But the Watcher must have arrived after M-pat, Dingo, and Pel went inside, or they'd have mentioned it. They probably didn't know it was there. She couldn't turn around and leave, though; that would arouse suspicion for sure.

"Is there a problem?" the guard said over the speaker.

"No problem." Waylee eased the Mustang through the open gate and headed for the six story broadcast building. Best to continue with the plan, and modify as needed. She'd do whatever it took to get her video on the air, but also whatever it took to make sure her friends escaped.

Once they arrived, as promised, all doors opened for her.

Every nerve in Waylee's body tingled when they entered the data center. Murky blue-lit walls of processors stretched into the distance, alive behind millions of green and red eyes.

Do not go quiet into Luxmore's night.

Rage, rage against the machines' false light.

Charles stood and stared.

"So this is where our souls go when we're in the Comnet," she said.

He looked around. "This is just to handle some video feeds. This place is like a shoe box compared to what they must have for BetterWorld."

"How do you know where anything is?"

"Doesn't matter. It's all virtual."

A silhouette emerged from the gloom cloaking the end of the nearest machine corridor. The figure strode toward them, soundless. Then it resolved into Pel/Nick Smith.

Waylee and Shakti once watched this cheesy Bollywood movie—she couldn't remember the name - in which two lovers ran toward each other through a field of flowers. This was the cyberstructure equivalent. Neither Waylee nor Pel actually ran toward each other – they walked. Nor did they embrace when they met at the midpoint. But even playing it cool and behind a mask, Pel's eyes cast a bond stronger than steel.

"There's a Watcher outside," she whispered in his ear.

His eyes widened. "So they didn't buy Kiyoko's story?"

She thought about it. "It doesn't seem like this place is on alert. I think the Watcher is part of Homeland's overall mobilization. It ignored us and we had no trouble getting in."

"I'm still afraid," he whispered, "your video might backfire, do more harm than good. Are you sure we want do this?"

She replied loud enough for Charles to hear. "I thought we resolved this. Have faith."

Charles shook his head. "I can't believe you're arguing now. Let's get this done."

Waylee agreed. "Yeah, what he said."

Pel nodded and smiled. "The majority rules." He cast his eyes down the corridor. "If you'll follow me, I'll show you to the administrative consoles."

Waylee opened her big leather purse and handed Pel the stun gun she'd brought in for him. She pulled out one of her own, plus a Heckler & Koch pistol M-pat had given her. She wasn't any good with a gun, but its only purpose was intimidation. She eyed Charles. "Take the rear."

Pel snickered. "That's what she said."

She sighed. "You really ought to work on your repertoire."

They followed Pel through the machine hive to an unmarked glass door with long windows on either side. Three people sat inside at computer consoles, a prim-looking Asian woman, a fortyish Latina with short hair, and a young bearded man with brass-framed data glasses. The Asian woman looked up.

Inside, someone, maybe everyone, was listening to the Super Bowl in progress.

"Dolphins start at their own twenty yard line," an announcer said. *"First time they've had the ball after stopping the Giants at midfield and forcing the punt. Three wide receivers..."*

Pel/Nick entered the room first and stood by the door.

"And Armstrong hands off the ball to Leggett... He's stuffed at the line of scrimmage for no gain."

Waylee/Tania followed Pel in. Charles entered behind her but remained in the doorway. Everyone stared at them.

Waylee nodded at the technicians. *What now?* She looked around.

Eight consoles sat in two rows, each topped by large curving glass displays. Half the consoles were on, each with multiple portals open, including video of the Super Bowl. The Latina and bearded guy, seated at the second row of consoles, returned their eyes to the game.

"Ten twenty two, ten twenty two..." A whistle blew. *"It looks like Mosby moved prematurely,"* the announcer said.

"Yeah, he's a little too anxious," his co-announcer said.

The Asian woman stood and crossed her arms. "What are you two doing here? You're not scheduled for today."

"Helping out," Waylee said.

"False start, number 76, offense," a referee shouted.

The woman's eyes narrowed. "Both of you? No, that's ridiculous. You work when you're scheduled to work."

Pel moved to the side and palmed his stun gun. He glanced out the spotless window.

Waylee's stomach tensed. "They called me up and asked me to come in."
"Who did?"

"Hut hut..." *"And Armstrong's fading back to pass..."*

"Fuck it," Pel said. "Knew she'd be a hassle." He raised his stun gun and shot the woman. She crumpled to the floor.

"Johnson's got it over the middle..."

The other two technicians jumped to their feet. Charles ducked out of the room. Waylee scrambled for her stun gun. It wasn't supposed to go this way.

The bearded guy grabbed a metal stapler on his desk and hurled it at her, then dashed to the right, away from her and Pel. Waylee flinched but the stapler caught her under the left eye, the sudden pain surprising her.

"He breaks one tackle, still going..."

Waylee ignored the pain. It would have been worse without the padding

Kiyoko had fattened the cheeks with. She ran after the man, who was headed for an open doorway on the right side. It smelled like coffee in there. She tried to aim the stun gun but her hand wouldn't stay still.

The man reached the doorway. She stopped, leveled her gun and pulled the trigger. His limbs stiffened and he dropped, head smacking against the door jamb on the way down.

"And down at the forty yard line. First down, Miami."

Eyes wide, the remaining tech raised her hands. "I just work here. I got a family."

"On the floor," Waylee said. *Someone's begging me for their life?* "I won't hurt you."

"And Armstrong's moved the Dolphins down field with a twenty-five yard gain."

The windows had no blinds so they'd have to hurry. Waylee ran from tech to tech, slapping on handcuffs. She and Pel dragged them into the adjoining kitchenette/lounge, where the bearded man had been headed, and fastened socks in their mouths with duct tape.

"You okay?" Pel asked her when they finished.

"Could have been worse."

"Your face is torn."

"How's it look?"

"Painfully obvious."

Waylee slapped a hand to her aching cheek and felt a loose flap of latex. *Fuck.* She looked at the employees on the tiled floor, trembling and stinking of sweat. "Stay chill, and you'll be free in less than an hour." They hadn't killed anyone, but a lot of people were hurt and terrified. These techs, the guards, especially the employees taped up since early morning, they were just regular people doing their jobs.

The government would call it "collateral damage" and say "the ends justify the means."

Did it?

* * *

Charles

Slipping back into the data room office, Charles felt like the biggest pussy-ass bitch on Earth. *I won't ever run away again. Gotta stand tall like M-pat and Dingo.*

He couldn't get used to Pel's new face. At least it didn't have a big rip like Waylee's. The fake MediaCorp admin ushered him to a console. "Have a seat. Everything's set up."

Masks worked both ways, and hid his shame. Charles took the driver's seat. *Game on!* Do this right, and people would talk him up for centuries. Biggest hack ever. Fuck up again, and their lives were over for nothing.

The console had all manner of command shells, network maps, and video feeds open. Three of the feeds displayed the game.

Pel turned the volume down on all the monitors so they could concentrate. He rolled a chair over and pointed to the left video on their console. "That's the data channel transmitting the Super Bowl from the control studio." He pointed to the other two. "Those are the echoes from the Comnet and satellite uplinks, so the technical director can verify what's being sent out."

Charles examined the transmission data. The signal was double encrypted, more than their usual layer. He showed Pel. "Looks like they're expecting us." *We should have locked that farm girl in a closet or some shit.*

"Same as with the Watcher," Waylee said. "They're covering their bases. Are we still good?"

"Encryption makes no difference. We ain't trying to change their signal, we're replacing it."

Other portals on the monitor displayed lists of running processes and scrolling lines of commands. "That's IT traffic between the studio and the data servers," Pel said. "The one on the bottom is our friend Hubert."

Hubert hadn't been on the broadcast system since the game started. Doing something else, or maybe in the bathroom taking a dump.

"'Kay, Waylee," Charles said, "let's see your video."

A huge grin stretched across her torn mask. She reached into a pocket and handed him a memory stick. He plugged it in to the console computer and copied her video to one of the servers out in the big room somewhere.

"Don't send it yet," she said.

"I know, we gotta spoof the return signals."

"But also, timing is everything. I want to break in someplace that won't piss people off too much. Maybe during a time out or when the refs are jabbering. Or when they go to commercial, that would be perfect."

"'Kay."

Charles plugged in a data stick of his own, a toolbox of hacking utilities and scripts. Pel had already done the hard part, figuring out where everything was. The rest was like putting a puzzle together.

The Chinese supervisor's monitor beeped. Pel rushed over to it. "Says unauthorized software detected on your console."

"Shit." *They've got hyped-up intrusion prevention systems.* His screen froze and wouldn't accept commands.

From behind, Waylee gripped his shoulder. "Can you get around it?"

Charles shook off Waylee's hand. He ran over to the supervisor's console and disabled the lock. "Why'd we even bother with this Nick Smith guy? Why not replace the supervisor?"

Pel threw up his arms. "Smith was the only one we could get to."

Charles brought up the system process list, killed the detection program, and hurried back to Smith's console. He loaded his pre-written code, called by a shell script that would do four things. First, it would notify their Collective friends to start jamming the incoming message and voice lines and the nearby cell network. To anyone calling in, the lines would seem busy.

Second, it would run a program to intercept any commands from the control studio and quarantine them without sending back any error messages. They'd figure out something was wrong when the commands didn't work, but there wasn't anything they could do about it.

A third program would reroute the Super Bowl feed from the control room to storage drives in the server room instead of the Comnet and satellite uplinks. In its place, it would transmit Waylee's video.

Finally, his script would replace the verification signal from the uplink stations with the control room's video, not Waylee's video which was actually being sent out to the world. All he had to do now was check the variable definitions, swiping over the right process names and pathways.

"Second quarter's started," Pel said. "We're behind schedule."

"What's the score?"

"No score yet. Can you believe that?"

It took a couple of minutes for Charles to finish modifying his script. "What's up with the local phones?" he asked Pel.

"That's Hubert's job; we can't access them from here."

Charles set up a chatbox, disabled the log, and invited Hubert, listed as superuser SU32.

```
SysAdmin3: Ready?
SU32: This on record?
SysAdmin3: MMDRND
```

"Inner Circle term," he told Waylee. "My mama didn't raise no dummies."

```
SU32: What about other admins?
```

"We got 'em all?" Charles asked Pel.
"The ones in the building, yeah, this is their office."

```
SysAdmin3: XO
SU32: All good here. When?
```

Charles looked at Waylee.
"Let's do it next commercial break," she said.
Pel leaned forward. "Ask him what he's doing."
Charles typed as fast as he could.

```
SysAdmin3: Whats yr game?
SU32: Sending worm to building's unified communications
server. Will stop all voice communications, email, ev-
erything. Easy-peasy for #1 engineer on campus.
SysAdmin3: Go as soon as the next commercial break
starts.
SU32: ok.
SysAdmin3: What about other buildings?
SU32: Can't access, but doesn't matter.
```

Pel edged forward in his seat and turned up the game volume. A receiver for the Dolphins was running down the sideline toward the end zone.

"And Freeman's got only one man to beat," the announcer said, *"but it looks like the safety's got a bad angle."*

"That's right," the other announcer said. *"Freeman burned the defensive back. He went for the interception and got out of position. Freeman could go all the way."*

"He's at the 20... the 10... Touchdown!"

Charles typed his shell script name at the root prompt, `# Touissant`

His finger shook, but he didn't press the enter key. He looked at Waylee. "Want to do the honors?"

Waylee gazed at him. "It's your program. Your honors."

As soon as the Dolphins kicked the extra point, Charles tapped the enter key.

Nothing happened. The outgoing feed replayed the touchdown, with the announcers saying what a great play it was and what it would do for momentum. *Too early.*

Waylee screeched. "Where's our video?"

Charles checked the system log. His script had been blocked by superuser syssec-d.

Da fuck? They'd taken care of all the humans. The mystery admin must be an AI daemon. He'd have to work fast, before Hubert ran his worm and tipped everyone off.

As an admin, Charles had virtually unlimited power. He tried to kill the syssec-d process.

```
Insufficient privilege.
```

It wasn't just a process, it was his artificial counterpart. He tried to delete the whole account.

```
Insufficient privilege.
```

A chatbox popped up.

```
SysSec-Daemon: What are you doing?
```

"Who's that?" Pel said behind him.

No time to explain.

```
SysAdmin3: Running system updates.
```

The Super Bowl feed began a car commercial. Hubert would set off his worm now.

One thing about AIs, they lacked imagination. Charles listed syssec-d's activities and found a 'centralized exceptions' folder, which contained files and processes exempt from security scanning. The folder was nearly empty. He copied his scripts to a definition file and dumped it in the folder.

"The new Yolo-X is our hottest car ever," the commercial promised.

Charles ran a configuration process, which would make sure syssec-d read the updated exemptions list. He crossed the fingers of his left hand and hit the up arrow until the prompt returned to `# Touissant`.

* * *

Waylee

Waylee's skin burned as Charles tried his program again. "Please work," she said. Her heart pounded out speedcore thrash beats. Getting shot at, chased out of their house through miles of stormwater pipes, thrown on the FBI's most wanted list, it couldn't be for nothing.

The left video, the feed from studio control, continued the car commercial. The two videos on the right, the signal going out to the world, began with a shrill emergency tone, a screen with the presidential seal, and a voice announcing, "This is an emergency message from the President of the United States. We apologize for the interruption. Please stand by. You must take immediate action following the end of this broadcast."

Waylee grabbed Charles's arm. "Is it working?"

He nodded.

The screen dissolved to President Rand speaking on the Smithsonian stage. A caption underneath listed the location, date and time. Floating name and affiliation tags followed everyone on camera other than wait staff and Pel.

"It looks like we've got more wealth gathered here than the rest of the country put together," the president said.

Cutaway to assembled guests in tuxedos and evening gowns.

Back to President Rand. "And everyone here has prospered during my first term. Am I right?"

Loud assents from the guests.

"Are you sure people are seeing this?" Waylee asked Charles.

He pointed to the right-most feed. "That's your video on the uplink verification. So yeah."

On the screen, Waylee/Estelle asked why ordinary Americans should vote for Rand.

"People are surprisingly easy to influence once you know how their minds work," his media advisor said.

Luxmore stepped forward. "People are generally stupid. That's why they need people like us to tell them what to do. Plato's philosopher-kings, bred and educated to make the right decisions."

"Exactly," the president said. "Most people don't know what's in their best interest."

"What about all men and women being created equal?" Waylee/Estelle said. "That governments should consent to the will of the governed?"

The president laughed.

"So MediaCorp persuades the public to support you…"

"Staying on message, we call it. We're headed toward a world where MediaCorp knows everything about everyone. But we're on the same side. We help each other out."

The feed split into three windows, the left-most displaying an email from the president's media advisor, the middle showing a memo from MediaCorp's news director to their staff, and the right playing the news as broadcast. All three contained the same content. Then it switched to their emails about Justice Consiglio's sex site visits, with the right window showing him shaking hands with the president.

The president re-appeared. "He can turn anything into a public issue. Name a person alive who doesn't have skeletons in their closet."

The video continued, detailing how MediaCorp and the president's party worked to suppress democracy, and what they planned for the future. At the bottom of the video, a caption invited viewers to virtual links administered by the Collective: "Discover more at /MenOfGold, and discuss at #FooledNoMore." Bots would swamp attempts to shut the links down or plant misinformation.

Waylee's stomach knotted with regret. *I'm slanting the truth just like MediaCorp.*

All she claimed to stand for, freedom to think and decide for oneself, she'd thrown aside as she clung to her quest. She and Bob Luxmore were one and the same, imposing their view of the greater good, manipulating others to fall in line.

But the video was just a wake-up shock. People could examine all the raw material and draw their own conclusions. And hopefully a critical mass would emerge, and bring down the plutocracy. She hugged Charles, then Pel. "I love you."

"Love you too. Now let's get the hell out of here."

Charles rolled his seat away from the console and thrust a finger at it. "Owned!"

"Just a sec," Pel said. "Gotta clean up." He changed the console login password and the root password, then brought up a file directory. He looked at

308 ♦ T.C. Weber

Waylee and spoke quietly. "If you go unplug all the consoles, we'll delete the password file. No one will be able to log in."

"Hell," Charles said, "just delete all the admin accounts entirely, the ones we can, anyway. That'll really slow 'em down."

Waylee left them to it and unplugged the other consoles. Then she peeked into the lounge. The handcuffed techs stared at her and made muffled noises. "Sorry about this," she told them. "You work for an awful company, that's why we're doing this." She really was sorry. Even for President Rand. But it had to be done.

Waylee hurried out of the office. Pel squirted Gorilla Glue in the entrance lock, then shut it behind them. "They can still get in by breaking a window, but it'll cost them a couple of minutes."

They walked, then sprinted, through the blue machine hive. Beyond, freedom awaited.

43

M'patanishi

Dolphins were up 7-0. The Super Bowl coverage broke for a car commercial.

But on the data center camera, which M-pat was using to monitor his friends, Waylee, Pel, and Charles leaned toward their screen. Pel flashed a thumbs up.

"Yo, over here," Dingo said from his console.

M-pat hurried over.

Dingo's display showed two camera feeds from the presidential booth. President Rand and a bunch of others stared at the screens above the big window overlooking the stadium. "...People are generally stupid," CEO Luxmore said on the screen within a screen. "That's why they need people like us to tell them what to do..."

"We did it, yo!" Dingo jumped up and smacked fists with him.

M-pat lost it. "Fuck yeah, I can't believe we pulled this motherfuckin' shit off!" He flashed all the B'more handsigns for solidarity, then actually hugged the motherfucker.

In the display of the president's suite, a woman asked, "Where is this showing?"

"Just here?" a chubby man said. "Or everywhere?"

"Can't get through to control," another woman said, staring at her comlink.

M-pat recognized Luxmore because his big-titty blonde was next to him. "Send everything you've got to the MediaCorp campus in Virginia," the CEO told someone out of view. He stared directly into the nearest lens. "And turn those cameras off." He yanked his comlink out of a coat pocket. The feeds went dark.

The world's biggest shitstorm was headed their way. M-pat threw on his data glasses. "DG, call 23." Pel's code number.

No connection.

He turned to Dingo. "Hey, I can't get anything on this."

Dingo put his glasses on. "Me neither."

They tried the phones on nearby consoles. No dial tone.

"Whole phone system's down," Dingo said.

"No wonder we're not getting calls now."

A handheld radio crackled on the supervisor's console. "A-28 to Nest One." One of the two guards patrolling the building. A-97 was the other.

M-pat picked up the radio, pushed in a trigger on the side, and lifted it to his lips. "A-28, this is Nest One. Go ahead." He had heard plenty of radio traffic on police scanner apps, but still had to guess at the lingo.

"Comms are down, other than radio. Can you advise? Over."

What a dumbass question. "A-28, where are you and A-97?"

"Sixth floor per your instructions. All clear, over."

"Uh, stay put. I'll notify dispatch about the comm problem." He had no intention of actually doing that. "Over."

"And out?"

"Yeah, yeah, over and out." *Fuck this radio shit.*

"Aren't you supposed to say 'Roger Wilco'?" Dingo asked.

"Ain't never heard no cop say motherfuckin' Roger Wilco. Ain't you got shit to do?" M-pat brought up the list of radio codes on the console. He called dispatch and used Luke Annlote's ID and the code for prowlers. "55 to Dispatch, 10-70, multiple suspects near the power plant, Priority 1." A long broadcast, so he added, "Over."

"55, 10-4" a male voice acknowledged over the speaker. "What's your 20?"

They wanna know where I am. "Uh, power plant parking lot."

"55, stand by." After a pause, the dispatcher called out five patrol IDs and directed them to the power station on the other side of the campus.

M-pat looked at Dingo. "Time to go."

"I'll kind of miss this place." Dingo gathered his gear together and pocketed the data stick with the stadium booth video.

Not me. M-pat sat back down at his original console. He disabled all the cameras and locks, shutting down all the security systems he could access. He turned off the radio and left it on the console, one less way they could be tracked.

On their way out of the security office, Dingo squirted half a tube of glue in the lock.

Waylee, Pel, and Charles, all wearing data glasses over their masks, emerged from the stairwell door down the hall. They ran toward each other, Waylee holding a hand against her cheek.

Pel knocked fists with Dingo. Waylee squeezed arms around M-pat. "I love you guys." A big flap of latex drooped from her face, exposing white foam underneath.

M-pat pulled Waylee's arms off his back. "Better do somethin' 'bout that mask. Authority's on the way, y'all."

The smiles disappeared, replaced by cringing jaws and tense shoulders. He could smell their fear, like cheap beer puked over moldy onions.

"I sent the guards to the power plant," he said, "but we gotta jet." If they caught him, he was going back to prison for keeps.

Pel's eyes widened and he started jogging toward the lobby, waving the others to follow.

M-pat caught up. "Yo, yo. Be cool." He looked around. "Act like your shift is over. And don't bunch up."

Pel's teeth scraped some of the color off his fake lips. "Waylee said there's a Watcher outside."

"You fuckin' serious?" They had worst-case plans for private drones, but not Watchers.

Waylee tapped a foot. "We should activate the planes." Her hands shook as she pulled the hand-sized radio out of her big purse. She extended the antenna and flipped the power switch on. The receive light turned green, meaning the satellite repeater in the Mustang trunk was still in range.

* * *

Kiyoko

Huddled in her blanket in the back of the moving truck, Kiyoko watched the Super Bowl feed in her immersion helmet. Waylee's video wrecked the president and MediaCorp for minute after minute. And all the raw material was out there for follow up. *I've got the most awesome sister ever.*

Nyasuke stared at her and meowed.

"I know. I should be there with them." She prayed to every god she'd ever heard of. "Please bring them all back safely."

She thought about searching the Comnet for gods she'd left out. Then Waylee's voice sounded in the helmet speakers. "There's a Watcher over the campus. Launch the planes." The connection ended before she could respond.

"VR, Spitfire." Kiyoko's helmet view switched to her model fighter plane, a replica British Spitfire from World War II. She lay on a grassy field a few hundred yards from the MediaCorp campus. Three identical drones sat parked next to hers. Pel had procured all four and set up the Comnet connections.

Her wingmates stood by on the Comnet: her BetterWorld dragon friend, Abrasax, and two hackers from the Collective, their avatars an Amazon warrior and a Japanese lolita. Kiyoko messaged them, "To battle we go."

Her wingmates appeared in 2-D popup windows. "It's a good day to fly." "Hoo-ah!" "Kiai!"

Kiyoko reduced the size of her other portals and focused on her Spitfire. Moving her left VR glove, she pushed the virtual throttle forward. "Go!"

Her engine started. The propeller whined and the plane tore across dead grass and bare dirt, bouncing up and down. She fought a surge of nausea.

She pulled back the stick and the plane rose from the ground. The vibrations dwindled and it climbed into the air. *I'm flying for real!*

The other planes followed on her left and right. Beyond the field, she kept low over treetops and roofs.

Just ahead, she saw the rear section of the MediaCorp campus. A wheel-shaped Watcher hovered overhead, black against the sky and brandishing antennae. No other enemy aircraft, at least for now.

"Spitfire Three, buzz the power plant. Four, take the satellite dishes." Both targets were well away from the front gate. "Two, you're with me. We're taking out that black dragon."

The Spitfires flew over the MediaCorp fences and climbed. Two security cruisers departed the single-story security headquarters in the center of campus and drove toward the power plant. The two planes piloted by the Amazon and lolita peeled off and headed for their targets, wagging their wings and weaving back and forth.

"Two, attack from above left. Ram if you can. I'm hitting from the right." According to Pel's Comnet research, the Watchers flew using a turbine that sucked air in through the top and forced it out through a skirt along the sides. So the top was the most sensitive place to hit.

In her popup window, Abrasax blew smoke from her nostrils. "Suicide girls, got it."

Abrasax's Spitfire climbed while Kiyoko flew straight at the Watcher, approaching faster than she would have thought.

The Watcher darted out of the way. Kiyoko flew past it, turned, and climbed, the Spitfire responding instantly to her virtual control stick.

Abrasax dove at the Watcher but it dodged again, scurrying to the right.

Further away, the other Spitfires flew loops and barrel rolls, making it nearly impossible for the guards to hit them with pistols. They tried anyway, flashes followed by *pops*.

"Drive the black dragon to me," Kiyoko told her friend.

Abrasax's Spitfire rolled and accelerated back toward the Watcher. It tilted away and flew up.

Kiyoko didn't have her friend's years of simulating flight, but probably the Watcher's pilot had never been attacked before. She kept climbing, then estimated an intercept vector.

The Watcher changed course again, but it moved like a jellyfish compared to the Spitfires. Abrasax slowly closed the distance, matching its maneuvers.

Kiyoko dove toward her quarry. Bullets whizzed past her. Within a shallow bowl on the top of the Watcher, blades spun too fast to see. She guided the Spitfire straight for them. The intake bowl filled her vision.

Everything turned black except for the popup windows.

"You got it!" Abrasax shouted, followed by "I just hit it too!"

* * *

Dingo

Striding down the antiseptic MediaCorp hallway, Dingo wondered if he should feel more scared. Pel and Charles darted their heads back and forth, panting like overheated stray dogs. Even Waylee and M-pat moved like zombiepocalypse survivors who'd just been bitten and shit in their pants.

Back in the reception area, a frumpy woman asked, "What's going on? The phones are down."

M-pat held up a hand. "Don't worry. We're on it. Just sit tight."

The three receptionists stared at Waylee, hand held against her torn mask. "What's wrong with you?" one said.

Waylee turned away and led Pel and Charles through the revolving front doors. M-pat followed, Dingo last.

Outside, cold air blasted Dingo in the face. He heard high-pitched engines, then distant gunshots, .45 pistols it sounded like. He glanced in their direction, but there were too many buildings in the way.

He heard a *smack* above, followed by another. A Watcher fell from the sky, trailing smoke, and crashed somewhere on the other side of the broadcast building. "Sweet."

M-pat walked toward Luke's Mazda. "Let's get out of here." The others headed for their cars, a little too fast.

M-pat hopped in the driver's seat, Dingo in the shotgun. They headed for the exit, thick bars in front, tire trap and chain link fence gate beyond, reinforced guard bunker to the left.

The gate didn't open when M-pat placed his badge against the reader. He tried again. No luck, and the gate was strong enough to stop a fully loaded 18-wheeler.

Dingo glanced over. "'Sup?"

"Should have opened." M-pat pulled the Mazda into one of the parking spaces behind the guard station.

Pel stopped Nick Smith's VW a few car lengths behind them. Charles sat in the passenger seat. No sign of Waylee or her blue Mustang.

M-pat held his badge up to the bulletproof windows of the bunker and pointed at the rear door.

The bald guard nodded and opened the door. He stayed just inside. "Sorry, Luke, we're on lockdown. Heard there's a break-in or something at the power station."

"Yeah, well my shift is over. Open the gate, would ya?"

"Are you kidding? Your shift isn't over 'til midnight."

M-pat frowned. He yanked his Glock out of its shoulder holster and pointed it at Baldy's face. "My shift ends when I say it ends, motherfucker."

The guard ducked behind the door and tried to slam it shut.

M-pat threw his body against the door, right leg back for leverage. "You supposed to surrender when a gun pointed at you." His eyes narrowed into homicidal determination.

If they killed someone, that would be the story, not Waylee's video. Dingo stormed past M-pat and into the small room.

Baldy pulled a pistol out of his belt holster but Dingo knocked it out of his hand. M-pat pushed his way in.

"Don't shoot," Dingo said. He threw a jab combo at the guard but he blocked the blows with his forearms. M-pat circled around them, searching for an opening.

The guard kicked Dingo hard in the shin. Burning pain shot through his leg. Then a fist smacked his jaw. He must have flinched, cause it was only a glancing blow and didn't knock him down.

M-pat grabbed Baldy's arm while it was still outstretched, twisted it, and pulled him off balance. He kicked against the back of the man's knee and down he went.

Dingo stepped forward and kicked a field goal against Baldy's head. It snapped to the side and he stopped moving.

"That might have been off the charts," M-pat said.

"Shit." Dingo felt the man's neck for a pulse. He was still alive, just out.

Dingo yanked the handcuffs from the guard's utility belt and snapped them around the man's wrists.

M-pat searched for the exit gate override. He found it in the center of the control panel. He pressed the button and the gate slid open. "Let's go," he said. "You a'ight?"

"Yeah." Except the pain was really kicking in now. It felt like his shin bone was broken.

He limped his way into the car, and heard distant sirens and helicopters. "Are we gonna make it?"

M-pat didn't answer. He slapped the start button and slammed down the accelerator. In the mirror, Dingo watched Pel follow them out the gate with Charles.

Where the hell was Waylee?

44

Waylee

Data glasses set to maximum magnification, Waylee watched from the Mustang as Dingo and M-pat forced their way into the guard station far ahead. Pel and Charles sat in the Volkswagen waiting for the gate to open.

After what they did, Homeland would bring down the hammer. It wouldn't take long, thanks to Amy's advance warning. Pel and the others needed a decoy. And she had the fastest car.

She had sent Charles with Pel. He was only seventeen, and incredibly smart, and deserved a life.

"But he came with you," Pel had objected.

She chose not to explain that if anyone deserved to get caught, it was her. This had all been her idea. If not for her, they'd all be living normal lives now. And she owed Dingo and Pel and M-pat for helping her escape the noose in West Baltimore. Even their dog, who had died for her. Time to repay her debts.

Waylee had just kissed Pel's latex lips and said, "Shut up and get the fuck out of here."

The gate opened and M-pat and Dingo returned to the Mazda. She heard faint sirens somewhere to the north.

M-pat tore off, Pel and Charles not far behind. She followed them at a discreet distance, passing farm fields and townhouse complexes.

Dingo's voice sounded in her bone transducers, clear despite the layers of encryption. "Yo, Mustang, where you at?" They must be on an outside network now.

"Shut up and drive faster. I'm behind you. I'm gonna take a different route, though."

As planned, the others took the first left. Waylee slowed, then stopped at the intersection, a convenience store on the right and shuttered garden center on the left.

She pulled off her ruined mask. *So long, Tania.* Chilly air caressed her face. She looked in the mirror and combed fingers through her fire red hair. The stapler had left a nasty bruise on her cheek.

Seconds later, a Watcher glided toward her, followed by a line of helicopters, their blades barely audible. *Here they come.*

Waylee stepped on the gas and swung the car to the right. She addressed her glasses, "DG, navigation." The navigation program appeared over her left eye. "Rendezvous Point Two," she said.

An arrow pointed down the road, with "Turn left in 3.2 miles" underneath. The helicopters grew louder, sounding like low-pitched lawnmowers. Tilting the side mirrors, she saw three following her. The Watcher too.

She accelerated. She passed a boxy Dongfeng sedan and a double-trailer truck. The old-fashioned speedometer pointer hugged the highest number, 140 miles per hour. Her data glasses said 160. Farm fields gave way to skeletal trees and interspersed houses.

The Watcher fell behind, but the three helicopters drew closer.

Let them. She would outrun the ground pursuit, and once inside the tunnel that was Rendezvous Point Two, she'd hop into the back of Shakti's van and they'd never see her again.

Waylee had to slow at the next intersection. She yanked the wheel to the left. The tires screeched, and she headed north on an empty two-lane road.

The signal icon disappeared from her data overlay, replaced by a flashing 'Connection lost.' *Fuck. They're jamming me.* How would she call Shakti now? She smacked a fist against the top of the dashboard.

Something caught her eye. One of the helicopters—sleek, gunmetal gray, and bristling with weapons—reached her car and dropped to treetop level just to the left. Its side door slid open.

Dread turned the world to ice. Her hypomanic brain had hugely exaggerated her chance of escape. She mashed the accelerator to the floor.

The helicopter fell behind, then caught up again. It flew alongside her, its rotor downdraft flagellating bare tree branches, bending and twisting them like an electric shock. High-pitched harmonics emerged beneath the quiet whirring of the rotor blades. Waylee couldn't see the other two. *They must be overhead.*

Waylee wanted to give her pursuers the finger. As long as the others got away, it didn't matter what happened to her. Her hands felt differently, though, and wouldn't budge from the steering wheel, too intent on survival.

"Pull over," an amplified voice roared from the helicopter.

She had no GPS signal either. She was supposed to turn east again somewhere. "DG, display route."

According to the map on her data glasses, she should turn at the next major intersection. Maybe another few miles. Then just ten minutes to the tunnel.

"Pull over. This is your last warning."

Her knees shook but her right foot didn't stray from the accelerator. She swerved around another truck. Oncoming SUV, closing fast. She darted back into her lane, just in time. The SUV and truck honked in anger.

She left the truck behind. Saw the intersection ahead in the distance.

Something flashed in the open helicopter doorway. A loud bang came from beneath. The Mustang jolted and jerked to the right.

Her heart seized. She pulled back her foot and spun the wheel to the left, but the car had a mind of its own and whipped back and forth along the road.

Another flash, another bang, and then the whole world turned over and over. *I'm going to die.*

* * *

Pain poked through the haze, sharpened into details, then overwhelmed Waylee entirely.

Pain meant life at least. She was strapped in her seat, facing a tortured web of cracks over gouged dirt. Blood dripped onto the glass and dyed the cracks red, flowing upward and irrigating the soil. Her breath sounded wet and raspy. No air bag had deployed.

Her left arm hurt more than the rest. Her neck was too stiff to move far, but her forearm seemed to jut out at a weird angle. Beyond it, beyond jagged remnants of the side window, the world was upside down, clear, the road angling off to the left.

Bright flares smacked against the inverted road, forming pickets of red flame. A helicopter landed in front of them, blowing clouds of dead leaves. Soldiers in form-fitting black armor and mirrored goggles leaped out the side and fanned out, pointing stubby rifles as they ran. Another helicopter flew past and landed somewhere out of sight.

No sign of her data glasses, no way to call Pel even if she wasn't being jammed. *So this is the end. For me, at least. If there even is a me. My brain's a hall of circus mirrors. I should have been a Buddhist—they say the self is just illusion.*

Cyborg soldiers reached the car. One kneeled next to the open window and poked a slate-gray gun barrel at her. "Just the one woman here," he spoke in his goggle mike.

Waylee felt no sense of impending depression. Nothing but peace. Maybe she'd snapped her head so hard, the warring homunculi inside had flown out of her mouth and into the roadside ditch, where they'd be devoured by vultures.

Fuck the both of them.

Waylee tried to say "I surrender" to the soldier in her window, but coughed up thick blood instead. *I'm fucked. But I gave Authority a bitch slap it'll never forget. And its docile enablers, the cowed, the distracted, maybe they won't be so docile anymore.*

45

February 19
Georgetown, Guyana

Kiyoko

The rotating pedestal fans did little to alleviate the sweltering heat in Shakti's aunt's house. Kiyoko's undergarments clung to her skin like a clammy blanket. It probably wasn't any hotter than in Baltimore during the summer, but no one in Guyana seemed to have air conditioning. There was never any relief.

Kiyoko stared out the living room windows down to the flooded street below. All the houses had their living quarters on the second floor, with a concrete block garage and storage space on the first. A good thing, since everywhere she could see, the city sat in several inches of foul-smelling water.

"Happens all the time now," Shakti's aunt had explained in her Caribbean accent when they arrived three days ago. "The pumps or the generators fail and since we're below sea level, everything floods."

Kiyoko turned back to the garish living room, with its long paisley rug and perimeter of sofas and chairs with scarlet slip covers. Nyasuke slept curled on the coffee table. Pel hunkered in the corner sofa, invisible from the screened windows. Dingo and Charles sat next to him, their eyes lidded with boredom. Shakti and several of her relatives occupied plush chairs and discussed the upcoming wedding.

"Stay away from the windows," Pel said from the corner.

"What, is someone gonna shoot me?" Kiyoko said. Except to visit embassies, Pel hadn't left the house since they arrived, and even then he wore fake dreads, dark makeup, and sunglasses. He got angry every time she and Charles accompanied Shakti to government offices or the market or friends' houses.

"Shoot or kidnap," Pel said. "We're worth a lot of money. We've gotta be careful."

Dingo looked over. "Damn, Pel, you full-on freaked, yo."

Pel's eyes narrowed. "Easy for you to say. For me and Charles, the CIA's either en route or already here."

Shakti's relatives ignored the exchange. "You simply can't have a proper wedding on such short notice," Shakti's grandmother told the others. "The preparations to be made, the food and clothes we need, the flights from U.S. America and Canada…"

Shakti waved a hand and spoke in the singsong voice she'd reacquired. "I've tried to explain, we just need to file the legal paperwork. There's plenty of time for ceremony later."

M-pat had returned to Baltimore, and as far as they knew, hadn't been picked up by the cops. Shakti had Guyanese citizenship and had been assured she wouldn't be extradited. Dingo either, once the two of them married. Shakti hadn't committed any extraditable crimes, and Dingo left no proof of his.

Kiyoko, Pel, and Charles, none of whom had passports, would have to move on. Guyanese authorities had granted them temporary asylum while they reviewed their case, but they wouldn't resist the U.S. government for long. Neighboring Brazil, on the other hand, was too powerful to be pushed around. And they had a vibrant music scene.

They would visit the Brazilian embassy tomorrow and hope for the best. To her great disappointment, Japan and China turned them down yesterday, saying they needed valid passports. But Brazil, Shakti's relatives insisted, delighted in tweaking their northern rival. If they got in, maybe Paulo could help set them up, pass along some friendly contacts.

Dingo turned to Pel and Charles. "You gotta throw me a stag party before you leave, yo."

Pel sighed. He hadn't smiled since they boarded the charter boat in Miami. "With what?"

They'd spent the rest of their money and traded their truck and most of their electronics, after wiping, to guarantee the crew's loyalty. The trip lasted forever, it was cramped and hot, and Kiyoko was seasick the entire time.

Dingo poked Pel in the arm. "Since when do we need money to have fun? Money is nothing but chains."

"Fun? Are you kidding? I can't believe we're sitting around here talking about a stag party and a stupid wedding."

Pel's collapse was a serious problem. Kiyoko stomped her foot. "Look. This marriage will keep Dingo out of jail. Case closed."

His eyes glistened with moisture. "We never should have left Waylee."

When Waylee didn't show up anywhere or respond to messages, they searched the Comnet until they discovered she'd been captured. Homeland had confirmed it in an announcement, "Terrorist leader apprehended."

Kiyoko kneeled in front of Pel and held his hand. "We'll free her."

Charles held up a fist. "Yeah. You broke me out, we can break Waylee out."

"I was thinking more like setting up a defense fund," Kiyoko said, "and getting people and foreign governments to apply pressure—"

"Are you kidding?" Pel interrupted. "When has that ever worked? Peltier, Abu-Jamal, Manning, Assange, they're rotting in jail or died there despite all the pressure."

Kiyoko stood and looked at Charles. Maybe Pel would come around in time. "Whatever it takes, I'm for it..."

Dingo threw two quick jabs to the air. "Let me know, I'll raise an army to bust her out."

Pel wiped his eyes and curled his lips into a sneer. "Don't be fools. Enough acting like fools."

"What are you talking about?" Charles said. "We totally owned the biggest bossmen in the world. It's all everyone's talkin' 'bout on the Comnet. All about our twelve minute Super Bowl broadcast and everything we released."

"And how MediaCorp should be dissolved," Kiyoko added, "and the president impeached."

Shakti's aunt looked over. "Yes, even here in Guyana people talk about it."

Pel shook his head. "I never would have agreed to Waylee's plan if I'd known I'd lose my house, never see my family and friends again, and see the woman I worship spend the rest of her life in prison."

Everyone stared at him. Kiyoko picked up her sleeping cat from the coffee table and squeezed onto the sofa between Pel and Dingo. "We don't know that, Pel. Have some faith. You saw. With faith and a plan, we can do anything."

He didn't respond.

"And if you asked Waylee," she said, "she'd say the sacrifice was worth it."

Pel stood. "You know MediaCorp's spin machine will bury everything we did. And the president will order a crackdown. I should have tried harder to stop her." He marched out of the room.

Kiyoko returned to the window. Shakti's aunt had pointed the way north, toward Virginia and Maryland. Beyond the white houses with red-shingled roofs, the tangles of electrical wires, and the scattered palm trees, beyond the leaky seawall and hungry Caribbean, her sister sat imprisoned somewhere.

Stay strong. We'll get you out.

* * *

March 1
Marine Corps Base Quantico, Virginia

Waylee

"You've got a visitor," the stocky female nurse told Waylee.

Who was it this time? Did they expect her to say anything without legal counsel?

At least it would be relief from the unending boredom. She lay in a white-walled hospital room by herself, with only medical staff and interrogators for company. No Comnet access, no entertainment channels or books even. And they'd completely immobilized her, strapping her limbs to the bed. Metal and plaster scaffolding clung to her neck and left arm.

The only good news was she could think clearly, not overcome by depression or anxiety. Her demons had died in the crash. Or at least entered a coma.

"Damn."

Waylee couldn't move her head to see who her visitor was, but the voice sounded familiar. "Who is it?"

"Your legal team." Francis Jones strolled into her field of view, dapper in a charcoal pinstripe suit.

"Oh my God." Waylee couldn't help it—tears of happiness welled up and streamed down her cheeks. And she couldn't wipe them away. "Look at me. This is so embarrassing."

"No need to feel embarrassed." Francis grabbed a tissue from the bedside table and dabbed her tears away. "Sorry it took so long to get access."

He introduced her to three lawyers licensed in Virginia, which he was not, he said. All three—two women and one man—looked fresh out of law school.

"I'm pretty fucked up, Francis. Doctors said my seatbelt saved me. But I won't be playing any gigs for a while."

"Well, we intend to sue the government for excessive use of force, among other things." He held up a finger. "Before we get started... I insisted that our conversation remain private, as a matter of attorney-client confidentiality. The authorities here agreed, but I can't promise they aren't watching or listening anyway. And obviously we couldn't bring any detection equipment, assuming we had any, on the base."

She couldn't move her head to nod. "I wouldn't trust them."

Francis sat in the metal chair next to the bed and pulled a data pad out of an inner pocket. He stretched it to lap size. "I understand you haven't been charged yet?"

"They said I was an enemy combatant and the Constitution didn't apply."

He huffed. "That's bullshit. The FBI tried that tactic with your sister and it didn't stick. You're an American citizen on American soil. You get due process."

"Homeland thugs come in almost every day and ask questions, but I haven't said shit. They say I was driving a stolen car, committed acts of conspiracy, fraud, and espionage, and I might as well confess." *Maybe I should.*

He leaned forward. "Have they described the proof?"

"No. I invoke the Fifth Amendment, and that's as far as the conversations get."

Fingers flew on his data pad. "Robert Luxmore's taken a special interest in your case. Said on camera you should get life in prison."

"I must have tweaked him good."

Francis looked up and smiled. "MediaCorp stock took a nose dive, and a lot of stockholders want Luxmore gone. The public is ready to tar and feather him. There's even talk of revoking their corporate charter."

"Do you think that'll happen?"

He frowned. "We'll see. Corporations have committed some horrific crimes—oil spills, poisoning, fraud, even mass murder—and received little more than a slap on the wrist, if anything at all. In this case, it's not clear that MediaCorp has actually violated any laws, although the People's Party and others are looking into it."

"What about President Rand?"

He leaned back in the chair. "His approval ratings are at an all-time low. Congress, believe it or not, plans to hold hearings."

So much for party unity. "Rats fleeing the ship. Any chance of impeachment?"

He shook his head. "None. Just righteous indignation so their constituents will think they give a damn."

Her skin tingled. "We've gotta break up MediaCorp and put the 'Net in the hands of the people. Give everyone an equal voice, like the original vision. Without freely shared, accurate information, we're doomed as a species."

He nodded. "I'll pass that along."

One of the Virginia lawyers stepped forward. "All this public outrage can help your case. Some say you're a political prisoner."

"Aren't we all." She looked back at Francis. "Well if they bury me, a lot of great writing's come out of prisons. Francis, promise you'll get me published?"

"If it comes to that, sure." He patted her hand. "You know, your band is getting quite popular."

"Fastest trending music on the Comnet," one of the other lawyers said.

"Kiyoko will be happy about that," Waylee said. *On to more important things.* "Promise me something else?"

"What's that?"

"They told me Pel and Kiyoko left the country."

"I haven't talked to them," he said, "but yes, they've all been granted asylum."

"Get them a message. It's important."

"Of course. What's the message?"

"Tell them I'm fine and I love them."

Francis nodded.

One of the other lawyers pulled a camera out of her bag. "Do you mind if I take some pictures? For the case?"

"Sure." She tried to sit up but had forgotten the restraints. "Could you unstrap my arms?"

Francis unbuckled her arm straps.

Waylee sat up in the bed, reveling in the slight freedom of movement. She met her lawyers' eyes. "Thank you for caring."

The female lawyer pointed the camera at her.

Waylee stared at the lens. *I didn't go quietly.* She clenched her right fist and thrust her unbroken arm up in defiance.

Then she spoiled the effect by smiling.